WAITING *FOR* SUNRISE

A Good Man in Africa

On the Yankee Station

An Ice-Cream War

Stars and Bars

School Ties

The New Confessions

Brazzaville Beach

The Blue Afternoon

The Destiny of Nathalie 'X'

Armadillo

Nat Tate: An American Artist

Any Human Heart

Fascination

Bamboo

Restless

Ordinary Thunderstorms

WAITING *FOR* SUNRISE

A Novel

William Boyd

HARPER

An Imprint of HarperCollins*Publishers*

www.harpercollins.com

HarperCollins books may be purchased for educational, business, or sales promotional use. For information, please write: Special Markets Department, HarperCollins Publishers, 10 East 53rd Street, New York, NY 10022.

First published in Great Britain in 2012 by Bloomsbury Publishing.

FIRST U.S. EDITION

Library of Congress Cataloging-in-Publication Data

Boyd, William, [date]
   Waiting for sunrise : a novel / William Boyd.
      p.   cm.
   ISBN 978-0-06-187676-9
   1. World War, 1914–1918—Fiction. I. Title.
   PR6052.O9192W35 2012
   823'.914—dc23
                                                    2011036857

---

12   13   14   15   16   OFF/RRD   10 9 8 7 6 5 4 3 2 1

For Susan

A thing is true at first light and a lie by noon.

ERNEST HEMINGWAY

Truly, to tell lies is not honourable; but when the truth entails tremendous ruin, to speak dishonourably is pardonable.

SOPHOCLES

PART ONE

VIENNA, 1913-1914

1. A Young, Almost Conventionally Handsome Man

IT IS A CLEAR and dazzling summer's day in Vienna. You are standing in a skewed pentangle of lemony sunshine at the sharp corner of Augustiner Strasse and Augustinerbastei, across from the opera house, indolently watching the world pass by you, waiting for someone or something to catch and hold your attention, to generate a tremor of interest. There's a curious frisson in the city's atmosphere today, almost spring-like, though spring is long gone, but you recognize that slight vernal restlessness in the people going by, that stirring of potential in the air, that possibility of audacity – though what audacities they might be, here in Vienna, who can say? Still, your eyes are open, you are unusually poised, ready for anything – any crumb, any flung coin – that the world might casually toss your way.

And then you see – to your right – a young man striding out of the Hofgarten park. He is in his late twenties, almost handsome in a conventional way, but your eye is drawn to him because he is hatless, an anomaly in this busy crowd of Viennese folk, all hatted, men and women. And, as this young, almost conventionally handsome man walks purposefully past you, you note his fine brown, breeze-blown hair, his pale grey suit and his highly polished ox-blood shoes. He's of medium height but broad-shouldered with something of a sportsman's build and balance, you register, as he goes by, a couple of paces from you. He's clean-shaven – also unusual in this place, the city of facial hair – and you observe that his coat is well tailored, cut tight at the waist. Folds of an ice-blue silk handkerchief spill easily from his breast pocket. There is something fastidious and deliberate about the way he dresses

3

himself – just as he's almost conventionally handsome, so is he also almost a dandy. You decide to follow him for a minute or so, vaguely intrigued and having nothing better to do.

At the entry to Michaeler Platz he stops abruptly, pauses, stares at something stuck to a hoarding and then continues on his way, briskly, as if he's running slightly late for an appointment. You follow him around the square and into Herrengasse – the slanting sunrays picking out the details on the grand, solid buildings, casting sharp, dark shadows on the caryatids and the friezes, the pediments and the cornices, the balusters and the architraves. He stops at the kiosk selling foreign newspapers and magazines. He chooses *The Graphic* and pays for it, unfolding and opening it to glance at the headlines. Ah, he's English – how uninteresting – your curiosity is waning. You turn round and wander back towards the pentangular patch of sunlight you abandoned on the corner, hoping some more stimulating possibilities will come your way, leaving the young Englishman to stride on to wherever and whomever he was so intently heading . . .

Lysander Rief paid for his three-day-old *Graphic* (overseas edition), glanced at a headline – 'Armistice Signed in Bucharest – Second Balkan War Ends' – and ran his hand unreflectingly through his fine straight hair. His hat! Damn. Where had he left his hat? On the bench – of course – in the Hofgarten where he'd sat for ten minutes staring at a flower bed in a fearful quandary, wondering agitatedly if he was doing the correct thing, suddenly unsure of himself, of this trip to Vienna and everything it portended. What if it was all a mistake, all vain hope and ultimately pointless? He looked at his wristwatch. Damn, again. He'd be late for his appointment if he went back. He liked that hat, his narrow-brim boater with the maroon silk band, bought in Lockett's, on Jermyn Street. Someone would have stolen it in an instant, he was sure – another reason not to retrace his steps – and he cursed his distractedness again, setting off once more up Herrengasse. It just showed you how tense he was, he thought, how preoccupied. To rise up and walk away from a park bench and not automatically set your hat firmly on your head . . . He was clearly more jittery and apprehensive about this meeting than even his obvious, perfectly understandable nervousness would indicate. Calm down, he said to himself, listening to the measured click of the metalled crescents set in the leather heels of his shoes as they struck the stone paving – calm down. This is just the first appointment – you can walk away, go back to London – no one is holding a loaded gun to your head, forcing you.

He exhaled. 'It was a fine day in August, 1913,' he said to himself out loud but in a low voice, just enough to change the subject and readjust his mood. '*Es war ein schöner Augusttag des Jahres* . . . ah, 1913,' he repeated in German, adding the date in English. He had trouble with numbers – long numbers and dates. His German was improving fast but he might ask Herr Barth, his teacher, to do an hour or so on numbers, to try and fix them in his head. '*Ein schöner Augusttag –*.' He saw another defaced poster on the wall, like the one he'd spotted as he'd walked into Michaeler Platz – that was the third he'd seen since setting out from his lodgings this morning. It had been clumsily torn from its hoarding, ripped away from wherever the glue was not strong enough to hold the paper fast. At the first poster – just next to the tram-stop near the room he was renting – his eye had been held by what remained of the body (the head had gone) of the scantily clad maiden it displayed. She was almost naked, cowering, hands pressed to her sizeable breasts, cupping them protectively, a semi-visible filmy swirl of self-supporting veil protecting her modesty at the plump juncture of her thighs. Something about the reality of the drawing was particularly compelling, however stylized the situation she was in (that airborne, handy veil) and he had paused to take a closer look. He had no idea what the context of this image was as everything else had been torn away. However, on the second defaced poster, the end of a scaly, saw-toothed

5

reptilian tail explained why the nymph or the goddess, or whatever she was, appeared so terrified. And now on the third poster some lettering was left: '*PERS –*' and below that '*und*' and below that, '*Eine Oper von Gottlieb Toll –*'.

He thought: 'Pers' . . . Persephone? An opera about Persephone? Wasn't she the one dragged off to the underworld and Narcissus – was it? – had to go and fetch her back without looking round? Or was that Euridice? Or something . . . Orpheus? Not for the first time he resented his eccentric and patchwork education. He knew a lot about a few things and very little about a great deal of things. He was taking steps to remedy the situation – reading as widely as he could, writing his poems – but every now and then his ignorance stared him candidly in the face. One of the hazards of his profession, he admitted. And classical myths and references were certainly a bit of a jumble, not to say a prominent hole.

He looked back at the poster. Only the top half of the head had survived the shredding on this one. Arabesques of wind-lashed hair and wide eyes peering over the ragged edge of the horizontal rip as if, Lysander thought, she was staring horrified over the top of a bedsheet. Piecing together the fragments of the three posters in his head to form a notional body of the goddess, Lysander found himself briefly stirred, sexually. A naked woman, young, beautiful, vulnerable, confronted by some squamous, no doubt phallic, monster about to ravish her . . . And no doubt this was the purpose of the posters and no doubt, furthermore, this was what had provoked the prudish bourgeois outrage that had made some good citizen decide to vandalize the display. All very modern – all very Viennese – he supposed.

Lysander strode on, deliberately analysing his mood. Why should this poster depicting the potential ravishment of some mythological woman excite him? Was it natural? Was it, to be more precise, something to do with the pose – the cupped hands both covering and holding the soft breasts, at once coquettish and defensive? He sighed: who could answer these questions anyway?

6

The human mind was endlessly baffling, complex and perverse. He stopped himself – yes, yes, yes. This was exactly why he had come to Vienna.

He crossed the Schottenring and the wide expanse of the square in front of the huge charcoal bulk of the university building. That's where he should go to find out about Persephone – ask some student specializing in Latin and Greek – but something was nagging at him, however, he couldn't recall a monster taking part in the Persephone story . . . He checked the streets he was passing – almost there. He stopped to let an electric tram go by and turned right down Berggasse and then left on Wasagasse. Number 42.

He swallowed, mouth suddenly dry, thinking: maybe I should just turn about, pack my bags, go home to London and resume my perfectly agreeable life. But, he reminded himself, there would still be the issue of his particular problem, unresolved . . . The main wide doors to the street at number 42 were open and he stepped through into the coach-entryway. There was no sign of a concierge or guardian. A steel-meshed elevator was available to carry him to the second floor but he opted for the stairway. One floor. Two. Wrought-iron banisters, varnished wooden handrail, some sort of speckled granite forming the steps, a dado rail, turf-green tiles below, white distemper above. He concentrated on these details, trying not to think about the dozens – perhaps the hundreds – of people who had preceded him up these stairs.

He reached the landing. Two solid panelled doors with fanlights stood side by side. One said '*Privat*'; the other had a small brass sign above the separate bell, tarnished, needing a polish. 'Dr J. Bensimon.' He counted to three and rang, confirmed suddenly in the rightness of what he was doing, confident in the new, better future he was setting out to secure for himself.

2. Miss Bull

DR BENSIMON'S RECEPTIONIST (a slim, bespectacled, severe-looking woman) had shown him into a small waiting room and mentioned, politely, that he was in fact some forty minutes early for his appointment. Therefore, if he wouldn't mind waiting until? My mistake – foolish. Coffee? No, thank you.

Lysander sat in a low armless black leather chair, one of four in the room, placed in a loose semi-circle facing an empty grate below a plaster mantelpiece, and once again called on calmness to soothe his agitated mood. How could he have been so wrong about the time? He would have assumed the hour set for this consultation would have been mentally carved in stone. He looked around and saw a black bowler hat hung on the hat-and-coat-stand in the corner. The previous appointment's, he assumed – then, seeing one hat, he realized he could have gone back to the park for his boater after all. Damn it, he said to himself. Then – fuck it – relishing the obscenity. It had cost him a guinea, that hat.

He stood up and looked at the pictures on the wall that were etchings of vast ruined buildings – moss-mantled, overgrown with weeds and saplings – all tumbled coping stones, shattered pediments and toppled columns that seemed vaguely familiar. No artist's name came to him – another hole in his moth-eaten education. He moved to the window that overlooked the small central courtyard of the apartment building. A tree grew there – a sycamore, he saw, at least he could identify some trees – in a square of tramped browning grass, edged by the disused carriage house and loose boxes, and, as he watched, an old, aproned woman appeared from them, effortfully limp-lugging a brimming coal scuttle. He turned away and paced around, carefully folding back with the toe of his shoe the flipped-over corner of the worn Persian rug on the parquet floor.

He heard some voices – unusually urgent, raised – from the receptionist's ante-room, then the door opened and a young woman came in and shut it behind her with a forceful bang.

'*Entschuldigung,*' she said, gracelessly, glancing at him, and sat down on one of the chairs and rummaged vigorously through her handbag before pulling out a small handkerchief and blowing her nose.

Lysander stepped quietly back to the window; he could sense this woman's unease, her tension, coming off her in waves, as if some dynamo inside her were generating this febrility, this – the German word came to him, pleasingly – this *Angst*.

He turned and their eyes met. She had the most unusual eyes, he saw, the palest hazel. And they were large and wide – the white visibly surrounding the iris – as if she were staring with great intensity or had been shocked in some way. Pretty face, he thought – neat nose, pointed, strong chin. Very olive skin. Foreign? Her hair was pinned up under a wide blood-red beret and she wore a dove-grey velvet jacket over a black skirt. On the jacket lapel was a large red-and-yellow shellac brooch of a crude-looking parrot. Artistic, Lysander thought. Laced ankle-boots, small feet. A very small, petite, young woman, in fact. In a state.

He smiled, turned away and looked at the courtyard. The stout old housekeeper was heading doggedly back to the stables with her empty scuttle. What did she want with all that coal in high summer? Surely –

'*Sprechen Sie Englisch?*'

Lysander looked round. 'I am English, actually,' he said, warily. 'How can you tell?' He felt annoyed that he clearly wore his nationality like a badge.

'You've a copy of the *Graphic* in your pocket,' she said, pointing at his folded newspaper. 'Rather gives you away. But, anyway, most of Dr Bensimon's patients are English so it was an easy guess.' Her accent was educated, she was obviously English herself, despite her somewhat exotic colouring.

'You don't happen to have a cigarette on you, do you?' she asked. 'By any faint and lucky chance.'

'I do, as it happens, but –' Lysander indicated a printed sign laid on the mantelpiece. '*Bitte nicht rauchen.*'

'Ah. Of course. Would it be all right if I filched one for later?'

Lysander took his cigarette case from his jacket pocket, opened it and offered it to her. She chose one cigarette, said, 'May I?' and took another before he could give her permission, slipping them into her handbag.

'I have to see Dr Bensimon very urgently, you see,' she said, briskly, in a no-nonsense manner. 'So I do hope you don't mind if I barge the queue.' At this she smiled at him a smile of such innocent brilliance that Lysander almost blinked.

On quick reflection, Lysander thought, he did rather mind, actually, but said, 'Of course not,' and smiled back, uncertainly. He turned again to the window pane, touched the knot of his tie and cleared his throat.

'Do sit down if you want to,' the young woman said.

'I'm very happy standing. I find these low armless chairs rather uncomfortable.'

'Yes, they are, rather, aren't they?'

Lysander wondered if he should introduce himself but then considered that a doctor's waiting room was the kind of place where people – strangers – might prefer to preserve their anonymity; it wasn't as if they were meeting in an art gallery or a theatre foyer, after all.

He heard a slight noise and looked over his shoulder. The woman had stood up and had gone to one of the etchings of ruins (what was that artist's name?) and was using its glass as a mirror, tucking fallen strands of hair back under her beret and pulling down small wispy curls in front of her ears. Lysander noticed how her short velvet jacket revealed the full swell of her hips and buttocks under the black skirt. Her ankle-boots had three-inch heels yet she was still very small in stature –

'What're you looking at?' she said abruptly, meeting his gaze in the reflection of the etching's glass.

'I was admiring your bootees,' Lysander improvised quickly and smoothly. 'Did you buy them here in Vienna? –'

She never answered, as the door to Dr Bensimon's consulting room opened at that moment and two men stepped out, talking and chuckling to each other. Lysander knew at once which one was Dr Bensimon, an older man in his forties, quite bald with a brown trimmed beard flecked with grey. Everything about the other man – to Lysander's eyes – shouted 'soldier'. A navy double-breasted suit, a banded tie below a stiff collar, narrow cuffed trousers above shoes so polished they might have been patent. Tall, ascetically lean with a small neat dark moustache.

But the young woman was immediately in a kind of frenzy, interrupting them, calling Dr Bensimon's name, apologizing and at the same time insisting on seeing him, absolutely essential, an emergency. The military man stepped back, leaned back, as Dr Bensimon – glancing at Lysander – swept the yammering woman into his room, Lysander hearing him say in a stern low voice as he did so, 'This must never happen again, Miss Bull,' before the door to his consulting room shut behind them.

'Good god,' said the military type, dryly. He was English as well. 'What's going on there?'

'She seemed very agitated, I have to say,' Lysander said. 'Cadged two cigarettes off me.'

'What's the world coming to?' the man said, lifting his bowler off its wooden hook. He held it in his hands and looked candidly at Lysander.

'Have we met before?' he said.

'No. I don't think so.'

'You seem oddly familiar, somehow.'

'I must look like someone you know.'

'Must be that.' He held out his hand. 'I'm Alwyn Munro.'

'Lysander Rief.'

'Now that does ring a bell.' He shrugged, cocked his head, narrowed his eyes as if searching his memory and then smiled as he gave up and moved to the door. 'Don't feed her any more cigarettes, if I were you. She looks a bit dangerous to me.'

He left and Lysander resumed his scrutiny of the small drab courtyard outside. He extracted every possible detail from the view – the basket-weave pattern of the paving stones, the dog-toothed moulding on the arch above the stable door, a damp streak on the brickwork under a dripping tap. He kept his mind occupied. A few minutes later the young woman appeared from Dr Bensimon's room, evidently much calmer, more composed. She picked up her handbag.

'Thank you for letting me barge ahead, ' she said breezily. 'And for the ciggies. You're very kind.'

'Not at all.'

She said goodbye and sauntered out, her long skirt swinging. She glanced back at him as she closed the door behind her and Lysander caught a final glimpse of those strange, light brown, hazel eyes. Like a lion's eyes, he thought. But she was called Miss Bull.

3. The African Bas-Relief

LYSANDER SAT IN DR Bensimon's consulting room, looking around him as the doctor wrote down his personal details in a ledger. The room was spacious, with three windows along one wall, simply furnished and almost entirely done in shades of white. White painted walls, white woollen curtains, a white rug on the blond parquet and a beaten silver-metalled primitive-looking bas-relief hung above the fireplace. In one corner was Dr Bensimon's mahogany desk, backed by floor-to-ceiling glass-fronted bookshelves. On one side of the fireplace was a soft high-backed armchair, loose-covered in coarse cream linen and on the other a divan under a thick, woollen fringed blanket and two embroidered pillows. Both were facing away from the desk and Lysander, who had chosen the armchair, found he had to crane his neck round uncomfortably if he wanted to see the doctor. The room was very quiet – double windows – and Lysander could hear no sound of the city streets beyond – no clatter of electric trams, no carriages or wagons clopping by, no automobiles – it was ideally calm.

Lysander looked at the silver bas-relief. Fantastic African figures, half-man, half-animal, with extravagant headdresses, pricked out with traceries of small holes punched through the soft metal. It was strange and very beautiful – and doubtless freighted with all manner of pertinent symbolism, Lysander thought.

'Mr L.U. Rief,' Bensimon said. In the quiet room Lysander could hear the scratch of his fountain pen. His voice was lightly accented, somewhere from the north of England, Lysander guessed, Yorkshire or Lancashire, but honed down so that placing the location was impossible. He was good at accents, Lysander flattered himself – he'd unlock it in a minute or so.

'What do the initials stand for?'

'Lysander Ulrich Rief.'

'Marvellous name.'

Manchester, Lysander thought – that flat 'A'.

'Rief – is that Scottish?'

'Old English. It means "thorough", some say. And I've also been told it's Anglo-Saxon dialect for 'wolf'. All very confusing.'

'A thorough wolf. Wolfishly thorough. What about the "Ulrich"? Are you part German?'

'My mother is Austrian.'

'From Vienna?'

'Linz, actually. Originally.'

'Date of birth?'

'Mine?'

'Your mother's age is hardly relevant, I would venture.'

'Sorry. Seventh of March 1886.'

Lysander turned again in the chair. Bensimon was leaning back in his seat, at ease, smiling, fingers laced behind his shining pate.

'Best not to bother turning round all the time. Just think of me as a disembodied voice.'

4. Wiener Kunstmaterialien

LYSANDER WALKED DOWNSTAIRS FROM Bensimon's apartment, slowly, his mind full of thoughts, some pleasurable, some dissatisfying, some troubling. The meeting had been brief, lasting only some fifteen minutes. Bensimon had written down his personal details, had discussed payment methods (bi-monthly invoicing and cash settlement) and then finally had asked him if he would like to discuss the nature of his 'problem'.

Lysander paused in the street outside and lit a cigarette, wondering if this process he had embarked on would really help or if he would have been better going to Lourdes, say? Or to have taken up some quack's remedy? Or become a vegetarian and wear Jaeger underwear like George Bernard Shaw? He frowned, uncertain suddenly – not a good mood to be in, not encouraging. It was his closest friend Greville Varley who had suggested psychoanalysis to him – Greville being the only other person aware of his problem (and only vaguely so, at that) – and Lysander had followed up the idea like a zealot, he now realized, cancelling all his future plans, withdrawing his savings, moving to Vienna, seeking out the right doctor. Had he been foolishly impetuous or was it merely a sign of his desperation? . . .

Turn left at Berggasse, Bensimon had said, then walk all the way down to the little square, to the junction of all the roads at the bottom. The shop is right in front of you – WKM – can't miss it. Lysander set off, his mind still full of the crucial moment.

BENSIMON: So, what seems to be the nature of the problem?

LYSANDER: It's . . . It's a sexual problem.

BENSIMON: Yes. It usually is. At root.

LYSANDER: When I engage in lustful activity . . . That's to say, during amatory congress –

BENSIMON: Please don't search for euphemisms, Mr Rief. Plain speaking – it's the only way. Be as blunt and as coarse as you like. Use the language of the street – nothing can offend me.

LYSANDER: Right. When I'm fucking, I can't do it.

BENSIMON: You can't get an erection?

LYSANDER: I have no problem with an erection. On the contrary – all very satisfactory there. My problem is to do with . . . with emission.

BENSIMON: Ah. Incredibly common. You ejaculate too soon. *Ejaculatio praecox.*

LYSANDER: No. I don't ejaculate at all.

Lysander strolled down the gentle slope of Berggasse. Dr Freud's rooms were here, somewhere – perhaps he should have tried for him? What was that French expression? 'Why speak to the apostles when you can go to God himself?' But there was the problem of language: Bensimon was English, which was a huge advantage – a boon, even – not to be gainsaid. Lysander recalled the long silence after he had told Bensimon the curious nature of his sexual malfunction.

BENSIMON: So – you're engaged in the sex-act but there is no orgasm.

LYSANDER: Precisely.

BENSIMON: What happens?

LYSANDER: Well, I can go on for a good time but the realization that nothing will happen makes me, eventually, slacken off, as it were.

BENSIMON: Detumescence.

LYSANDER: Eventually.

BENSIMON: I'm going to have to think about this. Most unusual. Anorgasmia – you're the first I've seen. Fascinating.

LYSANDER: Anorgasmia?

BENSIMON: That's what's wrong with you. That's what your problem's called.

And that was that, except for one further piece of advice. Bensimon asked him if he kept a journal, a diary, or a commonplace book. Lysander said he didn't. He did write poetry, he said, fairly regularly, some of which had been published in newspapers and magazines, but – he shrugged modestly – he was an amateur poet, he enjoyed trying his hand at verse and made no claims at all for the lines that ensued – and, no, and he didn't keep a journal.

'I want you to start writing things down,' Bensimon had said. 'Dreams you have, fleeting thoughts, things you see and hear that intrigue you. Anything and everything. Stimulations of every kind – sexual or olfactory, auditory, sensual – anything at all. Bring these notes along to our consultations and read them out to me. Hold nothing back, however shocking, however banal. It'll give me a direct insight into your personality and nature – into your unconscious mind.'

'My "id", you mean.'

'I see you've done your homework, Mr Rief. I'm impressed.'

Bensimon had told him to jot these impressions and observations down as close as possible to the time they occurred and not to alter or edit them in any way. Furthermore, they were not to be written down on scraps of paper. Lysander should purchase a proper notebook – leather-bound, fine paper – and make it a true personal document, something that was contained and enduring, not just a collection of random scribblings.

'And give it a title,' Bensimon had suggested. 'You know – "My Inner Life", or "Personal Reflections". Formalize the thing, in other words. Your dream diary, your journal of yourself – your *Seelenjournal* – it should be something you'll treasure and value in the fullness of time. A record of your mind during these coming weeks, conscious and unconscious.'

At least, Lysander thought, crossing the street to the artists' supplies shop that Bensimon had recommended – the Wiener Kunstmaterialien – at least it would be something concrete, a kind of permanent chronicle of his stay. All this talking – and all the talking he was bound to do – were simply words lost in the air. He was warming to the idea as he pushed through the swing doors into the shop, Bensimon was right, perhaps it would help him after all.

WKM was large and well lit – clusters of electric bulbs hung from the ceiling in modern, aluminium-spoked chandeliers, the gleaming coronas reflected in the shiny tan linoleum floor below them. The smell of turpentine, oil paint, untreated wood and canvas made Lysander feel welcome. He loved these kinds of emporium – alleyways of stacked artistic materials, like a cultural cornucopia, ran here and there: shelves of layered paper types, jars filled with sharp pencils, a small copse of easels, large and small, raked rows of tubes of oil paint laid out in chromatic sequence, fat gleaming bottles of linseed oil and paint thinner, canvas aprons, folding stools, stacked palettes, cobbled tins of watercolours, flat boxes of pastels, their lids open, displaying their bright contents like so many multi-coloured cigarillos. Whenever he came into shops like this he always resolved to take up sketching as a serious hobby, or watercolouring or lino-cutting – anything to give him a chance to buy some of this toothsome equipment.

He turned an aisle corner to find a small library of cartridge paper pads and notebooks. He browsed a while and picked up one with hundreds of pages, like a dictionary. No, no – too daunting, something more modest was required that could be realistically filled. He selected a pliable black leather-covered notebook, fine paper, unlined, 150 leaves. He liked its weight in his hand and it would fit in a coat pocket, like a guidebook – a guidebook to his psyche. Perfect. A title came into his head: '*Autobiographical Investigations* by Lysander Rief' . . . Now, that sounded exactly what Bensimon –

'We meet again.'

Lysander turned to see Miss Bull standing there. A friendly, smiling Miss Bull.

'You're buying your notebook, aren't you?' she said knowingly. 'Bensimon should have a commission in here.'

'Are you doing the same?'

'No. I gave mine up after a couple of weeks. Trouble is I'm not really verbal, you see. I visualize – see things in images, not words. I'd rather draw than write.' She held up what she was purchasing – a small cluster of dull oddly shaped knives, some tapered sharply, some with triangular ends, like miniature trowels.

'You can't draw with those,' Lysander said.

'I sculpt,' she explained. 'I'm just ordering more clay and plaster. WKM's the best place in town.'

'A sculptress – how interesting.'

'No. A sculp*tor*.'

Lysander inclined his head, apologetically. 'Of course.'

Miss Bull stepped closer and lowered her voice.

'I'd really like to apologize for my behaviour earlier this morning –'

'Couldn't matter less –'

'I was a bit . . . overwrought. I'd run out of my medicine, don't you see. That's why I had to get to Dr Bensimon – for my medicine.'

'Right. Dr Bensimon dispenses medicines as well?'

'Well, no. Sort of. But he gave me an injection. And more supplies.' She patted her handbag. 'It's marvellous stuff – you should try it if you're ever a bit low.'

She certainly seemed different as a result of Dr Bensimon's medicine, Lysander thought, looking at her, much more assured and self-confident. Somehow more in command of every –

'You've a most interesting face,' Miss Bull said.

'Thank you.'

'I'd love to sculpt you.'

'Well, I'm a bit –'

'No hurry.' She rummaged in her bag and came up with her card. Lysander read it: 'Miss Esther Bull, artist and sculptor. Lessons provided.' There was an address in Bayswater, in London.

'Bit out of date,' she said. 'I've been in Vienna for two years, now – my telephone number's on the back. We've just got a telephone installed.' She looked at him challengingly. Lysander hadn't missed the second person plural. 'I live with Udo Hoff,' she said.

'Udo Hoff?'

'The painter.'

'Ah. Yes, that does – yes. Udo Hoff.'

'Have you a telephone? Are you in an hotel?'

'No to both. I'm renting rooms. I've no idea how long I'll be staying.'

'You must come to the studio. Write your address down. I'll send you an invitation to one of our parties.'

She handed him a scrap of paper from her bag and Lysander wrote down his address. A little reluctantly, he had to admit, as he wanted to be alone in Vienna: to resolve his problem – his anorgasmia, now it had a name – himself, alone. He didn't really require or desire any kind of social life. He handed the scrap back.

'Lysander Rief,' she read. 'Have I heard of you?'

'I doubt it.'

'And I'm Hettie, by the way,' she said, 'Hettie Bull,' thrusting her hand out. Lysander shook it. She had a very firm grip.

5. The River of Sex

'WHY AM I TROUBLED by this encounter with HB? Why am I also vaguely excited by it? She's not "my type" at all, yet I already feel somehow drawn into her life, willy-nilly, her orbit. Why? What if we'd met at a concert or a house party? We wouldn't have thought anything of each other, I'm sure. But because we met in the waiting room at Dr Bensimon's we know something secret about each other, already. Does this explain it? The wounded, the incomplete, the unbalanced, the malfunctioning, the ill seek each other out: like attracted to like. She won't leave me alone, I know. But I don't want to go to Udo Hoff's studio, whoever he is. I came to Vienna to avoid social contact and told hardly anyone where I was going, just saying "abroad" to people who pressed for details. Mother knows, Blanche knows, Greville knows, of course, and a handful of essential others. I want to treat Vienna as a kind of beautiful sanatorium full of perfect strangers – as if I had consumption and had simply disappeared until the cure was effected. I don't think Blanche would like HB, somehow. Not at all.'

There was a barely audible knock at his door – more of a scratch than a knock. Lysander put his pen down and closed his notebook, his *Autobiographical Investigations*, putting it in a drawer of his desk.

'Come in, Herr Barth,' Lysander said.

Herr Barth tiptoed in and shut the door as softly as he could. For a man of significant bulk he tried to move unobtrusively and with as much discretion as possible.

'*Nein, Herr Rief*. Not "Come in". *Herein*.'

'*Verzeihung*,' Lysander apologized, drawing up an extra chair to the desk.

Herr Barth was a music teacher who came, moreover, from a long line of music teachers. His father had seen Paganini play in 1836 and, when his first son was duly born some years later, had called him Nikolas in honour of the event. As a young man Herr Barth had taken the identification to heart and wore his hair long and grew his cheek whiskers in the Paganini style, a homage he had never abandoned. Even now, approaching his seventies, he merely dyed his long grey hair and his whiskers black and still wore old-fashioned high collars and long coats with silver buttons. His instrument was not the violin, however, but the double bass – which he had played in the orchestra of the Lustspiel-Theater in Vienna for many years before he took up the family profession of music teacher. He kept his old double bass in its cracked leather case propped against the wall at the bottom of his bed in his small room at the end of the corridor, the smallest of the three rooms that were rented out in the Pension Kriwanek. He claimed to be able to teach any instrument that 'could be carried or held in the hand' to a level of competence – whether strings, woodwind or brass. Lysander was not aware of any pupils seeking out this offer but had happily accepted Herr Barth's diffident suggestion, made a day after he had moved into the pension, that he help Lysander improve his German – for the sum of five crowns an hour.

Herr Barth sat down slowly, flicked away the strands of hair resting on his collar with both hands and smiled, wagging an admonitory finger.

'Only German, Herr Rief. Only this way will you advance in our wonderful and beautiful language.'

'I'd like to practise numbers today,' Lysander replied – in German.

'Ah, numbers, numbers – the great trap.'

They duly practised numbers for an hour – counting, dates, prices, change, adding, subtracting – until Lysander's head was a reeling Babel of figures and the dinner bell rang. Herr Barth only paid for board and breakfast so he excused himself and Lysander crossed the corridor to the panelled dining room where Frau Kriwanek herself was waiting for him.

Frau K, as her three lodgers referred to her, was a woman of rigid piety and decorum. Widowed in her forties, she wore traditional Austrian clothes – moss-green dirndl dresses, in the main, with embroidered blouses and aprons, and broad buckled pumps – and projected a demeanour of excruciating politesse that was really only endurable for the length of a meal, Lysander had quickly realized. Her world admitted and contained only people, events and opinions that were either 'nice' or 'pleasant' (*nett* or *angenehm*). These were her favourite adjectives, deployed at every opportunity. The cheese was nice; the weather pleasant. The Crown Prince's young wife seemed a nice person; the new post office had a pleasant aspect. And so on.

Lysander smiled blandly at her as he took his accustomed seat at the dining table. He sensed the years falling from him: Frau K made him feel he was in his adolescence again – younger, even, pre-pubescent. He became unmanned in Frau K's presence, strangely cowed and respectful; he became someone he didn't recognize – a man without opinions.

He saw there was a place set for a third party – the other lodger in the pension, Lieutenant Wolfram Rozman, apparently absent or late. Dinner was at eight o'clock, sharp. Frau K approved of Lysander – he was nice and pleasant, and English (nice people) – but the lieutenant, Lysandser instinctively felt, did not meet with Frau K's full approval. He was not pleasant, perhaps not even nice.

Lieutenant Wolfram Rozman had done something wrong. It wasn't exactly clear what, but his presence in the Pension Kriwanek was a form of disgrace. It was a regimental matter,

Lysander had learned from Herr Barth. He had not been cashiered but had been temporarily expelled from barracks over this scandal, whatever it was, and forced to live here until judgement was delivered and his military fate decided. Lieutenant Rozman didn't seem unduly concerned, Lysander had to admit – apparently he'd already been in the pension for nearly six months – but the longer he stayed the more Frau K found him not a pleasant man, incrementally. Even in the two weeks Lysander had been witness to their exchanges he had detected a marked sharpness in address, an increase in frosty formality.

In fact, Lysander liked Wolfram – as he'd been invited to call him almost immediately – but he studiously kept this opinion from Frau K. She smiled her thin smile at him now and rang the bell for service. The maid, Traudl, appeared almost at once with a tureen – containing clear cabbage soup with croutons – in her hands. This was the first course of dinner in the Pension Kriwanek, summer or winter. Traudl, a round-faced girl of eighteen who blushed when she spoke and blushed when she was spoken to, plonked the tureen down on the table hard enough for two splashes of soup to leap out and land on the immaculate white nap of the tablecloth.

'You will pay for the cleaning of the tablecloth, Traudl,' Frau K said evenly.

'With pleasure, Madame,' Traudl said, blushed, curtsied and left.

Frau K said grace, eyes closed, head level – Lysander bowed his – and served them both clear cabbage soup with croutons.

'The lieutenant is late,' Lysander observed.

'He's paid for his meal, it's up to him if he eats it.' She smiled again at Lysander. 'Have you had a pleasant day, Herr Rief?'

'Very pleasant.'

After the meal (chicken stew with paprika) the custom was that Frau K left and the gentlemen were permitted to smoke. Lysander lit a cigarette and resumed his normal persona now Frau K had gone, and began wondering, as he was inclined to do after any time spent with her, whether he should move to a hotel or another boarding house but, as he ran through the pros and cons, he realized that actually he was comfortable at the Pension Kriwanek and that, apart from one meal a day with Frau K, life there suited him.

The pension was in fact a large apartment on the third floor of a newish block on the south side of a courtyard off Mariahilfer Strasse about half a mile from the Ring. It had hot-water heating and electric light; the large bathroom the lodgers shared was modern (flushing toilet) and clean. When Lysander had consulted the travel agency about his trip he had stipulated that the list of boarding houses he was given had to be able to provide a comfortable bedroom with a capacious wardrobe, offer professional standard laundry services (he had very precise demands about the use of starch) and be near a tramway halt. The first address he had visited was the Pension Kriwanek, where he saw that his room was comprised of a sitting room, a curtained alcove with a double bed and a small boxy annexe that served as a dressing room with plenty of shelves and cupboard space for his clothes. He hadn't bothered to look any further – and this was probably the fact that inspired his postprandial thoughts of leaving – should he have seen what else Vienna had to offer? Still, he had a tutor in residence, also, and that wasn't to be overlooked.

When you entered the apartment through double doors off the third-floor landing you were confronted by a wide hall – wide enough for two cane-backed bergères and a round table with a glass-domed stuffed owl as a centrepiece. From this hall a long corridor led away to the dining room and the three lodgers' rooms – Lysander's, Wolfram's and Herr Barth's – and the bathroom they shared. At the end of this passage there was a door marked '*Privat*' that must give on to the kitchen area, he assumed, as well as Frau K's rooms. He had never been through it, never dared. Traudl also lived in so she would have had a corner somewhere that was hers, as well. There seemed to be a narrow parallel service-corridor from the kitchen to the dining room – the dining room had two exits – but beyond that his sense of the pension's geography was vague – who knew what lay behind *Privat*? The place was comfortable, you could keep yourself to yourself. Breakfast was served in your room, dinner was a paid-for supplement, a packed lunch could be provided at a day's notice. He felt strangely at home, he had to admit.

Traudl came in and began to clear away the dessert dishes.

'How're you, Traudl?' Lysander asked. She was a solid, strapping girl and clumsy with it.

On cue she let a dessert spoon drop to the carpet.

'Not very happy, sir,' she said, picking it up and rubbing away the custard stain with a napkin.

'Why's that?'

'I've so many fines to pay Frau Kriwanek that I won't earn anything this month.'

'That's a shame. You have to be more careful.'

'Traudl? Careful? Totally impossible!' came a man's voice.

'Good evening, Lieutenant, sir,' Traudl said, blushing.

Wolfram Rozman hauled out a chair and sat down heavily.

'Traudl, my little fluffy chicken, bring me some bread and cheese.'

'At once, sir.'

Wolfram leaned across the table and clapped Lysander on the shoulder. He was wearing a pale-blue suit and a lilac bow tie. He was a very tall man, inches taller than Lysander, with the gangly, limber laziness of movement that very tall men display. He sprawled in his seat, one arm flung over the back of the adjacent chair, and thrust his legs under the table. Lysander saw his pale-blue trousers and spats emerge on his side. He had hooded, sleepy eyes and a dense blond moustache with its tips waxed upward over loose, full lips.

Lysander offered him a cigarette that he accepted and – after fruitless rooting in his pockets for a box of matches – lit with Lysander's lighter.

'I suppose I'm in her blackest books,' Wolfram said, blowing excellent smoke-rings. 'As black as night.'

'You're just not very "pleasant" – let's put it that way.'

'I was running back, trying not to be late and I thought – Jesus, God, no, *Herrgott Sakra*, I can't stand it. So I went to a café and drank schnapps.'

'Why don't you forget dinner, like Barth? Then you don't have to see her.'

'The regiment is paying for everything. Not me.'

Traudl came back in with a plate of black, sliced bread and some soft creamy cheese.

'Thank you, my little mongoose.'

Traudl seemed about to say something but thought better of it, curtsied and left by the service door.

Wolfram leaned forward.

'Lysander – you know you can mount Traudl if you give her twenty crowns. Yes?'

'Mount?'

'Possess her.'

'Are you sure?' Lysander calculated quickly: twenty crowns was less than a pound.

'I do it a couple of times a week. The girl's short of money – she's actually quite agreeable.' Wolfram put his cigarette out in the ashtray, spread cheese on his bread and began to eat. 'Big friendly country girl, they know a few special tricks, those girls – just to tell you, in case you felt like it.'

'Thanks. I'll bear it in mind,' Lysander said, a little bemused at this revelation. What would Frau K say if she knew about these goings-on? He would look at Traudl with new eyes.

'You look surprised,' Wolfram said, munching on his bread and cheese.

'Well, that's because I am. I had no idea. In this place of all places – the Pension Kriwanek – it's very deceptive.'

Wolfram pointed at him with his knife.

'This place – this Pension Kriwanek – is just like Vienna. You have the world of Frau K on top. So nice and so pleasant, everybody smiling politely, nobody farting or picking their nose. But below the surface the river is flowing, dark and strong.'

'What river?'

'The river of sex.'

6. The Son of Halifax Rief

'I AM IN THE stalls bar of the Majestic Theatre in the Strand. I am walking through a crowd of elegantly dressed society ladies – young and middle-aged. They gossip and chat and occasionally one of them glances at me. They pay me hardly any attention at all – even though I'm completely naked.'

Lysander paused. He was reading to Bensimon from *Autobiographical Investigations*.

'Yeeessss . . .' Dr Bensimon said, slowly. 'That's interesting. You dreamed this last night?'

'Yes. I wrote it down immediately.'

'But why a theatre, I wonder?'

'It's obvious,' Lysander said. 'If it *wasn't* a theatre – now, that would be more interesting.'

'I don't follow.'

'I'm an actor,' Lysander said.

'A professional actor?'

'I earn my living acting on stage, mainly in the West End of London.'

He heard Bensimon stand up and cross the room to sit down on the end of the divan opposite. Lysander turned in the armchair – Bensimon was staring at him eagerly.

'Rief,' he said. 'I thought it sounded familiar. Are you any relation to Halifax Rief?'

'He was my father.'

'My god!' Bensimon seemed genuinely astonished. 'I saw his King Lear in . . . Where was it?'

'The Apollo.'

'That's right, yes, the Apollo . . . He died, didn't he? Halfway through the run or something.'

'In '99. I was thirteen.'

'Good lord. You're Halifax Rief's son. How extraordinary.' Bensimon gazed hard at Lysander as if seeing him for the first time. 'I think I can spot a resemblance of sorts. And you're an actor as well, goodness.'

'Not as successful as my father – but I earn a fairly decent living.'

'I love the theatre. What was the last play you were in?'

'*The Amorous Ultimatum.*'

'Don't know it.'

'By Kendrick Balston – drawing-room comedy. It's just closed after four months at the Shaftesbury. That's when I came on here.'

'Goodness . . .' Bensimon repeated, nodding slightly, as if something had been revealed to him. He went back to his desk and Lysander looked at the silver bas-relief. He was becoming very familiar with it, he felt, even if this was only his second session with Bensimon.

'So – you're naked in the stalls bar of the Majestic. Are you aroused?'

'I'm enjoying being there, I suppose. I'm not ashamed of being naked in front of these people. Not embarrassed.'

'There's no laughing or sniggering, no pointing, no mockery.'

'No. They seem to take it perfectly normally. Idle curiosity would be the strongest emotion. They just glance at me and carry on their conversation.'

'Do they "glance" at your penis?'

'Ah. Yes. Yes, they do.'

There was a silence. Lysander closed his eyes, he could hear the

Bensimon pen scratching away. To take his mind momentarily off their discussion he forced himself to recall the pleasures of the last weekend. He had caught the train to Puchberg and stayed the night at the station hotel there. Then he had taken the funicular to the Hochschneeberg and had walked (he had brought his hiking boots with him) all the way to the Alpengipfel peak and back. He had felt his mind clear and his spirits lift as they always did when he was hiking in the mountains or on one of his walking tours. Maybe, he thought, this was the best reason to have come to Austria – new walks, new landscapes. Every weekend he could take a train and walk in the mountains, empty his head, ignore his problems. The walking cure –

'Is this a recurring dream?' Bensimon asked.

'Yes. With variations. Sometimes there are fewer people.'

'But it's essentially you – naked – amongst women, fully dressed.'

'Yes. It's not always in a theatre.'

'Why do you think you dream this?'

'I was rather hoping you might tell me.'

'Let's continue this conversation next time,' Bensimon said, bringing the session to an end. Lysander stood and stretched – he felt strangely tired, all that concentration. He slipped his notebook into his pocket.

'Keep writing everything down,' Bensimon said, showing him the door. 'We're making progress.' They shook hands.

'See you on Wednesday,' Lysander said.

'Halifax Rief's son, how incredible.'

Lysander sat in the Café Central drinking a Kapuziner and thinking about his father. As usual he tried to bring him to mind but failed. All he had was an image of a big burly man and a square fleshy face under thick greying hair. He could hear the famous voice, of course, the resonant bass rumble, but what lingered most fixedly in his memory of his father was his smell – the aroma of the brilliantine he used in his hair, his own mix, prepared by his barbers. A sharp initial astringent whiff of lavender underlayed by the richer scent of bay rum. A very perfumed man, my father, Lysander thought. And then he died.

Lysander looked around the big café with its high ceilings and glass dome. The place was quiet. A few people reading newspapers, a mother and two little girls inspecting the pastry trolley. Sun slanting through the tall windows, setting the ruby and amber lozenges of coloured glass in the panes aglow. Lysander signalled a waiter and ordered a brandy, feeling like sustaining the tranquil mood. When it arrived he tipped it in his Kapuziner and took out Blanche's letter. The first he'd had from her since arriving in Vienna – he had written to her four times . . . He flattened the sheets. Royal blue ink, her strong jaggy handwriting filling the page, going right up to the edge.

Darling Lysander,
You will be cross with me I know but I do miss you, my lovely man, honestly, and I keep meaning to write but you know me and how 'frantic' everything is. We had the copyright read-through of 'Flaming June' but something was wrong, apparently, and we all had to re-foregather two days later. It's a lovely part for me and I was thinking there's a young Guards officer that you'd be 'perfect' for. Shall I tell dear old Manley that you might be interested? He'll do anything I ask him, silly besotted dear. But you'd need to come home soon, my treasure. It would be lovely to work together again. Is your mysterious 'cure' going well? Will it last ages? Are you taking salt baths and having cold showers and drinking asses' milk and all that? I tell people you've got a 'condition' and they go – 'Oh. Ah. Right. I see,' and rush off looking serious. I'm going down to Borehamwood tomorrow to have a 'cinematograph test'. Dougie says I have the perfect face for the 'flickers' so we shall see. I had a lovely note from your mother asking me if we had decided on the 'great day'. Do think about it, sweetness mine. I show people the ring and they say

'When?' and I laugh – my bell-like laugh – and say we're in no hurry. But I was thinking that a winter wedding might be so special. I could wear furs –

He folded the letter and put it back in his pocket, feeling vaguely sick. It was as if he were hearing her voice in his ear, reminding him what had brought him to Vienna, forcing him to confront the reality of his particular problem. He could hardly marry Blanche in these circumstances. Imagine the honeymoon night . . .

He lit a cigarette. Blanche had had lovers before, he knew. She had practically invited him into her bed but he had insisted on being honourable, respectful – now they were betrothed. He took his notebook from his pocket and made a swift calculation. The last time he had tried to have sexual congress with a woman had been with a young tart he'd picked up in Piccadilly. He counted back: three months, ten days ago. It was days after he had proposed to Blanche and was purely by way of necessary experiment. He remembered the small frowsty room in Dover Street, the one gas lamp, cleanish sheets on the narrow bed. The girl was pretty enough in a lurid way with her paint on but she had a black tooth that was visible when she smiled. He had started well but the inevitable result ensued. Nothing. We can try again, the girl said when he had paid her, don't really count, do it, when nothing happens? You have to pay though – blank cartridge still makes a bang.

Lysander allowed himself a sour smile – some soldier-client had probably told her that and it had stayed in her head. He stubbed his cigarette out. Perhaps he should tell Bensimon he was engaged to Miss Blanche Blondel – it might impress him as much as Halifax Rief.

He paid his bill – remembered to put his hat on – and stepped out into the afternoon's warm sunshine, pausing on the café steps, thinking he might walk back to the Pension Kriwanek – maybe skip supper? – wondering also where he might go this coming weekend – Baden, maybe, or even Salzburg, make a short trip of it, the Tyrol –

'Mr Rief?'

Lysander jumped unconsciously. A tall man, lean hard face, neat dark moustache.

'Didn't mean to surprise you. How d'you do? Alwyn Munro.'

'Sorry – dreaming.' They shook hands. 'Of course. We met at Dr Bensimon's. Coincidence,' Lysander said.

'If you come to the Café Central you'll meet everyone in Vienna, eventually,' Munro said. 'How are you enjoying your stay?'

Lysander didn't want to make small talk.

'Are you a patient of Dr Bensimon?' he asked.

'John? No. He's a friend. We were at varsity together. I pick his brains sometimes. Very clever man.' He seemed to sense Lysander's reluctance to continue the acquaintance. 'You're in a rush, I can see. I'll let you get on.' He fished in his pocket for a card. Handed it over. 'I'm at the Embassy here, if you ever need anything. Good to see you.'

He touched the brim of his bowler with a forefinger and stepped into the café.

Lysander strolled back to Mariahilfer Strasse, enjoying the sun. He took his jacket off and slung it over his shoulder. The Tyrol, he thought, yes – real mountains. Then, as he was about to cross the Opernring he saw another of the defaced, ripped posters. This time the head of the monster was left – some kind of dragon-crocodile amalgam – and the composer's full name: Gottlieb Toller. He thought he might ask Herr Barth if he knew anything about him. He heard the sound of a band playing a militarized version of a Strauss waltz and he adjusted his pace to keep in step with the thump of the bass drum. He thought of Blanche's beautiful long face, her thin, bony wrists rattling with bangles, her tall slim frame. He did love her and he wanted to marry her, he told himself – it wasn't pretence or social convention. He owed it to her to try and become well again, to be a normal man happily married to a wonderful woman. He had to see this through.

He crossed the Ring with due caution and as he did so the band altered its tune to a quickstep or a polka. He felt his spirits lift with the rhythm as he ambled up Mariahilfer Strasse, the music fading slowly behind him, merging with the traffic noise, as the band marched off to its barracks, civic duty done, the good people of Vienna entertained for an hour or so. Lysander felt the sun warm his shoulders and a curious congregation of emotions assail him – pride in what he had done for himself, seeking his cure on his own terms, pleasure in strolling the now familiar streets of this foreign city and, as a muted undertone, a thin enjoyable melancholy at being so far from Blanche and her all-knowing, understanding eyes.

7. The Primal Addiction

'WHAT ABOUT MASTURBATION?' BENSIMON asked.

'Well, it usually works. Nine times out of ten, let's say. No real problems there.'

'Ah. The primal addiction.'

'Sorry?'

'Dr Freud's expression . . .' Bensimon held his pen poised. 'What's your stimulus?'

'It varies.' Lysander cleared his throat. 'I, ah, tend to think of people – women – that I've been attracted to in the past and then imagine a –' He paused. Now he understood why it was useful not to be facing one's interlocutor. 'I imagine a situation in which everything goes well.'

'Of course, that's a hypothesis. The hypothesized perfect world. Reality's far more complicated.'

'Yes, I do know it's a fantasy,' he said, trying to keep the irritation out of his voice. Sometimes Bensimon was so literal-minded.

'But that's useful, that's useful,' Bensimon said. 'Have you heard of "Parallelism"?'

'No. Should I?'

'No, not at all. It's a theory I've developed myself as a kind of adjunct to the main line of Dr Freud's psychoanalysis. Maybe we'll come back to it later.'

Silence. He could hear Dr Bensimon making little popping noises with his lips. Pop-pop-pop. Annoying.

'Is your mother alive?'

'Very much so.'

'Tell me about her. What age is she?'

'She's forty-nine.'

'Describe her.'

'She's Austrian. Speaks fluent English with hardly any accent. She's very elegant. Very fashionably smart.'

'Beautiful?'

'I suppose so. She was a very beautiful young woman. I've seen photographs.'

'What's her name?'

'Anneliese. Most people call her Anna.'

'Mrs Anneliese Rief.'

'No. Lady Faulkner. After my father died she married again to a Lord Faulkner.'

'How do you get along with your stepfather?'

'Very well. Crickmay Faulkner's older than my mother – considerably older. He's in his seventies.'

'Ah.' Lysander could hear the pen scratching.

'Do you ever think about your mother in a sexual way?'

Lysander managed to suppress his weary sigh. He had expected better from Bensimon, really.

'No,' he said. 'Not at all. Never. Ever. No.'

8. A Dashing Cavalry Officer

LYSANDER LOOKED AT WOLFRAM in astonishment. He was standing in the hallway in full military uniform, his sabre dragging on the floor, shako under his arm, spurred black boots with knee guards. He looked huge and magnificent.

'My god,' Lysander said, admiringly. 'Are you going on parade?'

'No,' Wolfram said, a little gloomily. 'My tribunal is today.'

Lysander walked round him. The uniform was black with heavy gold frogging, like writhing snakes, on the plastron front. A furred dolman jacket hung from one shoulder. His shako had a red plume matching the red facings on the jacket collar and the stripes down the side of his trousers.

'Dragoons?' Lysander guessed.

'Hussar. Have you got anything to drink, Lysander? Something strong? I must confess to having some nervousness.'

'I've got some Scotch whisky, if you like.'

'*Perfekt.*'

Wolfram came into his room and sat down, his sabre clinking. Lysander poured him some whisky into a tooth glass that he knocked back with one gulp and held out at once for a refill.

'Very good whisky – I think.'

'You don't want to have whisky on your breath at the tribunal.'

'I'll smoke a cigar before I go in.'

Lysander sat down, looking at this Ruritanian ideal of a dashing cavalry officer. When he puts his shako on, Lysander reckoned, he'll be seven feet tall.

'What's the tribunal about?' he asked. He felt he could reasonably try to ascertain what was the cause of Wolfram's limbo in Pension Kriwanek, now judgement day had arrived.

'A question of missing funds in the officers' mess,' Wolfram said, equably. He explained: the Colonel of the regiment was retiring and officers had contributed to a fund to buy him a splendid present. Donations were made anonymously, money being slipped into the slot of a locked cashbox set on a dresser in the mess dining room. When the box was finally opened they found only enough money to buy the colonel 'a medium-sized box of Trabuco cigars, or a couple of bottles of Hungarian champagne,' Wolfram said. 'Clearly we either gave very little money to our beloved Colonel or someone had been pilfering.'

'Who had the key to the box?'

'Whoever was on the rota to be supervisory officer of the mess each week. The box was there for three months. Three months equals twelve weeks, which equals twelve suspects. Any one of whom had plenty of time to make a copy of the key and take the money. I was one of those twelve supervisory officers.'

'But why do they suspect you?' Lysander felt a stir of outrage on Wolfram's behalf.

'Because I'm a Slovene in a German regiment. German-speaking Austrians, I mean. There's a couple of Czechs but the German officers will always suspect the Slovene – so I spent six months here while they decided what to do with me.'

'But that's ridiculous. Just because you're a Slovene?'

Wolfram smiled at him, tiredly.

'How many countries are there in our great empire?'

'Austria, Hungary and . . .' Lysander thought. 'And Croatia –'

'You haven't even started. Carnolia, Moravia, Galicia, Bosnia, Dalmatia – it's a vegetable soup, a great big stinking salad. Not to mention the Italians or the Ukrainians. I'll take one more whisky.'

Lysander poured it for him.

'You have Austria.' Wolfram moved the bottle and put down the glass beside it. 'You have Hungary. The rest of us are like the harem for these two powerful Sultans. They take us when they want, violate us when they feel the need. So – who stole the Colonel's money? Ah, must be the wily Slovene.'

There was a knock on the door and Traudl looked in, blushing.

'Lieutenant Rozman, sir, your *Fiaker* is here.'

Wolfram stood, did up the buttons on his collar, pulled on his gloves, grabbed his sabre.

'Good luck,' Lysander said and they shook hands. 'You're an innocent man, you've nothing to fear.'

Wolfram smiled, shrugged. 'No human being is entirely innocent . . .'

'True, I suppose. But you know what I mean.'

'I'll be fine,' Wolfram said. 'The wily Slovene has a few surprises up his sleeve.' He gave a little bow, clicked his heels – his spurs rattled, dryly – and he left.

Lysander returned to his desk and opened *Autobiographical Investigations*, feeling a certain mild despondency. Win or lose, Wolfram's stay at the pension must be nearly over – he would either be returning to barracks, vindicated, or, disgraced, be cast adrift on to the sea of civilian life. Back to Slovenia, probably . . . He would miss him. He began to jot down some of the facts in the case of Lt. Wolfram Rozman. 'No human being is entirely innocent,' he wrote, and the thought came to him that, if one were planning to steal something, it would indeed be a clever ploy to make sure that there were a dozen other potential suspects. A cluster of suspects obscuring the guilty one. He underlined the sentence: '<u>No human being is entirely innocent.</u>' Perhaps it was time to tell Bensimon his darkest, most shameful secret . . .

There was another knock on his door. He looked at his wristwatch – Herr Barth wasn't due for an hour. He said, 'Come in,' and Traudl appeared again and shut the door behind her.

'Hello, Traudl. What can I do for you?'

'Frau Kriwanek is visiting her sister and Herr Barth is sleeping in his room.'

'Well, thank you for the information.'

'As he was leaving Lieutenant Rozman gave me twenty crowns and told me to come and see you.'

'What for?'

'To give you some pleasure.'

At this she stooped and lifted her thick skirt and apron to her waist and in the penumbra they cast Lysander saw the pale columns of her thighs and the dark triangle of her pubic hair.

'It won't be necessary, Traudl.'

'What about the twenty crowns?'

'You keep them. I'll tell Lieutenant Rozman we had a very nice time.'

'You're a kind, good man, Herr Rief.' Traudl curtsied.

No human being is entirely innocent, Lysander thought, going to the door and opening it for her. He searched his trouser pockets for change, thinking to tip her, but all he found was a visiting card. She didn't need tipping anyway – she'd just earned twenty crowns.

'I can come another time,' Traudl said.

'No, no. All's well.'

He shut the door behind her. River of sex, indeed. He glanced at the card in his hand – whose was this?

'Captain Alwyn Munro DSO,' he read. 'Military Attaché, British Embassy, Metternichgasse 6, Vienna III.'

Another bloody soldier. He put it on his desk.

9. Autobiographical Investigations

IT IS THE SUMMER of 1900. I am fourteen years old and am living at Claverleigh Hall in East Sussex, the country seat of my stepfather, Lord Faulkner. My father has been dead for a year. My mother married Lord Faulkner nine months after my father's funeral. She's his second wife, the new Lady Faulkner. Everybody in the neighbourhood is pleased for old Lord Crickmay, a bluff, kindly man in his late fifties, a widower with one grown-up son.

I still don't really know what I feel about this new arrangement, this new family, this new home. Claverleigh and its estate remain largely *terra incognita* to me. Beyond the two walled gardens there are woods and fields, copses and meadows, paddocks and two farms spread out across the downs of East Sussex. It's a large well-run estate and I feel a permanent alien in it even though the servants in the house, the footmen, the housemaids, the coachmen and the gardeners, are all very friendly. They smile when they see me and call me 'Master Lysander'.

I have been removed from my school in London – 'Mrs Chalmers' Demonstration School for Boys' – and am being tutored by the local curate, the Reverend Farmiloe, an old and learned bachelor. My mother tells me that, most likely, I shall be sent to a boarding school in the autumn.

It is a Saturday so I have no lessons but the Reverend Farmiloe has asked me to read a poem by Alexander Pope called 'The Rape of the Lock'. I am finding it very hard-going. After lunch I take my book and wander out into the big walled garden, looking for a secluded bench where I can continue my laborious reading. I like poetry, I learn it easily by heart, but I find Alexander Pope almost incomprehensible – not like Keats or my favourite, Tennyson. The gardeners and the boys are out in the long herbaceous borders weeding and greet me as I pass: 'Good day, Master Lysander.' I say hello – I know most of them by now. Old Digby the head gardener, Davy Bledlow and his son Tommy. Tommy is a couple of years older than me and has asked if I would like to go out hunting rabbits with him one day. He has a prize ferret called Ruby. I said, no thank you. I don't want to hunt and kill rabbits – I think it's cruel. Tommy Bledlow is a big lad with a broken nose flattened on his face that makes him look strange – a threatening clown. I leave the walled garden and cross the fence into Claverleigh Wood by the stile.

The sun shines down through the fresh green leaves of the ancient oaks and beeches. I find a mossy angle between two gnarled buttressing roots of a big oak. I am lying in a patch of sunshine and enjoying the warmth on my body. There's a faint breeze. In the distance I can hear the sound of a train chuffing along the Lewes to Pevensey line. Birds are singing – a thrush, I think, a blackbird. It's ideally peaceful. A warm summer's day at the beginning of the new century in the south of England.

I open my book and begin to read, trying to concentrate. I stop and remove my boot and socks. Flexing my toes, I read on.

> 'Sol through white curtains shot a tim'rous ray
> And op'd those eyes that must eclipse the day.'

In eighteenth-century London, a beautiful young woman is lying in bed, about to wake up, dress herself and start her social life – that much was fairly clear. I ease back so my head is in shadow and my body in sunlight.

> 'Belinda still her downy pillow breast,'

Not 'breast', I see, but 'prest'. Why did I read breast? The association of downy pillow, a girl in her night clothes, disarrayed and open enough perhaps to reveal – I turned the page.

> '. . .*Shock*, who thought she slept too long
> Leapt up, and wak'd his mistress with his tongue.'

Who's this 'Shock'? But I am thinking of the downstairs maid – isn't she called Belinda? – I think so, the tall one with the cheeky face. She has 'downy pillows', all right. That time I saw her kneeling, relaying a fire, with her sleeves rolled up and her buttons undone. I know what a 'mistress' is – but how did he wake her with his tongue? . . .

I feel my penis stirring agreeably under my trousers. The sun is warm in my lap. I glance around – I'm quite alone. I undo my belt and fly buttons and pull my trousers and my drawers down to my knees. The sun is warm. I touch myself.

I think of Belinda the downstairs maid. Think of breasts, soft like pillows, of a tongue waking a mistress. I grip myself. Slowly I begin to move my fist up and down . . .

The next thing I remember is my mother calling my name.

'Lysander? Lysander, darling . . .'

I'm dreaming. And then I realize I'm not. I'm waking slowly, as if I've been drugged. I open my eyes, blink, and see my mother standing there silhouetted by the sun-dazzle. My mother standing there looking down at me. Very upset.

'Lysander, darling, what's happened?'

'What?' I'm still half asleep. I look down, following her gaze, my trousers and my drawers are still bunched around my knees, I see my flaccid penis and the small dark tuft of hair above it.

I drag up my trousers, curl up in a ball and begin to cry uncontrollably.

'What happened, darling?'

'Tommy Bledlow,' I sob, god knows why, 'Tommy Bledlow did this to me.'

10. A Peculiar Sense of Exclusiveness

LYSANDER STOPPED READING. HE felt the retrospective shame blaze through him, like the driest tinder burning, writhing, crackling hot. His mouth was parched. Come on, grow up, he said to himself, you're twenty-seven years old – this is ancient history.

Lysander sat quiet for a moment. Bensimon had to speak first.

'Right,' Bensimon said. 'Yes. So. This happened when you were fourteen.'

'I think I'd been asleep for about two hours. I was missed at teatime. My mother was worried and came out looking for me. The gardeners said I'd gone into the wood.'

'And you had begun to masturbate –'

'And had fallen asleep. A dead sleep. The sun, the warmth. A good lunch . . . And then my mother found me apparently unconscious with my trousers pulled down, half-naked, exposed. No wonder she panicked.'

'What happened to the young gardener?'

'He was dismissed immediately, by the estate manager, without pay and references. It was that or the police. His father protested that his son had done nothing – though he had to admit he hadn't been in the garden all afternoon – and he was dismissed as well.'

'Who could possibly disbelieve young Master Lysander?'

'Yes, exactly. I feel very guilty. Still do. I've no idea what happened to them. They lost their cottage on the estate, as well. I took ill – I remember crying for days – and I was in bed for a fortnight. Then my mother took me to a hotel in Margate. I was examined by doctors – I was given all kinds of medicines for my "nerves". Then I was packed off to my terrible boarding school.'

'It was never spoken of again?'

'Never. I was the victim, you see. Ill, shattered, pale. Every time someone asked me about the incident I started to weep. So everyone was very careful with me, very worried about what I had "endured". Walking on eggshells, you know.'

'Interesting that you blamed the gardener's son . . .' Bensimon wrote something down. 'What was his name again?'

'Tommy Bledlow.'

'You still remember.'

'I'm hardly likely to forget it.'

'He had asked you to go hunting with him – with his ferret.'

'I'd said no.'

'Did you have homosexual feelings for him?'

'Ah . . . No. Or at least I wasn't aware of any. He had been the

42

last person I had spoken to. In my panic, in the urgency of the moment, I just plucked his name from the air.'

Lysander took a tram back to Mariahilfer Strasse. He sat in something of a daze as they made their clattering and rocking way across town. Bensimon had been the only person to whom he had ever told the truth about that summer's day at the turn of the century and he had to admit that the recounting of his dire and dark secret had produced a form of catharsis. He felt a strange lightness, a distancing from his past and, as he looked around him, from the world he was moving through and its denizens. He contemplated his fellow passengers in Tram K – saw them reading, chatting, lost in their thoughts, staring blankly out of the window as the city flowed by – and felt a peculiar sense of exclusiveness. Like the man with the winning lottery ticket in his pocket – or the murderer returning unspotted from the scene of his crime – he sensed himself above and apart from them, almost superior. If only you knew what I have disclosed today; if only you knew how everything in my life was going to be different now . . .

This last was wishful thinking, he quickly realized. What had happened that afternoon in June 1900 was the erased passage in the narrative of his life, a long white gap between two parentheses in the account of his days as a fourteen-year-old boy. He had never thought about it subsequently – erecting an impenetrable mental *cordon sanitaire* – pre-empting all catalysts that might stir unwelcome memories. He had walked many times in Claverleigh Wood; he and his mother were very close; he had talked to gardeners and estate workers without once bringing Tommy Bledlow to mind. The event was gone, the incident banished – effectively lost in time – as if some diseased organ or tumour had been removed from his body and incinerated.

He paused, stepping down from the tram at his halt, wondering why he had unthinkingly chosen that image. No – he was glad that he had told everything to Bensimon. Perhaps, at root, this was

43

all psychoanalysis could really achieve: it authorized you to talk about crucially, elementally, important matters – that you couldn't relate to anybody else – under the guise of a formal therapeutic discourse. What could Bensimon say to him, now, that he couldn't say to himself? The act of confession was a form of liberation and he wondered if he needed Bensimon any more. Still, he did feel almost physically different from the man who had written down the events of that day. And writing it down was important, also, he could see that. Something had changed – it had been a purging of sorts, an opening up, a cleansing.

He walked slowly and thoughtfully home from the tram-halt to the pension, stopping only to buy a hundred English Virginia cigarettes from the tobacconist at the junction of Mariahilfer Strasse and the pension's courtyard. He wondered vaguely if he were smoking too much – what he needed was a bracing twenty-mile hike in the mountains. He started to contemplate pleasantly where he might go this weekend.

Traudl was dusting down the glass-domed owl when he pushed open the door. She didn't curtsey, he noticed, and her welcoming smile seemed a little more knowing. Not surprisingly, Lysander thought, now we both have our own new secret to share.

'The lieutenant would like to see you, sir,' she said, then, glancing around, whispered, 'Remember about the twenty crowns.'

'Don't worry. He'll just assume we – you know . . .'

'Yes. Good. Be sure to say this, sir, please.'

'I will, Traudl. Rest assured.'

'And I put your post in your room, sir.'

'Thank you.'

Lysander knocked on Wolfram's door and, summoned, went in. He could see at once from Wolfram's wide smile and the bottle of champagne in an ice-bucket that all had gone well at the tribunal. He was back in his civilian clothes – a caramel tweed suit with chocolate-coloured tie.

'Acquitted!' Wolfram said with a maestro's gesture, arms raised in a flourish, and they shook hands warmly.

'Congratulations. I hope it wasn't too much of an ordeal,' Lysander said.

Wolfram busied himself with the opening and pouring of the champagne.

'Well, they try to scare you to death, of course,' he said. 'All those senior officers in their dress uniforms and their most disapproving expressions – solemn, solemn faces. Keep you waiting for hours.' He topped Lysander up. 'If you keep your nerve, your dignity, you're halfway there.' He smiled. 'Your excellent whisky was most helpful in that department.'

They clinked glasses, drank.

'So, it's all over,' Lysander said. 'What made them see sense?'

'An embarrassing lack of evidence. But I gave them something to think about. It helped move the spotlight away from the wily Slovene.'

'Oh, yes – what?'

'There's this captain in the regiment, Frankenthal. Doesn't like me. Arrogant man. I found a way of reminding my superior officers that Frankenthal is a Jewish name.' Wolfram shrugged. 'Frankenthal had the key for a week, just like me.'

'What's his Jewishness got to do with it?'

'He's not a Jew – his family converted to Catholicism a generation ago. But still . . .' Wolfram smiled, mischievously. 'They should have changed their name.'

'I don't follow.'

'My dear Lysander – if they can't pin the crime on a Slovene then a Jew is even better.' Wolfram drained his glass. 'Serves the disagreeable fellow right. And I have a month's leave, by way of apology for my "ordeal". So – you'll still see a bit more of me. Then we go on manoeuvres at the end of September.' He smiled. 'How was the country girl, eh?'

'Oh, Traudl, yes. Most enjoyable. Thank you very much.'

Lysander changed the subject quickly. 'What would you have done if they hadn't acquitted you?'

Wolfram thought for a second. 'I would have killed myself, most likely.' He frowned, as though thinking through the options, rationally. 'A bullet to the head, most likely. Or poison.'

'Surely not? My god.'

'No, no – you have to understand, Lysander, here in Vienna, in this ramshackle empire of ours, suicide is a perfectly reasonable course of action. Everyone will know your true feelings and why you had no choice but to do it – no one will condemn you or blame you.'

'Really?'

'Yes. Once you understand that you will understand us.' Wolfram smiled. 'It lies very deep in our being. *Selbstmord* – death of the self: it's an honourable farewell to this world.'

They finished the bottle and Lysander went back to his room feeling the effects of the alcohol. He thought he might skip dinner tonight – maybe go out to a café and carry on drinking. He felt buoyant, pleased about Wolfram, of course, and pleased that he himself had finally opened up the sealed casket of his past.

Propped on his desk was his post. A letter from Blanche, one from his bank in London and one with an Austrian stamp and handwriting he didn't recognize. He tore it open. It was an invitation to the *Vernissage* of an exhibition of 'recent work' by the artist Udo Hoff at an art gallery – the Bosendorfer-Renz Galerie für moderne Kunst – in the centre of town. Written across the bottom in green ink in large bulbous letters was the injunction: 'Do come! Hettie Bull.'

11. Parallelism

LYSANDER HAD MOVED FROM the chair to the divan at Bensimon's suggestion. He wasn't sure yet what this displacement and change in bodily alignment would signify, but Bensimon had been insistent. His head propped on pillows, Lysander still had an excellent view of the African bas-relief.

'How old was your mother when your father died?' Bensimon asked.

'Thirty-five . . . Thirty-six. Yes.'

'Still a young woman.'

'I suppose so.'

'How did she take your father's death?'

Lysander thought back, remembering his own awful shock, his utter misery, when the news had been delivered. Through the dark mists of his own fraught recollection he remembered how abject his mother had been.

'She took it very badly indeed – not surprisingly. She adored my father – she lived for him. She abandoned her own career when they married. She travelled with him when he travelled. When I was born I went with them also. He had his own theatre company, you see, apart from his work in the London theatres. She helped him run it, did the day-to-day administration. We were touring constantly all over England, Scotland, Ireland. We lived in rented houses, flats – never really had a place of our own. When he died we were living in a flat in South Kensington. For all his fame and success my father died virtually bankrupt – he'd sunk all his money into the Halifax Rief Theatre Company. There was very little left over for her. I remember we had to move to lodgings in Paddington. Two rooms, one fireplace, sharing a kitchen and a bathroom with two other families.'

Lysander could recall those rooms vividly. Grimy, uncleaned windows, worn, patched oilcloth on the floor. The smell of soot from the station nearby, the hoot and whistle from the marshalling

47

yards, the metallic clash and thunder of railway wagons and the sound of his mother, morning and night, weeping quietly. Then somehow she met Crickmay Faulkner and everything changed.

Lysander thought before he added, 'For a while she rather took to drink. Very discreetly – but in the months after the funeral she drank a lot. She was never unseemly but when she came to bed I could smell it on her.'

'Came to bed?'

'We had a sitting room and a bedroom in those lodgings,' Lysander said. 'We shared the bed. Until Lord Faulkner proposed marriage and he set us up in a larger house in Putney where I had my own room.'

'I see. How did your mother meet your father? Did he come to Vienna?'

'No. My mother sang in a chorus of a touring German opera company. They were touring England and Scotland in 1884. She had – has – a very fine mezzo-soprano voice. She was in Glasgow performing in Wagner's *Tristan* at the King's that was alternating with the Halifax Rief Theatre Company's production of *Macbeth*. They met backstage. Love at second sight, my father used to say.'

'Why second sight?'

'Because he said that at first sight his thoughts were hardly "amorous". If you see what I mean.'

'I do, I do. "Love at second sight." A pretty compliment.'

'Why are you asking me all these questions about my mother, Dr Bensimon? I'm no Oedipus, you know.'

'Heaven forfend, I'm sure you're not. But I think what you told me – what you read out to me the last time – holds the key to your eventual recovery. I'm just trying to get more context about you, about your life.'

Lysander registered the sound of his chair being pushed back. The session was over.

'Do you remember I asked you if you'd heard of Parallelism?' Bensimon had crossed the room into the very edge of his field of vision. A shadow with his hand extended. Lysander swung his legs off the divan, stood up and was offered a small book, little more than a pamphlet. He took it. Navy-blue cover with silver lettering. *Our Parallel Lives, an introduction*, by Dr J. Bensimon MB, BS (Oxon).

'I had it privately printed. I'm working on the full-length version. My magnum opus. Taking rather a long time, I'm afraid.'

Lysander turned the book over in his hands.

'Can you give me the gist?'

'Well, bit of a challenge. Let's say that the world is in essence neutral – flat, empty, bereft of meaning and significance. It's us, our imaginations, that make it vivid, fill it with colour, feeling, purpose and emotion. Once we understand this we can shape our world in any way we want. In theory.'

'Sounds very radical.'

'On the contrary – it's very commonsensical, once you get to grips with it. Have a read, see what you think.' He looked at Lysander, searchingly. 'I hesitate to say this, and I very rarely make this leap, but I have a feeling Parallelism will cure you, Mr Rief, I really do.'

12. Andromeda

LYSANDER FELT UNEASY AND strangely unsure of himself on the day of Udo Hoff's *Vernissage*. He hadn't slept well and even as he shaved that morning he felt a little odd and jittery – uncharacteristically nervous about going to the exhibition, about meeting Hettie Bull again. He soaped his brush in his shaving mug and worked the lather into his cheeks, chin and around his jaw, wondering automatically, as he pursed his lips and ran the brush under his nose, whether he ought to grow a moustache. No, came the usual, instant answer. He had tried it before and it didn't suit him; it made him look dirty, he thought, as if he had forgotten to wipe away a smear of oxtail soup from his upper lip. He had the wrong colour of brown hair for a moustache. You needed stark contrast, he thought, to justify a moustache on a young face – like that chap Munro at the embassy, black and neat, as if he'd stuck it on.

He dressed with care, selecting his navy-blue lightweight suit, black brogues and a stiff-collared white shirt that he wore with a scarlet, polka-dotted, four-in-hand tie. A splash of bold colour to show how artistic he was. His father would not have approved – a natty and particular dresser himself, Halifax Rief always maintained that it should take a good five minutes before anyone noticed your style or the care and thought that lay behind the clothes a man wore. Any form of ostentation was vulgar.

Lysander decided to visit the Kunsthistorisches Hofmuseum on the Burgring. It was a gesture, he knew, and a futile one at that, but he was imagining himself at the gallery for Hoff's exhibition, the room full of people, all expert and opinionated about art, ancient and modern. What could he say to such intellectuals, art critics, collectors and connoisseurs? He was conscious again of the huge gaps in his knowledge of general culture. He could quote pages of Shakespeare, Marlowe, Sheridan, Ibsen, Shaw – or at least those parts of the playwrights' work he'd had to con in his career. He had read a lot of nineteenth-century poetry – poetry he loved – but he knew very little of what was perceived to be 'avant-garde'. He bought newspapers and magazines and kept up with world events and European politics, to a degree, and he realized that, on first impression, he presented a highly plausible rendition of a worldly, informed, educated man – but he knew how flimsy the disguise was whenever he encountered people with real brains. You're an actor, he rebuked himself, so act intelligent! There's plenty of time to acquire knowledge, he thought, you're not remotely a fool, there's a lot of native brain-power there. It's not your fault that you were badly educated, moving from school to school. Your adult life has been focussed on your theatrical career – auditions, rehearsals, small roles becoming more significant. Only in the last play he'd been in, *The Amorous Ultimatum*, could he have been legitimately considered a leading man – or second leading man, at any rate – his name on the poster in the same type-size as Mrs Cicely Brightwell, no less, and no better benchmark to show how far he'd come in only a few years. His father would have been proud of him.

In the museum he wandered through the grand galleries on the first floor, looking at the gloomy, varnished images of saints and madonnas, mythical gods and melancholy crucifixions, stepping close to read the names of the artists on the bottom of the frame and mentally checking them off. Caravaggio, Titian, Bonifazio, Tintoretto, Tiepolo. He knew these names, of course, but he could now say, 'Do you know Bordone's *Venus and Adonis*? I was looking at it just today – yes, funnily enough – in the Hofmuseum. Splendid, very affecting.' He began to relax a little. It was just an act, after all, and that was his *métier*, his talent, his calling.

He wandered on. Now all the painters were Dutch – Rembrandt, Franz Hals, Hobbema, Memling. And what was this? *Attack by Robbers* by Philip Wouverman. Dark and powerful, the swarthy brigands armed with silver cutlasses and spiky halberds. 'Do you know Wouverman's work? Very striking.' Where were the Germans? Ah, here we are – Cranach, D'Pfenning, Albrecht Dürer . . . But names were beginning to jumble and distort in his head and he felt a sudden tiredness hit him. Too much art – museum-fatigue. Time for a cigarette and a Kapuziner. He had enough names in his head to sustain any fleeting social chit-chat – it wasn't as if he was going to be interviewed for a job as a curator, for heaven's sake.

He found a coffee stall on the Ring and leaned on its counter, smoking a Virginia and sipping his coffee. It really was a splendid boulevard, he thought – nothing remotely like it in London, the Mall was the only contender, but feeble in comparison – the great circular sweep of the roadways girdling the old town, the careful positioning of the huge buildings and palaces, their parks and gardens. Very beautiful. He looked at his wristwatch – he still had an hour or so to kill before he could reasonably make an entrance at the gallery. He wondered what Udo Hoff would be like. Bound to be very pretentious, he imagined, exactly the sort of man who could lure and impress a Hettie Bull.

He sauntered along the Ring towards the steepling tower of the Rathaus. He could hear, as he approached, an amplified voice shouting and he saw, as he drew near, a crowd of some hundreds gathered in the small park in front of the town hall. A wooden stage had been erected, some six feet high, and on it a man was giving a hectoring speech through a megaphone.

Automobiles and motor diligences whizzed by as the day began to lose its heat. The evening rush homeward had begun. Tourists in horse-drawn carriages clip-clopped along the pavement edge like vestiges of another age. Bicycles everywhere, swerving through the traffic. Lysander crossed the boulevard over to the Rathaus, watching the oncoming vehicles carefully, and joined the murmuring crowd.

They were all working men, it seemed, and they had come to this meeting symbolically wearing their work clothes. Carpenters in dungarees with hammers hooked to their belts, masons in leather aprons, motor engineers in their bib-and-brace overalls, chauffeurs in gauntlets and double-breasted overcoats, foresters with long two-handled saws. There was even a group of several dozen miners, black with coal dust, their teeth yellow in their smirched faces, the whites of their eyes stark and disturbing.

Lysander moved closer to them, curious, strangely fascinated by their black faces and hands. He realized this was the first time he had seen real miners close to, as opposed to images of them in magazines and books. They were paying concentrated attention to the speaker, who was barking on about jobs and wages, about immigrant Slav labour that was undercutting the rightful earnings of the Austrian working man. Cheers and clapping broke out as the speech became more incendiary. A man bumped into him and apologized, politely, not to say effusively.

Lysander turned. 'It's quite all right,' he said.

He was a young man, in his early twenties, with a grey felt hat, minus its band, and his long dark hair hung over his collar – his beard was patchy and unbarbered. Oddly, because the weather was fine, he was wearing a short, yellow rubberized cycling-coat. Lysander saw that he was shirtless under the cycling-coat – a vagrant, a madman – the sour smell of poverty came off him.

Loud cheers rose from the crowd at some sally from the speaker.

'They just don't understand,' Cycling-coat said fiercely to Lysander. 'Empty words, hot air.'

'Politicians,' Lysander said, rolling his eyes in ostensible sympathy. 'All the same. Words are cheap.' He was beginning to be aware of glances coming his way. Who is this smart young man in his polka-dot tie talking to the madman? Time to leave. He walked away around the group of miners – black troglodytes come up from the underworld to see the modern city. Suddenly Lysander felt the idea for a poem grow in him.

The Bosendorfer-Renz gallery was in a street off Graben. Lysander hovered some distance away at first, watching to see that guests were actually going in – he needed the security of other bodies. He approached the door, invitation in hand, but no one seemed to be checking on the identity of invitees so he slipped it back in his pocket and followed an elderly couple into what seemed more like an antique shop than an art gallery. In the small window were a couple of ornately carved chairs and a Dutch still life on an easel (apples, grapes and peaches with the inevitable carefully perched fly). At the rear of this first room was a corridor – bright lights beckoned and a rising hum of conversation. Lysander took a deep breath and headed on in.

It was a large high-ceilinged room, like a converted storage area, lit by three electric chandeliers. Long sections of wooden partitions mounted on small wheels broke up the space. It was busy, forty to fifty people had already arrived, Lysander was glad to see – he could lose himself. Hoff's canvases were hung from a high picture rail; here and there small sculptures and maquettes stood on thin chest-high plinths. He decided to do a quick tour of the paintings, say hello to Miss Bull, congratulate Hoff and disappear into the night, duty done.

Hoff's work, at first glance, appeared conventional and unexceptional – landscapes, townscapes, one or two portraits. But on closer inspection Lysander registered the strange and subtle light effects. A view of a meadow with a wood beyond seemed bathed in the glow of powerful arc-lights, the shadows cast densely black, razor-edged, turning the banal panorama into something sinister and apocalyptic, making you wonder what blazing light in the sky caused this baleful iridescence. A Saharan sun shining on a northern European valley. There was another sunset which was so lurid that it seemed the sky itself was diseased, rotting. In a townscape – *Village in the Snow* – Lysander suddenly noticed that two houses had no doors or windows and the village church had a round 'O' on its steeple, not a cross. What secrets were harboured here in this humble village?

As he went round the room spotting these potent anomalies, Lysander found that he was growing impressed with Hoff's subtly oblique and disturbing vision. The largest painting was a full-length portrait of a heavily made-up woman in an embroidered kaftan sitting in a chair – *Portrait of Fräulein Gustl Cantor-De Castro* – but a second glance revealed that the kaftan was unbuttoned in her lap to reveal her pubis. The arrowhead of dark hair had seemed part of the decorative frieze-motif on the richly embroidered kaftan. When he saw this, Lysander felt a genuine frisson of shock as he realized what he was looking at. The flat stare of the hard-faced woman appeared to be directed exclusively at him, making him seem either complicit in the exposure of her sex – she had undone these buttons just for him – or else he was a voyeur, caught in the act.

He turned away and saw a waiter circulating with a tray of wine glasses. Lysander helped himself to one – it was a Riesling, a little too warm – and moved away to a corner to survey the crowd, most of whom seemed more interested in talking to each other than looking at Udo Hoff's new paintings. He wondered who was Hoff. You could spot the artists – one with a shaven head, one with no tie, one bearded fellow in a paint-spattered smock as if he'd just come from his studio. Absurd to demarcate yourself so obviously, Lysander thought – no class. He could see no sign of Miss Hettie Bull, however.

He set down his empty glass on a table and wandered off to glance at what was hanging on the mobile partitions. He jerked to a halt, almost comically, at what he saw next. Turning a corner to investigate what was on the reverse side of a partition filled with small, framed drawings of jugs and bottles he found himself in front of the cartoon, the original design, of a theatre poster. There it was – a near-naked woman cupping her breasts as some blunt-faced rearing dragon-monster, like a scaly eel, threatened her – one orange eye glowing and a snake's forked tongue extended in the direction of her loins. Written on it was *'ANDROMEDA UND PERSEUS eine Oper in vier Akten von GOTTLIEB TOLLER'*. So Udo Hoff had designed the offending poster, the shreds and scraps of which he had seen throughout Vienna . . . One mystery solved. And Perseus not Persephone.

Lysander stepped back for a better view. It was a provocative and disturbing image, no doubt. The scaly neck and head of the monster with its solitary septic eye. Even the most innocent bourgeois could see what was meant to be symbolized here, no doubt about it. And the woman pictured, Andromeda, she seemed –

'Did you ever see it?' An English voice – Manchester accent.

Lysander turned. Dr Bensimon stood there in evening dress – white bow tie, tailcoat – his beard recently trimmed and neatened.

They shook hands, Lysander finding it strange to see his doctor here, out of his context. Then he remembered Miss Bull was a patient, also.

Bensimon had obviously been thinking along similar lines. 'Never thought to find you here, Mr Rief. Took me aback when I saw you.'

'Miss Bull invited me.'

'Ah. All is explained.' He looked again at the poster and gestured at it. 'The opera only had three performances in Vienna – at a *Kabarett* called "Hell" – *die Hölle*. It was the only place that would put it on. Then it was banned by the authorities.'

'Banned? Why?'

'Gross indecency. Mind you, I would have banned it for the music. Intolerable screeching atonality. Richard Strauss gone insane.' He smiled. 'I'm very old-fashioned in only one thing – music. I like a good melody.'

'What was indecent about it?'

'Miss Bull.'

'She sang?'

'No, no. She was Andromeda, sort of. Can't you see the likeness in the portrait? You know the myth: Andromeda is chained to some rocks by the seashore as a placatory offering to a sea-monster, Cetus. Perseus comes along, kills Cetus, rescues her, they get married, etcetera, etcetera. Well, the soprano playing Andromeda – forget her name – could have passed easily for a heavyweight boxer. So Toller came up with the idea of a stand-in Andromeda for the monster-attack – our Miss Bull. There was an actually very impressive shadow-play – an Oriental puppet-effect for the monster projected somehow on the back wall – huge. Perseus was stage-front singing some interminable tenor aria – twenty minutes it seemed like – while Andromeda was being menaced. The soprano was off stage wailing and screaming. Cacophony, is the only word.'

Lysander was curious. 'What was so indecent about Miss Bull's Andromeda?'

'She was entirely naked.'

'Oh. I see. Right, yes . . .'

'Well, she had a few yards of some semi-transparent gauze around her. Left nothing to the imagination, let's say.'

'Very brave of her.'

'Not short on audacity, our Miss Bull. Anyway, you can imagine the outrage. The brouhaha. They closed the theatre, ripped down every poster they could find. Poor Toller was charged with everything – immorality, indecency, pornography. Threw the book at him.' Bensimon shrugged. 'So he killed himself.'

'What?'

'Yes. Hanged himself in the actual theatre – in "Hell". Very dramatic statement. And sad, of course.'

They stood there for a few seconds looking at the poster in silence. There was a distinct resemblance to Hettie Bull, Lysander saw, now he looked at Andromeda's face and not her naked body.

'I'd better be going,' Bensimon said. 'I've an official dinner, hence the get-up. Dozens of doctors, for my sins. Have you seen Miss Bull yet?'

'No,' Lysander said. They looked around the crowded room. Lysander suddenly saw her – her small figure. He pointed. 'There she is.'

'We should say hello,' Bensimon said, and they made their way across the room towards her.

Hettie Bull was standing with three men. As he and Bensimon crossed the room through the crowd towards her, Lysander noticed that she was wearing billowing cerise harem-style pantaloons, a short black satin jacket with diamanté buttons and a collar and tie. Her mass of hair was loosely piled up on her head and secured with many tortoiseshell combs. A small appliquéd bag hung from her shoulder on a braided cord reaching almost to her knees. When she turned to greet them Lysander heard a soft tinkling from ground level and looked down to see small silver bells sewn to the front of her shoes. Bensimon made his farewells and left. Hettie Bull turned to Lysander. Her big hazel eyes.

'What do you think of Udo's paintings?' she asked.

'I like them. Very much. No, I do.'

She was staring at him intently but her mood seemed calm and assured. Perhaps she'd taken some more of Dr Bensimon's medicine. She looked vaguely androgynous in her little jacket with its collar and tie.

'Then you must tell him yourself,' she said and moved off on chiming feet to tap the elbow of a man standing a few yards away, engaged in a conversation with two women wearing wide floppy hats. Hettie brought him over.

'Udo Hoff – Mr Lysander Rief.'

Lysander shook hands. Hoff was a very thick-set, burly man in his thirties, shorter than Lysander, with an immense breadth of chest and shoulder, a shaven head and a pointed russet beard. He seemed over-muscular, like a circus strong-man, almost bursting the stressed buttons of his shirt front, his thick neck straining at his collar.

'Mr Rief's also with Dr Bensimon,' Hettie explained. 'That's how we met.'

Lysander immediately wished she hadn't explained as Hoff seemed to look him up and down with new hostility and something of a sneer crossed his features.

'Ah, the Viennese cure,' he said. 'Is this the latest fashion in London?' He spoke good accented English.

'No. Not at all,' Lysander said, defensively. The man seemed suddenly keen to provoke him. So – mollification, charm. He would be pleasant and nice, Frau K would be proud of him.

'I really admire your paintings – very striking. Most intriguing.'

Hoff made a flipping gesture with the palm of one hand as if a fly were bothering him.

'How are you enjoying our city?' he asked in a flat voice.

Lysander wondered if this was some kind of joke or test. He decided to take it as genuine.

'Very much. I was just thinking this evening, as I walked along the Ring before coming here, how impressive it was. Exceptionally well laid out with a generosity of scale that you won't find in –'

'You like the Ring?' Hoff said, incredulous.

'Emphatically. I think it's –'

'You do realize these are new buildings, only a few decades old, if that?'

'I have read my guidebook carefully –'

Hoff actually prodded him on the arm with a finger, his eyebrows circumflexing in a strange anguished frown.

'I abominate the Ring,' Hoff said, a little tremor in his voice. 'The Ring is a grotesque bourgeois sham. It's an offence to the eye, to one's sense of what is right, one's most basic values. I close my eyes when I see the Ring. New buildings masquerading as something ancient and venerable. Shameful. We Viennese artists live in a permanent sense of shame.' He poked him again in the arm as if to add emphasis and walked away.

'Good god . . . Sorry about that,' Lysander said to Hettie. 'I had no idea it was a sensitive subject.'

'No, we artist types aren't meant to "like" the Ring,' she said, then lowering her voice, added, 'But I have to say I do, rather.'

'Same here. There's nothing like it in London.'

She raised her face to him. She's so *gamine*, Lysander thought, I feel I could pick her up with one hand.

'When am I going to sculpt you?' she said. 'You're not leaving town, are you?'

'No – no plans. Actually, things are going rather well with Dr Bensimon – I'll be here for at least another month.'

'Then come to my studio one afternoon, I can do some preliminary drawings.' She rummaged in her little bag and scribbled down an address on a scrap of paper.

'It's on the outskirts. You can get the train to Ottakring and walk from the station. Maybe take a cab the first time just to be sure. Shall we say Monday at four?'

'Ah, yes,' Lysander looked at her address. Was this wise? – but he was oddly tempted. 'Thank you.'

She put her hand on his arm. 'Wonderful. You've a most interesting face.' She glanced around. 'I'd better go and find Udo in case he gets even angrier. See you on Monday.' She smiled and walked away, the tinkle of her bells swiftly lost in the hum and chatter of the conversation.

13. Autobiographical Investigations

When God turned his hand from the making of man
And woman, of matter much finer,
Some black flux and rust, well seasoned with dust
Remained – so he fashioned the miner.

Miner – delver not climber
Miner – world's underground designer
Miner – ocean liner (?)
Miner – confine her/repiner/incliner/diner

QUITE PLEASED WITH FIRST verse. Bit stuck.

Hettie Bull. Bullish man – Udo Hoff. Bull in a china shop. Bull fighter. Matador. Little jacket. White shirt and tie. Bull fighting bull.

'Happy people are never brilliant. Art requires friction.' Who said that? Nonsense. Art is the pursuit of a kind of harmony and integrity. A harmonious life full of integrity is artistic. Ergo. Q.E.D.

Dream. I was shaving and then in the mirror my face turned into my father's. How are you, old son? he said. I'm well, father, I said. I miss you. Step through the mirror and join me, then, he said, come on, lad. I touched the mirror and his face turned back to mine.

I remember an argument I had with Blanche because she'd left me a note written in pencil. I said that was disrespectful – she wrote to me as if she were jotting down a list of groceries – you didn't write in pencil to someone you loved. She called me a silly arrogant prig. She was right – sometimes I think a fundamental priggishness is my worst feature. Not priggishness, so much, as worrying or making a fuss about things that are of no consequence at all.

Great acting is being able to say 'Pass the salt, please,' without sounding weird or odd or stupid or portentous. Great acting is being able to say 'Horror! Horror! Horror!' without sounding weird or odd or stupid or portentous.

Life is more than love. Turn that around. Love is more than life. Makes just as much sense. This is less true if you say LOVE = SEX-LOVE. Life is more than sex-love. Sex-love is not more than life. True. Didn't Dostoevsky say something similar? You never step into the same river twice, similarly there is never a simple, single thought. The simplest thought can be qualified again and again and again. I have a headache – because I drank too much schnapps with Wolfram, who made me laugh. The simple headache has its history, its penumbra, and is touched by my pre-headache life and (I hope) my post-headache life. Everything is unbelievably complicated. Everything.

14. The Fabulating Function

'I READ YOUR LITTLE book,' Lysander said, stretching himself out on the divan. 'Most interesting. I think I understand it. Well, sort of.'

'It's basically about using your imagination,' Dr Bensimon said. 'I'm going to pull the curtains today, if you don't mind.'

Lysander heard him drawing the curtains on the three windows and the room grew dim and tenebrous, lit only by the lamp on Bensimon's desk. As he crossed back to his seat his giant shadow flicked across the wall by the fireplace.

As far as Lysander was able to comprehend, Bensimon's theory of 'Parallelism' worked approximately along the following lines. Reality was neutral, as he had explained – 'gaunt' was a word he used several times to describe it. This world, unperceived by our senses, lay out there like a skeleton, impoverished and passionless. When we opened our eyes, when we smelled, heard, touched and tasted we added the flesh to these bones according to our natures and how well our imagination functioned. Thus the individual transforms 'the world' – a person's mind weaves its own bright covering over neutral reality. This world is created by us as a 'fiction', it is ours alone and is unique and unshareable.

'I think I find the idea of the world being "fictive" a bit tricky,' Lysander said, with some hesitation.

'Pure common sense,' Bensimon said. 'You know how you feel when you wake up in a good mood. The first cup of coffee tastes extra delicious. You go out for a stroll – you notice colours, sounds, the effect of sunlight on an old brick wall. On the other hand, if you wake up gloomy and depressed, you have no appetite. Your cigarette tastes sour and burns your throat. In the streets the clanging of the trams irritates you, the passers-by are ugly and selfish. And so on. This happens unreflectingly – what I'm trying to do is make this power, that we all have in us, a conscious one, to bring it to the front of your mind.'

'I see what you mean.' This made a sort of sense, Lysander acknowledged. Bensimon continued.

'So – we human beings bring to the world what the French philosopher Bergson calls "*La Fonction Fabulatrice*". The fabulating function. Do you know Bergson's work?'

'Ah. No.'

'I've rather appropriated this idea of his and reworked it. The world, our world, is for each one of us a unique blend – a union, a fusing – of this individual imagination and reality.'

Lysander said nothing, concentrating on the bas-relief over the fireplace, wondering how Parallelism was going to cure his anorgasmia.

Bensimon was speaking again. 'You know that old saying: "The gods of Africa are always African." That is the fiction the African mind has created – its fusing of imagination and reality.'

Perhaps that explains the bas-relief, Lysander thought.

'I can understand that,' he said, cautiously. 'I can see how that works. An African god will hardly be Chinese. But how does that apply to my particular problem?'

Lysander heard Bensimon move his chair from behind his desk and set it down close to the end of the divan. Heard the creak of leather as he sat down.

'In precisely this way,' he said. 'If the everyday world, everyday reality, is a fiction we create then the same can be said of our past – the past is an aggregate of fictive realities we have already experienced – our memories. What I'm going to try and make you do is change those old fictions you've been living with.'

This was all becoming a bit complex, Lysander thought.

'I'm going to use a bit of very mild hypnosis on you. A very gentle and shallow hypnotic state. That's why the room is dark. Close your eyes, please.'

Lysander did so.

Bensimon's voice changed register, going deeper and strangely monotone. He spoke very slowly and deliberately.

'Relax. Try to relax totally. You're inert, lying immobile. You feel that total relaxation begin in your feet. Slowly it begins to travel up your legs. Now you feel it in your calves. Now it's reached your knees . . . Your thighs . . . Breathe as slowly as possible. In – out. In – out. It's climbing your body, now it's in your chest, filling your body, total relaxation.'

Lysander felt a kind of swoon flow through him. He was completely conscious but he felt in a form of semi-paralysis, as if he couldn't lift a finger, floating an inch above the blanket. Bensimon began to count down in his deep, monotone voice.

'Twenty, nineteen, eighteen . . . You are completely relaxed . . . Fifteen, fourteen, thirteen . . .'

Now Lysander felt fatigue envelop him, his eyes locked shut, Bensimon's voice oddly distant and muffled as he counted down to zero.

'Think back to that day,' Bensimon went on. 'You're a young boy, fourteen years old. You have your book in your hand, "The Rape of the Lock". You walk through the walled garden. You greet the gardeners. You climb the stile into the wood. It's a glorious sunny day, warm and balmy, the birds are singing. You walk into the wood and you sit down at the foot of an ancient oak. You start to read. The sun warms you. You begin to nod. You fall asleep. Fast asleep. You sleep for two hours, you're late for tea. You wake up. You pick up your book and you go back to the house where your mother is waiting for you. You apologize for being late and the two of you go into the drawing room to have your tea . . .'

'Open your eyes.' A dry slap. Slap-slap.

Lysander did so at once, suddenly tense, forgetting where he was for an instant. He'd fallen asleep. Had he missed something crucial? Bensimon opened the curtains and daylight filled the room again.

'Did I fall asleep. I'm terribly sorry if I –'

'For a matter of seconds. Quite natural. You'll remember everything I said.'

'I remember apologizing for being late for tea.'

'Exactly.' Bensimon crossed the room. 'You weren't in a trance. You were simply imagining being in a parallel world. A world where you went to sleep in a wood on a sunny afternoon, woke up and returned home for tea. Concentrate on that day in your parallel world. Fill it with detail and concentrate on the emotions that day generated. Use your *fonction fabulatrice*. In this parallel world nothing happened. Reality and imagination fuse to form the fiction that we live by. Now you have an alternative.'

Lysander ordered a brandy in the Café Central. He thought about what had happened in that session, obeying Bensimon's instructions to concentrate on the details of the parallel world he had created – that sunny day where nothing happened except that he nodded off over his book as he lay under an oak tree in Claverleigh Wood. Yes, he could see himself waking, rubbing his eyes, rising to his feet a little stiffly and unsteadily, picking up his book and walking home. Over the stile, through the walled garden – all the gardeners gone – and into the Hall through a side door, clattering up the stairs to the green drawing room where his mother was waiting and tea had been laid out on the circular table. Thinking – yes, she has rung the bell for more hot water to freshen the pot because I was late and the tea had cooled. There would be triangles of buttered toast and strawberry jam and a slice of seed cake, my favourite. I sit down and brush a blade of grass off my trousers. My mother picks up the silver teapot – no, it's the pale-green china one with the pattern of coiling ivy leaves and the chip in its lid – and as she pours my cup of tea she asks me, 'How's the reading going, darling?'

Lysander paused, brandy glass held halfway to his lips. It was so real. Completely real and, to him, entirely true. He had chosen to go into a parallel world and had brought his imagination to bear.

Extraordinary. His mother was wearing . . . What? A tangerine rest-gown with wide Magyar sleeves. A jade bracelet that clinked against her teacup. Stevens, the footman, cleared away the tray. It was so easy. What was it called? His *fonction fabulatrice*. He had made a familiar world and created a day in it where nothing untoward had happened. He felt only happiness . . . Maybe he should read some more of this Bergson person. He sipped his brandy, felt its warmth slide down his throat, its sweet smoky mellowness, and smiled to himself.

15. The Studio at Ottakring

THERE WAS A LETTER from Blanche in Lysander's post that morning. He ripped it open with his thumb and for a brief second he caught a residual odour of rose water, the scent she used. She had covered four leaves of lilac writing paper, dense with her big, jagged scrawl.

> Darling One and Only,
> Flaming June is going to be an enormous success – I can feel in my bones that it's going to run and run for months. When are you coming home? Are you feeling better in yourself? Your little kitten wants to curl up in your lap again. I have a part in a 'film' – can you believe it? Loads of lovely money. You must have a test when you come back. It's so easy – no lines to learn! I think your handsome face will be perfect and the whole experience is simply fun, as easy as pie compared to what we do night after night in the theatre –

He put the letter down, deciding to finish it later, and noticing with some irritation that Blanche hadn't bothered to answer any of his questions. Writing letters to each other was meant to be a form of dialogue, a conversation – but Blanche wrote as if the traffic was one way, a declamation about her feelings and what she was up to that paid not the slightest notice to his replies. When he wrote to her he always had her latest letter by his side. A correspondence should feed off its two parts; monologues – however lively and intimate – were not necessarily interesting.

His mood of mild irritation persisted as he walked to the *Stadtbahn* station and bought his return ticket to Ottakring. He looked out of the window at the western suburbs of Vienna as the little train chuffed around its branch line to its destination. Suddenly he didn't feel like posing for Miss Bull and being drawn by her – why had he agreed? But Miss Bull was persistent, it was hard to say no to her – this much he'd already learned.

At Ottakring he showed the driver of a two-horse *Fiaker* the address of the studio and climbed up into the cab. They rattled further westward, past rows of allotments and orchards of apple trees and a large graveyard with a wooden paling fence before turning up a muddy farm lane. The cab stopped at a gate painted a vibrant scarlet and Lysander stepped down and paid the modest fare. Already he was thinking of his journey home: it was all very well taking a cab from the station but how did one return to the station? He would stay an hour – no more.

From the gate, a clinker path led to what looked like an old stone barn at the edge of a tree-lined field in which two shire horses grazed. Flower pots were clustered round the front door to the barn, bright with marguerites and zinnias. He pushed the gate open and set a brass bell, mounted on a whippy length of curved metal, clanging loudly. Miss Bull appeared at the doorway almost immediately. They shook hands. She was wearing a knee-length canvas smock covered in splashes of clay and plaster.

'Mr Lysander Rief, you're actually here. I can't believe it!' she cried and led him into her studio.

The old barn had been converted into a capacious, windowless, ceilingless sculpture-room. A wide section of the tiled roof had been removed and replaced with glass panes. In the corner was a large squat cast-iron stove with a tall thin chimney pipe climbing up in a series of angled lengths to the roof. Along one wall ran a line of trestle tables covered with trays and pots and variously sized blocks of wood. Twisted wire armatures were stacked at one end. In another corner was a seating area – four cane chairs round a low table with a bright throw on it and a jug of anemones. In the very middle of the room on a high turning table was a crude clay sculpture, three feet tall, of a crouching minotaur – a blunt bovine head with stubby horns set on a massy, muscled body beneath. Beside it stood a small dais, with a square of carpet cut to fit the surface. Lysander looked around.

'Marvellous light,' he said, thinking this was the sort of remark to make on entering an artist's studio.

Miss Bull removed her smock to reveal that she was wearing a cream muslin blouse over a mid-calf black serge skirt. She had wooden clogs on her feet. Her dark hair was tousled, pinned and piled up on her head with long strands falling from it carelessly. There were no paintings on view.

'Does Hoff work here?' Lysander asked.

'No, no. We live across the field, about half a mile away. Udo's family home. We both tried working in his studio but it was a disaster – we did nothing but fight. So I rented this old place and renovated it after a fashion.' She pointed up. 'Got some proper light in.' She indicated a door at the far end. 'There's a bedroom in there, if I feel like a snooze, and a sink and scullery. Thunderbox outside round the back.'

'Very nice.' He corrected himself. 'Ideal.'

'Have a glass of Madeira,' she said, going to the trestle table and pouring the wine into two small tumblers. Lysander wandered over and they clinked glasses and drank. He didn't really like fortified wines – sherries and ports and the like – and immediately felt a small dry headache form over one eye.

'This is impressive,' he said, gesturing at the crouching minotaur.

'I'm going to cast it in bronze,' Miss Bull said. 'If I can afford it. Udo posed – never again. Moaning, complaining. I pose nude for him all the time. Most unfair.' She put her glass down and picked up a large drawing pad and a stick of charcoal. 'Talking of which – shall we get to work?'

'Should I stand on the dais?'

'Yes. But once you've got your clothes off.'

Lysander smiled reflexively, assuming this was a typical Miss Bull-style risqué joke.

'Clothes *off*?' he said. 'Most amusing.'

'I don't sculpt the clothed figure. So there's no point in me drawing you with your clothes on.' She smiled and pointed to the door at the end of the big room. 'You can change in there.'

'Fine. Right.'

It was a small basic bedroom with whitewashed walls and rough planked floor covered with a rag-rug. There was a single iron-framed bed with a brown blanket and a dresser with a plain jug and ewer. On the ledge of a small window that looked over a vegetable garden lost amongst its rank weeds was a small glass jar filled with dried grasses, the only sign of individuality.

Lysander stood in the middle of the room thinking what to do. What was going on here? For a second he considered the option of opening the door again, striding out and telling her that it was impossible and that he had to leave. But he knew Miss Bull would think the less of him if he did that. He didn't want her to see him as a prig or an insecure stuffed-shirt. He emptied his mind as best he could and began to undress.

When he was down to his socks and his drawers he began to feel a stirring of excitement at the audacity of what he was about to do. He looked at his clothes laid neatly on the bed. Last chance. He slipped off his socks and tugged at the bow of the waistcord. As his drawers fell he felt his genitals cool. There was a towel on a towel-rail by the dresser and he tied it around him and stepped back into the studio. Miss Bull was sitting in a wicker chair that she'd drawn closer to the dais. She held out something that looked like a small leather sling.

'It just struck me. Would you prefer a *cache-sexe*? I don't mind.'

'No, no. *Au naturel* – all the same to me.'

He stepped up on to the dais, feeling the coarse carpet under the soles of his feet and hearing his suddenly thumping heart in his ears.

'Ready when you are,' Miss Bull said, calmly.

He let the towel fall and concentrated his gaze on the sooty chimney rising from the stove opposite, hearing only the hurried scratch of the charcoal on Miss Bull's sketch pad. He squared his shoulders and told himself to relax, once more. He was not the tallest of men but he knew he had a good slim-waisted, broad-shouldered figure – certainly his tailor was always complimenting him on his build. 'Classic, Mr Rief. The "manly ideal" – you should see my other customers. Gor blimey.'

'Could you turn to your left slightly? Perfect.'

Lysander turned, trying to think of himself as some kind of Greek Olympian, a discus-thrower or javelin-hurler, stripped off for the games. What was all the fuss about the naked body, anyway? Especially in the context of art – think of all the nudes ever painted, the unclothed statues in public gardens, Michelangelo's David, the innumerable Venuses and bare-buttocked gods and gladiators. He took a deep breath, allowing his fingers to graze his thighs. Relax, relax, relax.

'Could you put your hands on your hips?'

He did so, clenching his buttocks involuntarily, suddenly chastened by the thought of Udo Hoff, crossing the meadow from his own studio to see how his mistress was getting on . . . No, don't let your thoughts go there. Think of a parallel world, your parallel world . . . He shut down his mind.

He heard the legs of the wicker chair scrape back and the wooden clattering sound of Miss Bull's footsteps – walking away and then returning.

'Shall we have a break?' she said. 'You've earned another glass of Madeira.'

Now he could look at her. She stood there smiling, holding out the glass for him. He stooped and picked up the towel, holding it casually in front of him, and stepped down to the floor, taking the glass from her. But now he couldn't tie the towel around him, he had no hands free – but what the hell, he thought. He was enjoying the sensation – they might as well be standing at the bar of a café, chatting. Miss Bull seemed totally unperturbed. It was just another life-class to her, of course.

'You stood admirably still.'

'Thank you.'

'Anyone would have thought you'd done this before.'

'It's a definite first.' He took a huge gulp of Madeira and then another – too sweet for his taste but he needed the rush of alcohol.

'D'you want to see what I've done?' Miss Bull was holding out the sketch pad, a strange smiling expression on her face. It seemed both absurd and yet entirely natural that he was standing here naked in this room with only a hanging towel 'to protect his modesty', as the saying went, three feet away from a young woman, fully clothed in a muslin blouse, a serge skirt and wooden clogs. She took the glass from his hand and replaced it with her sketch pad.

Lysander looked at the drawing. Very detailed and three-dimensional, the charcoal shaded and blurred by the rub of her fingertips. A strong confident hand, a very capable draughtswoman. He felt his throat close and a nerve-tremor run across his shoulder blades.

He cleared his throat. 'What would you call this? "A study of male genitalia"?'

'You have a shortish foreskin, I noticed,' she said, lowering her voice confidentially. 'For a moment I thought you must be circumcised, like Udo.' She took a step towards him. 'But as I looked more closely I saw that you weren't.'

'No. I'm not circumcised,' he managed to say, feeling a warm flush spread across his neck and chest – the gulps of Madeira only now working on him. He felt his penis stir and thicken, as though aware it was being discussed and responding.

Miss Bull allowed her gaze to drop below his waist and with one hand moved the hanging towel aside.

'Now that's what I call a study in male genitalia,' she said. He felt her other hand run softly down his back making him shiver. Her fingertips scraped across his buttocks.

'Shall we go to bed?' she asked, leaning into him, looking up, smiling, her big hazel eyes full of laughter.

16. A Devilish Plan

DR BENSIMON LOOKED AT Lysander quizzically.

'Well, that's somewhat extraordinary. I have to say.'

'I know,' Lysander admitted, shaking his head in similar bafflement.

'Everything functioned?'

'Absolutely problem-free. As normal. In fact I did it again – just to prove to myself that it wasn't some kind of fluke.'

'Twice?'

'Within the space of forty minutes, say.'

Lysander thought back – two days after the event he still felt bemused and marvelling. They had gone into the small bedroom and then, in a maelstrom of his clothes being flung off the blanket and Miss Bull ridding herself of blouse, skirt, camisole, shift and knickers, they found themselves in the iron bed, her little slim lithe body tense and squirming in his arms, his arousal insistent and demanding. Certain details initially printed themselves on his mind – her dark hair spread wide on the pillow, her surprisingly full breasts with perfectly round small nipples, her fingertips sooty with charcoal – but from then on he seemed to go into a form of sexual trance, everything blurring as he concentrated. And when the release came and his orgasm arrived it took him by complete surprise, so much so that he shouted – '*MY GOD!*' – in astonishment and pleasure, that made her ask him if he was all right.

They separated, rolled apart and Lysander buried his face in the thin pillow, feeling tears in his eyes as Hettie – Hettie, now, no longer Miss Bull – went to fetch the Madeira bottle and the glasses. They drank, they caressed each other, they talked.

'This was all a devilish plan, wasn't it?' he accused her.

'Yes. I admit – I confess. Ever since that first day when we met in Dr Bensimon's rooms. When I was in such a state, remember?'

'Yes.'

'But, even so, I found I couldn't get you out of my mind, for some reason. Maybe because you let me barge in and were so understanding. Not horrible, but kind. And pretty.'

'And so you plotted and planned and came up with this diabolical scheme.'

'But I was worried it might not work. You might have stormed off in a fit, outraged. But, I thought, seeing as you're an actor –'

'How did you know I was an actor?'

'I asked Dr Bensimon what you did . . . I thought, seeing as you were an actor, you might rise to the challenge.'

'No pun intended.'

'I can call you Lysander, now, can't I?' she said, kissing his chin and reaching down for him.

'I think you'd better.'

And then they made love again and Lysander experienced and enjoyed his second orgasm, somehow even more satisfying than the first because it was prefigured and if his mind was going to interpose itself it had had plenty of warning. Miraculously, he climbed steadily to a second climax of sensation and duly climaxed.

Dr Bensimon was tapping the end of his pen on his desk pad of blotting paper, thinking hard.

'Who was your partner? A prostitute?'

'Ah . . . No.'

'Was she someone who conformed to your sexual preferences, your "type", I mean.'

'Actually, no . . . Not really my type at all.'

'Most intriguing. Can you explain it?'

Lysander thought again. 'I don't know. Perhaps you helped in some way – all our conversations. Perhaps it was Parallelism . . .'

17. Autobiographical Investigations

HETTIE BULL – WHO WOULD have thought? . . . But how to explain it? How to describe and understand the effect she has on me? I was attracted to her from the outset, I now see, which defies logic – or my emotional logic, anyway, as I know my eye veers towards those tall rangy girls and women, with long necks and thin wrists – tall rangy women like Blanche. How and where do these sensual tastes generate themselves? Why does one respond to dark hair rather than blonde? To plumpness rather than slimness, say? What is it about the configuration of a face – of eyebrows in relation to a nose, the height of a forehead, the fullness of lips, the changing geometry of a smile – that makes me, in particular, and not someone else, quicken and react? Is it the stirring of some atavistic notion of the ideal mating partner, our primitive sexual nature superseding the rational civilized mind – 'That's the one, that's the one' – and thereby leading us astray?

So – Hettie Bull. I wonder if it began with the juxtaposition of the staid, solid name – daughter of John Bull, England's icon – and the olive-skinned, big-eyed, eldritch, psychologically unbalanced *gamine* that is the physical reality of the young woman you see. Was ever a name less suited to a person? So many questions. But I have to testify here to the potent, unignorable catalyst of her slim naked body – so small and lissom, so *enthusiastic* . . . perhaps that's the key? She is so unabashed and brazen. When a man knows he is wanted – when a man knows he is wanted so much that an elaborate trap is laid for him, a trap so devious that he voluntarily sheds his clothes and stands naked before the woman who is hunting him . . . Aching physical presence, plus manifest desire, plus absence of shame, plus perfect opportunity. Impossible to resist.

Have I been cured by Hettie Bull? Can I go back to London now and be with Blanche, full of sexual confidence at last? She will take me to her bed, I know, she's practically said as much. So why don't I just go home?

Be honest. Hettie Bull has cast some kind of spell over you. Her sorcery works and you want to see her again, you have to see her again, you can't wait to see her again . . . But two afterthoughts nag at me: the sense that my involvement with Hettie Bull – wherever it goes from here – will bring me trouble in some form or other; and the fact that the more I become involved with Hettie the more grievous my betrayal of Blanche.

When I came home that afternoon – the little train carrying me back to Vienna through the encroaching dusk – I went to my room and, locking the door, stripped off my clothes. My body was marked with sooty fingerprints, like the lightest clustered bruises, charcoal dust from her fingertips tracing the passage of her rapid hands over my body. I washed them away with a damp flannel and put on fresh clothes, the impress of her fingers easily effaced. But as I sit here writing this I see in my mind's eye tantalizing glimpses of her body, remembering vividly moments that we shared. The hang of her breasts as she reached over me for her Madeira glass. The way she stayed naked as I dressed, watching me from the tangled sheet and blanket, head propped on a hand. Then as I left how she slipped out of the bed and reached beneath it for the chamber pot. I stood watching her as she squatted over it, then she shooed me from the room, laughing. I think I am in serious trouble. I know I am. But what can I do?

18. Mental Agitations

LYSANDER BEGAN TO SEE a pattern in Dr Bensimon's questioning, began to sense the direction in which he was being gently led.

'What was your mother wearing when you came home that day?'

'She was wearing a teagown, one of her favourites – satin, a kind of coppery colour with a lot of lace and ribbon at the neck.'

'Anything else you can remember about it?'

'There was a sable trim on the sleeve and the hem. A lot of beading on the bodice.'

He looked at his notes again.

'You ate buttered toast and strawberry jam.'

'And seed cake.'

'Were there any other jams or condiments?'

'There was anchovy paste – and honey. My mother always eats honey at breakfast and teatime.'

'Describe the room you were in.'

'We call it the Green Drawing Room, on the first floor at the side off the landing on the west stair. The walls are lacquered an intense emerald green. On one wall are about thirty miniature paintings – landscapes of the estate and the house in its setting – I think done by an aunt of Lord Faulkner. Competent but rather flattered by their framing, if you know what I mean. It's a small but comfortable room – the main drawing room is vast and looks over the south lawn – you can sit forty people easily.'

'So you made instinctively for the Green Drawing Room.'

'We always had tea there.'

'What's on the floor?'

'A rather fine carpet – a Shiraz – and standard parquet.'

Slowly but surely the questions drew out more and more precise details. Lysander saw how this parallel day, during which nothing happened, was slowly acquiring a tactile reality – a texture and richness – that began completely to outstrip the original, disastrous day with its cluster of jangling, indistinct memories. That fatal afternoon began slowly to fade and disappear, buried under the accumulating facts and minutiae of the new parallel world. As the sessions continued, he found that he could summon up this new world far more effectively than the old; his new fictive memories, spurred on by his *fonction fabulatrice*, became concrete, overthrowing his painful recollections, making them vague and shadowy, to the extent that he began to wonder if they were simply the half-remembered details of a bad dream.

Soon, when tea was over, he had his mother going to the piano – a baby grand – and singing a Schubertlied in her rich mezzo-soprano. Lord Faulkner, lured by the music, joined them and smoked a cigar as he listened, the smoke making Lysander sneeze. Lord Faulkner called for another pot of tea, asking for Assam, his favourite. The fact that all this was an exercise in auto-suggestion didn't devalue these 'memories' at all, Lysander saw. By a sheer act of will, persistence and precision his parallel world came to dominate his memory, exactly as Bensimon had predicted, and the bland domestic emotions of that new fictive day supplanted everything that had caused anguish and provoked insupportable shame.

As he left, retrieving his Panama hat from the hat-stand, Bensimon's stern, bespectacled secretary appeared, an envelope in her hand. A receipt, he supposed, for last month's fees.

'Herr Rief,' she said, not meeting his eye. 'This was left for you.'

Lysander took it and read it on the stairs going down to the street. It was from Hettie.

'Come next Wednesday at six pm. U is going to Zürich. Pack an overnight bag.'

Lysander acknowledged the irrepressible surge of excitement. He felt like a boy legitimately excused school in the middle of term – that sense of unlooked-for freedom, unexpected release. Then more reproachful thoughts intruded as he strolled homeward. It was all very well feeling grateful to Hettie for 'curing' him but he had been snared, after all, and had tumbled guilelessly into her trap – everything had been contrived to make what took place inevitable. In his conscience he could just about forgive himself – it had been a momentary fall, his honour tarnished but not irreparably – one moment of uncontrollable passion that could be consigned to history and forgotten. No one knew, no one had been hurt. But if he went back to her and spent a night or two then that was another matter. For the sake of his engagement, his relationship and future with Blanche he should write back and say no – it couldn't happen again or he'd be lost, he knew.

He crossed the Ring by the Burg Theatre and was instantly reminded of Udo Hoff and his architectural recriminations. And with that trigger came the fizzing surge of elation at the idea of seeing Hettie again. He began to imagine what it would be like to spend a night with her in that narrow bed, to wake in the morning, sleepy and warm, thigh to thigh, to roll over and reach for her . . .

Back at the pension he sat down and wrote immediately to Blanche, breaking off their engagement. It was the only honourable course to take, even if the lies were fluent. He said that various consultations with doctors and psychoanalysts in Vienna had convinced him that any cure, if it were to work, would be lengthy and complicated. Furthermore, he was troubled by the depth and severity of his 'mental agitations' and therefore, under these circumstances, he felt it was only fair to you, dearest Blanche, to release you from your promises and vows. He begged her forgiveness and understanding and urged her to do what she wished with the ring he had given her – throw it in the Thames, sell it, bequeath it as an heirloom to a niece or a goddaughter – whatever seemed apt. He would remember her kindness and beauty as long as he lived and he was abjectly sorry that his 'particular unfortunate circumstances' forbade him from becoming her devoted husband.

He sealed the envelope with a mixture of emotions – guilt, sadness and exhilaration – also modest self-satisfaction at promptly ending the duplicity combined with a thrilling sense of liberation. He was a free man now – his wretched anorgasmia a horrible memory, a thing of the past. Who could say where this liaison with Miss Hettie Bull would lead? But he made a promise to himself not to look any further into the future than his next encounter with her. There was a real element of danger added to the excitement, of course – a cuckolded lover in the wings – not to mention Hettie's own deep instabilities (he had witnessed them breaking through – he wasn't ignoring them) but for the moment next Wednesday at 6.00 p.m. was all he could think about.

At dinner that night, Wolfram said to him, 'You seem in excellent spirits this evening, Lysander.'

'I am,' he confessed. 'I've realized that coming to Vienna was the best thing I've ever done in my life.'

'I'm glad to hear that, Herr Rief,' Frau K said. 'I've always said that Vienna is the most pleasant city in Europe.'

'In the world,' Lysander added. 'The most pleasant city in the world.'

19. The Arc of a Love Affair

IN LATE SEPTEMBER LYSANDER arranged with Hettie to meet for a long weekend in Linz. They travelled there separately and each, for the sake of appearances, booked a separate room in the

Goldener Adler Hotel. Hettie told Hoff that she wanted to look at a seam of marble that had been unearthed in a quarry near Urfahr. He didn't seem in the least suspicious, she said.

The change in being away from Vienna would be marked, Lysander thought. Their snatched afternoons and rare nights in the barn always suffered from a persistent undercurrent of anxiety – fear of discovery. It wasn't just the prospect of Hoff finding them together – it could just as easily be a neighbour or a friend dropping by unannounced. To spend two entire nights as normal lovers would surely affect their moods. Everything would be different. Lysander was entranced by the prospect but initially Hettie seemed oddly edgy and nervous. For the first time he saw her inject Bensimon's medicine. She poured some white powder from a small envelope into a glass of water to make a solution, then filled her syringe with it, injecting it with practised ease into a vein in the crook of her elbow.

'What's it called?'

'Coca.'

'Does it hurt?'

'Not in the least. It calms me down,' she explained. 'It makes me more confident and sure of myself.'

'It's not morphine, is it?'

'You can buy it at a chemist. But then you have to leave your name and address – but I don't want to do that so I get it from Dr Bensimon. His is better quality, anyway, so he says.'

It worked fast. Soon she was smiling and kissing him. She said she'd had a 'blazing row' with Hoff before she left and that had unsettled her. On the train to Linz she became convinced someone was following her and had taken a very roundabout route from the station to the hotel to throw any such person off the scent.

'I felt all raggedy and nervy,' she said. 'And now I don't. I'm all calm. See? Do you want to try some?'

Lysander took her in his arms. 'If I felt any happier, I'd explode.' He kissed her. 'You're my medicine, Hettie. I don't need a drug.'

'Dr Freud uses Coca as well,' she said, a little defensively. 'That's how Bensimon knows about it.'

They walked along the promenade by the Danube and ate Linzer Torte in the Volksgarten, where a band was playing military marches. Back in Lysander's room – the bigger of their two – Hettie undressed him, removing his shirt and tie, unbuckling his belt and unbuttoning his flies. It was something she liked to do, she said, before she removed her own clothes. For Lysander it was an unconscious echo of that first day, the day his anorgasmia left him for ever, so he had no complaints.

On the Sunday he took the opportunity of being in Linz to look up a cousin of his mother – a Frau Hermine Gantz. His mother had given him the address when he said he'd like to meet some of his Austrian family. He was going to call and leave his card but at the house on Burger Strasse they had never heard of a Frau Gantz. Lysander assumed his mother had made a mistake – she hadn't been in Austria for over twenty years, after all.

The next day, as they were packing their valises for the return to Vienna, he saw Hettie preparing her Coca solution. A precaution, she said, Hoff might still be in a bad mood – he was a very angry man.

★ ★ ★

My darling Lysander,
It won't work. I'm going to ignore your letter. Don't think of me, think of yourself. Find your health and your good, kind nature again and come home to your girl. I love you, my Darling One, and if I can't stand by you in your hour of trouble and distress then what kind of a wife would I make you? No, no, a thousand times no! We are meant to be with each other and while I applaud your sweetness and unselfishness in offering to let me 'renounce my vows' I will not hear of such a thing again. Take your time, my

love, all the time you need – three months more, six months, a year. I will be waiting for you. Everyone tells me that Vienna has the best doctors in the world so I'm sure you are absolutely in the right place to find the right answers. I'm going to tear up your letter and burn it right now (London is beastly cold, I have a fire lit at breakfast). It never happened, you never wrote it, I never read it, my love for you is as constant and sure as the 'Rock of Gibraltar' (you know what I mean).

All my fondest love, my darling,

Your own, Blanche.

★ ★ ★

The Café Sorgenfrei became their post office. It was a small, dark, rather grimy bohemian place in a little street near the Hoher Markt. Hoff had been banned from the café when he was an art student and had vowed never to set foot in it again, Hettie said, so it was perfect. She would leave messages for Lysander behind the bar – places and times they could meet, when she thought it was safe for him to come to the barn. Lysander communicated with her in the same way. Sometimes he left a message saying simply, 'I have to see you,' and gave the name of a shabby hotel near the railway station or overlooking the Danube canal and let her know he had booked a room a couple of days hence, hoping that she could find a way of being there. Invariably, she did and Lysander began to worry that Hoff would grow suspicious of these comings and goings. No, she said, he only ever thinks of one person – himself. As long as he wasn't inconvenienced by any of her absences he remained entirely indifferent as to what she was doing or her whereabouts.

★ ★ ★

The girl of my dreams do you know her?
She smiles 'neath the diamonds of dew

When morning breaks over the moon-mists
And the stars fade away in the blue.

Sometimes in the sunshine I see her,
And hear her low song in the breeze,
Then in her wide eyes glimpse the wonder
The smile from the blue of the seas.

She's always my beautiful girl
Bewitchingly lovely and true
Perhaps if I name her you'll know her:
She answers to 'Love' – and she's You.

★ ★ ★

Lysander evolved a plan of self-improvement to fill in the days that intervened between his meetings with Hettie. He couldn't just moon away the hours in cafés writing love poetry so he set himself a diligent programme of self-education. He increased the German lessons with Herr Barth and also began conversation classes in French – his French was at a reasonable standard – with a retired schoolteacher, one Herr Fuchs, who lived a few blocks further up Mariahilfer Strasse.

He made daily visits to Vienna's many museums, attended the opera and concerts, went to exhibitions in art galleries and wandered the city with his guidebook, going into every church of note that was recommended. From time to time he would take a day trip out of town to tramp the pathways of the Wienerwald or stride along mountain tracks heading for distant peaks, map in one hand, a stout ash walking stick in the other.

Wolfram eventually quit the pension – to Frau K's evident pleasure – rejoining his regiment for extensive manoeuvres in Galicia. It was something of an emotional farewell, but he and Lysander resolved to stay in touch however their respective lives might separate them. Wolfram vowed to come by on his next leave – 'We'll go to Spittelberg, get drunk and find ourselves two lively young girls.' The lodger who replaced him was a middle-aged engineer called Josef Plischke. Taciturn, upright and faintly pompous he was the perfect companion for Frau K at her dinners. Lysander changed his pension rates to breakfast only, pleading poverty rather than terminal boredom. He had to budget, alas, he told Frau K, and it was true – his funds were diminishing. His affair with Hettie was costing him money – he paid for everything as she was entirely dependent on Hoff for money. Hoff, Lysander learned, was a surprisingly wealthy man, enriched by an inheritance from his late parents as well as by the increasingly high prices his paintings were fetching.

Lysander sent a telegram to his mother and asked if she could wire him another £20.

★ ★ ★

Winter arrived with full force in December – heavy frosts and snow flurries – and the stove in the old barn, for all its redoubtable size, proved an inadequate source of warmth. When he stayed there, Lysander would haul the mattress off the bed and drag it through to the main room, laying it in front of the stove, twin doors open so the flames could be seen.

Hettie found a book of pornographic Japanese prints in Hoff's library and brought them to the barn so they could experiment. She took his penis in her mouth. He tried and failed to sodomize her. They had a go at emulating the contorted positions illustrated, studying the pages as if they were architects inspecting a blueprint.

'Your leg is meant to be over my shoulder not under my armpit.'

'I'll break my leg if I put it there.'

'Are you inside me? I can't feel you.'

'I'm about three inches away. I can't reach, it's impossible.'

She still chose to undress him, loving the moment, she said, when she could tug down his trousers and drawers and his 'boy' would sway free.

One day she said to him as they lay in bed in their shabby hotel overlooking the Danube canal, 'Why don't you kiss my breasts? Every man I've known likes to do that.'

Lysander thought: all the better to keep anorgasmia at bay – but said, 'I don't know why I don't . . . Maybe it seems a bit infantile to me.'

'Nothing wrong with being infantile. Come here.'

She sat up in bed and, at her beckoning, he nuzzled up to her. She cupped her breast and carefully offered the nipple – pert between two fingers – to his mouth.

'See? It's nice. I like it anyway.'

★ ★ ★

Hettie insisted that he come to the New Year party at Hoff's studio. Lysander was very reluctant at first but Hettie encouraged him.

'It's even *less* suspicious if you come, don't you see? He doesn't suspect a thing. You have to come – I want to kiss you at midnight.'

So Lysander duly went and felt out of place at this loud gathering of artists, patrons and gallery owners. He hugged the corners of the large studio, content to keep his eyes on Hettie as she patrolled the room in her Balinese pantaloons and chequerboard jacket and her tinkling shoes. Udo Hoff didn't seem to know who he was – several times their eyes met, Hoff's blankly taking in another stranger in his house.

Immediately after midnight Hettie led him down a dark passageway bulky with hung coats, scarves and hats and kissed him, her tongue deep in his mouth, his hands on her breasts. Seconds later the light went on and Hoff appeared, evidently quite drunk. Hettie was searching the coats.

'Ah there you are, *mein Liebling*, Mr Rief is going – he wanted to say hello and goodbye.'

'It's easier to find a coat when you've got the light on.'

'Mr Rief couldn't find the switch.'

Lysander and Hoff shook hands, Hoff now gazing at him intently, though a little unfocussed.

'Thank you for a wonderful party,' Lysander said.

'You're the Englishman, aren't you?'

'Yes. That's me.'

'A happy new year to you. How is your cure going?'

'I'm pretty well cured – I should say. Yes, I think that's a fair comment.'

Hoff congratulated him and then demanded Hettie help him find more champagne, he said. When his back was turned, Hettie blew Lysander a kiss and left with Hoff. Five minutes later Lysander managed to find his coat and hat and he wandered outside, still trembling from the narrow escape. A love affair wasn't an arc, as he'd heard it described, it was a far more variable line on a graph – undulating or jagged. It wasn't smooth, however much pleasure one was deriving from it, day by day. He headed down the drive. Snow was falling, big soft flakes, the road to the station whitening in front of his eyes, unsmirched by wheel tracks, the world going quiet and muffled as a few final, distant bells continued to ring in 1914.

★ ★ ★

'I think you're right,' Bensimon said. 'We've done everything – been very thorough. We might as well admit it and call it a day.'

'I can't thank you enough, doctor. I've learned so much.'

'You're absolutely convinced the problem has completely gone.'

Lysander paused – sometimes he wondered if Bensimon had any inkling that he and Hettie Bull were lovers. How could he tell him that Hettie had proved that his problem had gone, dozens and dozens of times? She was still Bensimon's patient, of course.

86

'Let's say recent experience – recent experiences – have convinced me all is functioning normally.'

Bensimon smiled – man to man – letting his inscrutable professional mask slip for a moment.

'I'm glad Vienna provided other compensations,' he said, dryly, walking him to the door. 'I'm going to write up your case if you don't mind – anorgasmia cures are worth documenting – and present it as a paper at our next conference, maybe publish it in some learned journal.' He smiled. 'Don't worry, you'll be thoroughly disguised by an initial or a pseudonym. Only you and I will know who's being discussed.'

'I'd like to read it,' Lysander said. 'I'll give you my address – my family home, I can always be reached there.'

They shook hands and Lysander thanked him again. He liked Dr Bensimon, he had told him his most intimate secrets and he felt he could trust the man absolutely – and yet he had to acknowledge that he didn't really know him at all.

He settled his final account with the stern secretary, earning a wan smile as they shook hands in farewell, and he took his now familiar stroll from the consulting rooms on Wasagasse along the Franzenring. This is the last time, he realized, a little saddened but at the same time pleased that his essential purpose in coming to Vienna had been so thoroughly achieved. What was it Wolfram had said? A 'river of sex' flowing underneath the city. That had been his salvation – along with Dr Bensimon's Parallelism. He was well, life should be simpler, the way ahead obvious yet, since coming here, everything was a hundred times more complex. He had Hettie in Vienna and Blanche in London and absolutely no idea what he should do.

He walked past the big café – Café Landtmann – and realized that in all these months of passing it he'd never once gone in and so retraced his steps. It was roomy and plain, a little faded and grander than the cafés he chose to frequent – a place to come in the summer, he thought, and sit outside on the pavement. He took a seat in a booth with a good view of the traffic whizzing by on the Ring, lit a cigarette, ordered a coffee and a brandy and opened his notebook. *Autobiographical Investigations* by Lysander Rief. He flicked through the pages, full of notes, descriptions of dreams, a few sketches, drafts of poems – it was another legacy of his stay in Vienna. Bensimon had urged him to continue writing in it as part of his therapy. 'It may seem a bit banal and inconsequential,' Bensimon had said, 'but you'll come back to it once a few months have gone by and be fascinated.'

The café was quiet, caught in that lull between the bustle of lunch, the great Viennese punctuation mark in the day, and the first arrival of those seeking coffee and cakes in the afternoon. Waiters polished cutlery and folded napkins, others flapped out clean linen tablecloths or leaned on their serving stations, gossiping. From somewhere in the rear came the ceramic clatter of plates being stacked. The maître d' combed his hair discreetly, using a silver tray propped against the wall as a mirror. Lysander looked around – very few customers – but then his eye was caught by a man a few tables away, wearing a tweed suit and an old-fashioned cravat tie, reading a newspaper and smoking a cigar. He was in his late fifties, Lysander guessed, and had fine greying hair combed flat against his head; his beard was completely white and trimmed with finical neatness. Lysander put his notebook down and sauntered over.

'Dr Freud,' he said. 'Forgive me for interrupting but I just wanted to shake your hand. I've been most successfully treated by one of your ardent disciples, Dr Bensimon.'

Freud looked up, folded his newspaper and rose to his feet. The two men shook hands.

'Ah, John Bensimon,' Freud said, 'my other Englishman. We've had our disagreements, but he's a good man.'

'Well, whatever they may be I've had the most rewarding psychoanalytical sessions with him. I know how much he respects you – he refers to you constantly.'

'Are you English?'

'Yes. Well, half. And half Austrian.'

'Which explains your excellent German.'

'Thank you.' Lysander took a polite step backwards ready to take his leave. 'It's an honour to shake your hand. I won't keep you from your newspaper further.'

But Freud seemed not to want to let the conversation end. He stayed him with a little gesture of his cigar.

'How long have you been seeing Dr Bensimon?'

'Several months.'

'And you've finished?'

'I feel − let's say − as far as I'm concerned my psychosomatic problem is a thing of the past.'

Freud drew on his cigar, thinking. 'That's very swift,' he said, 'impressive.'

'It was his theory of Parallelism that finally made all the difference. Remarkable.'

'Oh "Parallelism",' Freud almost scoffed. 'I'll make no comment. Good day to you, sir. I wish you well.'

The great man himself, Lysander thought, going back to his seat, pleased he'd had the courage to approach him. Definitely an encounter for the memoirs.

★ ★ ★

He hadn't seen Hettie for four days and he was missing her badly. In fact, he calculated, he hadn't seen her for a week . . . It was the longest period since the affair began that they had been apart. He scribbled a note to her and decided to go at once to the Café Sorgenfrei. Perhaps there would be something there from her, also. Out in the streets it was cold but not freezing and the new year's snow was turning to slush, the tyres of the passing automobiles splattering the brown muck on the legs of pedestrians who ventured too close to the roadway.

Watching the passing motor cars carefully, Lysander wondered, not for the first time, if he should learn to drive. Perhaps that could be another part of his Viennese education – then he realized he could hardly afford the price of driving lessons. He had just paid Frau K his next month's rent in advance and found himself left with only just over a hundred crowns. He'd cancelled his German and French classes until further notice and had telegraphed his mother once again for more money. It made him feel inadequate – why should his mother be subsidizing his love affair with Hettie, he thought. He admitted to himself that he'd been living these last weeks in a self-imposed decision-free limbo, happy to drift in the here-and-now. The problem was – and he had to face it as his money ran out and a return to London beckoned – that he was finding it very hard to imagine a future without Hettie. Was this the beginning? Sexual infatuation shading into love? And yet, during all the weeks of the affair, despite all the endearments and confessions of powerful emotion on both their parts, she had never once spoken of leaving Hoff.

What to do? . . . he pushed his way through the swing door of the Café Sorgenfrei and elbowed aside the heavy velvet curtain that kept the draughts out. Grey strata of smoke hung in the air and made his eyes smart as he approached the bar to hand over his envelope. There was the young barman in his puce waistcoat – what was his name? – and his preposterous dragoon-guardsman's whiskers.

'Good afternoon, Herr Rief,' he said, taking Lysander's letter. 'And we have a little package for you.' He reached below the bar and drew out a flat parcel tied with string. Lysander felt a small surge of joy. Bless Hettie – they must have been thinking of each other, simultaneously. He ordered a glass of Riesling and took the package over to a table by the window. He opened it carefully to see that it contained a libretto. *Andromeda und Perseus eine Oper in vier Akten von Gottlieb Toller*. The cover was a colour reproduction of Hoff's poster – Hettie in all her nakedness . . . He riffled through the pages, imagining a note would fall out and when nothing did he then turned back to the title page to look for an inscription. There it was; 'For Lysander, with all my love, Andromeda.' And below that in a series of distinct lines, he read,

There are times when I am wholly confident in the destiny of HB
But there are other times when I find that I am
not completely honest
Superficial
Facing-both-ways
Cowardly.

★ ★ ★

Lysander wondered why, given his reduced financial resources, he had decided to pay the two-crown supplement to have dinner that night with Frau K and Josef Plischke. Perhaps he just wanted some company, however trying and mediocre. The main course – after the cabbage soup with croutons – was *Tafelspitz*, a boiled-beef stew of ancient lineage, Lysander thought, concocted days ago and allowed to simmer endlessly on a stove in the invisible kitchen. And still the gravy was watery and the meat sinewy and stringy. Plischke ate with enthusiasm, complimenting Frau K on her cuisine in a tone of leaden sycophancy that drew Frau K's most pleasant thin smile from her.

As they chatted, about some aerial demonstration this summer at Aspern with a dozen flying machines, Lysander mentally did his accounts – he had telegraphed his mother two days ago asking for another £20. With luck that should arrive in his bank tomorrow and, with further luck and careful husbandry, that amount should keep him going for another month or two. He decided not to think what might occur beyond that time when his money would run out yet again. Perhaps he should try and find a job himself – maybe teach English to the Viennese? But two months more in

Vienna meant two months more of Hettie. He realized, with a small shock of self-awareness, that he was beginning to define his life around her –

There was a loud banging at the door and he heard Traudl go to answer it. For a second he imagined it might be Wolfram, drunk, come to carry him off to the bordellos of Spittelberg.

Traudl appeared at the dining-room door, flushed and trembling.

'Madame,' she said in a small voice. 'It's the police.'

Frau K's face pinched itself into a rictus of disgust at this violation of her pension's probity and marched out into the hall. Plischke burrowed in his mouth with a toothpick, searching for shreds of *Tafelspitz*. Lysander looked at him – that imperturbability was a bit too swiftly donned. What have you been up to, Josef Plischke?

Frau K reappeared in the doorway.

'They wish to see you, Herr Rief.'

Lysander made the instant assumption and felt the shock in his gut. His mother. Dead? Fatally ill? He felt sick and threw down his napkin.

There were three policemen in the hall. Grey uniforms, black leather belts. Shiny, peaked, badged helmets with flat tops. One man wore a short cape and it was he who saluted and introduced himself as Inspector Strolz.

'You are Herr Lysander Rief?'

'Yes. What's happening? Is there some kind of problem?'

'I'm afraid so.' Strolz smiled, apologetically. 'You are under arrest.'

Lysander heard Frau K's shocked gasp from the door to the dining room behind him.

'This is completely ridiculous. What are you arresting me for?'

'Rape.'

Lysander thought for a second that he might fall over. 'This is absurd. There's obviously been some kind of mistake –'

'Please come with us. There will be no need for handcuffs if you do exactly as we say.'

'May I collect a few possessions from my room?'

'Of course.'

Lysander went to his room, his brain a babbling confusion of supposition and counter-supposition. He stood there frozen – Strolz watching him from the doorway – trying to think what he might need. His overcoat, his hat, his wallet. His notebook? No. He suddenly felt very fearful and alone and had an idea. He rummaged in his desk drawer, finding what he was looking for.

He went back into the hall, avoiding Frau K's eye, and asked Strolz if he could be permitted to say a word to his friend, Herr Barth.

'As quickly as possible.'

Strolz stood behind him as Lysander knocked on Herr Barth's door and heard him say, 'One minute,' then, 'Come in.'

Lysander realized that for all the months they had been living next door to each other this was only the second time he had been in Herr Barth's tiny bedroom. He saw the piled, tottering towers of sheet music, the music stand with his damp woollen combinations draped over it to dry, the huge double bass in its container in the corner by the sagging bed with its embroidered coverlet.

'Did I hear the word "police", Herr Rief? They're not after me, are they?'

'No, no. I'm the one who's been arrested – it's a ghastly mistake – but I have to go with them. Could you contact this person and say I've been arrested? I'd be most grateful. They'll know what to do.'

He handed over Alwyn Munro's card. 'He's at the British Embassy.'

Herr Barth took it, beaming at this deliverance.

'Count on me, Herr Rief. First thing in the morning.' He glanced over Lysander's shoulder, spotting Strolz standing there a few paces back, and lowered his voice. 'They are fools, ignorant fools, the police. Just be extremely polite, that's all they understand. They'll be impressed. You'll be fine.'

Lysander went back into the hall where he saw that the front door was now open. Frau K stood by it, hands clenched together, a look of pure hatred in her eyes directed at the man who had brought this disgrace on her establishment.

'It's all a terrible mistake,' Lysander said as he walked past her, followed by the three policemen. 'I've done nothing. I'll be back tomorrow.'

But something in him told him he wouldn't and he knew also that, had there been no witnesses present, Frau K would have spat in his face.

The policemen took him downstairs to a police van parked at the junction with Mariahilfer Strasse. They opened rear doors and he clambered in. Through the small paneless barred window cut in one side he watched the snowy vistas of Vienna roll by – the opera house, the Hofburg palace, the Hofburg Theatre – all the monuments of this old/new city flashing by like something in a stereoscope – until they arrived at the *Polizeidirektion* on the Schottenring.

20. Little Boy or Little Girl?

THE VAN TURNED OFF the Schottenring and drove through a giant archway into a central courtyard and the huge wooden doors swung – slowly, soundlessly – shut behind it. Lysander was led into the building and along a wide passageway to an interview room. There was a smell of disinfectant in the air and the empty corridors were disconcertingly full of the sound of footsteps echoing from elsewhere in the building, as if the place were populated by the ghosts of prisoners past forever being marched to and from their cells.

Lysander took his seat and faced impassive, efficient Inspector Strolz across a desk. Strolz took down his details, writing in a thick

94

ledger with a dipping-pen and inkpot like a Victorian clerk. Lysander sat there in his overcoat, hat on his knee, trying to keep his mounting sense of outrage – accompanied by flickering undertones of panic – under control. When he was formally charged he decided the time had come to ask a few salient questions.

'Whom, exactly, am I meant to have raped?'

Strolz consulted his notebook.

'Fräulein Esther Bull. On or around the third of September, last year, 1913.'

'That's completely impossible.' He was thinking back. The third of September had to be that first time, that first day he went to the barn. 'It's impossible because . . .' he continued, unable to keep the tremor of offence, of injustice, out of his voice, 'because Fräulein Bull and I have been engaged in . . .' He paused. 'We have been lovers for four months. In these circumstances I don't understand how she can accuse me of rape. Don't you see, inspector? You don't "rape" someone and then enjoy a love affair – a warm, passionate, affectionate love affair – with the victim, subsequently, for many months thereafter. It defies logic and justice.'

Strolz took this in, nodding. 'Be that as it may, this information has no relevance here and now, Herr Rief. In a courtroom it may carry more weight.'

'But why would she come up with this rape story?'

'Fräulein Bull is four months pregnant. She alleges that she was raped by you that day, September the third. That was the day the child was conceived, apparently.'

Lysander sat there, wordless, deeply shocked. *Conceived?* He had seen Hettie a week ago and she'd said nothing . . . Four months pregnant? What was going on?

'If you bring Miss Bull here,' he finally managed to speak. 'Then everything will be sorted out. This farce, this farrago will –'

'Unfortunately that won't be possible. Furthermore, the charge against you is a joint one, brought by Fräulein Bull and her

95

common-law husband . . .' Strolz looked at his notebook again. 'Herr Udo Hoff. In fact it was Herr Hoff who contacted the police.' He closed the ledger and stood up. 'You'll be taken to a magistrate's court tomorrow for the formal arraignment – so tonight you'll be our guest. Do you have everything you need? Cigarettes? May I have some coffee sent down?'

Lysander was escorted to his cell down a flight of stairs to the semi-basement area of the building. The door was locked behind him. There was a glassed-in electric bulb recessed in the ceiling, a wooden bed with a straw mattress and a blanket, a sink with a single tap and a tin chamber pot with a hinged lid. In the exterior wall there was a small, high, barred window. Through a slotted vent in the door a voice informed him that the light would be turned off in ten minutes.

Ten minutes later, he lay in his bed, in the dark, in his overcoat, smoking, trying to work out a possible sequence of events. Importunate questions gabbled in his head. When had Hettie discovered she was pregnant? Why did she tell Hoff? She must have decided to – for some unimaginable personal reason, he supposed – at which point the scandalized Hoff went to the police. Then Hettie must have lied, he reasoned on, in order to save herself and concocted this story about his visit to the studio during which, at some time in the afternoon, he – Lysander – had sexually assaulted her. She couldn't have confessed to the subsequent affair, obviously. But why not, when she knew she was pregnant? But how could she be pregnant? She had told him she was infertile – she claimed her menses came, if at all, months apart, and she hardly noticed them. Consequently he had never used a prophylactic. Had she been lying? Had she wanted to trap him, somehow?

Then for a minute or two he experienced a kind of incoherent rage at Hettie; a sense of injustice being done to him that made him almost breathless at the effrontery, the crazy malice that was involved. He sat up, gasping physically for his breath, as though he had been stifled somehow, and ordered himself to calm down. He felt light-headed, almost dizzy and began to worry about his blood pressure. There was nothing to be gained by allowing his feelings to surge so tumultuously out of control. Clear logical thought was his best weapon – making himself ill would gain him nothing.

He calmed himself, yet he grew increasingly worried as the night wore on and as he went over the different narratives and options again and again. It became clear to him that his only defence was to expose the affair – to let the world (and Hoff) know the precise details of the liaison. And what could Hoff say in the face of that evidence? Nothing. The case would be thrown out, surely?

He lay in the dark and periodically paced around his small cell. He finished his pack of cigarettes, waiting for sunrise, unable to sleep or rest, his mind frenetically, pulsatingly active. There was only this one course of action – to destroy Hettie's preposterous story and expose her as a liar. He thought of her gift of the *Andromeda* libretto and its cryptic message on the title page. It was her pre-emptive confession to him, he now saw, and he wondered also if she had meant it to serve as a warning.

The van took him and two other shabby villains to a magistrate's court early in the morning. At 8.10 a.m. Lysander found himself facing a sleepy presiding judge who had a fragment of egg-white lodged in the bristles of his wide tobacco-stained moustache. Lysander was formally charged with rape, bail was denied – bail was not permitted in cases of rape, he was told by the judge – and the date for his trial was established as May 17 1914. He had no lawyer, and so was taken back to the central police station and re-deposited in his small cell. At ten o'clock he was given a bowl of carrot soup and a hunk of black bread. He asked if he could speak to Inspector Strolz but was told that Inspector Strolz had left on a fortnight's leave.

Lysander began to experience a form of creeping terror at his impotence that he recognized as the beginnings of despair. How could he possibly find a lawyer? He supposed the court would appoint one for his trial in May. The trial was over three months away. Was he going to be kept in this cell until then or transferred to a prison? He began to curse Hettie for this hideous, ridiculous lie. Why not tell Hoff the simple truth? What did she think would be achieved by this god-awful nightmare of a mess that she had landed him in?

He banged on the door until someone came and he asked for paper and pencil and was refused.

He urinated in his chamber pot.

He washed his hands and face in the sink and dried them on the lining of his greatcoat.

He lay down and managed to doze for an hour.

He took off his coat and tie and did some basic gymnastic exercises – press-ups, star-jumps, running on the spot until he was breathless.

He urinated in his chamber pot.

He sat on his bed and forced his brain into activity, trying to recall the sequence and detail of the affair. Dates, times, places. He remembered the names of all the hotels they had stayed in – every fact that made the affair concrete and irrefutable. Then he found his thoughts straying to Hettie herself and the unignorable new fact that she was carrying his child. He almost wept. He sniffed, coughed, inhaled and willed himself to anger, stirred by the thought that the foetus would almost certainly be aborted, another ghastly consequence of this hideous predicament she had created. Hoff would see to that, oh yes. Boy or girl, he found himself wondering? Little boy or little girl? . . .

He was given a thick slice of cold fatty sausage, a chunk of cheese with black bread and a lukewarm mug of coffee.

He looked at his wristwatch. It was 2.30 in the afternoon.

The day seemed to take a week of subjective time to crawl to its conclusion. He watched the small rectangle of sky that was visible through his cell window darken as the sun began to set. A little vermilion touched the cloud base. The aural sub-current of the cell wing continued without change as the hours maundered by. Clangs, shouts, footsteps, the rumble of trolley wheels, the occasional laugh, the rasping of a stiff-bristled brush sweeping the corridor outside again and again.

When it was quite dark the electric light was switched on. He did some more press-ups, wondering where this fitness urge had sprung from. With the edge of a button he scored a dash in the plaster of the cell wall. Day one. He managed an ironic smile at this melodramatic gesture. Why had he smoked all his cigarettes last night?

The door was unlocked and a policeman looked in.

'Follow me,' he said.

Lysander duly followed him up the stairs and into another corridor, where he was shown into a windowless room with a table and two chairs. He sat down, keeping his mind empty. Could this be Hettie, decided to rescue him? Two minutes later Alwyn Munro entered the room.

Lysander felt like embracing him. Herr Barth had done what he had promised – wonderful, salt-of-the-earth, true friend Herr Barth. How he loved that man! He shook Munro's hand warmly.

'Bit of a pickle, eh?' Munro said, jocularly, sitting down and offering him a cigarette.

'It's not true. All lies. I've been having an affair with her for months.' Lysander drew on his cigarette so avidly his head reeled.

Munro slid a business card across the table.

'This is your lawyer. A very good man. He couldn't make them set bail, I'm afraid. That's the problem with rape cases. Luckily for you it seems Miss Bull has suddenly altered the charge to "assault". The bail for assault is very high – ten thousand crowns.'

'But that's absurd!' Lysander complained. 'Assault? I'm meant to have "assaulted" Miss Bull? I'm not a criminal. How is one meant to lay one's hands on that kind of money? Why's it been set so high?'

'It seems Hoff's father was a very respected District Commissioner. Friends in high places. Ministers, senior civil servants, judges . . . Does seem a bit punitive.'

'I can't raise that amount – who do they think I am?'

'Don't worry – we've paid it.' Munro smiled. 'Consider it a loan – but not interest-free, alas.'

Lysander experienced a jolt of elation. He swallowed. His hands were shaking.

'My god . . . I'm incredibly grateful. Does this mean I can go?'

'Not exactly. There are special conditions.' Munro leaned back in his chair as if to gain a more objective view. 'You're to be confined to the grounds of the British Embassy until your trial. Actually, it's not the embassy but the temporary consulate where we attachés work.' He smiled. 'A little bit of *Grossbritannien* in Vienna, all the same.'

'Why keep me there?'

'They obviously think you'll make a run for it rather than stand trial. And as we've put up the bail they're making us responsible for seeing that you don't escape.'

Lysander's elation began to drain away.

'So I'm swapping an Austrian cell for a British one.'

'I think you'll be much more comfortable.' Munro shrugged. 'Best we could do. They're very serious here about crimes like rape, sex-murders, assaults and so on.'

'I haven't raped or assaulted anyone.'

'Of course. I'm just explaining why they've demanded these conditions. We've got a little place for you out at the back. Small garden. You won't be locked up but you can't leave the premises.' Munro stood. 'Shall we go?'

21. A Small Villa in the Classical Style

THE TEMPORARY CONSULATE BUILDING was in fact a small villa in the classical style, somewhat dilapidated, some three streets away from the embassy itself in Metternichgasse, opposite the botanical gardens. Lysander's 'prison' was a two-storey, octagonal stone summerhouse at the end of a high-walled parterre that ran from the rear terrace of the villa. He had an octagonal bedroom on the top floor and an octagonal sitting room on the ground floor with a small fireplace. No lavatory and no bathroom but it was comfortable enough, he had to admit. He could walk the gravelled, weedy pathways of the neglected parterre whenever he felt like fresh air or needed exercise. Food was brought to him on a tray from a nearby restaurant three times a day, his fire was lit, a jug of hot water provided every morning for his ablutions, his laundry was collected and returned (he had sent for his clothes and belongings from the Pension Kriwanek) and his chamber pot was discreetly emptied and replaced by a variety of embassy servants who seemed to change almost daily. He rarely saw the same face more than twice. He had been told that he would be charged for food and laundry services. All costs accrued would be added to the 10,000 crowns already owed to His Majesty's Government – not to mention his steadily accumulating legal fees.

Lysander had several meetings with his lawyer, a Herr Feuerstein, a serious young man, about Lysander's age, who wore a pince-nez and a neat beard, and who tutted and frowned darkly and muttered to himself as he went over the facts of Lysander's case as if determined not to provide his client with a scintilla of hope or optimism. He did agree, however, that the best defence was the revelation of the affair. And so he took down everything, in his tiny copperplate hand, that Lysander could remember of his dozens of encounters with Hettie. He volunteered to visit the hotels they had frequented in Vienna, Linz and Salzburg to make copies of the register and perhaps even take clandestine photographs of Hettie's barn/studio. He asked

Lysander to draw him a detailed plan of the barn and provide the best inventory he could of its contents. He may be a pessimist, Lysander thought, but at least he's a thorough pessimist.

Lysander also had daily visits from Alwyn Munro and the other attaché – the naval attaché – a man called Jack Fyfe-Miller. Fyfe-Miller was a blond, burly young man in his early thirties, with a full, fair beard – ideally seafaring for a naval attaché, Lysander thought – who had won a rugby blue at Cambridge. After their first few encounters Lysander decided to label him 'stupid'. Fyfe-Miller had seen him on stage in London (in *The Taming of the Shrew*) and seemed only curious about theatre-life and actresses in particular. He kept asking; do you know Ellen Terry? Have you ever met Dolly Baird? What's Mrs Mabel Troubridge really like? But from time to time he would make a remark that showed deeper intellectual reserves and Lysander began to think that the bluffness and the heartiness was something of an act.

After a week in the summerhouse at the end of the parterre he felt thoroughly settled in, routines were established and he was living an approximation of a normal life. He decided to ask Munro if there was any way a meeting with Hettie could be arranged.

'Not sure that's a good idea,' Munro said.

'If I could speak to her – even for a few minutes – I'm sure we could sort out everything.'

They were walking the tufted, mossy pathways of the parterre around the small cement basin of the dry fountain at its centre. On a pile of tumbled, parched boulders a lichened stone cherub held a gaping fish aloft as if it were gasping for air rather than providing the conduit for the fountain's water that would never spout and flow again.

'Look,' Lysander said, pointing to a small paint-blistered door in the garden's back wall. 'Smuggle her in through there and no one will be the wiser. Just give me a moment alone with her – she'll drop the case.'

Munro thought, smoothing his neat moustache with a forefinger.

'Let me see what I can do.'

22. Autobiographical Investigations

HETTIE. THIS UTTER MADNESS – how could you have done this to me? Stop. No. First the facts, the dialogue. She came, last night, just before eleven o'clock. Jack Fyfe-Miller brought her in through the door in the back wall and waited outside in the cab as we talked. She stayed for twenty minutes.

We kissed, like old and practised lovers, with real passion, as if none of this craziness had happened. She clung to me, telling me how much she was missing me and asked me how I was. I felt the grotesque absurdity of the situation – as if I'd had a bout of flu and she hadn't seen me while I convalesced. For a few seconds the mad raging anger took me over and I had to step away and turn my back on her.

HETTIE: Is everything all right? Are you well?

ME: How am I ? How am I? I'm terrible. I'm miserable. I'm abject. How do you think I am?

HETTIE: Seems a nice little house you have here. It's sweet. Is this your garden?

ME: Hettie, I'm a prisoner on bail. I'm going to be tried for assault. For 'sexually assaulting' you.

HETTIE. I know. I'm so sorry. I couldn't think what to say when Udo found out. So I just blurted out anything that came to mind. Anything to make him stop shouting at me.

In the fraught emotion of the reunion I forgot that she was pregnant – carrying our child. I put my hand on her belly – it seemed very flat.

ME: You don't feel pregnant.

HETTIE: I hadn't a clue I was. You know I thought I was infertile. I was convinced I was – truly. I didn't feel sick or anything. Didn't put on weight, nothing, not the slightest indication. But then my nipples began to go darker and Udo saw and took me to the doctor who examined me and said I was four months pregnant.

ME: I never noticed your nipples.

HETTIE: Because you saw them all the time. You hadn't noticed the gradual change. I hadn't either, to be honest. Udo hadn't seen my breasts for weeks. He was shocked – took me straight to the doctor. When Udo heard I was pregnant he got in this towering rage so I said it was you.

ME: But I didn't rape you, or assault you, if I recall. If I recall you undressed *me* – effectively.

HETTIE: Because I knew you liked that sort of thing.

ME: What're you talking about?

HETTIE: I read your file – when I was at Dr Bensimon's. He had to leave the room when I was there for a consultation and he left your file on his desk. He was gone for about ten minutes and I got bored, saw your file. I was curious –

ME: That's completely outrageous!

HETTIE: I don't recall you complaining. Just because I knew about your dreams, your fantasies . . .

ME: No, no. All part of the therapy. No extra charge –

HETTIE: Don't be cynical. But it was Udo who said you must have attacked me and I sort of said, well, yes, I suppose so, yes, he must have. I don't know why. He was in such a fury. I said you'd overpowered me and before I knew it I was agreeing with him. Anything to stop him shouting. I'm really sorry, my darling. You have to forgive me – I was in such a panic.

I felt an immense lassitude pour through me, a kind of terminal fatigue.

ME: Why didn't Udo think it was his child?

HETTIE: Because – well – we don't have normal sexual relations any more. Not for over a year now. He knew at once he wasn't his.

ME: What do you mean, 'he'?

HETTIE: He's a boy – the baby – I know.

ME: But you realize that when I go on trial I'm going to tell the truth – about you and me and our affair.

HETTIE: No! No, you can't do that. Udo will kill me – and the child.

ME: Nonsense. He can't do that. He's not a monster.

HETTIE: You don't know what he's capable of. He'll throw me out, destroy me somehow. He'll find a way of punishing me and the baby – our baby.

ME: Then leave him. Walk away. Come to London and live with me. What do you owe him? Nothing –

HETTIE: Everything. When I met him in Paris I was . . . I was in serious trouble. Udo saved me. Brought me to Vienna. Without him I'd be dead – or worse. I implore you, Lysander, I beseech you – don't let him know about us.

ME: You're not going to have an abortion.

HETTIE: Never. He's ours. Yours and mine, my darling.

Just at that moment Fyfe-Miller appeared and rapped on the French window. Hettie kissed me goodbye and her last whispered words were, 'I beg you, Lysander. Say nothing. Don't destroy me.'

★ ★ ★

This morning I had a meeting with Herr Feuerstein. I asked him, assuming I was found guilty, what sentence I could expect. 'Eight to ten years, if you're lucky,' he said. Then added: 'But you're not going to be found guilty, Herr Rief. The case will fall apart the minute you give your evidence.' He flourished his dossier. 'I've got everything. The hotels in Vienna, in Linz, in Salzburg. Testimonials from the staff. How do you say it in English? A "cakewalk".' He allowed himself a rare smile. I thought – if Feuerstein is that confident then it's all over for Hettie. 'I'm really looking forward to it,' Feuerstein added. 'May 17th can't come quickly enough.'

Now I'm waiting for Munro and Fyfe-Miller to come for a meeting, here in the summerhouse. I'm going to tell them there's only one thing I can do. This case must never come to trial.

23. A New Brass Key

LYSANDER SAT IN HIS octagonal sitting room facing Alwyn Munro and Jack Fyfe-Miller. Snow flurries swooped softly against the French windows and the fire in the grate struggled against the cold of the day. For some reason Fyfe-Miller was in his naval uniform – a row of medal ribbons on his chest – that had the effect of making him more serious and noteworthy, a serving officer of the line. Munro was in a three-piece, heavy tweed suit as if he were off for a shooting weekend in Perthshire.

'I've been thinking, over these last few days,' Lysander said carefully. 'And one thing has become absolutely clear to me. I can't risk going to trial.'

'Feuerstein tells me your defence is impregnable,' Munro said.

'We all know how easy it is for things to go wrong.'

'So you want to run for it,' Fyfe-Miller said, lighting a cigarette.

Once again Lysander saw how the bland exterior concealed a quick mind.

'Yes. In a word.'

The two looked at each other. Munro smiled.

'We had a private bet about how long it would take you to arrive at this conclusion.'

'It's the only way, as far as I'm concerned.'

'There are real problems,' Munro said, and proceeded to outline them. The British Embassy, like every embassy in Vienna, was riddled with informers. One in three of the Austrian staff, he reckoned, was in the pay of the Interior Ministry. He added that this was completely normal and only to be expected – the same conditions applied in London.

'Therefore,' he added, 'if you left us you would be missed very swiftly. You're being watched all the time, even though it doesn't seem like it. Someone would alert the police.'

Fyfe-Miller spoke up. 'Also, as your gaolers, as it were, we would be honour-bound to report your absence to the authorities. And, of course, your bail would be forfeit.'

Lysander decided to ignore this last point. 'But what if I slipped away in the middle of the night? It'd be hours before I was noticed.'

'Not so. The middle of the night would be the worst possible time. The watchmen, the police at the gate, the night staff – everyone's more alert at night. I'm pretty sure there are a couple of police plainclothesmen out there, sitting in a motor, twenty-four hours, waiting, watching. The middle of a working day is far more discreet.' Munro smiled. 'Paradoxically.'

'If you left,' Fyfe-Miller said, speculatively, 'you'd have the maximum of an hour's start, I'd say. If no one else had reported you then we would have to – after an hour.'

'Better to assume a fifteen-minute start,' Munro said. 'They're not fools.'

'Where would *you* head for, Alwyn?' Fyfe-Miller asked, disingenuously.

'Trieste. It's practically Italian anyway – they hate the Austro-Hungarians. Head for Trieste, take a steamer to Italy. That's what I'd do.'

Lysander picked up the sub-textual message. He was by now fully aware of what was taking place here; Munro and Fyfe-Miller were laying out a course of action, almost a set of instructions for him to follow. Do what we tell you, they were saying, and you will be safe.

'What station serves Trieste, by the way?' Lysander asked in the same spirit of innocent enquiry.

'The *Südbahnhof*. Change at Graz. Ten-, twelve-hour journey,' Fyfe-Miller said.

'I'd go straight to the Lloyds office in Trieste and buy a steamer ticket to . . .' Munro frowned, thinking.

'Not Venice.'

'No. Too obvious. Maybe Bari – somewhere much further south than anyone would expect.'

Lysander said nothing, content to listen, aware of what was going on in this duologue.

Munro held up a warning finger. 'You'd have to assume that the police would go straight to every station.'

'Yes. So you might need some form of disguise. Of course, they'd also presume you'd be heading north, back to England. So heading south would be the right option.'

'You'd need money,' Munro said, taking out his wallet and counting out 200 crowns, laying the notes on the table in a fan. 'What's today? Tuesday. Tomorrow afternoon, I'd say. Be in Trieste by dawn on Thursday.'

'Bob's your uncle.'

The two men looked at Lysander candidly, no hint of conspiracy or collusion in their eyes. Their pointed absence of guile carried its own message – we've been having a conversation here, pure and simple. A conversation about a hypothetical journey – read nothing more into it. We take no responsibility.

'The risks are grave,' Munro said, as if to underline this last fact.

'If you were caught it would rather look like an admission of guilt,' Fyfe-Miller added.

'You'd need to be clever. Think ahead. Imagine what it would be like – what to do in any eventuality.'

'Use your ingenuity.'

Munro stood and headed for the door, Fyfe-Miller following. The money was left lying on the table.

Lysander went to the door and opened it for them. He knew exactly what was expected of him, now.

'Most interesting,' he said. 'Thanks.'

'See you tomorrow,' Munro said. Fyfe-Miller gave a smart salute and Lysander watched them stride briskly back to the consulate through the falling snow.

At the end of the afternoon, the snow having abated, leaving the low box-hedges of the parterre with an inch of white icing, Lysander went for a stroll around the garden, thinking hard. He had the money in his pocket, Munro and Fyfe-Miller had outlined the best route out of Austria. Once he was in Trieste he would be safe – Italians outnumbered Austrians there twenty-to-one. Some tramp-steamer or cargo ship would take him to Italy for a few crowns. Then his eye was caught by something unfamiliar – a glint, a gleam of light. He wandered over.

In the lock of the small door in the back wall was a new brass key, bright and untarnished, shining in the weak afternoon sun. Lysander slipped it in his pocket. So, that was it – tomorrow afternoon, after lunch, he thought. The dash for freedom.

24. Ingenuity

LYSANDER DELIBERATELY LEFT HALF his lunch – stewed pork with horseradish – uneaten. He told the surly fellow with buck teeth who came to take it away that he wasn't feeling well and was going to bed. As soon as he was alone again he slipped on his coat, gathered up a few essential belongings that could be distributed amongst his various pockets, lifted his hat off the hook on the back of the door and stepped outside.

It was a breezy day of scudding clouds and almost all the snow had melted. He took a turn around the garden to make it seem he was on his usual post-prandial walk and, as he reached the small door in the back wall, unlocked it and was through in a second, pulling it to and locking it again from the outside. He threw the key back over the wall into the garden. He looked around him – an anonymous side street in the Landstrasse district, not a part of Vienna he was familiar with. He walked up to a main road and saw that it was named Rennweg – now his bearings returned. He was about five minutes walk from the South Railway Station where he could catch his train to Trieste – but he knew he had to use his ingenuity, first. He saw two cabs waiting outside the State Printing Works and ran across Rennweg to hail one.

He was at Mariahilfer Strasse in fifteen minutes. Fifteen minutes was the start that Munro and Fyfe-Miller said he should allow himself. He could be sitting in the *Südbahnhof* now with a ticket to Trieste in his hand. Was he making a mistake? Use your ingenuity, Munro had said. It wasn't so much advice as a warning, he thought.

Lysander rang the bell at the landing door of the Pension Kriwanek, saying a small prayer. Let Frau K be out (she was usually out after lunch, shopping or visiting) and let Herr Barth be in.

The door opened and Traudl stood there – her face rapidly pantomiming surprise and shock. Her blush rose to her hairline.

'Oh my god!' she said. 'Herr Rief! No!'

'Hello, Traudl. Yes, it's me. Is Frau Kriwanek in?'

'No. Please, what are you doing here, sir?'

'Is Herr Barth in?'

'No, he's not in, either.'

Good and damn, Lysander said to himself and gently pushed his way past Traudl into the hall. There were the two bergères and the stuffed owl under its glass dome, relics of his former happy life, Lysander thought, feeling a spasm of anger that he'd been forced to relinquish it.

'Would you open Herr Barth's room, please, Traudl?'

'I don't have a key, sir.'

'Of course you have a key.'

Meekly, she turned and headed down the corridor to Herr Barth's room, removing the bunch of house keys from her apron pocket, and unlocked the door.

'Don't tell anyone I was here, Traudl. Understand? I'll explain everything to Herr Barth later – but you mustn't say a word to anyone else.'

'Frau Kriwanek will know, Herr Rief. She knows everything.'

'She doesn't know everything. She doesn't know about you and Lieutenant Rozman . . .'

Traudl hung her head.

'I would hate to have to tell Frau Kriwanek what you and the lieutenant got up to.'

'Thank you, Herr Rief. I would be most grateful for your silence on this matter.'

'And remember you owe me twenty crowns, Traudl.'

'I'll tell no one. Not a soul. I swear.'

Lysander gestured for Traudl to enter Herr Barth's little room. 'After you,' he said, and followed her in.

25. Trieste

LYSANDER SAT LOOKING OUT of the window of the Graz express, watching the early morning sunlight glance and shimmer off the Golfo di Trieste as he caught glimpses of the sea in between the numerous tunnels the train barrelled through on its descent to the coast and the city. These vistas of the Adriatic and its rocky coastline were symbolic of his salvation, he told himself; he should store them away in his memory-archive. Here he was, arriving at the very edge of Austria-Hungary and he would be leaving it for ever in a matter of hours. He was hungry – he hadn't eaten since his abandoned lunch the day before and he promised himself a decent breakfast at the station restaurant as soon as they arrived. He had just over 100 crowns left, more than enough to book passage on a steamer to Ancona – no need to go as far south as Bari. Once in Ancona he would go to Florence and have money wired to him there, then he would make his way home through France. Now he was almost in Trieste all these plans seemed entirely feasible and logical.

With complaining groans of braking metal the Graz express slowed to a halt at Trieste's Stazione Meridionale and Lysander stepped out on to the platform. Seeing signs in Italian was already enough for him. He had made it, he was free –

'Rief?'

He turned very slowly to see Jack Fyfe-Miller stepping down from the first-class carriage with a small leather grip in his hand.

Lysander felt his bowels ease with this small deliverance.

'Bravo,' Fyfe-Miller said, clapping him on the shoulder. 'Bet you're hungry. Let me buy you breakfast.'

They went to the Café Orientale in the Lloyds building on the Piazza Grande where Lysander ordered and ate a six-egg omelette with a ham steak and consumed many small sweet bread rolls. Fyfe-Miller drank a spritzer and smoked a cigarette.

'We were very impressed,' he said.

'What do you mean?'

'Munro and I were there at the *Südbahnhof* looking out for you. We thought you were never coming, I must say – thought you'd left it too late. They had the police there very quickly. We were beginning to get worried – then along you came, swearing in Italian, carrying a double bass.'

'I was using my ingenuity, as instructed.'

Lysander had stuffed a pillow from Herr Barth's bed under his shirt and buttoned his overcoat around this new pot-belly. He had taken Herr Barth's ancient hard-felt top hat and punched a dent in it. The big double bass in its leather container was surprisingly light, though bulky. He had locked Traudl in Herr Barth's room and had hailed a cab on Mariahilfer Strasse for the station. Once there, he bought his ticket for Trieste (third class) and with many a '*Mi scusi*', '*Attenzione*' and '*Lasciami passare*' had made his way noisily to the platform. People looked round, he saw children smiling and pointing, policemen glanced at him. A station porter helped him heave the double bass on board. No one was looking for a plump Italian double-bass player in a greasy topper. He found a seat by the window and waited, as calmly as he could, for the whistle-blast announcing their departure.

'Sometimes being ostentatious is the best disguise,' Lysander said.

'So we saw . . . What happened to the double bass?'

'I left it on the train when we changed at Gratz. Feel a bit guilty about that.'

'We were very impressed, Munro and I. We had a good laugh before I jumped on the train after you.'

'Did you report me missing?'

'Of course. After an hour – but they already knew. The informers in the embassy were miles ahead of us. However, we were suitably outraged and very apologetic. Very shamefaced.'

After breakfast Fyfe-Miller bought him his ticket to Ancona and they walked along to the new port to find the mole where the mail-steamer was berthed.

Fyfe-Miller shook his hand at the foot of the gangway.

'Goodbye, Rief. And damned well done. I'm sure you've made the right decision.'

'I'm sorry to leave,' Lysander said. 'There's a lot of unfinished business in Vienna.'

'Well, you won't be able to go back, that's for sure,' Fyfe-Miller said with his usual bluntness. 'Now you're a fugitive from Austro-Hungarian justice.'

The thought depressed him. There was a toot from the steam whistle on the smoke-stack.

'Thanks for all your help – you and Munro,' Lysander said. 'I won't forget.'

'Neither will we,' Fyfe-Miller said, with a broad smile. 'You owe His Majesty's Government a considerable sum of money.'

They shook hands, Fyfe-Miller wished him *bon voyage* and Lysander boarded the scruffy coastal cargo vessel. Steam was got up and the mooring ropes were cast off, thrown on board and the little ship left the busy harbour of Trieste. Lysander stood on the rear deck, leaning on the balustrade, watching the city recede, with its castle on its modest hill, admiring the splendour of the rocky Dalmatian coastline. All very beautiful in the winter sunshine, he acknowledged, feeling a melancholy peace overwhelm him and wondering if he would ever see this country again, thinking ruefully that his business with it – Hettie and their child – had every chance of remaining unfinished for ever.

PART TWO

LONDON, 1914

1. Measure for Measure

LYSANDER CLEARED HIS THROAT, blew his nose, apologized to the rest of the cast and picked up his playscript once more. The doors and windows were wide open so the room, Lysander reasoned, would have almost as much summer pollen blowing around it as the garden outside – hence his sneezing fit. He could see Gilda Butterfield at the far end of the long table fanning her moist neck with her fingertips. Flaming June, all right, he thought and his mind turned immediately to Blanche. Her prediction had been absolutely right – the play was an enduring and superlative success and she was off on an endless tour of it. Where now? Dublin, he thought, or was it Edinburgh? Yes, he really ought to try and –

'Ready when you are, Lysander,' Rutherford Davison said. Lysander noticed he still had his jacket on while all the other men had shed theirs because of the heat. He picked up the text.

'You must lay down the treasures of your body
To this supposed, or else to let him suffer –
What would you do?'

Davison held up his hand.
'Why do you imagine he says that?'
'Because he's frustrated. Consumed with lust. And he's bitter,' Lysander said, without really thinking.
'Bitter?'
'He's a disappointed man.'
'He's an aristocrat, he's running the whole of Vienna.'
'Vienna's no protection against bitterness.'

Everyone laughed, Lysander was pleased to note, even though he hadn't intended to be humorous at all and had spoken with unconscious feeling. He had completely forgotten that *Measure for Measure* was set in Vienna – this strange play about lechery and purity, moral corruption and virtue – that made him think uncomfortably about the place and his recent history there. Too late to back out now, and he could hardly explain why. Davison hadn't even smiled at his inadvertent sally, however. He was determined to be combative and provocative, Lysander could tell, following the new lead among theatre managers. He and Greville had discussed how tiresome and unnecessary this trend was just last night.

'We'll call it a day,' Davison said, as if he sensed how stifling and uncomfortable it was to be sitting here late on a Friday afternoon. 'Have a restful weekend. We'll make a start on *Miss Julie* on Monday.'

The rehearsal broke up in a chatter of exultant conversation and the sound of chairs scraping back. They were in a church hall in St John's Wood – a good rehearsal space with a small garden at the rear when some fresh air was required. The 'International Players' Company', as they were known, had been formed by Rutherford Davison himself in an attempt – as he put it – to present the best in foreign drama to the sated and complacent London audiences. It was quite a clever plan, Lysander had to admit, taking his jacket off the back of the chair. The idea was to run an established, well-respected play in a repertory double bill with a new, more challenging foreign one. Last season's offering had been a Galsworthy, *The Silver Box*, alongside Chekhov's *The Cherry Orchard*. This season they were presenting *Measure for Measure* with Strindberg's *Miss Julie*. Or rather, *Fröken Julie* as Davison insisted, thinking the foreign title would hoodwink the censor. Apparently the play had been banned in 1911. Davison had acquired a new translation from an American company and thought that the Swedish title might divert attention from its salacious reputation. Lysander hadn't read *Miss Julie* yet but was planning to do so this weekend, if time permitted. His role was Jean, the valet, something of a challenge because he was also Angelo in *Measure*. He and Gilda Butterfield were the most experienced actors in the International Players so he should be flattered, he supposed, and if the plays were well received it would advance his career and reputation significantly. All very well, he thought, but if Davison kept goading him it might not be as stimulating a job as he had imagined.

'Any plans this weekend?'

Lysander turned to see Gilda Butterfield, Miss Julie herself – and Isabella in *Measure*. They were destined to spend a lot of time in each other's company over the coming weeks. She was very fair with a mass of curly blonde hair tied back in a velvet bow – very Scandinavian, he supposed. A few freckles were visible across the bridge of her nose and cheeks, unmasked by her powder – a busty, hippy young woman. Strapping, outdoors-y. She was interested in him, he could tell, wondering if the job might deliver up a little romance as a bonus.

'Going down to Sussex,' he said, fishing out his cigarette case and opening it. She took a cigarette and he lit it for her. 'My uncle's back from two years exploring Africa. We're welcoming him home.' He took one himself, lit it and they wandered towards the front door.

'Whereabouts in Sussex?' she said, adjusting her bow at the nape of her neck with both hands, leaving the cigarette in her mouth – both hands moving behind her head caused her breasts to rise and flatten against the pleated front of her blouse. For a second, Lysander acknowledged the careless carnality of the pose then reminded himself that he wasn't ready for another dalliance. Not after Hettie.

'Claverleigh,' he said. 'Do you know it? A little way beyond Lewes. Not far from Ripe.'

'My brother lives in Hove,' she said, happy now with the tightness of her bow. She exhaled, pluming the smoke away from him. 'Perhaps we might find ourselves down there at the same time, one weekend.'

'That would be lovely.' Really, this was almost brazen, Lysander thought, she was giving actresses a bad name. Wait until he'd told Greville. He held the door open for her and Rutherford Davison came through.

'Ah, Lysander, can I have a quick word?'

Lysander felt sweat trickling down his spine – he should have taken a bus home, not the Tube. It was hot, of course, but he knew he was sweating more than usually because he'd allowed himself to become irritated. Davison had kept him back twenty minutes after the others had left asking a lot of damnfool questions about his character, Angelo. Was he an only child or did he have siblings? If so, how many and of what sex? What did Lysander think he'd been doing before his big speech in Act II? Was he well travelled? Did he have any health problems he might be concealing? Lysander had done his best to answer the questions seriously because he knew that Davison had gone to Russia a year before, had met Stanislavsky and had fallen under the sway of his new theories about acting and drama, and was convinced that all this extraneous material and information that one invented fleshed out the character and bolstered the text. Lysander felt like saying that if Shakespeare had wanted us to know that Angelo was well travelled or suffered from piles he would have dropped in a line or two in the play to that effect. But in the interest of good relations and a peaceful time he had nodded and said 'good point' or 'intriguing idea' and 'let me think a bit more about that'. It was a big role, Angelo, and it would be better and easier all round to have the director on his side.

At one stage, Davison had said, 'There's a book you might like to read, that you might find useful for Angelo – *Die Traumdeutung* by Sigmund Freud. Heard of it?'

'I've met the author,' Lysander had said. That shut him up.

He smiled at the memory of that afternoon in the Café Landtmann. Davison had looked at him with new respect. Perhaps they would rub along after all.

The Tube train pulled in to Leicester Square and Lysander stepped out, jamming his boater on to his head. He thought he might drop into a pub for a cooling pint of shandy and quench his thirst – try to reduce the sweatiness and discomfort he was experiencing. He came up from the station and sniffed the air – London in June, a hot June, the smell of horseshit stewing.

He and Greville Varley rented a flat on Chandos Place and there was a pub, the Peace and Plenty, round the corner from William IV Street, that he liked. Small and plain, with scrubbed floorboards and wainscotting, not tarted up with etched glass and velveteen wallpaper like so many in London. Greville wouldn't be in, anyway, he had a matinée today. No, couldn't be, it was Friday. Matinée tomorrow.

'Afternoon, Mr Rief. Hot enough for you?'

'Yes, thank you, Molly, but could you cool it down for tomorrow, please? – I'm off to the country.'

'All right for some, Mr Rief.'

Molly was the barmaid and the landlord's niece, up from Devon – or was it Somerset? A round-faced, plump girl who reminded him of Traudl.

Obliging, blushing Traudl in the Pension Kriwanek, Lysander thought, taking his pint to a seat in the corner, thinking – that was my life not so long ago, those were its familiar details and textures. Someone had left a newspaper and Lysander picked it up to read the headlines and tossed it down almost immediately. He wasn't interested in Irish Home Rule or the threat of a coal strike. So what *are* you interested in, he asked himself, aggressively. Your life? Your job? Your friends? Your family?

Good questions. He sipped his beer, analysing his distractions, his pleasures . . . Since he'd come back from Vienna so precipitately he'd moved flat and found the new place with Greville – that was good. He'd won a part in a three-reeler film and earned £50 for two days' work – no complaints. He'd been to numerous auditions and landed this plum double role with the International Players'

Company – not to be sniffed at. And, oh yes, Blanche Blondel herself had called off their engagement.

He leaned back and took his boater off. Blanche . . .

He had rather dreaded their first encounter, and with good reason, as it turned out. He had been nervous, oddly tongue-tied, moody and irritable.

'There's somebody else, isn't there, in Vienna?' Blanche had said after five minutes.

'No. Yes, well . . . There was. It's over. Completely.'

'So you say – but you're giving a very good impression of a lovelorn fool pining for his girl.'

She took his ring off and handed it to him. They were in a chop-house on the Strand, dining after her show.

'I'm going to stay your friend, Lysander, ' she had said, amiably. 'But not your fiancée.' She reached over and squeezed his hand. 'Sort yourself out, darling. And, if you still feel like it, propose to me again and we'll see what I say.'

Lysander went up to the bar for another pint. Only four o'clock and here he was on his second. He watched Molly pour it – two long hauls at the lever and there it was, a sudsy head at the very rim. He pushed over a handful of coppers lifted from his pocket and she picked out the right change. The unnatural curls at Molly's temples were damp with perspiration, sticking to her skin. He should marry Blanche, he thought, to hell with it – everything about that woman was right for him.

'Greville? You in?' Lysander called, closing the door to the flat behind him. No reply. He dropped his keys into a bowl on the hall table. Mrs Tozer, the housekeeper, had been in cleaning and tidying and the smell of beeswax polish hit his nostrils. She had organized the post into two distinct piles for her 'gentlemen' and he was vaguely annoyed to see that Greville had twice as many letters as he did. The flat was on the top floor of a mansion block no more than ten years old. From Greville's bedroom you could just see Nelson standing on his column in Trafalgar Square. There was a sitting room, two fair-sized bedrooms, a small kitchen-scullery and a bathroom with WC. A maid's room had been converted into a joint dressing room and walk-in wardrobe – both he and Greville had far too many clothes. All the belongings he had left in the summerhouse in Vienna had been promptly shipped back to London by Munro – it was as if he had never been there at all.

Lysander shuffled through his post – bill, bill, postcard from Dublin ('Wish you were here. B'), a telegram from his mother ('PLEASE COLLECT PLOVERS EGGS FORTNUMS STOP') and – his mouth went dry – a letter with an Austrian stamp, Emperor Franz-Josef in profile, forwarded on to him from his previous flat, the postmark over two weeks old.

He went into the sitting room and cut the letter open with a paper knife. He knew what news it contained and he sat there at the writing desk for a minute, somehow not daring to reach in and draw the slip of paper out.

'Come on!' he urged himself out loud. 'Don't be pathetic.'

One sheet of paper. Hettie's unformed, childish handwriting.

Dearest Lysander,

It is with great happiness that I write to you with the news that our son is born. I told you he would be a boy, didn't I? He came into this world at 10.30 p.m. on the twelfth of June. He's a big baby, almost nine pounds, and has a powerful pair of lungs. I wanted to call him Lysander – but that was obviously out of the question – so I have decided on Lothar, instead. If you say Lysander–Lothar quickly a few times they almost blend together – or so I like to believe.

I miss you very much and I thank you from the bottom of my heart for what you did. Your escape was a great scandal here in Vienna and was written about in some newspapers. The police were roundly condemned for their uselessness and inefficiency.

You can imagine my feelings when I heard you had gone and that there would be no trial.

You can always write to me care of the Café Sorgenfrei, Sterngasse, Wien. But I assume that your heart is only full of hate for me now, after what I did to you. Love our little boy, Lothar, instead of me. I will send you a photograph of him soon.

With our love,

Hettie and Lothar.

He closed his eyes and felt the warm tears well and run down his cheeks. Hettie and Lothar. He blubbed like a baby for a few minutes – like baby Lothar – head in his hands, leaning forward on the writing desk. Then he stood, went to the drinks' cabinet and poured himself an inch of brandy, toasted Lothar Rief, wishing him a long life and good health, and drank it down. He heard Greville's key in the lock and wiped his eyes but it was no use. Greville came in, said, 'Good god, man, what's happened?' and Lysander started weeping again.

2. Summer Evening

He took a taxi from Lewes station to Claverleigh Hall. As he went through the gates into the park, past the Elizabethan gatehouse with its twisted brick chimneys, he felt he was coming home, although, after registering the emotion initially he then questioned it, as he always did. For half his life it had been his home, true – if you defined 'home' as the place your surviving parent lived. He still kept his old room above the L-shaped kitchen wing that had been built on to the back when the house was extensively remodelled in the 'Italian' style towards the end of the last century – the façade was stuccoed, a four-columned Tuscan porch was added – but after that first recognition the sensation that he was somehow just visiting re-established itself. It would always be the domain of the Faulkners – even a long-standing stepson called Rief was something of an interloper.

Claverleigh Hall was a moderately-sized mansion house of two storeys with added dormers in the roof. Its most striking architectural feature was its main staircase – 'important' – curving up towards a small Soaneian dome from the entrance hall. And on the first floor was a galleried drawing room that ran the length of the building and its nine tall windows. This gallery had two fireplaces and the ceiling was regarded as over-decorated, all swags, scrolls and festoons of plaster, crests, flowers, fruit and putti crammed into the corners. It was a comfortable home, all the same, and Faulkners had been living in it for over a century since the second Baron bought it with a fortune made from a wise investment in sugar plantations in the Caribbean.

The front door was opened by Lord Faulkner's butler, Marlowe, who took his suitcase and led him to his old room.

'How's everything, Marlowe?'

'Very well, sir. Except the Major has cancelled for this evening.'

'That's a shame. What's happened?'

The Major was his uncle – Major Hamo Rief, VC, the not particularly famous explorer.

'He's indisposed,' Marlowe confided, 'but nothing serious, we're informed.'

'So who do we have for dinner, then?'

Marlowe said it was just the family – Lord and Lady Faulkner, the Honourable Hugh Faulkner (Crickmay's son) and his wife, May, and the 'two little girls'. The local dignitaries who had been hoping to greet Major Rief had been postponed until the Major felt better again. Lysander relaxed. He liked his stepbrother, Hugh. A tall, genial, balding man in his forties who seemed to blink twice as much as anyone else he'd ever met. He was known as the grandest dentist in Harley Street. Lysander supposed dentistry was an odd job for someone who would be the sixth Baron Faulkner one day, but he made an excellent living and, because of his rank, was much sought after on dental matters by London high society. His wife, May, was jolly and energetic, and their two girls, Emily (12) and Charlotte (10), were funny and unspoilt.

So, a family dinner, Lysander thought – good. Perhaps he might walk over to Winchelsea the next day and pay a visit on the Major. It was a good twenty miles from Claverleigh to Winchelsea by country lanes – a day's walk – but nothing could be better for him in his current mood, Lysander thought. He would send a telegram and alert the Major that he'd be coming.

He took two dozen well-wrapped plovers' eggs out of his suitcase and handed then to Marlowe.

'Where can I find my mother?' he asked.

'Lady Faulkner is in the small walled garden, sir.'

Lysander pushed through the door in the high brick wall that led to the smaller walled garden and found his mother vigorously dead-heading dahlias. She was wearing a billowy, chartreuse, light-canvas dust-coat over her frock and a wide straw hat held down on her head by a silk scarf. He kissed her cheek and smelled her perfume, violets and lavender, a little ghostly trace of his father that still clung to her.

She took his hand and led him to a wooden bench set in the right angle at the corner of the garden wall and sat him down, staring at him intently. It had been some weeks since they had seen each other and Lysander thought she was looking very well, suiting the casual informality of her gardening clothes, with wisps of her greying hair hanging down unrestrained, stirred by the breeze. Tonight at dinner she would appear entirely different, he knew, with heavy powder and rouged lips, tall and handsome, her hair wound up in an onion-shaped bun, her tightly waisted dress with its broad sash emphasizing her still youthful hour-glass figure. In the evenings she wore her décolletage cut low, the generous swell of her breasts only half hidden by some diaphanous material. She used to be on the stage, Lysander reminded himself on these occasions, and this glamorous night-time persona that she transformed herself into was her only chance to perform, these days, to be covertly stared at and desired.

'You're looking weary, my darling,' she said, touching his cheek with her knuckles. 'Working too hard, I bet. What's the play?'

'Two plays, that's the problem. *Measure for Measure* and a Swedish one called *Miss Julie*.'

'Isn't it terribly immoral? How wonderful.'

'I haven't read it yet. I've got it with me.'

'I remember when your father did Ibsen. *Hedda Gabler*. Everyone was very disturbed. What is it about these Scandinavians?'

'We're trying to provoke a reaction, I think. Anyway, it should be interesting.' He paused. 'Mother . . . I've got some rather momentous news.'

He had told his mother nothing about why and how he had had to leave Vienna – she thought it was simply the planned end of his stay. He had hinted at an entanglement – a flirtation – and she also knew that his engagement to Blanche was over. She was sorry – she liked Blanche a lot.

'You know that I told you I became involved with a young woman while I was in Vienna.'

'This English girl, Miss Bull. How could I forget a name like that? The one that made Blanche so cross – and I'm on Blanche's side, by the way.'

'Yes. Well, I've had a letter from Miss Bull. She's had a child.'

His mother looked at him. Her eyes widened, then narrowed.

'She's not saying it's yours.'

'It is mine. Indisputably. It's a boy, called Lothar. Your first grandchild.'

His mother stood up, took a handkerchief from her sleeve and walked away, rather dramatically dabbing at tears, he thought.

'I knew a boy at school called Lothar,' she said, throwing the words over her shoulder. 'Lothar Hinz.' She composed herself and came back over to the bench, sat down and took both his hands. 'Let's speak straightforwardly, darling, with honesty. Remember, I'm an actor's wife so nobody could be more broad-minded. What are the problems looming over this wonderfully happy occasion?'

'The boy is mine but I don't know when and how I'm ever going to be able to see him.'

'Another man in the picture?'

'Yes. Miss Bull's common-law husband – as the expression goes. An unpleasant fellow, a painter called Udo Hoff.'

'Painters are always difficult. But you're in touch with Miss Bull, at least. What's her Christian name?'

'Esther.'

'Sounds religious to me. Is she religious?'

'Not in the least. She's known as Hettie.'

'Hettie Bull. We have a chambermaid here called Hettie.'

'Hettie Bull is an . . . extraordinary person. I was completely . . .' Lysander paused. 'She was helpful to me and I rather lost my head. She overwhelmed me. We overwhelmed each other.'

'So it was very passionate.'

'Very.'

'And little Lothar is the outcome.'

They sat there in silence for a while.

'Have you a photograph of this Hettie Bull?'

'Do you know, I haven't. I left in such a hurry. All I have is this.'

Lysander took the libretto of *Andromeda und Perseus* out of his pocket and handed it to her.

'That's her. She posed for Andromeda.'

'Very daring. She's completely naked. She looks pretty anyway. Is she tall?'

'She's tiny. A little slip of a thing – *gamine*. Electric.'

Lysander suddenly thought this was a good sign, a further indication of the success of his Vienna cure, in that he was practically talking with his mother about sex. She reached out and removed some thistle down from his lapel.

'I thought you liked tall girls, like Blanche.'

'I did. Until I met Hettie.'

She looked at the cover of the libretto again.

'Can I borrow this? It seems interesting. Did you hear the music? I don't know the composer.'

'It was very modern, apparently. But, no, I didn't. Do take it.'

'Lysander! Why did no one tell us you were here?'

They looked up to see, coming through the door from the large walled garden, the lanky figure of the Hon. Hugh Faulkner. He turned and shouted back through the open door.

'Girls! Uncle Lysander's here!'

Squeals of delight followed this announcement and, seconds later, Emily and Charlotte came racing across the lawn towards them.

'I think we'll keep this news from the rest of the family for a while,' his mother said, quietly. 'Careful, girls, don't fall and spoil your lovely dresses!'

Crickmay Faulkner offered Lysander a cigar.

'Your mother tells me you're acting in an indecent play.'

'I'll take a cigarette, thank you. Yes, it's Swedish, called *Miss Julie*.'

'I like the sound of that already. I want tickets for the first night, front row.' Crickmay smiled. 'I want to be corrupted before I die.'

'Me too,' Hugh added, lighting his cigar. 'I want to be corrupted too – but you've got a good few years left in you, Papa.' He passed the port decanter to Lysander. 'What's it about?'

'It's about a rich, well-born woman who has an affair with a valet.'

'Marvellous. But they'll never let you put it on.'

They laughed. Crickmay lit his cigar, coughed and slapped his chest.

'Don't tell your mother, she'll get cross with me.'

He was looking decidedly older these days, Lysander thought, his face slowly collapsing, big bags under his rheumy eyes and sagging cheeks. His thick white moustache needed clipping.

The three men were sitting in the dining room in their dinner jackets, smoking and drinking port, the women having retired to the drawing room. Lysander topped up his glass, feeling a little drunk. Telling his mother about Hettie and Lothar had encouraged him to drink more than he meant. Brandy and soda before dinner, too much claret with the roast lamb and now port. Better stop if he was going to walk to Winchelsea tomorrow.

'Shall we join the ladies?' Crickmay said, heaving himself to his feet with difficulty and limping out of the room.

'Bring the port, Lysander,' Hugh said. 'Are you thinking about going to church tomorrow? If you won't, I won't.'

Lysander picked up the port decanter.

'No. I'm walking to Winchelsea tomorrow, check up on the Major.'

'Amazing fellow. Where's he been to now?'

They walked down the wide corridor towards the Green Drawing Room.

'Somewhere in West Africa, I think. Exploring the upper reaches of the Benue River, the last I heard. He's been away for two years.'

They turned into the drawing room, where May was playing the piano and his mother was searching through sheet music looking for a song. It was her party piece, a nod to her past that everyone indulged and enjoyed. Lysander went and stood by the fireplace, looking at her with admiration as she stood in the ogival curve of the piano, one hand resting on the music stand, and raised her chin firmly, ready to sing. It was still light outside – the deepening blue of the short summer night just beginning to overcome the last of the sun's iridescence in the sky. Lysander felt a pressure at the base of his spine and a feeling of peace flow through him. He had a son – it was as if the news had only just registered. He had a son called Lothar. He wondered if one day he would ever bring him to Claverleigh Hall to meet his grandmother. It seemed an impossible dream. His mother began to sing and her warm vibrant voice filled the air.

> *'Arm und Nacken, weiss und lieblich,*
> *Schimmern in dem Mondenscheine. . . '*

Brahms, he recognized, one of his favourites. 'Summer Evening'. 'White and lovely, her arms and neck glimmer in the moonshine.' He felt the emotion well and brim in him – such a simple poem. Hettie, he thought at once – it wasn't over, clearly. He stood and crossed to the window as his mother continued singing. He looked out through his reflection in the panes to the darkening park beyond, the sun below the horizon now, though its light still charged and brightened the blue-grey air. The ancient limes, oaks and elms in the fenced enclosure seemed to solidify, losing their individual character as trees, and became great opaque shaggy monoliths that, as the remaining sunglow removed itself from them, somehow better revealed the true artful geography of the landscape gardener who, a century before, had placed the feathery saplings here and there – on the sides of hillocks, on the edge of the small lake, and grouped them in gentle valleys – to make a near-perfect man-made landscape that he would never see.

3. The Walk to Winchelsea

Lysander was up at six o'clock and went down to the kitchen, where he gulped a quick cup of tea and had two rounds of cheese-and-pickle sandwiches made up for him. He had found a pair of corduroy trousers and some mountain boots in his wardrobe and with a linen jacket and a Panama hat he was ready for the day. He reckoned it was a twenty-three-mile walk to Winchelsea, more or less straight across country, following lanes and tracks via the villages of Herstmonceux and Battle before he briefly joined the main trunk road that would lead him down to the coast at Winchelsea.

The day was warm but there was a threat of showers, according to Marlowe, so he stuffed a rubberized cycling cape in his rucksack, along with his sandwiches and his playscript of *Miss Julie*, and set off across the park looking for the first of the cart-tracks that would lead him east to Herstmonceux.

He made good going in the early morning freshness over the downland, catching glimpses of the silvered sea to his right whenever he hit higher ground and the unfolding valleys opened up to afford him a view southwards. He felt good in himself, as he always did when he was walking with purpose, his mind emptying of everything except what he could see and hear around him, as he skirted the oak and beech copses, following sunken lanes hedged with hornbeam and blackthorn, hearing a late cuckoo piping its two-note song, looking down on small farms from ridge-paths, crossing trunk roads as quickly as he could, eager to remove himself from traffic and the noisy reminders of the twentieth century.

They were beginning to cut hay in the fields as he passed, the haymakers scything down the meadows and filling the air with the sweet, pungent scent of cut grass. Around the middle of the morning he realized he had slightly lost his bearings. He hadn't seen the sea for an hour and, although he knew he was heading broadly east – the position of the sun told him that – he hadn't come across a fingerpost or a sign for a village for a mile or two. He met a four-horse wagon jingling up a lane and asked the carter's boy who was leading the team where he could find the road to Herstmonceux. The boy told him he'd passed

Herstmonceux and he should turn back. If he went on aways he'd come to a country church. There was a signpost there that would tell him the directions.

He paused at the church, ancient and solid, faced with grey-blue flint, with a battlemented tower and a graveyard half overgrown with nettles, long grass and cow parsley. Gnarled, bent apple trees flanked the cemetery wall. He ate the first of his sandwiches here and the cheese and pickle gave him a thirst so he strode on to Battle, finding an old milestone on the verge that told him Battle was two and a half miles away. Battle with its pubs. He was making good time – a pint of ale, a cigarette and he'd be ready to move on again.

In Battle he found a quiet pub called The Windmill – it was only just noon – not far from the abbey. He bought a pint of cloudy ale for sixpence and sat down on a bench seat by the window and watched three haymakers in dirty smocks play dominoes. He took *Miss Julie* out of his haversack, thinking he really should try and read it through before the first rehearsal tomorrow afternoon in St John's Wood. He read a page or two then closed the book, thinking that August Strindberg was not part of this world and it was something of an affront to both Strindberg and The Windmill pub in Battle to introduce them to each other.

Sitting in this small pub with its cool flagged floor, listening to the murmuring voices of the haymakers and the click of dominoes falling, drinking beer here in the middle of summer in England in 1914, he suddenly felt a stillness creep up on him as if he were suffering from a form of mental palsy – as if time had stopped and the world's turning, also. It was a strange sensation – that he would be for ever stuck in this late June day in 1914 like a fly in amber – the past as irrelevant to him as the future. A perfect stasis; the most alluring inertia.

And then suddenly it was over, the mood passed, as a lorry rumbled by, tooting its horn and the world began to move again.

He picked up his rucksack, eased himself into its straps and took his empty pint glass back to the bar.

As he left Battle it began to drizzle but he decided to press on, turning off the busy Hastings road as soon as he could and following a cart track that a group of foresters – cutting lengths of alder – told him would see him clear across country to Guestling Thorn. Once he was there he'd have to brave the verge of the main road to Rye with its motor traffic for a mile or two but it would lead him straight to Winchelsea and the Major.

He liked Winchelsea, he thought, as he entered the village, striding down one of its wide streets to Hamo's cottage. All village streets should be this wide, he thought: the village was full of light, open to the sun on its high bluff. Hamo's white weatherboarded cottage was on the western edge with a fine view over Rye Bay to Camber Sands and the expanses of Romney Marsh beyond. He knocked on the door.

4. A Very Sweet Boy

'WELL, I THOUGHT YOU should be aware of the situation,' the Major said. 'You know what I always say, Lysander – honesty is everything in life. The bedrock of all relationships. I make no bones about it, as I'm sure you'll agree. Never have, never will.'

The Major stood with his back to a small fire in the grate of the sitting room. He was wearing an old quilted red velvet smoking jacket with a cravat and a small, white, beaded skullcap on his bald head. He looked lean and weatherbeaten, still heavily tanned, with deep lines scoring either cheek as if he'd spent months gritting his teeth. His eyes, in his dark face, were a disconcertingly pale blue.

'I totally understand, Hamo,' Lysander said. 'You know that. It couldn't matter less to me.'

A young African boy came into the room with a tray bearing a whisky bottle, two glasses and a soda siphon.

'Thank you, Femi,' the Major said.

The boy – who looked seventeen or eighteen – smiled, and set the tray down.

'Femi – this is my nephew, Lysander Rief.'

'Pleased to meet, sar,' Femi said and shook Lysander's offered hand. He was wearing a khaki-drill suit and a knitted black tie. He was tall with a high forehead. A fine handsome African face, Lysander thought.

'Of course, it causes a bit of a stir when we go shopping in Rye, as you can imagine,' the Major said with some glee. 'However, I just tell everyone he's a visiting African prince and they calm down quickly enough.'

Femi gave a small bow and went back into the kitchen.

'Let me just go and see how our supper's coming along,' Hamo said, and followed Femi out. Lysander stood and prowled around the room. It was full of artefacts from Hamo's trips to west and central Africa – sculptures, pottery, calabashes, animal hides on the floor – including an entire zebra skin in front of the fire. On one wall was a glass case full of weapons – ceremonial axes and daggers and long bladed, finely etched spears as well as Hamo's muzzle-loading elephant gun and his Martini-Henri Mark II rifle from the South African War. 'The world's most accurate rifle up to a quarter of a mile,' Hamo had told him once. 'Soft lead bullet makes one hell of a mess.' Next to it was a carved ebony frieze full of fantastic creatures – huge-eared, multi-limbed goblins and what looked like hermaphrodites – it reminded Lysander of Bensimon's bas-relief. He missed his meetings with Bensimon, he realized.

He turned as he heard Hamo come back into the room.

'Femi was my guide on the Niger,' Hamo went on. 'Saved my life at least three times,' he added matter-of-factly. He looked fondly towards the kitchen. 'He's a very sweet boy. His English is coming along remarkably well.'

He poured Lysander another whisky and topped it up with soda.

'So you walked all the way from Claverleigh? I'll have to take you on my next expedition.'

Hamo Rief had won his Victoria Cross in 1901 during the South African War. At the beginning of the raising of the siege of Ladysmith he had seen a troop of Boer horsemen seize two field artillery pieces and he single-handedly drove off the raiding party, recovering the guns, killing four and wounding five, but not before being wounded himself, three times. Honourably discharged from his regiment as a result of his injuries he found that the wanderlust that had taken him into the army in the first place still remained so he decided to become an amateur explorer, joining the Royal Geographical Society, and, in 1907, privately funded an expedition to West Africa, attempting to travel across the continent from the Niger River to the Nile. In fact he only managed to reach Lake Chad – where he fell ill with dengue fever – and spent several months there recuperating, using the time to gather specimens and make anthropological studies of the local tribes. The book he wrote and published on his return, *The Lost Lake of Africa*, became a surprise bestseller and funded this last and latest expedition, exploring, not the upper reaches of the Benue River as Lysander had thought, but various islands in the Bight of Benin.

Lysander was very glad to be with his uncle again after a gap of two years. Though he had been something of a distant figure to him during his childhood – Hamo had spent many years with his regiment in India – Lysander had grown very fond of his uncle as he'd come to know him better after his father's death. He was full of admiration for his absolute fearlessness, military and social. Hamo didn't resemble his older brother – he was bald and naturally skinny with a small head – but, for Lysander, he was the only remaining blood link with his dead father. Hamo talked about him without need of prompting and would regularly repeat the fact that the only person he had ever, truly loved was his brother, Halifax.

'Halifax understood me completely, you see, from a very early age,' Hamo had once confided to Lysander. 'When I told him – I must have been fourteen or so – that I thought I wasn't interested in girls he said neither was Alexander the Great. Then he read me some of Shakespeare's sonnets – and I never looked back.'

They ate a supper of cold mutton and boiled potatoes, Femi joining them at the table. Then Hamo brought out half a Stilton cheese and a plate of hard biscuits and decanted another bottle of claret in front of a candle, showing Femi how the light at the neck of the bottle ensured that you didn't allow the sediment to flow into the decanter.

'I'm sorry I had to cancel my "Welcome Home" dinner at Claverleigh,' he said. 'I'll write to your mother in a day or two and explain. I just couldn't face it – d'you know what I mean?'

'I completely understand.'

'I simply didn't want to meet the mayor of Lewes or Sir Humphrey Bumphrey and his lady wife, etcetera, etcetera. And I don't think young Femi was quite ready for that ordeal by fire, either.'

'To be honest, I don't think old Crickmay was bothered – gets easily tired these days. Neither was my mother. I think they thought you might like it – you know, kill the fatted calf, lay on a bit of opulence after your lean years in Africa.'

Hamo poured more wine.

'She's a sensible, lovely woman. I appreciated the gesture. Anyway, I've got to give a lecture in London – I'll invite everyone to that.' He turned to Femi and put his hand on his arm. 'Are you all right, my dear boy?'

'Yes, sar. Very good.'

Hamo swung his gaze back to Lysander.

'So, what's going on in the wicked world of the theatre? Did you know Ellen Terry used to have a cottage here in Winchelsea? Lived in sin with Henry Irving. Used to dance on her lawn in bare feet and her nightdress. We're a very tolerant little village. Broad streets, broad minds.'

Femi went up to bed once the dishes were cleared away and Hamo and Lysander sat on in front of the small fire, smoking and chatting. As Lysander hoped, the conversation began to revolve around Halifax Rief.

'It's a source of enormous regret. It keeps happening. I said to Femi without thinking – you must meet my brother, Halifax. And then I remembered he was dead and gone, all these years. I keep saying – I must tell this to Halifax. How he'll laugh. Hopeless.'

'You see, I was too young,' Lysander said. 'I never really saw enough of him to fix him in my head. He was just "Father", you know. Always off to the theatre or on tour.'

Hamo pointed the stem of his pipe at Lysander. 'They have great respect for actors, Femi's people. In fact throughout Africa – actors, dancers, musicians, showmen. You should see some of these chaps in Femi's tribe, how they can imitate animals – egrets, leopards, monkeys. Incredible. A few daubs of paint, some feathers and a stick. And then a few gestures, the way they hold themselves – uncanny. You think you're watching a heron, say, picking its way through marshy water, stabbing at fish with its beak. Halifax would have been amazed.'

'What was the last thing you saw him in?' Lysander knew the answer to this question but he wanted to prompt reminiscences.

'It was his Lear. Yes . . . About a week before he died. I was on leave in London, going back to India and the regiment. Absolutely terrifying performance. He was a big man, your father, you know, but in that play you saw him shrink, with your own eyes, saw him diminish physically. You know that speech, "Blow, winds and crack your cheeks!"'

'The storm scene.' Lysander spread his arms and declaimed, '"Rage! Blow! You cataracts and hurricanoes spout till you have drenched our steeples, drown'd the cocks!"'

'Exactly. Except he did it in a quiet voice. Stood very still, hardly moved – no bombast. Sent shivers up your spine. Do you want another whisky, old chap?'

'I will, actually – I've got some rather momentous news. And I want to ask your advice.'

Over two more glasses of whisky Lysander told Hamo the whole story about Hettie, the rape and assault charge, his arrest and flight from Vienna to Trieste. And the birth of Lothar.

'What's the name? Say again.'

'Lothar. Lothar Rief.'

'But now you can't go back to Austria, I suppose. Not even disguised?'

'I don't think I can risk it.'

'Then why don't I go in your place? Find this girl, Hettie, and make contact discreetly. No one'll suspect an old fellow like me.'

'Would you?'

'Like a shot.' Lysander could see the excitement glitter in his pale blue eyes. 'I could find the boy. Check out what this artist, Hoff, is like – pretend to buy a painting. See what the set-up is and report back to you.'

'It might work . . .' Lysander began to think himself, his own excitement building. 'And I've a friend out there,' he added. 'A lieutenant in the hussars. Could be useful.'

'I don't speak the language of course.'

'Wolfram Rozman – he speaks excellent English.'

'We'll make a plan, Lysander, we'll sort it out. Get young Lothar back where he belongs. Maybe I'll kidnap him . . .' He shot Lysander one of his rare lopsided smiles and winked.

The next morning Lysander was up and left early to catch the train from Rye back to Claverleigh. Femi was in the kitchen wearing a crudely patterned cotton robe down to his ankles, with bare feet. Suddenly he looked very African in the small cottage kitchen, with the kettle boiling on the range, the stacked dishes on the wooden draining board. He shook Lysander's hand.

'The Major, he talk of you, many, many,' Femi said.

Lysander was touched and left the house with a new sense of

purpose and for the first time since he'd heard of Lothar's birth he felt stirrings of hope. A plan was forming. He picked up a trap waiting outside the inn at Winchelsea and was at Rye station in time for the 7.45 to Brighton, calling at Hastings and Lewes, with the rest of the Monday morning commuters, empty-faced men in their grey suits, stiff collars and bowler hats, reading their newspapers, counting down the hours until they could catch the train home again. Lysander stood amongst them, an incongruous figure with his baggy corduroy trousers and Panama hat, his rucksack slung over one shoulder, thinking of Hamo's plan, his singing heart making him smile spontaneously.

5. A Grotesque Insult to the Bard

LYSANDER'S HEAD WAS STILL buzzing. He was experiencing that strange combination of huge mental fatigue with sheer, adrenalin-fuelled exhilaration that occurred whenever he came off stage after a first night – particularly if his role had been a sizeable one. It could last for an hour or more, he knew, as he felt his eyelids flicker and grow irresistibly heavy. Gilda was saying something to him but he couldn't find the energy to listen. He was thinking back over his performance as Angelo, worrying that he'd rather gabbled his big speech in Act II. No doubt Rutherford would tell him in the morning . . .

The cab rattled over some cobblestones and woke him up. Gilda swayed with the motion and grabbed his arm to keep herself upright.

'Oops, sorry,' she said. 'But don't you think so?'

'Think what?'

'You're not listening to me, you beast.'

'Do you think I went too fast through, "Is this her fault or mine? The tempter or the tempted, who sins most?" I thought I may have rushed it.'

'Not to my ear. No, I was saying – are we mad?'

'In what way?'

'To be doing *Miss Julie* as well. The first night's in two weeks, I can't believe it.'

'It's only ninety minutes and there's no interval.'

'I suppose so . . . But it's very intense – I think we'll be exhausted. What have we taken on?'

The back of the cab was full of her scent – a clinging, farinaceous odour of lilies and cinnamon –'Matins de Paris' she had said it was called when he asked. He had agreed to wait for her after the show but she had taken forty minutes to put on her finery. She was looking in her compact-mirror now, checking her hair, her lip-rouge – the palest pink. It suited her.

'We're going to be the last there,' Lysander said.

'Then we can make an entrance. It *is* our night.'

'Don't let Rutherford hear you say that.'

She laughed – her real laugh, Lysander noted, rather deep and raucous, not like her fake laugh, a kind of girly trill. He could easily distinguish them, now they had spent so much time together rehearsing *Measure for Measure* and *Miss Julie*, just as he could distinguish the real Gilda Butterfield from 'Miss Gilda Butterfield', the latter overlaid with many veneers of faux-gentility, pretension, archness and other affectations, the laugh being the least of it. She was talking again.

'Rutherford asked me one of his questions about *Miss Julie* that I really didn't know how to answer.'

'Oh, yes, one of his "Stanislavsky" questions.' He was awake now – exhilaration had vanquished fatigue. 'What was it?'

'He said: what do you think happens when Julie and Jean go outside – just before the ballet sequence?'

'And you said?'

'I said I assumed they kissed.'

141

'Come on, Gilda. You're a woman of the world.'

'What do they do, then?'

Lysander decided to take the risk. Something about Gilda dared him to say it. She was an actress, for god's sake. He lowered his voice.

'They fu – they fornicate, of course.'

'*Lysander!* Talk about calling a spade a spade.' She laughed again, however.

'Excuse my Anglo-Saxon. But it's very obvious. It's very important also, for when they both come back on, that the audience realizes this. When *we* both come back on.'

'Now you put it that way I see what you mean, yes . . .' She busied herself with her mirror again, embarrassed, he supposed, wondering if he'd gone too far.

'When Jean and Julie come back on after the ballet. Everything's changed,' he said. 'They haven't just been billing and cooing in the rose garden. They've been – you know, passionately, irresistibly . . .' He paused. 'It affects the whole play. That's why you commit suicide.'

'You sound like Rutherford,' she said. 'Or have you been reading too much D. H. Lawrence?'

They were rolling down Regent Street towards the Café Royal. It was a warm clear night, not too muggy for late July. The cab pulled up and Lysander paid the driver and helped Gilda down carefully. She was wearing a very tight hobble-skirt that gave her a footstep of no more than eighteen inches and a sleeveless silk blouse freighted with flounces and ribbonry. She had a pearl choker at her throat and long white gloves almost to her armpits. Her curly blonde hair had been subdued under numerous hair-ornaments. He handed over her chiffon stole and she wound it loosely around her bare shoulders.

'You look very beautiful, Gilda,' he said. 'And you were superb tonight as Isabella,' he added, sincerely.

'Stop. You'll make me cry.'

He offered her his arm and they went into the Café through the revolving doors to be met by a manic babble of talk and laughter and a blurry wall of smoke.

'We're with the Rutherford Davison party,' Lysander said to the maître d'.

'Upstairs, first floor,' the man said. 'The smaller of the two private rooms.'

They walked up the stairs. On the landing they could hear the excited talk and laughter coming from the rest of the company through the open door of the private room, left ajar as if in welcome, expecting them. There was a pop of a champagne bottle opening and the sound of people clapping. Gilda tugged on his elbow and held him back, pausing them both in the gloom of the corridor. She looked around and took his hand and drew him to her. Their faces were close.

'What's going on?' Lysander said.

She kissed him hard on his lips and pressed herself against him. He felt her tongue pushing, flickering, and he opened his mouth. Then she stepped back, checked the copious frilling of her blouse and readjusted her chiffon stole. Lysander took out his handkerchief and dabbed at his lips in case there were any traces of her lip-rouge. She looked at him squarely – a look that came from the real Gilda Butterfield.

'We'd better go in,' she said, 'or they'll wonder what's become of us.'

She linked arms with him again and they walked into the room together. The company rose to their feet and applauded.

Lysander allowed a waiter to pour him more champagne as he tried to listen to what Rutherford Davison was saying. He was very aware of Gilda across the room and the many glances she was throwing his way. He felt in something of a quandary. He decided to see simply where the evening would lead. A night for instincts, not rationality, he decided.

'No,' Rutherford was saying, 'I think we'll do two full weeks of *Measure* and then very quickly announce *Miss Julie*. I have a horrible feeling they'll close us down as soon as the reviews start appearing so we want to have as many performances as possible.'

'But it was done in Birmingham this year, you said. So there's a precedent.'

'A precedent for a very boring, prudish, safe-as-houses production. Wait till you see how we do it – what I've got planned.'

'It's your company.'

Lysander had grown to like Rutherford – perhaps 'like' was the wrong word – he had grown to trust his intuition and his intelligence. He was not naturally a warm or open person but he seemed to know what he was doing and didn't waver from his purpose. He had said that *Measure for Measure* and *Miss Julie* were a perfect double-bill as both plays were fundamentally about sex, even though they were written three centuries apart. Certainly the emphases and undercurrents that had been revealed this evening had set audible mutterings running through the audience a few times. He wondered what the reviews would be like – not that he'd be reading them. Rutherford said he only read reviews for adjectives and adverbs – he was hoping for 'shocking' and 'daring' – even 'disgraceful' would suit. We're here to stir things up, he had said to the company. Let's show them a Shakespeare as troubled and worldly as the sonnets. This Swan of Avon has paddled through a sewer.

Lysander moved off and wandered round the room. He ate a couple of canapés and chatted to some of the other actors and their friends, aware of Gilda circling the room in the other direction – anti- to his clockwise. It was after midnight. He went back to the bar and ordered a brandy and soda.

'Would you light my cigarette, please, kind sir?' Cockney accent. Lysander turned.

Gilda stood there, a cigarette in a jet holder, poised. A little tipsy, he thought. He took out his lighter and clicked the flame into life and offered it to the end of her cigarette. She inhaled, checked the fit of the cigarette in the holder and blew smoke from the side of her mouth. She lowered her voice to an intimate near whisper, moving her mouth close to his ear. He felt her warm breath on his neck. Goosebumps.

'Don't you think, Lysander dear, purely in the interests of dramatic authenticity, we should practise our "Miss Julie" fornication? Perhaps?'

'As long as it's purely in the interests of the drama. What could be wrong with that?'

'Nothing. Even Rutherford would approve.'

'Then I think it's an excellent idea. My place isn't far. I'm alone tonight. We can practise there undisturbed.' Greville was in Manchester, touring in *Nance Oldfield* with Virginia Farringford.

The tempter or the tempted, who sins most? he thought to himself, feeling very tempted. He looked her in the eye – she didn't flinch

'Why don't you go down,' Gilda said, smiling, 'find a cab and I'll be there in five minutes?'

She blew him a kiss, making a moue with her lips, and glided away from him. Lysander felt that breathless pressure in his chest and blood-heat around the neck and ears that signalled his excitement. It was probably a very, very bad idea and no doubt he would curse himself for the rest of the run but for the first time since Vienna and Hettie he felt like being with a woman – felt like being with Gilda Butterfield, to be precise.

He said his goodbyes and went downstairs. The maître d' sent a boy out to hail him a cab and he stood there waiting, humming a song to himself – 'My Melancholy Baby' – full of eager anticipation and pushing the thought to the back of his mind that this evening would also be the acid test of his Bensimon cure. There had never been a problem with Hettie but then there had never been anyone since Hettie . . . He saw a man he vaguely knew collecting his hat and coat from the cloakroom. Their eyes met and recognition was immediate. Alwyn Munro sauntered over towards him.

'Lysander Rief, the great escapologist, as I live and breathe.'

They shook hands. For some reason, Lysander noted, he was pleased to see Munro.

'Celebrating?' Munro said, indicating his dinner jacket and buttonhole.

'First night. *Measure for Measure.*'

'Congratulations. Funnily enough we were just talking about you today,' Munro said, looking at him shrewdly. 'Where're you living now? I've something to send you.'

Lysander gave him his address in Chandos Place.

'Still in Vienna?' Lysander asked.

'No, no. We've almost all got out now. Now the war seems inevitable.'

'War? I thought it was just general sabre-rattling. Austria and Serbia, you know.'

'And the Russians and the Germans and the French rattling their sabres too. It'll be us in a few days. You wait and see.'

Lysander felt something of a fool. 'I've been very caught up in rehearsals,' he said, feebly.

'Everything is moving incredibly fast,' Munro said. 'Even I can't keep up.'

'Cab's here, sir,' the boy said and Lysander searched his pocket for some pennies to tip him. He was aware, out of the corner of his eye, that Gilda was coming slowly down the stairs. He'd better jump into the cab quickly – it wouldn't do for them to be seen leaving together.

'Must dash,' he said to Munro, touching him apologetically on the elbow. 'Good luck with your war.'

Gilda's body was quite extraordinary, Lysander thought. Like nothing he'd seen or experienced before – not that he was any kind of expert on women's naked bodies, having only studied half a dozen or so, in his time. But Gilda seemed to him almost as if she were another species of woman, so incredibly pale was she with a rash of freckles over her chest and between her small, uptilted breasts, the nipples the palest rose, almost invisible. Freckles dusted her back and shoulders and here and there – on her ribs, on her upper arms, on her thighs – were small flat moles, pinheads, constellations of them, like flicked brown paint. Just the body's pigmentation gone a bit awry, he supposed, the freckles like tiny faded tattoos. He had wondered, when she began to undress, how he would react to her translucent pallor but he found her whiteness and her stippling of pale brown very alluring.

He had insisted on wearing a preservative so she had insisted on rolling it on. This set the tone of genial amusement for the rest of the night – 'Fits you like a one-fingered glove, sir,' she said in her Cockney accent – and they continued to talk banteringly throughout.

'I love your markings,' Lysander said as she eased her legs wide to receive him. 'You're like a banana that's been too long in the fruitbowl, you know – sort of sea-creature.'

'Thanks a lot. I don't.'

'I feel I should be able to read you like tea-leaves.'

'Ha-ha. I'm thinking of getting them removed.'

'Don't you dare. You're unique. Like a quail's egg.'

'What lovely compliments. Sea-creature, quail's egg. Quite the charmer, Mr Rief, oh yes . . .'

His orgasm duly came – to his intense pleasure – but they didn't try for a second time. It was late and they were both tired, they admitted, what with the first night and the party. Maybe in the morning.

And now she was sleeping in his bed as he dressed, one long white haunch revealed, the rumpled sheet just failing to cover the clean edge of her golden triangle of hair. Miss Julie . . . Well, well, well. He knotted a cravat at his throat and pulled on a jacket. He had no milk or tea, no coffee, sugar or bread and butter in the flat – just a pot of marmalade. He thought he would run out for some provisions. They could have breakfast in bed and see what led on from there. Rutherford didn't want them back at the theatre until the afternoon.

He stepped over the tangled pile of her clothes – skirt, blouse, shift, corset, camisole, knickers, hosiery, shoes – and let himself quietly out of the room. He trotted down the stairs in a fine mood. Maybe it wouldn't be such a disaster, after all, to start a brief affair with Gilda, he thought. Might make Blanche jealous if people gossiped and whispered about it.

He stepped out on to Chandos Place. He'd run up to Covent Garden, that would be quickest – buy her a bunch of flowers.

Jack Fyfe-Miller, in naval uniform, was crossing the street towards him.

'Rief! Good morning! I was just going to slip this through your letter-box. Munro wanted you to have it as soon as possible.' He handed him a stiff brown envelope.

'What's this?'

'A surprise . . . You're looking very well. Your play had an extremely bad review in the *Mail* this morning. "Shocking," it said. A grotesque insult to the Bard.'

'We were rather hoping for that.'

Fyfe-Miller seemed to be looking at him intently.

'Is everything all right?' Lysander asked.

'I was just thinking – I last saw you on the quayside at Trieste. Somehow I knew we'd meet again.'

'And now we have. You and Munro, both, in under twelve hours. Quite a coincidence, isn't it?'

'Isn't it?'

'You taking up a life on the ocean wave again?'

'No, no. All British fleets have been ordered back to war bases. I'm off down to Portsmouth.'

'War bases? Really? Does that mean –'

'Yes. It's looking rather serious.' He smiled and gave him a salute. 'See you again soon, no doubt,' he said, and headed back towards Trafalgar Square.

Lysander put the envelope in his pocket and hurried up to Covent Garden to do his shopping. He didn't want Gilda to wake before he came back.

6. Autobiographical Investigations

I COULDN'T BELIEVE WHAT was in the envelope that Fyfe-Miller handed to me. I opened it after Gilda had gone (around ten o'clock – second time, very satisfactory) to find a formal invoice from the War Office detailing the amount I owed to His Majesty's Government. The 10,000 crowns of forfeited bail came to £475. Herr Feuerstein's legal fees and expenses were totalled at an exorbitant £350 and food, drink and laundry were estimated at an equally preposterous £35. No rent charged for the summerhouse, I noted, gratefully. Grand total: £860. I laughed. 'Full remittance would be appreciated at your earliest convenience.' I am earning £8 10 shillings a week in the International Players' Company. My savings are virtually exhausted because of my lengthy stay in Vienna. I owe my mother over £100. The expenses of my daily life (rent, clothing, food, etcetera) are considerable. Roughly calculating, I reckon that if I could stay working fifty-two weeks of the year (and name me an actor who can or does) I might be able to pay off this debt in five years – in 1919. Compound interest, moreover, is being added at 5 per cent per annum. I tore the invoice up.

I'm deeply grateful to Munro and Fyfe-Miller – they were crucially instrumental in my escape from Vienna but, from one jaundiced angle – mine, I admit – the whole ploy looks like a clever money-making scheme for the Foreign Office. I could spend most of my life paying this off.

★ ★ ★

Rehearsal for *Miss Julie* this morning. I must say I'm having no problems learning the lines, unlike Gilda. I find the two idioms – Shakespeare and Strindberg – ideally distinct, the lines learned seeming to occupy different cubbyholes of my brain. Not so Gilda, who is still reading from the script, much to Rutherford's annoyance. His exasperation this morning almost made her cry. I consoled her and we stole a kiss – as much as we've managed to achieve since that first night (and morning) of the First Night party. If anything she seems to have cooled somewhat, as if regretting giving herself to me. She's perfectly friendly but she always seems busy after the show. Sick mother, friends in town – there's always a good excuse.

Rutherford wants us both to re-enter after the ballet with our clothes in disarray and with wisps of straw in our hair. He actually suggested I come on stage buttoning my flies. Gilda is advocating more decorum but I can see how adamant Rutherford is – there will be battles ahead. He is determined to have us banned within twenty-four hours.

Strange dream about Hettie. I was drawing her – she was naked – in the barn. There was a banging at the door and we both cowered down, expecting it to be Hoff. But instead my father walked in.

I overheard this conversation at Leicester Square Tube station as I waited for a train. It was between two women (working class, poor), one in her twenties, one younger, sixteen or so.

WOMAN: I saw her up Haymarket, then in Burlington Arcade.

GIRL: She told me she had a job hat-binding in Mayfair.

WOMAN: She's not hat-binding, all painted like that.

GIRL: She said she was sad. That's why she was drinking.

WOMAN: I'm sad. We're all sad – but we don't carry on like that.

GIRL: She could've been a lady's maid, she said. Five pound a year and all her grub. Now she makes five pound a week, she says.

WOMAN: She'll end up in a rookery. I bet my life. Selling herself for thruppence to a shoe-black.

GIRL: She's a good soul, Lizzie.

WOMAN: She's half mad and three parts drunk.

A subject for Mr Strindberg, perhaps, were he still with us. The river of sex flows as strongly in London as it does in Vienna.

August the fifth. War was declared on Germany last night at 11.00 p.m., Greville said when he came in. I went out this morning to find a paper but they had all been sold. This evening we had barely twenty people in the auditorium but we performed the play with as much zest as if it had been a full house. Rutherford very cast down – says we're bound to close at the end of the week. So, the world will be denied Lysander Rief and Gilda Butterfield in August Strindberg's *Miss Julie*. Gilda was upset. I said German troops had advanced into Belgium and attacked Liège, a fact that made our little theatrical problems and regrets seem insignificant. 'Not to me,' she said fiercely. For a second I thought she was going to slap my face.

7th August. I see in the paper that HMS *Amphion* has been sunk by a mine off Yarmouth. For some odd reason I wondered if the *Amphion* had been Fyfe-Miller's ship – and that thought suddenly brought the war alive to me in a way that days of shouting headlines hadn't. It was personalized in the shape of an imagined Fyfe-Miller drowned at sea off Yarmouth. It made me cold and fearful.

★ ★ ★

I was being measured for a new suit at my tailor's yesterday and I said to Jobling that I rather fancied a 'waist-seam' coat. 'Very American, sir,' he said, as if that was an end to the matter. I said I thought the waist-seam was flattering. 'You'll be wanting slanting pockets next,' Jobling said, with a chuckle. Not a bad idea, I retorted. 'Your father would turn in his grave, sir,' he said and went on to talk about Grosvenor cuffs and double collars. And that was that. My father's ghost is still determining what I can wear.

A letter from Hettie arrived in this afternoon's post. The stamp was Swiss.

My dear Lysander,
Isn't this the most terrible business? I cry all day at the awful folly of it all. Why would Britain declare war on us? What has Vienna done to London or Paris? Udo says this is a purely Balkan affair but other countries are just using it as an excuse. Is this true?

I'm very, very frightened and I wanted to send this letter to you with all urgency to tell you what I have decided to do in these awful circumstances. My position is difficult, as you will be well aware. I am a British subject living in a country with which Britain is in a state of war. Udo has offered to adopt Lothar, the better to protect him and to make his nationality secure. I may be interned but Lothar would be safe – so of course I agreed. Once the papers are drawn up he will take Udo's name and become 'Lothar Hoff'. It's for the best, my dear one – I can and must only think of Lothar, I mustn't think of myself nor of your feelings, though I can easily imagine them.

Lothar is very well, a happy healthy boy. I wish us all happier and more secure times.

With love from us both, Hettie.

★ ★ ★

Hamo tried to console me – he was very affectionate and warm. Think of the little chap, he said, it's for the best. I came down last night (Sunday) to stay in Winchelsea with Hamo and Femi. Hamo is thinking of adopting Femi himself, he said, as there has already been fighting in West Africa between the British and the German colonies. Togoland has been invaded by British and Empire forces.

Last night we stayed up late, talking. I said that I assumed all his plans for making a trip to Vienna must now be abandoned.

'No can do, dear boy,' he said. 'But as soon as this damn war ends, I'll be there. With a bit of luck it might not last that long.'

I sit in the spare bedroom, under the eaves of this little cottage, writing this up, wondering what to do as everything seems to conspire against me. There is a stiff gale blowing up tonight, ripping the first leaves off the trees. I suppose I should try to find another job as the theatres show no sign of closing but the thought of auditions makes me feel sick. From somewhere in the lane the lid of a dustbin has been lifted off and sent clattering and spinning down the alleyway, its tinny percussion discordant and unnerving beneath the sudden giant rushings of the wind off the sea.

7. Illegal and Enemy Aliens

A FINE RAIN HAD started falling as the lorry shuddered to a halt outside the camp. Lysander and the new detachment of guards jumped down from the rear.

'Fuck me,' Lance Corporal Merrilees said. 'Fucking rain.'

'Meant to clear up this afternoon,' Lysander said, taking his cap off and looking up at the mass of grey clouds above his head. Cold drops hit his upturned face.

'All right for you, Actor, ain't it? All fucking warm and cosy.'

Merrilees led his section off around the perimeter wire and Lysander kicked the mud of his boots before going up the steps into the clubhouse.

The Bishop's Bay Internment Camp had been the Bishop's Bay Golf Club before the war started and before it was requisitioned by the Home Office as a holding facility for 'illegal and enemy aliens'. A few miles west down the coast from Swansea, round the headland from the Mumbles, it had been transformed into a fenced prison camp of some forty wooden huts, each sleeping twenty people on bunk beds, constructed along the length of the eighteenth fairway. The clubhouse became the administrative centre and the members' lounge was reconfigured into the camp's canteen, capable of serving three sittings of two hundred prisoners a time, if required. The camp's population fluctuated between four hundred and six hundred internees, men, women and children. Other areas of the golf course had been wired off as football and hockey pitches but there was not much demand for these, Lysander had noticed. The prevailing mood amongst the internees was one of glum injustice; grumbling and petulant lethargy their principal pastimes.

Lysander knocked on the camp-commandant's door. 'Capt. J. St.J. Teesdale' it said on a temporary sign outside. Lysander stepped inside on Teesdale's cry of 'Enter!' and forced himself to smile and say, 'Good morning, sir.' Teesdale had arrived only two weeks before and was finding his new authority something of a trial and a burden. He was nineteen years old and having some trouble growing his first moustache.

'Morning, Rief,' he said. 'Nasty-looking one for the middle of May.'

'Ne'er cast a clout 'til May be out,' Lysander said.

'Say again?'

'An ancient adage, sir. Summer doesn't start until May is over.'

'Right.' He looked at some papers on his desk. 'I'm afraid it's Frau Schumacher, first up. Insisting on seeing a doctor again.'

Lysander collected his ledger and a bundle of files and empty forms and followed Teesdale from the Club Secretary's office to the '19th Hole' bar. Here a couple of middle-aged typists from Swansea coped with the camp's administration, with the help of a solitary telephone, seated at desks at one end of the long room, while at the other, in front of a wide bay window, was a long trestle table where the day's meetings and interviews took place. Through the window was a panorama of a choppy Bristol Channel with its massed continents of clouds – mouse-grey and menacing – beyond the links and the first tee. The walls were covered with framed photographs of golfers past – foursomes and monthly medal winners and amateur champions of the South Wales golfing fraternity holding silver trophies aloft. The bar had been cleared of its bottles and glasses, its shelves filled with rows of cardboard box files, one for each internee. Lysander found it one of the most depressing rooms he'd ever occupied.

Frau Schumacher sat at the trestle table, her back to the window, her arms folded across her chest belligerently, her chubby features set in a dark, implacable frown. She started to cough as she saw Lysander and Teesdale come in. Lysander took his seat opposite; Teesdale drew his chair out of range of Frau Schumacher's staccato volley of dry coughs. Lysander opened Frau Schumacher's file.

'*Guten Morgen, Frau Schumacher, wie geht es Ihnen heute?*'

It took an hour to persuade Frau Schumacher to go back to her hut with the promise, in writing, that she would see a doctor within twenty-four hours, or sooner, if one could be found in Swansea. Lysander didn't dislike her, even though he saw her almost every two days, as almost everyone who was held in Bishop's Bay Internment Camp had a long line of genuine grievances, not least their incarceration. There were merchant seamen – including half a dozen morose Turks – whose German colliers had been impounded in Swansea docks at the declaration of war; some twenty schoolchildren from Munich (awaiting repatriation) who had been visiting Wales on a late-summer cycling holiday; many proprietors of local businesses – butchers, tea-shop owners, an undertaker, music teachers – who had German names or ancestry. Frau Schumacher herself had been visiting her cousin in Llanelli, who was married to a Welshman named Jones. The household had been woken on the morning of August 5 and Frau Schumacher arrested – she had been due to return to Bremen on the sixth.

Bad luck, Lysander thought, rotten luck, stepping outside for some fresh air, already feeling tired after an hour's translating of the Schumacher gripes and grudges. He turned up the collar of his tunic and jammed his cap on his head, searching his pockets for his cigarettes. He found them, lit one and wandered down a fairway towards the line of low dunes and the narrow beach beyond. Somebody shouted, 'Hey, Actor!' from one of the watchtowers and he replied with a cheery thumbs-up.

It was still drizzling but he didn't really care, content to stand alone on the beach and watch the wind whip the foam from the waves of the restless, steely sea. Ilfracombe was just about opposite, he calculated, many miles away out of sight on the other side of the wide channel. He'd been on holiday there once, in 1895, when he was nine. He remembered trying to persuade his father to come shrimping with him and failing. 'No, darling boy, shrimping's not for me.' He finished his cigarette and threw it towards the waves and strolled back towards the clubhouse. A small queue of internees had formed and they looked at Lysander expressionlessly as he walked past.

'Busy day,' Teesdale said, as they watched the first man shuffle in. 'How come you speak German so well, Rief?'

'I lived in Vienna before the war,' Lysander said, thinking – what a simple expression, seven words, and what multitudes did they contain. He should have them carved on his tombstone.

'Better get started,' he said, sensing that Teesdale wanted to chat.

'What school did you go to, by the way?'

'I went to many schools, sir. Peripatetic childhood.'

Of all the stupid decisions he had made in his life, Lysander thought, perhaps the stupidest had occurred that morning he had left Hamo's cottage in Winchelsea and went to Rye to catch the train back to London. He had half an hour to wait and so had wandered aimlessly into town, his head full of bitter thoughts of Hettie and his unseen baby boy, Lothar, soon to be Udo Hoff's son, in name, at any rate. In the window of an empty greengrocer's shop he saw a large printed banner. 'E.S.L.I. "THE MARTLETTS". DO YOUR BIT FOR ENGLAND, LADS!' A plump sergeant lounged in the doorway and caught Lysander's eye.

'You're a fine-looking fellow. Strong and lively, I'll warrant. Just the sort we need.'

And so Lysander had heeded this unlikely siren, had entered the shop and enlisted. He became Private 10099 in the 2/5th (service) battalion of the East Sussex Light Infantry regiment. Two days later he reported to the E.S.L.I. depot in Eastbourne for six weeks of basic training. It was an act of penance more than one of duty, he told himself. At least he was doing something and all he craved was mindless routine and mindless discipline. He would go to France to fight the common foe and somewhere in the romantic back of his mind he had a vision of himself marching triumphantly into Vienna to claim a first joyful meeting with his little boy.

'Night, Mr Rief,' one of the typists said as she left. Lysander was standing in the entry hall of the clubhouse waiting for the lorry to take him back to the company billet in Swansea. The romantic vision had faded fast. Swansea was as close as he'd come to France and the front line. The 2/5th (service) battalion of the E.S.L.I. had been assigned to guard coastal defences in South Wales. After a few months of patrolling the quaysides of Swansea and Port Talbot, laying barbed-wire entanglements on beaches or sitting in freezing trenches dug beside gun batteries overlooking the Bristol Channel, relief of sorts had come when 'C' company of the battalion, his company, had been ordered to provide shifts of perimeter guards and prisoner escorts for the newly established Bishop's Bay Internment Camp. Lysander had volunteered to help with the translating of the internees' many problems, had become indispensable, and so began to spend his days on duty sitting at the long table in the bar of the golf club. It was now May 1915. Greville Varley was in Mesopotamia, a lieutenant in the Dorsetshire regiment. The *Lusitania* had been sunk. The landings at Gallipoli did not seem to have gone well. Italy had declared war on Austro-Hungary. This monstrous global conflict was in its tenth month, and he had never even –

'Got a couple of minutes, Rief?' Teesdale was leaning out of his doorway. Lysander went back into the office, where Teesdale offered him a seat and a cigarette. Lysander felt very old sitting opposite young Teesdale with his near-invisible moustache. Old and tired.

'Have you ever thought of putting yourself up for a commission?' Teesdale asked.

'I don't want to be an officer, sir. I'm happy as an ordinary soldier.'

'You'd have a more comfortable life. You'd have a servant. A proper bed. Eat food off a plate.'

'I'm perfectly content, sir.'

'It's all wrong, Rief. You're a fish out of water – an educated man who speaks a foreign language with enviable fluency.'

'Believe it or not I'm actually very happy,' he lied.

'What did you do before the war?'

'I was an actor.'

Teesdale sat up in his chair.

'Lysander Rief. Lysander Rief . . . Of course. Yes! D'you know, I think I actually saw you in a play.' Teesdale frowned and clicked his fingers, trying to remember. '1912. Horsham College Sixth Form Dramatic Society. We had a trip up to London . . . What did we see?'

Lysander ran through the plays he had been in during 1912.

'*Evangeline, It Was No One's Fault, Gather Ye Rosebuds* . . .'

'That's it – *Gather Ye Rosebuds*. Blanche Blondel. Gorgeous woman. Stunning creature.'

'Very pretty, yes.'

'Lysander Rief – how extraordinary. I say, you wouldn't sign me your autograph, would you?'

'A pleasure, sir.'

'Make it out to James.'

Lysander sat on his bed, took his boots off and began to unwind his puttees. 'C' company was billeted in the warehouse of a former sawmill and the place was redolent of sap, freshly planked wood and sawdust. It was dry and well sealed, containing four rows of wooden-frame chicken-wire beds with a big communal latrine dug outside. They were fed copiously and regularly and there were many pubs in the neighbourhood. Most of the men in 'C' company spent their off-duty hours as drunk as possible. There were always a dozen or so men on a charge. The warehouse yard had been swept hundreds of times, its walls and building benefitting from at least seven coats of whitewash. Idle drunken hands were put to hard work by the NCOs. Lysander kept out of trouble.

He lay down, hearing the chicken wire beneath his palliasse creak and ping under his weight, and closed his eyes. Two more days and he had a week's leave coming. London.

'Oi, Actor!'

He looked up. Lance Corporal Merrilees stood there. Frank Merrilees was very dark with a weak chin, in his early twenties, with a sharp, malicious mind.

'Coming to the pub?'

They liked drinking with Lysander, he knew, because he had more money and would stand extra rounds. He was happy to conform to their expectations, buying, not popularity, but peace. The other men left him alone; he didn't have to participate in the mindless bickering, persecution and mockery that occupied the others.

'Good idea,' he said, sitting up again and reaching for his boots.

The pub Merrilees liked was called The Anchor. Lysander wondered if it was anywhere near the port – he had no sense, even after weeks at the sawmill, what district of Swansea they lived in. He was shuttled to and from the billet to the camp in the back of a lorry, Swansea's modest, rain-bright streets visible through the flapping canvas opening at the rear – that was the geographical extent of his war.

The Anchor was only a few streets' walk away – no public transport required, which perhaps explained why it was so favoured. There was a saloon bar and a small snug, entry to which was denied the E.S.L.I soldiers. Along with Merrilees came four others of his cronies, all well known to Lysander, his drinking companions – Alfie 'Fingers' Doig, Nelson Waller, Mick Eltherington and Horace Lefroy. When they bought a round Lysander paid for the tumblers of spirits – whisky, brandy, rum, gin – that accompanied the pints of watery beer. That was why they tolerated him. The language as they chatted was always richly profane – fucking this and cunting that – and like the internees their conversation was a coarse litany of resentments and slights suffered, posited acts of brutal revenge or fantasies of sexual fulfilment.

'Taps shut, lads,' the barmaid called.

'Let me get the last round in,' Lysander suggested.

'You're an officer and a gentleman, Actor,' Merrilees said, his eyes unfocussed. The others loudly agreed.

Lysander took the tray of six empty pint glasses and five tumblers up to the bar and gave his order to the barmaid, looking at her again as she pulled the pints. He recognized her, but her hair had changed colour since he was last here – it was now dyed a strange carroty-auburn. He seemed to remember she used to be fair-haired. She was petite but her stays gave her a hitched-up shelf of bosom, half-revealed by the V-neck of her satin blouse. Petite like Hettie, he found himself thinking. Her nose was bent slightly askew and she had a cleft in her chin that echoed the visible crease between her breasts. She had thick dark eyebrows.

'And three gins and two whiskies,' he added as she finished the pints. 'I like your hair,' he said. 'It's changed.'

'Thank you,' she said. 'I'm a redhead, really, going back to nature.' She had a strong Welsh accent.

Lysander took his pint off the tray and signalled to Waller to come and pick it up. The pub was slowly emptying but he'd rather talk to this girl than swear and curse with the soldiers.

'You come in here a lot, you soldier-boys.'

'It's our favourite pub,' he said. 'We're billeted at the old sawmill, down the road.'

'But you're not like them lot, are you?' she said, looking at him shrewdly. 'I can hear it in your voice, like.'

'What's your name?' he asked.

'Cerridwyn,' she said. 'Old Welsh name – it means "fair poetess".'

'Cerridwyn,' he repeated. 'Lovely name for a poetess. I write a bit of poetry, myself.' He didn't know what made him tell her that.

'Oh, yes? Don't we all?' Heavy scepticism. 'Give us a line or two then.'

Lysander, almost without thinking, began:

> 'She's always the most beautiful girl,
> Bewitchingly lovely and true,
> Perhaps if I name her, you'll know her:
> She answers to "Love" – and she's You.'

Cerridwyn was impressed, he saw – moved, even. Perhaps no one had recited poetry to her before.

'You never writ that,' she said. 'You learned it.'

'I can't prove it. But it's all mine, I'm afraid.'

'Well – sounds lovely to me. What's that last line again?'

'"She answers to 'Love' – and she's You."'

Suddenly he felt the urge to possess her, to unfasten that satin blouse and unpin her lurid hair. In an instant, also, he saw that she had registered this change in the look he was giving her. How does this happen, he wondered? What atavistic signals do we inadvertently send out?

'It's my day off on Monday,' she said, meaningfully.

'I'm going to London on leave on Monday,' he said.

'Never been to London.'

'Why don't you come with me?'

'You could show me around, like.'

'I'd love to.' This was madness, Lysander knew. 'I'll meet you at Swansea station. Nine o'clock. At the ticket office.'

'Ach. You won't be there.'

'Yes, I will.'

'What's your name?' she asked making it sound like a challenge, a test of his sincerity.

'Lysander Rief.'

'Strange name.'

'No stranger than Cerridwyn.'

Merrilees lurched up and said they'd better be getting back.

'Nine o'clock, Monday morning,' Lysander said, over his shoulder, taking Merrilees's elbow and helping him out.

On the way back to the sawmill there was a lot of foul-mouthed lewd banter about Lysander and the barmaid. Lysander switched his mind off and let the speculation swirl around him. He was thinking, pleasurably: train to London, slap-up lunch in a chop-house or an oyster bar. A little hotel he knew in Paddington. Ticket home to Swansea on the milk train for Cerridwyn. An adventure for them both.

Sergeant Mott was standing at the sawmill gates, his long baton twirling in his hand. They were all dead drunk except Lysander. Merrilees saluted and fell over.

'Fuck off out of it, you scum,' Mott said. 'It's the actor I'm interested in.'

The others disappeared in a second.

'I'm not drunk, Sarge,' Lysander said. 'Honest. Just had a couple of pints.' He was frightened of Mott.

'I don't care,' he said. 'Someone wants to see you in the office.'

Captain Dayson, company commander, had his billet in the sawmill office building across the yard. Lysander buttoned his tunic, straightened his cap on his head and knocked on the door.

'Ah, Rief, there you are,' Dayson said, in his usual drawl. He was a lazy man, more than happy with the internment camp job, hoping it would see the war out. 'You've a visitor.'

Lysander stepped into the room.

Alwyn Munro rose to his feet. He was in uniform and Lysander saw that he had Lieutenant-Colonel's pips on his shoulders. Promoted. Lysander remembered to salute.

'Hard man to find, Rief,' Munro said, and they shook hands.

'What can I do for you?' Lysander asked, his mind frantic with other questions.

'I'll tell you on the way back to London,' he said. 'I've a motor car waiting outside. Do you want to get your kit together?'

8. Autobiographical Investigations

THE JOURNEY BACK PROVED strangely uneventful. I sat in the rear of a large military staff car beside Munro, with some sort of pennant fluttering on the front mudguard, as it sped towards London. As we left the outskirts of Swansea, Munro offered me a cigarette and I asked him what was going on.

'You know what?' he said, as if the idea had just come to him. 'Why don't you just enjoy your well-earned leave? Relax, indulge yourself. Next Monday morning report to this address. In civilian clothes.'

He took out a little notebook and wrote down a number and a street.

'And what will happen then?' I asked.

'You'll be given new orders,' he said, a little coldly, I thought, implying I would have no choice in the matter. 'You're a serving soldier, Rief, don't forget.'

And he wouldn't divulge anything else. We talked in desultory fashion about the course of the war – the big attack at Aubers Ridge – and my experiences in the E.S.L.I. and my work at the Bishop's Bay Camp.

'I think you can consider that chapter in your life closed,' was all he said.

So here I sit in a small hotel in Bayswater (Greville and I have sublet the Chandos Place flat) with a week of leave awaiting me. My mind is empty – I have no expectations and speculation would be fruitless. God knows what Munro has lined up for me but it must be more interesting than Frau Schumacher's constant health issues.

Funnily enough, my little nugget of regret about my Swansea life concerns Cerridwyn. I can see her – all dressed up for her trip to London – standing outside the ticket office at Swansea station waiting to meet me. And then the nine o'clock train will leave. Of course, she'll wait for the next one just in case, but with hope dwindling as time goes by, and, after an hour or so when I don't appear, she will go home, cursing the tribe of men and their endless, selfish duplicities.

9. The Claverleigh Hall War Fund

'IT'S A HUGE SUCCESS. I could never have predicted it. We've already made over £200 and it's not even lunchtime. We made £500 yesterday,' Lysander's mother said, speaking in tones of humbled incredulity, as they stood on the main drive looking at the rows of parked motor cars and charabancs and a hundred-yard queue of people waiting to pay their shilling entrance fee to the 'CLAVERLEIGH HALL GRAND FÊTE' – as the banner at the gateway to the park proclaimed.

'Bravo,' Lysander said. 'Lucky Belgian refugees.'

'Oh no,' she said. 'We're much bigger than that now. We've just sent another six ambulances to France.'

The Claverleigh Hall charity had started shortly after the outbreak of war as a blanket-drive, a local scheme to provide warm clothing, blankets and tents for Belgian refugees. Anna Faulkner had been galvanized by their initial success and the Claverleigh Hall War Fund, as it then became, provided her with a focus for her energies and her organizing capacity that Lysander had not seen demonstrated for years – not since she had effectively run the administrative side of the Halifax Rief Theatre Company, anyway. Suddenly she had a cause and the considerable sums of money she raised meant that her voice was listened to. She started going up to London once or twice a week for meetings with civil servants at the Home Office and then senior soldiers at the War Office once the Claverleigh Hall Field Ambulances came into being. Her new plan was to open a training school for nurses to deal specifically with the most common wounds and ailments suffered by the troops on the Western Front. Who needs a midwife when you're suffering from trench-foot? was one of her more memorable slogans and she began to be invited to sit on committees and add her name to petitions and other good causes. She was looking even younger, if that were possible, Lysander thought. That's what having a purpose in life gave you.

'How's Crickmay today?' he asked. He hadn't seen his stepfather since he'd arrived.

'No change. Very poorly. Wheezing, coughing. He can hardly get out of bed, poor darling.'

'I've got to go back to London after lunch,' he said.

'He won't be at lunch,' she said. 'I'll pass on your best wishes. He'll see you next time you're down.'

Then she hurried away to change the brimming cash-box at the entry-gate and Lysander set off on a wander round the park, past the stalls selling jams and cakes, the coconut shy, the beer tent, the dog show, the jokey races – egg-and-spoon, three-legged, sack – the livestock exhibits and the gymkhana – keeping an eye out for Hamo, who had arrived an hour earlier and had gone in search of some seed potatoes for his vegetable garden.

He found him at the cricket nets where, for sixpence, you were granted the chance to bowl at two of Sussex County Cricket Club's leading batsmen – Vallance Jupp and Joseph Vine.

Hamo was looking on in some amazement.

'Some of these kids are astonishing,' he said. 'That nipper there just bowled out Jupp twice in one over. Very embarrassing for him – the ball span two feet.'

'Any news of Femi?' Lysander asked. He knew that Femi had gone back to West Africa, homesick and unhappy in Winchelsea.

'He's arrived in Lagos. But I don't suspect I shall hear much more. He's got money and he speaks good English now – he'll be fine . . .' Hamo looked south, towards the Channel, towards Africa, symbolically. 'It was last winter that finished him – that and being stared at all the time. It's amazing how rude the English can be when they see something unfamiliar. As soon as this war's over I'll go out and join him. Set up a business together, bit of trading.' Hamo turned his burning pale blue eyes on Lysander. 'I do love him dearly, you know. Miss him every second of the day. A completely honest, sweet person. Straight and true.'

'You're very lucky,' Lysander said and changed the subject. 'I hear Crickmay's not well at all.'

'He can hardly breathe. Some sort of terrible congestion of the lungs. Walks ten paces – has to rest for five minutes. Just as well your mother's got this great charity thing going. Otherwise she'd just be sitting around waiting for him to die.'

They wandered through the fête. There was a big crowd gathered round an artillery piece – a howitzer – and a small, sturdy aeroplane with a blunt nose, all doped canvas and stretched wires. Lysander saw that the East Sussex Light Infantry had a recruiting tent erected and a sizeable queue of young men had formed in front of it. Swansea was waiting for them.

'I haven't had the most exciting war, I realize,' Lysander said as they passed the queue.

'I wouldn't complain,' Hamo said. 'It's a filthy awful business.'

'However, I've a feeling it's all going to change.'

He told Hamo about Munro's visit to Swansea and his new instructions.

'Sounds very rum to me,' Hamo said. 'Civilian clothes? Don't agree to do anything rash.'

'I don't think I've much choice,' Lysander said. 'It was made very clear that these were orders to be obeyed.'

'Any fool can "obey" an order,' Hamo said, darkly. 'The clever thing is to interpret it.'

'I'll remember that.'

Hamo stopped and touched his arm.

'If you need my help, my boy, don't hesitate. I've a few friends in the military, still. And remember I've been in a scrape or two, myself. I've killed dozens of men, you know. I'm not proud of it – not in the least. It's just a fact.'

'I don't think it'll come to that, but thanks all the same.'

They left the crowded park, shouts and cheers rising in the air as someone breasted the tape in the sack race, and walked up the drive to the Hall where luncheon was waiting for them.

10. The One-on-One Code

THE NUMBER AND THE street turned out to be a four-storey terraced house in Islington with a basement below a finialled iron railing, a stuccoed first floor with a bay window, and the top two of soot-blackened brick. Completely normal and undistinguished, Lysander thought, as he rang the bell. A uniformed naval rating let him in and showed him into the front room. It was virtually empty – there was a chair in the middle of the floor facing a gate-legged table with three other chairs set around it. Lysander took off his raincoat and hat and sat down to wait. He was wearing a three-piece suit of lightly checked grey flannel, a stiff-collared shirt and his regimental tie. The E.S.L.I would be proud of him.

Munro came in, also suited, and shook his hand. He was followed by an older man in a cutaway frock coat – very old-fashioned – who was introduced as Colonel Massinger. Massinger had a sallow, seamed face and a rasping voice as if he were recovering from laryngitis. His thinning dark hair was flattened against his skull with copious, gleaming oil and his teeth were noticeably brown as if stained from chewing tobacco. Then Fyfe-Miller appeared, jovial and energetic, and Lysander's mind began to work faster. Tea was offered and politely declined. In fact he realized he was suddenly feeling a little nauseated – this encounter seemed more like a tribunal – he doubted if he'd be able to drink a cup of tea without heaving.

After a few pleasantries ('Enjoy your leave?') he was handed a piece of paper by Massinger. Written on it were columns of numbers. He studied it – it made no sense.

3 14 11 2
11 21 2 3
24 15 7 10
3 2 2 7

And so on.

'What do you make of that?' Munro asked.

'Some sort of code?'

'Precisely. We have an agent working for us in Geneva who, over the last few months, has intercepted six letters containing sheets of paper like this.'

An 'agent', Lysander thought? 'Intercepted'? What is this, he wondered, some War Office intelligence briefing?

'This type of code is classic,' Munro said. 'It's called a one-on-one cipher because it can't be cracked – impossible – as its key is known only to the person sending it and the person receiving it.'

'Right.'

'What we need you to do, Rief,' Massinger butted in, as if he was in a hurry and had to go off to another appointment somewhere, 'is to go to Geneva, meet our agent there who will then lead you to the man who is receiving these messages.'

'May I ask who this man is?'

'A German consular official.'

Lysander felt a near-uncontrollable urge to begin laughing. He wondered if refusing a cup of tea had been a mistake. He would have liked something to sip.

'And what would I do then?'

'Persuade this consular official to give us the key that will allow us to decrypt this cipher.'

Lysander said nothing. He nodded his head a few times as if this were the most reasonable task in the world.

'How do you imagine I might "persuade" him?'

'Use your ingenuity,' Fyfe-Miller interrupted.

'A large bribe would probably be the most effective method,' Munro said.

'Why me?'

'Because you're completely unknown,' Colonel Massinger said. 'Geneva is like a cesspit of spies and informants, agents, couriers. Buzz, buzz, buzz. Any Englishman arriving in the city, whatever his cover story, is noted within minutes. Logged, investigated and, sooner or later, exposed.'

Lysander was fairly sure that his features remained impassive.

'I'm English,' he said, reasonably. 'So surely the same thing will inevitably happen to me.'

'No,' Massinger said, showing his stained teeth in a faint smile. 'Because you will have ceased to exist.'

'Actually, I wouldn't mind a cup of tea after all.'

Fyfe-Miller went to the door and tea was ordered, duly appeared, and they all helped themselves to a cup from the pot.

'Maybe I put that last statement a little over-dramatically,' Massinger said, stirring his tea endlessly. Clink-clink-clink. 'You would be reported "Missing in Action". And during that time you would journey to Geneva under a different identity. Clandestinely.'

'Your new identity will be that of a Swiss railway engineer,' Munro continued. 'Your arrival in Switzerland, your "return home", as it were, will cause no notice. You will contact our agent and receive further instructions.'

'Am I allowed to know what this is all about?'

Munro looked at Massinger. Massinger stopped stirring his tea.

'It's very complicated, Rief,' Massinger said. 'I don't know if you've been following the war news closely, but this year we have embarked on several significant "pushes" – big attacks – at Neuve Chapelle, Aubers Ridge and recently at Festubert. They haven't been complete disasters but let's say we failed signally in almost all of our objectives.' He put his cup down. 'It was as if we were expected, if you know what I mean. Trenches opposite were reinforced, new redoubts built, reserves were in place for counter-attacks, extra artillery behind the support lines. Almost uncanny . . . We suffered very, very heavy casualties.'

His voice trailed off and he looked, for a second, a worried and almost desperate man.

Munro took over.

'We think – to be blunt – that, somewhere in our high command, there is . . .' He paused, as if the concept were eluding him. 'No, there's no other way of putting it – there's a traitor. Passing on intelligence of our forthcoming attacks to the enemy.'

'And you think these coded messages are evidence,' Lysander said.

'Exactly.' Fyfe-Miller leaned forward. 'The beauty of this is that, as soon as we have these codes deciphered, we'll know who he is. We'll have him.'

Fyfe-Miller was staring at him with that odd hostile-friendly intensity he had. Lysander felt his mouth go dry and a muscle-tremor start up in his left calf. Fyfe-Miller smiled at him.

'We know what you can do, Rief – remember? We've seen your capabilities in Vienna, seen you in action. That's why we thought of you. You speak excellent German and you're an unknown face and an unknown quantity. You're intelligent, you think on your feet.'

'I don't suppose I can do anything but volunteer.'

Munro spread his hands apologetically.

'It's not an option available to you, I'm afraid,' he said. 'Not volunteering.'

Lysander exhaled. In a way, he thought, being backed into a corner was better than being asked to do your duty.

'However,' Massinger said, 'there is the matter of your outstanding debt to His Majesty's Government since the Vienna business. Somewhere above one thousand pounds, now, I believe.'

'We would see this mission as payment in full,' Munro said. 'A recognition of the somewhat unorthodox nature of the task we're asking you to perform.'

'Fair exchange is no robbery,' Fyfe-Miller said.

Lysander nodded as if he knew what he was talking about. He kept hearing Hamo's words: any fool can obey an order – it's how you interpret it that counts.

'Well, that's an incentive, at any rate,' he said, with admirable calm, he thought. 'I'm ready when you are.'

Everybody smiled. Another pot of tea was called for.

11. Autobiographical Investigations

FYFE-MILLER THEN TOOK ME upstairs to a bedroom. On the bed was a suitcase that he flipped open.

'It's your new uniform,' he said. 'You're now a lieutenant – on lieutenant's pay – attached to the General Staff. We'll take you up to the line – we think we've calculated the best place – and you can go out on a patrol one night –' He stopped and smiled. 'Don't look so worried, Rief. You're going to have masses of briefings before you go. You'll know the plan better than your family history. Why don't you try it on?'

Fyfe-Miller stepped out on to the landing while I undressed and put on my new uniform, complete with red, staff-officer flashes on the lapels. It fitted perfectly and I said as much to Fyfe-Miller.

'Your tailor, Jobling, was very helpful.' He looked at me and smiled one of his slightly manic grins. 'To the manor born, Rief. Very smart.'

Once again I wonder what machinations have been going on behind the scenes. How had they known about Jobling? Perhaps not so hard to find out, I suppose. I think of these three men and their new influence over me and my destiny: Munro, Fyfe-Miller and Massinger. A duo I know – a little – and an unknown. Who's in charge of this show? Massinger? If so, whom does he report to? Is Fyfe-Miller a subordinate to the other two? Questions build. My life seems to be running on a track I have nothing to do with – I'm a passenger on a train but I have no idea of the route it's taking or its final destination.

I've moved hotel, from Bayswater to South Kensington. I have a bedroom and a small sitting room with a fireplace – should I need a fire. The days are growing noticeably milder as summer begins to make its presence felt.

And for me, suddenly – as someone who's about to go there – the news from the front seems acutely relevant. I find I am following the bloody, drawn-out end of the battle of Festubert with unusual interest. I read the news of this great triumph for the British and Empire troops (Indians and Canadians also participated) but even to the uninitiated the cavils and the qualifications in the accounts of the battle stand out. 'Brave sacrifice', 'valiant struggle', 'in the face of unceasing enemy fire' – these tired phrases give the game away. Even some semi-covert criticism: 'insufficient numbers of our heavy guns'. Casualties acknowledged to be in the tens of thousands. Maybe more.

Mother has forwarded my mail. To my surprise there's a letter from Dr Bensimon which I here transcribe:

My dear Rief,
I trust all is well, in every sense of the word. I wanted to let you know that I and my family left Vienna as soon as it was clear that war was inevitable. I have set up practice here in London should you ever have the need to avail yourself of my professional services. In any event, I should be pleased to see you. My consulting rooms are at 117, Highgate Hill. Telephone: HD 7634.
    Sincere salutations, John Bensimon

PS. The results of our Vienna sessions in 1913 were published in this year's Spring number of *Das Bulletin für psychoanalytische Forschung*. You go by the pseudonym 'The Ringmaster'.

I feel warmed and touched by this communication. I always liked and respected Bensimon but I was never quite sure what he thought about me. 'In any event, I should be pleased to see you.' I take that as clear encouragement, almost friendly, an explicit invitation to make contact.

Every day, Monday to Friday, I go to the house in Islington to be briefed by Munro, Fyfe-Miller and, increasingly, Massinger. I study maps and, in the basement, familiarize myself with a detailed sand-model of a portion of our front line. I thought this must be a War Office intelligence operation but I'm beginning to suspect it originates in some other secret government department. One day, Massinger referred inadvertently to a person known as 'C' a couple of times. I overheard him say to Fyfe-Miller, with some fervour, even suppressed anger, 'I'm running Switzerland but "C" thinks it's a waste of time. He thinks we should be concentrating our efforts in Holland. We're counting on Rief to prove him wrong.' What the hell does that mean? How am I meant to respond to that challenge? When I had an opportunity I asked Fyfe-Miller who this 'C' was but he said simply, 'I don't know what you're talking about. Stuff and nonsense.'

My Swiss railway engineer identity takes rapid shape. It's based closely on an actual engineer – a man suffering from chronic duodenal ulcers in a Belgian sanatorium. We have quietly borrowed much of his identity as he lies in his ward, semi-conscious, suffering, hope fading. My name is Abelard Schwimmer. I'm unmarried, my parents are dead, I live in a small village outside Zürich. I saw my passport today – a very authentic-looking document filled with stamps and frankings from the borders I've crossed – France, Belgium, Holland and Italy. I'm to arrive in Geneva by ferry from the French side of the lake at Thonon and make my way to a medium-sized commercial hotel. The agent I'm to contact goes by the name of

'Bonfire'. The Ringmaster meets the Bonfire. Bensimon would chuckle at that if he knew.

This morning Munro took me to a military firing range east of Beckton and instructed me in the use of the Webley Mark VI Service Revolver. I fired off many dozens of rounds at the targets and was fairly accurate. It was a powerful weapon and my forearm began to ache.

'I hope I won't be called upon to use this thing,' I said.

'We try to foresee every eventuality, Rief,' was all he replied. 'Have you ever thrown a grenade?'

'No.'

'Let's have a try, shall we? The Mills bomb. Very straightforward as long as you can count from one to five.'

Back in Islington he gave me certain crucial pieces of information. The address of a safe house in Geneva. The secret telephone number of the military attaché at the consulate – 'Only to be used in the most dire emergency'. The number of an account at the Federal Bank of Geneva where I could draw the funds necessary for the bribe. And an elaborate double-password that would enable me to identify Agent Bonfire – and vice versa, of course.

'Take your time but commit them to memory, I suggest,' Munro added. 'Or if you can't rely on your memory have them tattooed on a very private part of your anatomy.'

I think I can certify that this is Munro's first attempt at a joke.

I dined with Blanche last night at Pinoli's in Soho, one of her favourite places. She was about to start a run of *The Reluctant Hero* at the Alhambra and told me that the theatres were as busy as peacetime. I felt envious, experiencing a sudden urge to rejoin my old life, to be back on stage, acting, pretending. Then it struck me that this was precisely what I was about to do. Even the title of her play was suddenly apt. It rather sobered me.

'I do like you in your uniform,' she said. 'But I thought you were a private.'

'I've been promoted,' I said. 'I'm off to France soon. In fact . . .'

She looked at me silently, her eyes full of sudden tears.

'Oh, god, no,' she said, then gathering herself added, 'I'm so sorry . . .' She looked at her hands – at her missing engagement ring, I supposed – then she said, abruptly, 'Why did it all go so wrong for us, Lysander?'

'It didn't go wrong. Life got in the way.'

'And now a war's got in the way.'

'We can still be –'

'Don't say it!' she said sharply. 'I detest that expression.'

So I said nothing and cut a large corner off my gammon steak. When I bit into it I felt my crown go.

'I can make you another,' the Hon. Hugh Faulkner said to me. 'But, in the present unfortunate circumstances, it'll take a while.'

'Just stick it back on if you can,' I said. 'I'm off to France any day now.'

'Five of my Varsity friends are dead already,' he said gloomily. 'I don't dare to think how many from school.'

There was no reply I could reasonably make so I stayed silent. He said nothing either, kicking at the chrome base of the chair with the toe of his shoe. I was sitting in Hugh's special reclining chair in his clinic in Harley Street.

'We all need a bit of luck,' I said, to bring him out of his lugubrious reverie and to stop the tap-tap-tapping of his toe.

'Well, you were damn lucky you didn't swallow it, there's a stroke of luck for you,' he said, holding the crown up to his powerful overhead light. 'Amazing to think they used to make these out of ivory.' He unbuttoned the cuffs of his coat and rolled them back. 'Open wide and let's have a look.'

I did so and Hugh brought the big light close and peered in my mouth. He was wearing a three-piece dark suit and a tie I recognized but couldn't place. He started to poke around in my mouth with his sharp metal probe.

'Actually, I have to say that your teeth look in fairly good condition –'

'*Aaargh!*'

'Sorry, sorry!'

He had touched a nerve or else pushed his pick deep into a soft smudge of decay.

I was pale and sweaty. Rigid.

'My god, Hugh . . . Jesus! That was agony.'

'Sorry. I just touched that big filling at the back – upper right second molar.'

'Is it rotten?'

'No, no. There's nothing wrong with the tooth,' Hugh said, chuckling. 'What you felt there was an electric shock. Two bits of metal touch and the saliva acts as an electrolyte. Ouch! It's like a piece of silver foil when you break off a chocolate bar. You know, sticking to the chocolate. You start to eat and – a little electric shock. Nothing wrong with your teeth.' He stepped back and ran his hands through his hair, smiling apologetically. 'Anyway, let's stop messing about and stick the thing back on.'

THE ELECTROLYTE

When I saw your face at the door
In a dancing dream of dervishes
It was like a probe touching a molar
(Electrolyte of love).
Then I saw you true.

The evening mist gathers in the valley
My hands I move
And fold it flat
Into a neat square bundle
And give it to you.

★ ★ ★

I'm sitting in my old bedroom at Claverleigh. I've just been in to see Crickmay to say goodbye. I'm off tomorrow – to France. The sound of Crickmay's breathing is like some ancient wheezing pump trying to empty a flooded mine. Air and water intermixed.

He managed to gasp goodbye and squeeze my hand.

Outside in the corridor Mother seemed upset but under control.

'How long will you be away?' she asked.

'I'm not sure. A month or two, maybe a bit longer.' Massinger had not been precise. All duration would be determined by operational necessities and by Agent Bonfire.

'He won't be here when you come back,' she said, flatly.

'What will you do?'

'I'll be fine. I could spend twenty-four hours a day on the charity, if need be. I don't know what I'd have done without it, actually. We've a staff of six now in the office at Lewes.'

'That's wonderful.' I kissed her cheek and she took my hands, stepping back to look me up and down.

'You look very handsome in your uniform,' she said. 'Your father would have been very proud.'

I feel hot tears in my eyes just thinking about this.

12. L'Officier Anglais

MUNRO AND LYSANDER lunched in Aire, a dozen miles behind the front line. Apart from the fact that everyone in the restaurant was male and in uniform, Lysander thought, the gustatory and vinous experience was pretty much the same had they been there in 1912. They ate an excellent *coq au vin*, drank a carafe of Beaujolais, were presented with a selection of a dozen cheeses and rounded the meal off with a *tarte tatin* and a Calvados.

'The condemned man ate a hearty meal,' Lysander said.

'I admire your gallows humour, Rief, but I have to say it isn't called for. You're going to experience no – or at least minimal – risk. We're going to a quiet sector – only three casualties in the last month.'

Lysander wasn't particularly reassured by Munro's palliative: a casualty was a casualty. There might only be one casualty this month – and it might be him. And yet everyone would be applauding the increasing quietness of the quiet sector all the same.

They were driven by staff car to the rear-area of the southernmost extremity of the British lines, where the British Expeditionary Force's First Army abutted the French Tenth Army. They passed through the town of Béthune and turned off a main road to drive down farm tracks until they reached the billet of the 2/10th battalion of the Loyal Manchester Fusiliers. A log-and-fascine road led them to a meadow fringed with apple orchards and filled with rows of bell tents. A sizeable field kitchen was in one corner and from a neighbouring pasture came the shouts and cheers and thumps of leather on leather that signalled a football match was taking place.

Lysander stepped out of the car feeling like a new boy on his first day at school – excited, apprehensive and faintly queasy. He and Munro were directed to the battalion H.Q. situated in a nearby requisitioned farmhouse, where Munro handed over the official papers to a taciturn and clearly disgruntled adjutant – who took his time reading what they contained, making little gasping sounds in his throat as he did so, as if they substituted for the expletives he'd have preferred to use.

'Signed by Haig himself,' he said, looking at Lysander with some hostility. 'You're to be "afforded every assistance" you require, Lieutenant Rief. You must be a very important man.'

'He is,' Munro interrupted. 'It's essential that everything is done to help the lieutenant in every possible way. Do you understand, Major?'

'I understand but I don't understand,' the major said, laconically, rising to his feet. 'Follow me, please.'

Well, that's it, Lysander thought. That's done it: Munro's pushed it too far, it's like being blackballed at a club – the major's face was a picture of superior disdain. He took them along a brick path to a cow-byre where several camp beds were set up. He pointed one out to Lysander.

'Dump your kit there. I'll have a servant assigned. Dinner at six in the mess tent.'

'Leave him to me,' Munro said as they watched the major stroll off. 'I'll have another quiet word with our fine fellow.' He smiled. 'Scare him to death.'

Sometimes, Lysander thought, it was an advantage having someone like Munro on your side. All the same, he sat in silence throughout the meal in the mess tent. No other officer made any effort to engage him in conversation, but more, he thought, out of extreme caution than contempt. God knows what Munro had said. So he tackled his meal, a beef stew with dumplings and a steam pudding with custard, feeling full and uncomfortable but sensing it would only incur further opprobrium if he pushed his plates away half-eaten.

As soon as was polite, he went back to his camp bed in the cow-byre and smoked a cigarette.

'Mr Rief, sir?'

He sat up. A sergeant stood in the doorway.

'I'm Sergeant Foley, sir.'

They saluted each other. Lysander still felt a little strange being addressed as 'sir'. Foley was a squat dense man in his late twenties, he guessed, with a pronounced snub nose. He had a thick Lancashire accent that somehow suited his muscled frame.

'There's a wiring party going up. We can follow them.'

They didn't waste any time getting rid of me, Lysander thought, as he quickly gathered up a few essential belongings – a bottle of whisky, cigarettes, torch, compass, map, his kitbag with the two grenades, a scarf and spare socks. He left his raincoat behind – it was a warm clear night – and followed Foley out, feeling sudden misgivings stiffen his limbs and making his breathing a task he had to concentrate on. Keep calm, keep calm, he said to himself, remember it's a quiet sector – all fighting is elsewhere – that's why you're here. You've been fully briefed and trained, you've studied maps, you've been given simple instructions – just follow them.

He and Foley stayed at the rear of the wiring party as they tramped up a mud road and turned off it into a communication trench, waist-deep at first but gradually deepening until breastworks on each side reduced the evening sky to a strip of orange-grey above his head.

By the time they reached the support lines Lysander was beginning to feel tired. Foley showed him to the officers' dugout and there Lysander introduced himself to a Captain Dodd, the company commander – an older man in his mid-thirties with a drooping, damp-looking, curtain moustache, and two very young lieutenants – called Wiley and Gorlice-Law – who could barely have been twenty, Lysander thought, like senior prefects at a boarding school. They knew who he was, word must have been sent ahead, and they were polite and welcoming enough, but he could see them eyeing the red staff-officer flashes on his lapels with suspicion, as if he were contagious in some way. He was assigned one of the bunk beds and took his whisky bottle out of his kitbag as a donation to the dugout. Everyone had a tot immediately and the atmosphere became less chilly and formal.

Lysander relayed his cover-story – that he was here from 'Corps' to reconnoitre the ground in front of the British and French trenches and to try and identify, if possible, the German troops opposite.

'They've burnt off most of the grass in front of their wire,' Dodd said, pessimistically. 'Difficult to get close.'

Lysander took out his trench map and asked him to identify the precise section of the trenches where the British line ended and the French began. Dodd pointed to a V-shaped salient that jutted out into no man's land.

'There,' he said. 'But they've filled it with wire. You can't get through.'

'Never the twain shall meet,' Wiley said, cheerily.

'Foley's the man to take you out,' Gorlice-Law said. 'Apparently he loves patrolling.' He was spreading anchovy paste on a hard biscuit and he bit into it with relish, like a boy in the school tuck-shop, munching away. 'Delicious,' he said, adding in apologetic explanation, 'I'm always starving – can't think why.'

Dodd sent Wiley out to walk the front-line trench and check on the sentries. Lysander topped up their mugs with more whisky.

'They say it's bad luck when staff come up to the line from Corps,' Dodd remarked, gloomily. He wasn't exactly a ray of sunshine, Lysander thought.

'Well, I'll be gone the day after tomorrow,' Lysander said. 'You won't remember me.'

'That's all very well, but you'll have still come up, don't you see? Right here, to us,' Dodd said, persistently. 'So what kind of attack are you planning?'

'Look, it's just a recce,' Lysander said, wanting to tell him he wasn't a real staff officer at all, therefore there would be no malign curse involved. 'Nothing may come of it.'

'You wouldn't tell us anyway, would you?' Gorlice-Law said, reaching for another biscuit. 'Deadly secret and all that. Hush-hush.'

'Have another drop of whisky,' Lysander said.

He slept fitfully in his thin hard bunk, kept awake by his ever-turning mind and by Dodd's long, deep snores. He heard the whistles of the dawn 'stand-to' and breakfasted on tea and jam sandwiches brought to him by Dodd's batman. Foley arrived and offered to show him the front-line trench, to 'have a gander' at no man's land.

The trenches at this, the furthest right-hand wing of the British Expeditionary Force, were narrow, deep and well-maintained,

Lysander saw. Dry too, with a duckboard floor and a solidly revetted fire-step and a thick crowning berm of sandbags. Apart from the sentries standing on the fire-step the other soldiers huddled in scrapes and small half-caves hollowed out from the facing wall – eating, shaving, cleaning their kit. Lysander was amused to see that most of them were wearing shorts and their knees were brown – as if they were on a strange sort of a summer holiday – as he followed Foley along the traverses to a net-covered loophole. He was handed a pair of binoculars.

'You're safe enough from snipers,' Foley said. 'You can see through the net but they can't see in.'

Lysander raised the binoculars and peered out over no man's land. Long grass and self-seeded corn badged with rusty clumps of docks. In the middle distance, directly in front of them, was a small ruin – more like a pile of smashed and tumbled stones – and some way off were three leafy, lopsided elms with some of their main branches blasted off. It looked tranquil and bucolic. A warm breeze was blowing, setting the rough meadow that was no man's land in easy flowing motion, the tall grasses and the docks bending before the gentle combing wind.

'How far are their trenches?' he asked.

'Couple of hundred yards away, here. You can't see them, the ground rises in the middle, ever so slightly.'

Lysander knew this, just as he knew that the shattered masonry was the remains of a family tomb. This was to be his reference point at night.

'What about that ruin?'

'They ran a sap out to it for a listening post but we bombed them out a month ago. They haven't come back.'

'I want to have a good look at it tonight, Sergeant. Are there drainage ditches?'

'A few. Quite choked and overgrown. See that clump of willows – to the right?'

Lysander swivelled his binoculars. 'Yes.'

'That's the start of the deepest one. Runs across our front then dog-legs into Frenchie's wire.'

Lysander made some token notes on his map – he had his bearings clearer now – and he had his little torch and his compass. He should be all right.

'What time do you want to go out?' Foley asked. Lysander noticed the pointed absence of 'sir', now.

'When it's darkest. Two o'clock, three o'clock.'

'It's a very short night. Summer solstice's just gone.'

'We won't be out long. I just have to confirm a few details. You'll be back in half an hour. We'll be back,' he added quickly.

'Mr Gorlice-Law is coming with us, it seems,' Foley said. 'He's not done any patrolling yet. Captain Dodd thought it might be a nice dry-run for him.'

'No,' Lysander said. 'Just you and me, Foley.'

'I'll look after the little chap, don't you worry, sir.' He smiled. 'Best to keep the captain happy.'

In the afternoon two RFC spotter aeroplanes flew over the trenches and for the first time Lysander heard gunfire from the German lines. Then there was a distant shouting from somewhere in no man's land. A solitary voice. The men began to laugh among themselves.

'What's he shouting? Who is it?' Lysander asked Foley.

'He crawls out most afternoons when it's quiet and abuses us. You could set your watch by him.'

Lysander stood up on the fire-step and listened. Faintly but distinctly from the long grass came the cry of, 'Hey, English cunts! Go home, fucking English cunts!'

Lysander thought he could hear laughter from the German lines also.

After the evening 'stand-to', he began to feel his nervousness increase again. Once more he silently ran through his instructions, mentally ticked off everything he had to do. Covertly, he checked the two Mills no. 5 bombs in his pack and verified, for the twentieth time, that the detonators were in. Gorlice-Law was full of enthusiasm for the patrol, blackening his face and cleaning and loading and reloading his revolver.

'We're just looking at the ground,' Lysander felt obliged to tell him. 'I don't think it's worth your while.'

'I only arrived two days ago,' Gorlice-Law said. 'I can't wait.'

'Well, the first sign of trouble and we run for it.'

Dodd made him clean his face and set up the 'dining table' – half a door placed on two ammunition boxes – saying, 'I don't intend to sit down to eat with a blackamoor, Lieutenant,' and they were served up a supper of tinned stew and biscuits followed by tinned plum-duff and the rest of Lysander's whisky. As it grew darker, Foley arrived with the rum ration. It was strong liquor, Lysander thought, with a powerful odour of molasses and thick like cough medicine. He could see that Gorlice-Law was feeling the effects on top of the whisky – he had a glazed expression on his face and it was visibly obvious when he tried to concentrate – eyebrows buckling in a frown, lips pursed, his speech slow and deliberate.

Towards half past two in the morning, Lysander steered him up the trench to join Foley at the jumping-off point. A short wooden ladder was set against the facing wall opposite the gap in the wire. Foley wore a rolled-up Balaclava on his head, a dirty leather jerkin with a webbing belt around it, shorts, sandshoes and extra socks tied round his knees. He had a revolver in his pocket and a whistle on a lanyard round his neck.

'Three blasts and we head for home,' he said, looking at Lysander, askance.

'What is it, Foley?'

'You're fully dressed, sir. Like you were going on parade.'

'I don't have any other kit with me.'

Foley had a tin of black candle grease and he painted some stripes on Lysander's face. He turned to look at Gorlice-Law, who had stripped himself of jacket, webbing and puttees and had thrust his revolver in his belt.

'You do everything I say, now, Mr Gorlice-Law. Understand?'

'Yes, Sergeant.'

Foley put up a pink Verey rocket to let the battalion front know that a patrol was going out and they clambered up the ladder and over the sandbags, advancing at a crouch through the wire and on into the engulfing darkness of no man's land.

It was a moonless night and yet Lysander was still astonished at how quickly he lost his bearings as they crawled through the long grass. After a minute or so he had no idea in which direction he was heading as he followed Foley – with Gorlice-Law bringing up the rear. A white flare went up from the German lines and for a few seconds the world turned brightly monochrome. He had a sudden temptation to stand up and see where he was. They all froze.

'Where's the ruin?' he hissed at Foley as the glaring light dimmed and fizzled out.

'About fifty yards, diagonal, right.'

'Take us towards it.'

Foley changed course and they crawled on. A few miles north some kind of 'stunt' was taking place – star shells and distant artillery, the throat-clearing expectoration of machine-gun fire. Lysander glanced back – nothing was happening in the 2/10th Loyal Manchester Fusiliers' trenches, however. Black sleeping countryside. Even the precautionary, exploratory rocket-flares seemed to have died down. Everybody keen on a good night's sleep.

'How far are we now?' Lysander tapped Foley's ankle.

'Over that little rise and you're there.'

It was time.

'Stay here,' he said to Foley. 'Don't leave him.'

'No, sir. Don't go alone. Let me come with you.'

'It's an order, Foley. Look after the lieutenant.'

Lysander crawled away from them up the slope – just the smallest undulation, but it gave him enough height to see the pale tumbled blocks of stone from the demolished tomb. He looked right for the ravaged elms and thought he saw their darker shape against the night sky. Ruins, elms, drainage ditch – at least he had physical reference points to aim for in the fluid blackness and the whispering grass all around him.

He slithered down the reverse side of the slope towards the ruined tomb. It must have been quite an edifice, he thought, as he drew nearer, some local dignitary who wanted his family name to last. Well, he hadn't reckoned for –

Lysander froze. He heard a squeaking noise. Rats? . . . But it was too sustained. Dripping water? Then it stopped. He slipped his torch out of his kitbag and the two Mills bombs. Pull the pin, count to three, throw and move away, smartly. These explosions would be the diversion, the cause of his 'death' that would allow him to make the French lines.

The squeaking noise started again. It was very faint. He was up against the first blocks of stone from the crumbled wall. He aimed his torch in the direction he thought the noise was coming from and switched it on for a second. In the brief flare of light he saw two white faces turn and look up from a trench-sap dug deep under the base of the tomb. He saw a man with a black moustache and a very fair young boy's face and the turning spindle of a roll of telephone wire being unwound – squeaking quietly.

He switched off the torch, pulled the pin out of the bomb and tossed it into the sap. Clatter. Oaths. He did the same with the second and, in a running crouch, scrambled off in what he thought was the direction of the elms.

After what seemed an eternity he heard the bombs detonate – seconds apart – the flat *blap! blap!* of the explosions in the confined space below the tomb. Somebody started to scream.

Lysander dropped to his knees. The screaming continued, ragged and high-pitched. Almost immediately random gunfire began to come from both lines of trenches – sentries shocked awake by the bombs going off. Rockets curved up into the night sky – green, red, white. Suddenly he was in a world of glaring primary colours. Then came the whistle and thud of rifle grenades. A machine gun began to traverse. Lysander was now crawling on his belly, not daring to look up. He reckoned he must be sixty or seventy yards south of the ruin. Where were the fucking elms? Then he heard, in a moment's silence, the anguished shout of, '*Foley? Foley! Where are you?*' A powerful white light from a rocket showed him he was past the elms. He had gone further than he thought – now he needed to change course to find the willows and the drainage ditch. He huddled in a ball and shone his torch on his compass. He was heading straight for the German lines – east – he should be going south. He turned through ninety degrees and set off again. There was a cacophony of shooting coming from behind him and now he could hear the bass crump of big mortars being fired. His little diversion had got somewhat out of hand – he hoped Foley and Gorlice-Law had made it back safely.

He fell into the drainage ditch and thoroughly soaked himself from the four inches of water in the bottom. He squatted and leaned back against the bank, allowing his breathing to calm. A few more rockets were going up but the shooting seemed to be dying down. False alarm. Nothing of consequence. Just a scare.

He took out his map again, hooded his torch with his cupped hand and tried to see where he was. If this ditch was the one Foley had described then he had only to follow it a hundred yards or so before it began to angle right and bring him up to the French wire. Then all he needed to look out for were the green rockets from the French lines that would tell him where to come in. Assuming all was going to Munro's plan . . . He looked at his watch. 3.30. It would begin to grow light in an hour or so – time to make a move.

He sloshed his way along the ditch and, sure enough, it did begin to bear right but then it seemed to come to an abrupt halt in the face of some ancient culvert. Lysander peered into the blackness. In theory, the front-line wire of the French Tenth Army should be facing him. But no sign of any of the green rockets that Munro had promised. Every ten minutes one would go up, he had said. Surely they would have heard the noise and the fuss caused by his bombs going off?

He thought then about the two bombs he had thrown into the sap below the tomb. He saw in his mind's eye the snapshot of the two faces looking up at him – the man with the moustache and the fair boy – utterly shocked, astonished. Two signallers laying a telephone wire, setting up the listening post again, he assumed. He also had to assume that his bombs had killed or seriously wounded them both. There had been that screaming. Anguished, feral. The panic in the dark as the Mills bombs clattered off the stone. Fingers groping, searching, swearing frantically, then – BOOM! . . .

He felt himself start to shiver and he hugged his knees to his chest – no point in thinking about that, of what had happened to those two signallers. How was he to know that they would be there? No, he decided, the best course of action was to stay put and wait until sunrise. Then he might know what to do next.

It was rather eerie and beautiful to watch the sky begin to lighten behind the German lines and as the dawn advanced he was able to make out the key features of the landscape – there were the three elms to his right and in front of him the dark cross-hatchings of the French wire. The culvert mouth was a crude stone arch and rushes were growing thickly around it, drawing on the extra moisture the drainage ditch provided. A breeze sprang up and he began to smell the smoke drifting across no man's land as braziers were lit in the trenches. He felt hungry – some crispy rashers of bacon and a hunk of bread dripping with hot fat would do nicely, thank you.

Very carefully he parted the rushes above the culvert and saw the dense wire of the French lines about twenty yards away. Very thick and professionally laid, he thought. He couldn't squirm through that. He saw a grey column of smoke rise from the trenches beyond, snatched at by the breeze, but no sign of a breastwork of sandbags or a sentry's loophole.

He cupped his hands around his mouth and shouted.

'*Allo! Allo! Je suis officier anglais!*'

After about five seconds he shouted '*Allo!*' again and was answered by the crack of a rifle shot.

'*Je suis un officier anglais! Je ne suis pas allemand!*'

More shots followed but none came near him. Then he heard a shout from the French lines.

'*Tu pense que nous sommes crétins, Monsieur Boche? Vas te faire enculer!*'

Lysander felt a moment of helplessness. Maybe talking in French was wrong.

'I'm English!' he shouted. 'English officer. I'm lost! *Perdu!*'

There were some more haphazard rifle shots. He looked over his shoulder at the German lines, hoping the Germans wouldn't be provoked into shooting back, or else he'd find himself in a cross-fire.

'*Parlez-vous anglais?*' he shouted again. 'I'm an English officer! I am lost!'

There was more swearing at him − colourful expressions he didn't know or vaguely understood to do with various sexual acts involving animals and close members of his family.

He sat back in some despair. What should he do? He thought he might have to wait until night fell and make his way back to the Manchesters. Then it would be just his filthy luck to be shot by a nervous sentry, jumpy after last night's exchange. But assuming he made it back how would he explain himself − the whole Geneva operation might be put at risk? Stupid fucking plan, he thought, anyway. Why did he have to disappear, 'missing in action'? Why not simply go to Geneva as Abelard Schwimmer?

'*Officier anglais?*' The shout came from the French lines. Then, 'Are you there?' in English.

'Yes, I'm here! In the ditch! *Le fossé!*'

'Move to your left. When you are seeing . . .' The voice stopped.

'Seeing what?'

'*Un poteau rouge!*'

'A red post! *Je comprends!*'

'That is the entry to come through the . . . Ah, *notre barbelé.*'

'I'm coming! Don't shoot! *Ne tirez pas!*'

'Coming ver' slow!'

Lysander hauled himself out of the drainage ditch and began to crawl to his left, staying as flat as he could, suddenly feeling very exposed. He squirmed and wriggled along for a minute or so until he saw a red post hammered in by a gap in the maze of wire. He changed course and crawled towards it – now he could see it marked a zigzag path through the labyrinth.

'*Je suis là!*' he shouted.

He crawled slowly into the wire entanglement and saw the sandbagged breastwork up ahead.

'I'm coming!' he shouted, suddenly completely terrified, convinced he was being lured close just to be picked off. He held his cap up, his khaki English army cap, and waved it above his head. Strong arms reached for him as he gained the sandbags and hauled him over, lowering him gently to the bottom of the trench.

He lay there on the ground for a moment, his breath coming back, looking up at giants standing over him – bearded filthy men in dirty blue uniforms, all of them smoking pipes, bizarrely. They stared back at him, curious.

'*C'est sûr,*' one of them said. '*Un véritable officier anglais.*'

He was sitting in a dugout in the support lines, an enamel mug of black unsweetened coffee in his hand, experiencing a level of exhaustion that he'd never encountered before. It was all he could do to raise the mug to his lips, like lifting a heavy boulder or lead cannonball. He put the mug down and closed his eyes. Sleep. Sleep for a week. He had handed the sealed letter from his pack to the officer whose dugout this was – where the bearded blue giants had led him. Cigarette, that's what he needed. He patted his pockets – then remembered he'd left them behind in Dodd's dugout. Dugout Dodd. Wiley and Gorlice-Law. Was that Gorlice-Law's shout for Foley? He just hoped that all –

'There he is. Our bad penny.'

He looked round, blinking. Fyfe-Miller stood there in the doorway. Smart in a jacket with leather cross-belting, jodhpurs and highly-polished riding boots. The French officer stood behind him.

'*Notre mauvais centime*,' Fyfe-Miller translated for the French officer, making no attempt at an accent. He helped Lysander to his feet, grinning his wild grin. Lysander felt like kissing him.

'Phase one completed,' Fyfe-Miller said. 'That was the easy bit.'

PART THREE

GENEVA, 1915

1. The Glockner Letters

THE FERRY FROM THONON nosed into the quayside at Geneva, then its engines were thrown into reverse to bring its stern round and the whole little ship shuddered. Lysander – Abelard Schwimmer – almost lost his footing and held on tight to the wooden balustrade on the top deck as thick grey ropes were slung out on to the dock and seamen hitched them to bollards, making the ferry hold fast. The gangway was lowered and Lysander picked up his tartan suitcase and found a place in the disorderly queue of people hurrying to disembark – then it was time for him to move down the wooden incline and take his first steps on Swiss soil. Geneva lay in front of him in the morning sunshine – big apartment buildings fronting the lake, solid and prosperous – set on its alluvial plain, only the bulk of the cathedral rising above the level of the terracotta and grey rooftops, reminding him vaguely of Vienna, for some reason. Low hills and then the dazzling snows of the mountains beyond in the distance. He took a deep breath of Swiss air, settled his Homburg on his head and Abelard Schwimmer wandered off to look for his hotel.

After they had made their way from the front line to the rear, Lysander and Fyfe-Miller had been driven to Amiens, where a room had been booked for him in the Hôtel Riche et du Sport. He went straight to bed and slept all day until he was shaken awake by Fyfe-Miller in the evening and was informed that he had a train to catch to Paris and then on to Lyons. He changed into Abelard Schwimmer's clothes – an ill-cut navy-blue serge suit (that already felt too hot), a soft-collared beige shirt with ready-knotted bow tie and clumpy brown shoes. If Fyfe-Miller had been planning to offend his dress sense, Lysander thought, then he had done a first rate job. He was given a red tartan cardboard suitcase – with some spare shirts and drawers in it – that also had, hidden behind the lining, a flat bundle of Swiss francs, enough to last him two weeks, Fyfe-Miller said, more than enough time to finish the job. The outfit was completed by a Lincoln-green raincoat and a Homburg hat.

'Every inch the "*homme moyen sensuel*",' Fyfe-Miller said. 'What a transformation.'

'You've an appalling French accent, Fyfe-Miller,' Lysander said. 'The *Hhhhom moyn senzyul* – shocking.' He repeated it in the Fyfe-Miller style and then as it should be correctly pronounced. 'The "h" is silent, in French.'

Fyfe-Miller smiled, breezily.

'*Quel hhhhorreur.* I can make myself understood,' he said, unashamedly. 'That's all I need.'

They shook hands on the platform at Amiens.

'Good luck,' Fyfe-Miller said. 'So far, so good. Don't delay in Paris – you've forty minutes between trains. Massinger will meet you in Lyons.'

'Where's Munro?'

'Good question . . . In London, I think.'

Lysander travelled to Paris, then to Lyons, overnight and first class – a railway engineer's perk, he assumed. He shared a compartment with two French colonels who looked at him with overt contempt and never addressed a word to him. He didn't care. He nodded off and dreamed of throwing his bombs into the sap – seeing the two startled faces of the signallers looking up at him before he switched his torch off. When he woke at dawn the colonels had gone.

Lyons station was crowded with French troops about to entrain for the front. Lysander was reminded that the front line was still not far away, extending down through Champagne and the

Ardennes, curving in a meandering doodle from the North Sea to the Swiss border, almost five hundred miles, of which the British Army was responsible for about fifty. Massinger was waiting for him at the station buffet – drinking beer, Lysander noticed. They took the stopper train all the way to Lake Geneva, to Thonon on the south bank, and checked into the Hôtel de Thonon et Terminus, conveniently placed for the station in the lower town.

Massinger's mood was fractious and ill at ease. When Lysander started to tell him about his fraught night in no man's land he seemed only to half-listen, as if his mind were on more pressing matters. 'Yes, yes. Indeed. Most alarming.' Lysander didn't bother explaining in more detail, told him nothing about the bombing, about watching the dawn rise over the German lines as he crouched amongst the rushes of the drainage ditch.

They dined together but the atmosphere was still unnatural and forced. They were like vague acquaintances who – as ill luck would have it – found themselves as the only two Englishmen in a small French town. They were polite, they feigned conviviality, but there was no denying that, given the choice, they would far rather have dined alone.

Massinger at least had more information and instructions to give him about his mission. Once Lysander had arrived in Geneva and had settled in his hotel he was to go to a certain café every day at 10.30 and again at 4.30 and stay for an hour. At some stage he would be approached by Agent Bonfire, they would exchange the double password and new instructions would be given, if Bonfire felt that the moment was opportune.

'Bonfire seems to be calling all the shots,' Lysander said, unthinkingly.

'Bonfire is probably our key asset, currently, in our entire espionage war,' Massinger said with real hostility, his raspy voice even harsher. 'Bonfire reads all the correspondence going in and out of the German consulate in Geneva – how valuable do you think that is? Eh?'

'Very valuable, I would imagine.'

'Just make sure you're at the Taverne des Anglais at those hours, morning and afternoon.'

'Taverne des Anglais? Don't you think that's a bit obvious?'

'It's a nondescript brasserie. What's its name got to do with anything?'

They ate on in silence. Lysander had ordered a fish, under a local name he didn't recognize, and found it overcooked, bland and watery. Massinger had a veal chop that, judging by the effort he was deploying to cut it up, must be extremely tough.

'There's one thing that's worrying me, Massinger.'

'What's that?'

'When I come to bribe this official . . . What if he won't accept my bribe?'

'He will. I guarantee.'

'Indulge me in the hypothesis.'

'Then cut his fingers off, one by one. He'll spill the beans.'

'Most amusing.'

Massinger put his knife and fork down and stared at him, almost with dislike, Lysander thought, it was disturbing.

'I'm deadly serious, Rief. You have to return from Geneva with the key to that cipher – don't bother coming back if you haven't got it.'

'Look –'

'Have you any idea what's at stake here?'

'Yes, of course. Traitor, high command, etcetera. I know.'

'Then do your duty as a British soldier.'

After dinner, Lysander went for a calming stroll along the quayside and smoked a cigarette, looking across the vast lake – Lac Léman as it was known from this side – towards the shadowy mountains in Switzerland that he could still just make out in the gloaming. There was a strange light in the evening sky, the palest blue shading into grey – the *Alpenglühen*, he knew it was called, a unique admixture of twilit purple valleys combining with golden sunlit mountain tops. He felt excitement build in him – he would be off to Geneva on the first steamer tomorrow, more than happy to say farewell to Massinger with his tetchiness and insecurity. As Fyfe-Miller would have eagerly reminded him, phase two was waiting for him across the still black waters. He was ready for it.

As he strolled back to the hotel he found his thoughts returning to the Manchesters and the brief experience of trench warfare he'd undergone. He thought of the equally brief but intense acquaintances he'd made – Foley, Dodd, Wiley and Gorlice-Law. They were as familiar to him here, as he walked the streets of Thonon, as old friends, his memories of them as vivid as members of his family. Would he ever see them again? Probably not. It was inevitable, he knew, this dislocation and sudden rupture in war – still, the fact that it was did not console. Back at the hotel a note from Massinger was handed to him with his room key, reminding him that his steamer left at 6.30, but that he, Massinger, would not be present for his embarkation as he was feeling unwell.

The Hôtel Touring de Genève was a disappointment. Almost two years of war in the rest of Europe had effectively killed off the trade of regular visitors – tourists, alpine climbers, invalids seeking medical cures – all the customers that this type of establishment relied on. The atmosphere in the lobby was defeatist – it seemed uncleaned, dusty, waste-paper baskets unemptied. Geraniums were dying unwatered in the planters on the small terrace and this was midsummer. The hotel had eighty rooms but only five were occupied. Even the surprise arrival of a new client for an unspecified length of stay raised no glad smile of welcome.

That first evening he was the only diner in the dining room. The waiter spoke to him in clumsy German (asking him some question about Zürich that Lysander deflected) but he saw the logic in Munro's choice for his identity – as a germanophone Swiss railway engineer in francophone Switzerland, and in a mid-level establishment like the Touring, Abelard Schwimmer was entirely unremarkable, run of the mill – almost invisible.

The Hôtel Touring was on the Left Bank, two blocks back from the lake front, in a street with a tram-line and some sizeable shops. On his first morning Lysander bought himself a pair of black shoes, some white shirts and a couple of silk ties and replaced his Homburg with a Panama. He changed clothes and felt more like himself – a well-dressed Englishman abroad – until he remembered that was exactly whom he wasn't meant to be. He put the brown shoes back on and the Homburg but he refused categorically to wear a ready-knotted bow tie.

He went to the Taverne des Anglais at 10.30 and drank two glasses of Munich lager as he waited the hour out. Nobody came, and nobody came at 4.30, either. That evening he went to a cinema and watched, unsmiling, a comedic film about a botched bank robbery. He reminded himself that when the day came for him to return to his old profession he really must follow up some more cinema-acting opportunities – it looked ridiculously easy.

During lunchtime the next day (the 10.30 rendezvous was also not kept) he bought himself a sandwich and hired a rowing boat at the Promenade du Lac and rowed a mile or so along the length of the right bank. It was a sunny day and the white and pink stucco façades of the apartment blocks, with their steep roofs, cupolas and domes, their curious splayed tin chimney pots, the quayside promenades and the Kursaal theatre with its cafés and restaurants spoke only of a world of prosperity and peace. As he rowed he could see beyond the city and the low bluffs that surrounded it to the almost searing-white peaks of Mont Blanc and its chain of mountains to the west. He came to a halt for a minute or two in front of the tall façade of the Grand Hôtel du Beau-Rivage – or the Beau-Espionage, as Massinger referred to it. 'Keep out of it at all costs. Very dubious women of all nationalities, swarming with agents and informers, everybody with some story that they'll try to sell you for a few francs – from the manager to the laundry maids.

It's a sink.' Children were screaming and splashing in the big swimming bath by the Jetée des Paquis and for a moment Lysander wondered if he should buy a swimming costume and join them – the sun was hot on his back and he felt like cooling off. He thought of rowing on to the Parc Mon Repos – he could see its woods and lawns beyond the jetée but he looked at his watch and realized that 4.30 was not far away. He'd better return to the Taverne des Anglais and make do with a cold beer.

It turned out to be another non-encounter, so he had an early meal in a grill-room and went to hear an organ concert at the cathedral with music by Joseph Stalder and Hans Huber, neither of whom he'd ever heard of. He changed rooms in the Touring, asking to be moved to the back where it was quieter as the trams woke him early. He noticed he was beginning to sleep badly – he kept dreaming about throwing his bombs into the sap below the tomb. Sometimes he saw the starkly lit faces of the fair boy and the moustachioed man – sometimes it was Foley and Gorlice-Law. It wasn't sleep that he was being denied, so much as that he didn't welcome the dreams that sleep brought – the idea of sleeping and therefore dreaming was off-putting and disturbing. He decided to start delaying going to bed; he would walk the streets until late, stopping in cafés for hot drinks or a brandy, until boredom drove him back to his room in the hotel. Perhaps he might sleep better then.

The next morning, after another fruitless hour in the Taverne (he was being welcomed as a regular by the staff), he went to a pharmacy to buy a sleeping draught. As he wrapped the powder of chloral hydrate, the chemist recommended that he visit a health resort – but one that was above 2,000 metres. Insomnia could only be cured at that altitude, he insisted. He suggested the Hôtel Jungfrau-Eggishorn high on the Rhône Glacier – very popular with the English before the war, the man said with a knowing smile. Lysander realized he was unthinkingly letting his disguise drop – he had to concentrate on being Abelard Schwimmer and speak French with a German accent.

As he left the pharmacy his eye was held by the sign of another, nearby shop: 'G.N.LOTHAR & CIE' – and seeing this name, his son's name, he felt the acid pang of this strange loss, the love-ache for someone he'd never seen, never known, who was present in his life only by virtue of the conferred familial role: this 'son' of his – this abstraction of a son – destined to be identified by inverted commas to distinguish his purely notional presence in his affections. Of course, new anger for Hettie returned – her callow ineptitude, her absolute thoughtlessness – but he quickly recognized this was fruitless, also. A waste.

However, sitting in the Taverne that afternoon, waiting for another hour to go by uninterrupted, and thinking frustratedly about this child that he had and did not have, he began to think how foolish and absurd this process was, like some child's game of espionage. He'd been for a row on the lake, watched a film in a cinema and attended a concert in the cathedral. Perhaps he might visit an art gallery, or enjoy a drink in the bar of the Beau-Rivage and fend off the 'dubious' women.

In fact there were two young, rather attractive women sitting in the window taking tea. One of them, he thought, kept glancing over at him as he sipped his beer. But no, that would be too risky, even for this child's game –

Somebody sat down on the next table blocking the view. A widow in black crêpe, he saw, with a flat straw hat and a small half-veil. Lysander signalled a waiter – one more beer and he was off.

The widow turned to look at him.

'Excuse me, are you Monsieur Dupetit?' she asked in French.

'Ah . . . No. My apologies.'

'Then I think you must know Monsieur Dupetit.'

'I know a Monsieur Lepetit.'

She came and sat at his table and folded up her veil. Lysander saw a woman in her thirties with a once handsome face now set in a cold mask of resignation. Hooded eyes and a curved Roman nose, two deep lines on either side of her thin-lipped mouth, like parentheses. He wondered if she ever smiled.

'How do you do?' she said and offered her black-lace-gloved hand. Lysander shook it. Her grip was firm.

'Have you come to take me to him?' he asked.

'Who?'

He lowered his voice. 'Bonfire.'

'I am Bonfire.'

'Right.'

'Massinger didn't tell you?'

'He didn't specify your gender.'

She looked around the room, seemingly exasperated, thereby offering Lysander a view of her profile. Her nose was small but perfectly curved, like a Roman emperor's on a coin, or like some photographs he'd seen of a captured Red Indian chief.

'I am Madame Duchesne,' she said. 'Your French is very good.'

'Thank you. May I offer you something to drink?'

'A small Dubonnet. We're quite safe to talk here.'

She wasted no time. She would meet him tomorrow at his hotel at 10.00 in the morning and would show him the apartment where the consular official lived. He was a bachelor, one Manfred Glockner. He usually left for the consulate around noon and returned home late in the evening. She had no idea what his official diplomatic role was, but to her eyes he seemed a 'smart, bourgeois, gentleman-type – something of an intellectual'. When he started to receive letters from England she became curious and decided to open them. She had missed the first three but she had opened the six subsequent ones. Nine letters in all over a period of eight months from October 1914 to June 1915.

'Opened?' Lysander asked. 'Do you work in the consulate yourself?'

'No,' she said. 'My brother is a senior postmaster here in Geneva, at the central sorting office. He brings me all the letters I ask for. I open them, I read them, I make copies if they're interesting, then

I close them again and they go to the recipient. Letters coming in, letters coming out.'

No wonder she was Massinger's prize agent, Lysander thought.

'How do you open them without people knowing?'

'It's my secret,' she said. Here a normal person might have allowed themselves a smile of satisfaction but Madame Duchesne just raised her chin a little defiantly. 'Let's say it's to do with the application of extremes of heat and coldness. Dry heat, dry cold. They just pop open after a few minutes. No steaming. When I've read them I stick them down again with glue. Impossible to tell they've been opened.'

She reached into her handbag and took out some sheets of paper.

'Here are the six Glockner letters.'

Lysander took them and shuffled through them – six pages dense with columns of numbers like the one he'd seen in London. He folded them up and slipped them in his pocket, suddenly feeling unusual trepidation – the child's game had become real.

'I'll show you where Glockner lives tomorrow. I would suggest your visit be either at the dead of night or perhaps a Sunday – when the building is quiet.'

Tomorrow's Friday, Lysander thought. My god . . .

'I'd better get to the bank,' he said.

'It's up to you,' she said, unconcernedly. 'I'm just going to show you where he lives. What you do next is your affair.' She finished her Dubonnet and stood up. She was tall, Lysander noticed, and he spotted that the material of her dress was of good quality and well cut. She pulled down her half-veil and screened her eyes.

'You're obviously in mourning . . .'

'My husband was an officer – a captain – in the French army. We used to live in Lyons. He was killed in the second week of the war in the retreat from Mulhouse. August 1914. He was shot and badly wounded, but when they captured him they left him to die. Untended. I'm originally from Geneva so I came home to be with my brother.'

'I'm very sorry. My sympathies,' Lysander said, a little lamely, wondering what genuine condolences one could offer to a stranger almost two years after such a bereavement.

Madame Duchesne flicked her wrist as if batting the formulaic remark away.

'This is why I'm happy to help you in this war. To help our allies. I'm sure that was your unasked question.'

It was, as it happened, but Lysander thought of something more.

'These letters to Glockner – was there a postmark?'

'Yes, all from London West – English stamps, of course, which alerted me. I have the names of all the staff at the German consulate, my brother brings me their letters first as a matter of routine. See you tomorrow, Herr Schwimmer.'

She gave him a little bow – the slightest inclination of her head – turned and left. She had a firm confident stride – a woman of real convictions. There was something attractive about her bitter severity, he had to admit, her unshakeable sadness and profound melancholy. He wondered what she would look like in bed, naked, helpless with laughter, tipsy on champagne . . . He called for another glass of Munich lager. He was developing quite a taste for this beer.

2. The Brasserie des Bastions

LYSANDER AND MADAME DUCHESNE sat in a café almost directly opposite the entry to Glockner's apartment building. It was noon. Madame Duchesne was inevitably in black, though this morning she had dispensed with the veil. Lysander wondered what her first name was but felt it impossible to ask such a question on so slight an acquaintance. Madame Duchesne did not invite familiarity. As he thought further, he realized that once Glockner had been identified it would probably be the end of their contact – she would have done her duty.

'He's later than usual today,' she said.

Lysander noticed she had a closed gold cameo on a chain around her neck – doubtless containing a photo of the late Capitaine Duchesne.

'Here he comes,' she said.

He saw a smartly dressed man of medium height come out of the building. He was wearing a lightweight fawn Ulsterette overcoat and a Fedora. Lysander noted the spats, also, and that he carried an attaché case and a cane. He couldn't see if he had a moustache or not as he had turned and headed off down the street.

'Is there a concierge?' he asked.

'I would imagine so.'

'Hmmm. I'd have to get past her, wouldn't I?'

'I'm afraid that's your problem, Herr Schwimmer.' She stood up. 'Good luck,' she said in English, then, '*Bon courage.*'

Lysander rose to his feet as well, thinking that he didn't want this to be their last encounter.

'May I offer you dinner tonight, Madame Duchesne? I've been in this city for four days now and I'm getting bored with my own company.'

She looked at him intently, her hard face expressionless. She had dark brown eyes, he saw. Fool, he thought – you're not on some kind of a holiday.

'Thank you,' she said. 'That would be most agreeable.'

He felt a boyish lightening of his heart at this response.

'Wonderful. Where would you like to go?'

'There's a place near the museum with a very nice terrace that's only open in the summer. The Brasserie des Bastions. Shall we meet there at 7.30?'

'Perfect. I'll find it – see you there.'

That afternoon Lysander went to the bank and drew out 25,000 francs in 500 franc notes – approximately £1,000. He had been offered 1,000 franc notes but he suspected that, when it came to being tempted by a bribe, the bigger the wad of money on display, the better. He wondered what made Massinger so sure that Glockner was that biddable – perhaps it was a lazy assumption he made about poorly recompensed embassy functionaries. But Glockner didn't seem down at heel or exhausted. He looked smart and spry – he wasn't wearing celluloid cuffs or a spongeable cardboard shirt-front – there was nothing, at first glance anyway, that suggested he was corruptible.

He made sure he was early at the Brasserie, which turned out to be a wood and cast-iron building with two wide verandas extending from an ornate conservatory set back from the edge of the Place Neuve amongst the greenery of the gardens around the museum, yet far enough away from the circling omnibuses and automobiles of the busy square not to be disturbed by their noise or the dust raised by their tyres. He had changed his loathsome brown shoes for his black ones and his Homburg for his Panama and was wearing one of his new silk four-in-hand ties with a white soft collared shirt. He felt more like debonair Lysander Rief, the actor, and not stolid Abelard Schwimmer, the railway engineer. He wondered if Madame Duchesne would notice the subtle –

'Herr Schwimmer? You're early.'

He turned to see Madame Duchesne walking along a white gravelled alley of young lime trees towards him. She was still in widow's weeds, of course, but she was carrying an open fringed parasol against the evening sun and her fine taffeta dress was trimmed with lace at throat and wrists, falling fashionably short to her ankles to reveal gunmetal, buttoned boots with a neat French heel. She may be grieving still two years on, Lysander thought, but she was grieving in style. As they greeted each other and shook hands Lysander found himself speculating about her corsetry – she was very slim – and what chemise and bloomers might be underneath that rustling, close-fitting dress. He checked his thoughts, vaguely ashamed and surprised that Madame Duchesne brought out such lechery in him. As they were led to their table for two he caught a hint of her perfume – musky and strong. She wore no lip rouge or powder but the perfume was a gesture of sorts – perhaps she had put it on for him. He imagined her checking her appearance in the mirror before she set off and reaching for her scent bottle – a dab at the neck and the inside of her wrists . . . Enough. Stop.

'Shall we order a bottle of champagne?' he suggested. 'I don't think Massinger would object.'

'I don't drink champagne,' she said. 'Some red wine with the meal will be perfect.'

They each decided on the *menu du jour*: a clear soup, *blanquette de veau*, cheese and an apple tart. The wine he chose was rough and on the sour side, however, and they left it half-finished. Lysander felt increasingly tense and nervous and their conversation never really advanced beyond the formal and unrevealing.

As they ordered their coffee, Madame Duchesne asked if he was a soldier.

'Yes,' Lysander said. 'I joined up soon after war was declared.' He didn't expand on what kind of soldier he had been, telling her only that his regiment was East Sussex Light Infantry, but simply conveying that information seemed to make a difference. He thought Madame Duchesne looked at him differently, somehow.

'And what did you do before you became a soldier?' she asked.

'I was an actor.'

For the first time her impassivity wobbled and she registered surprise for a second or two.

'A professional actor?'

'Yes. On the London stage. Following in my father's footsteps as best I can. He was a real giant of an actor – very famous.'

'How interesting,' she said, and he felt it wasn't just a token remark. He had indeed become more interesting to her as a result, he was sure, and he felt pleased, calling for the bill and thinking he would go off somewhere for a cigarette and a couple of brandies.

At least the evening had ended on a better note – better than he had expected. And what *had* you expected? he asked himself, aggressively. Idiot. Time had been filled, that was the main thing. Tomorrow he would reconnoitre Glockner's apartment building and its environs and make a decision about what the best time to make a move would be on Sunday.

As they waited for his change, Madame Duchesne placed a small cardboard box on the table.

'A present from Massinger,' she said.

He picked it up – it was heavy and it rattled.

'Perhaps you should wait to open it when you return to your hotel,' she said.

But he was too curious and placed the box on his knee below the level of the table and lifted the lid back. He saw the gleam on the short barrel of a small revolver. There were some loose bullets beside it that had caused the rattling.

'What do I need this for?' he asked.

'It may be useful. Who knows? Massinger gave one to me, as well.'

Lysander slipped the box in his jacket pocket and they walked out into the formal gardens – box hedges, the trained rows of limes and planes, raked gravelled paths. There was still some light in the sky and the air was cool.

'Thank you for my dinner,' she said. 'It was a pleasure to get to know you better.'

They shook hands and he felt the squeeze of her firm grip. Again he sensed this curious desire for her – this woman who apparently had no desire in her life.

'By the way, my real name is Lysander Rief.'

'You probably shouldn't have told me that.'

'May I know your first name? Forgive me, but I'm curious. I can't gain a full idea of a person without knowing their full name.'

'Florence.' French pronunciation, of course, so much nicer than the English – *Florawnce*.

'Florence Duchesne. Lovely name.'

'Goodnight, Herr Schwimmer. And I wish you good luck for Sunday.'

3. 25,000 Francs, First Instalment

ON SUNDAY MORNING AT 9.45 Lysander saw the concierge and her husband leave Glockner's building for church. He had gone in the day before with a fake parcel for a Monsieur Glondin and had been assured by the concierge that there was no one of that name in the building – a Monsieur Glockner on the top floor, but no Glondin. It was definitely Monsieur Glondin, he said – must be a mistake, sincere apologies. He had gained a good sense of the entry floor and the stairway up to the apartments and, judging by the heavy cross the concierge wore around her neck and the larger cross on the wall of her cubby-hole, he suspected that a pious absence might be likely as the church bells began to chime on Sunday morning.

After a minute or so he pushed open the small street door and strode to the stairway, unnoticed by the little boy who was sitting in the concierge's seat with his head down scribbling in a book. He climbed the stairs to Glockner's apartment on the fourth floor.

Standing outside the door, ready to ring the bell, he paused a moment, running through the plan of action he had made, mentally ticking off everything he had brought with him in the small grip he was carrying – every eventuality covered, he hoped. He took the revolver out of his pocket and rang the doorbell. After a while, he heard a voice close to the door.

'*Oui? Qui est là?*'

'I'm a plumber sent from downstairs. There's a leak coming from your apartment.'

Lysander heard the key turn in the lock and the door opened. Glockner stood there in a silk dressing gown.

'A leak? Are you –'

Before Glockner could register that he didn't look in the least like a plumber Lysander pointed his gun at his face.

'Step back inside, please.'

Glockner did so, clearly very alarmed, and Lysander locked the door again behind him. Gesturing with the gun, he steered Glockner into his sitting room. Glockner was recovering his composure. He put his hands in his dressing-gown pockets and turned to face Lysander.

'If you're an educated thief you might find some books that are worth stealing. Otherwise you're wasting your time.'

The room was lined with bookshelves, some glass-fronted, some open. A blond parquet floor with a self-coloured navy rug. A deep leather armchair set beneath a standard lamp with a pliable shade to direct the light for well-illuminated reading. A writing desk with a chair and on the one clear wall a line of framed etchings – cityscapes. An intellectual's room – Florence Duchesne's pen-portait was correct. Glockner spoke good French with a slight German accent. He was an even-featured, clean-shaven man in his mid-thirties with a slight cast in his right eye that made his gaze seem curiously misdirected, as if he wasn't paying full attention or his mind had wandered.

Lysander pulled the hard chair away from the writing desk and set it in the middle of the room.

'Sit down, please.'

'Are you German? *Wir können Deutsch sprechen, wenn Sie das bevorzugen.*'

Lysander stuck to French.

'Sit down, please. Put your hands behind your back.'

'Ah, English,' Glockner said knowingly, smiling widely and nodding as he sat down, revealing some extensive silver bridgework at the side of his teeth.

'You've just signed your own death warrant,' Glockner said, with too evident bravado. 'I don't have the key – I just pass the letters on to Berlin.'

'Yes, yes, yes. Why don't I believe you?'

Lysander took the wad of money off Glockner's knees and reached into his grip and drew out a bundle of washing line, unspooling it and then roping Glockner securely to his chair – his chest and arms, his thighs and shins – bound tight like a spider spinning the filaments of sticky web around a pinioned fly. Then he tipped the chair back until Glockner was lying on the floor.

Lysander stood over him, looking down. In reality, he had no sure idea what he was going to do next – though it was clear that the bribe option had failed. However, having Glockner helpless like this served to make the obvious point that there would be alternative attempts at 'persuasion' imminently.

'It doesn't need to be this hard, Herr Glockner,' he said, as persuasively as he could. 'You don't need to suffer. You shouldn't suffer.'

He wandered round the apartment and looked at the etchings on the wall – street scenes of Munich, he saw.

'*Münchner?*'

'You'll be dead by the end of today,' Glockner said. 'They'll find you and kill you – they know everything that's going on in this town. I've an appointment at 11.00. If I don't show up they'll come directly here.'

'Well, that gives us less than an hour for you to make up your mind and see sense, then.'

Lysander paced about the room. He drew the curtains and switched on the electric side-lights, wondering what to do. What was it Massinger had said? Cut off his fingers, one by one . . . Oh yes, very straightforward. Right, where do we start? Obviously, he wasn't going to be able to mutilate the man and he felt a useless anger rise in him, directed at Massinger and his brutal complacency. This was *exactly* the situation he'd posited to Massinger – what if

213

the bribe was not accepted? – and he had been mocked for his scepticism. In a mood of mounting frustration he walked out of the sitting room and went to find the kitchen.

The flat was small – apart from the sitting room there was a bedroom, a bathroom and a small clean kitchen with a stove and a soapstone sink and a meat-safe. He began to open drawers, looking for knives or shears – those kitchen shears for boning chickens – they'd snap a finger off at the joint. He would threaten Glockner – perhaps squeeze a fingertip between two blades of the scissors; perhaps that would work, terrorize him enough. The imagined snip would perhaps be more disturbing than anything real.

The first drawer revealed cleaning equipment – bleach, wire-wool pan scourers, scrubbing brushes of various sizes. In the second drawer he found the knives – no shears – but they were sharp enough. He looked under the sink and found a bucket – a bucket would be a good prop, as if there would be blood to mop up, that might add to the conviction of the whole charade, he thought. He stopped and stood up.

He was thinking. An idea had come to him – from nowhere. He opened the first drawer again and took out the two pan scourers and held them in each hand – a coarse steel mesh shaped into a squashy sphere. He began to think further – no need to shed a drop of blood at all . . . Then he ran them under the tap, shook the water from them, slipped them into his pockets and wandered back into the sitting room.

'Last chance, Herr Glockner. Give me the key to the code.'

'I tell you I don't have it. I pass the letters on to Berlin where they're decoded.'

'Last chance.'

'How do you say it in English? Fuck your mother, fuck your sister, fuck your wife, fuck your baby daughter.'

Lysander stooped over him.

'You've just made a terrible mistake. Terrible.'

He pinched Glockner's nose shut with two fingers and, as he

reflexively opened his mouth to breathe, Lysander rammed the first of the kitchen scourers deep into Glockner's mouth – and then the second.

Glockner gagged and heaved. The bulk of the two scourers had forced his jaws wide apart, belling his cheeks. He was trying to force them out with his tongue but they were too firmly wedged in behind his teeth.

Lysander strode over to the armchair and unplugged the standard lamp, ripping the flex from its base. The flex was a simple, wound double-cable, covered in a fine gold-coloured thread. With his fingernails he picked the ends clear, exposing the wires and bending them into a rough Y-shape.

He dragged Glockner and his chair closer. Then he plugged the flex back into its socket and held the now live 'Y' in front of Glockner's eyes.

Suddenly the thought came to him that he might not be capable of going through with this. But then he argued with himself – it would be just a touch, after all, no severing or cutting, nothing unseemly, no blades gouging flesh, just something that occurred as a matter of unfortunate consequence on a doubtless daily basis in dentists' surgeries the world over. Glockner was going to the dentist – no one liked it particularly, no one knew what pain would be associated with the visit. It was a risk.

'You look like a man who's taken good care of his teeth. Admirable. Unfortunately all that expensive dental work is now going to cause you intense, unspeakable pain. Every tooth in your head is in contact with the wire mesh of the scourer. Your copious saliva – look, it's already dripping from the side of your mouth – is a very efficient electrolyte. When I touch this live electric wire to the scourers in your mouth . . .' He paused. 'Well, let's say you're going to remember this agony for the rest of your life.'

He waved the wire right in front of Glockner's eyes.

'Just give me the key to your code, then I'll be out of here in five minutes. Nod your head if you agree.'

Glockner made some grating sound in his throat but it was clear from the way his forehead buckled and his crazy eyes glared that he was trying to swear at him again.

Without thinking further, Lysander touched the exposed live wires to the scumbled edge of the kitchen scourer visible between Glockner's bared teeth. Just for a second.

Glockner's inhuman throat-tearing roar of pain was hugely disturbing, made him flinch and wince in sympathy. It was the aural representation of his awful torment. He whipped the wires away and, in some disarray himself, watched Glockner writhe in his bonds, banging the back of his head against the parquet, his eyes weeping, overflowing. My god. Jesus.

Lysander fetched a pad-cushion from a chair and slipped it under Glockner's head. He didn't want anyone coming up from down below to see what the noise was. He held another cushion in his hand to muffle Glockner's eventual screams.

'Now, Herr Glockner, that was just a split second. Imagine if I apply the wires and count to ten.'

He didn't give him time to make any response – get this over with – he jammed the wire into the scourer and slammed the cushion over Glockner's face. One second, two – no, he couldn't go on. He pulled the wire away and kept the cushion in place. Glockner's screams died away to rhythmic sobbing sounds, almost like a kind of animal, panting. He felt himself trembling as he removed the cushion.

Glockner's face was slumped as if the muscles weren't working, had gone terminally slack. His eyes were half-closed, blinking frantically.

'Nod your head if you agree.'

He nodded.

Carefully, quickly, Lysander picked out the scouring pads from his gaping mouth with his fingers. Glockner dry-heaved, turned his head and spat on the parquet. Lysander rose to his feet and carefully placed the live wire on the desk top, securing it with a paperweight.

'See?' he said accusingly. 'If you'd just told me when I asked you first none of this would have happened – and you'd have been a rich man. Where's the key?'

'Central bookcase . . .' Glockner coughed and moaned.

Lysander walked over to the central bookcase and opened it. It was full of German literature – Goethe, Schiller, Lessing, Schopenhauer, Liliencron . . .

'Second shelf from the top. Fifth book along.'

Lysander ran his finger along the spines. The classic book-cipher. The PLWL code, as it was also known, so Munro had told him – page, line, word, letter. Unbreakable unless you had the book.

Fifth book along, there it was. He drew it out.

Andromeda und Perseus.

Andromeda und Perseus. Eine Oper in vier Akten von Gottlieb Toller.

He felt a coldness grip him as if his organs had been suddenly packed in ice. He felt his bowels turn and flex with a powerful urge to shit.

He stopped the questions screaming at him. Not now. Not now. Later.

He turned back to Glockner. He seemed to have passed out. His eyes were closed and his breathing was shallow. With an effortful heave, Lysander righted the chair and Glockner's head lolled, a length of thick saliva falling from his mouth and dangling there, swaying like a lucent pendulum.

Lysander untied him quickly and dragged and laid him back on the rug again. He unplugged the flex and wound it round his palm before stuffing it in his pocket. He found Glockner's attaché case on the floor by the desk and flipped it open, sliding the wad of 25,000 francs into an internal pocket. He closed it and replaced it on the floor. He gathered up the lengths of rope and the scouring pads and threw them in his grip along with the libretto of *Andromeda und Perseus.* He had a final check of the room and the kitchen. He smoothed some ripples in the rug and straightened the books on

217

the second shelf from the top so there was no noticeable gap. He closed the glass door. An unconscious man on his back, with not a mark on him. 25,000 francs inside his attaché case. A standard lamp without a flex. Solve that mystery.

He stood for a moment in the hall, running through everything for a final time. Thank you, the Hon. Hugh Faulkner, thank you. He felt himself beginning to shiver. It was terrifying how easy it had been – no blood, no effort, even – just some logical thought and the application of electric current. Stop. Concentrate. From his grip he took a light Macintosh and a flat cotton golfing cap and put them on. The man leaving the building wouldn't look like the man who entered. He pulled the door to behind him, leaving the key in the lock on the inside. He went down the stairs calmly, meeting no one and was glad to note that the concierge was still at church and the little boy had left his post. Lysander stepped out on to the street and strode away. He looked at his wristwatch – 10.40 – he hadn't even been in Herr Glockner's apartment for an hour.

4. The Fiend

HE SPENT THE AFTERNOON painstakingly decoding the Glockner letters – it kept his mind on the job. As the contents slowly revealed themselves – it was laborious work – it became obvious to him that what was being detailed in them was the movement of munitions and *matériel* from England to various sections of the front line.

On one page: 'Fifteen hundred tons HE six inch to St Omer to Béthune.'

On another: 'Twen five thou coffins to Allouagne.'

And more of the same: 'One mil five thou three oh three Aubers

Ridge sector'; 'Six field dressing stations villages behind Lens'; 'Ammo railheads St Venant Lapugnoy first army Strazeele cavalry'; 'Sixteen adv dressing stns Grenay Vermelles Cambrin Givenchy Beuvry'; 'Fourteen trch mortar La Bassee canal'.

The list grew in astonishing, minute detail as he worked steadily through the close columns of numbers in the six letters. Assuming that the dates were recorded when these letters were intercepted, he reasoned, then this data would give a very intriguing picture of the focus of an impending attack. Artillery shells, small arms ammunition, food and rations, signalling equipment, field hospitals, pack animals, transportation – it seemed almost too random but anyone who knew what was involved in a 'push' would be able to read the signs and narrow the sector down with remarkably precise accuracy.

It was also clear to him that this information must have been generated far behind the lines – the scale and the quantities applied to armies and brigades, not regiments and battalions. Battalions drew their supplies from dumps that these movement orders fed. And even further away – there was mention of ten batteries of 18-pounder guns being shipped from Folkestone to Havre and then entrained for Abbeville; a loco shop was being established at Borre; a new forage depot at Mautort; summary of shunts at the Traffic Office, Abbeville; total of remounts sent from England to the First Army in May. Some of these facts and figures would be known to senior supply officers in France but the range and the scope of the knowledge displayed in the Glockner letters spoke instead – as far as Lysander's ill-informed mind could determine – of a far greater overview of the whole movement and ordnance operation for the British Expeditionary Force on the Western Front. The writer of these coded letters wasn't in General Sir John French's high command in St Omer, he reckoned, but safely at home in the War Office or the Ministry of Munitions in London.

He put his pen down and, with some unease, picked up the source text – *Andromeda und Perseus*. He turned to the title page, noting with some relief that this edition wasn't the same as the one he had. It had been published in Dresden in 1912, a year before his trip to Vienna, and had the title and author as simple text on the cover with no illustration. He knew that the fatal Viennese performances of Toller's opera were not its premiere, so he assumed that must have taken place in Dresden, whence this copy originated . . .

Malign coincidence? No, impossible. As obscure texts went, *Andromeda und Perseus* was about as recherché as you could find. But the more questions he asked himself about the conceivable provenance of this, the key text in the PLWL cipher, the more confused and troubled he became. Why this particular, forgotten opera? And how come he was the one to discover it? The unwelcome thought came to him that the only other person he knew who possessed a copy of this libretto was one Lysander Rief. And what did that imply? . . .

He decided that it was pointless speculating further. He had to return home and, with Munro and Fyfe-Miller, thoroughly analyse all the ramifications of this discovery. There was nothing much he could do on a Sunday afternoon in Geneva – the Hôtel des Postes closed at midday so he'd have to wait until tomorrow to telegraph Massinger in Thonon. It opened at 7.00 in the morning – he would be there. He sealed his transcripts of the six letters in an envelope and wrote his name and the Claverleigh Hall address on the front. Best for the precise details to be kept out of everyone's hands for the moment, he reckoned, at least until he had decided what to reveal – or not – about the key to the cipher.

He went out for a stroll in the late afternoon, thinking that perhaps he would have liked to have talked over the matter – discreetly – with Florence Duchesne but he realized that he didn't know where she lived. Then again, perhaps it was best that she knew as little as possible.

He took a tram across the Arve River and disembarked at one of the entrances to the Bois de la Bâtre on the far bank from the city. He wandered into the thick woods and left the pathway to find a secluded spot – far from any picnickers or strolling families – and patiently burned Glockner's copy of *Andromeda und Perseus* a page at a time. He kicked the small pile of frail ashes here and there, stamping them into the turf as though they might somehow be reconstituted and read once more. He was beginning to think that the crucial course of action was to keep the cipher text a secret that only he knew – he wasn't quite sure why, but out of the jabber of questions and answers that raged in his mind an instinctive way forward seemed to be emerging. Make himself the only keeper of the secret – who knew, in that case, what others might inadvertently reveal? The minute he saw Massinger he would be asked for it – he was fully aware of that – still, he had plenty of time to concoct a plausible story.

He ate an omelette in a brasserie by the steamer jetties and checked the departure times of the express steamers that did a round trip of the lake in a day. He drank too much wine and found his previous clarity of purpose begin to cloud as he wandered the streets, as if suddenly cognizant of the fact that, this Sunday morning in Geneva, he had tortured a man and extracted information from him. What was happening to him? What kind of fiend was he becoming? But then he thought – was 'torture' the right word? He hadn't bludgeoned Glockner's head to a bloody pulp; he hadn't mangled his genitalia, or torn out his fingernails. He had given him every warning, also, every chance to speak . . . But he was disturbed, as well, he had to confess – disturbed by his own swift ingenuity and resourcefulness. Maybe it was the very absence of blood – and of mucus, piss and shit – that made his own . . . he searched for the word – device – that made his device so distancing and therefore easier to live with. What he had done seemed more like an experiment in a chemistry laboratory than the wilful inflicting of pain on a fellow human being . . . But then another voice told him not to be so stupid and sensitive: he was under orders, on a mission and the knowledge he had gained by his clever, robust and admittedly brutal actions had been vital for the war effort and, conceivably, could save countless lives. Of course it could. He had been told in no uncertain terms – do your duty as a soldier – and he had.

The night porter at the Hôtel Touring sleepily and grudgingly opened the main door for him after midnight. Lysander went up to his room, feeling tired but sure he would be denied even a minute of sound sleep, such were the relentless churnings of his thoughts. They were added to, considerably, when he saw that a note had been pushed under his door. It was unaddressed but he tore it open, knowing who had sent it.

'Your brother Manfred is gravely ill. Leave for home at once. People are very <u>concerned</u>.'

It could only be Florence Duchesne. Manfred – how did she know about Glockner? And what was the significance of that underscored 'concerned'? . . . He lay on his bed fully clothed, running through the possibilities for the following day – what he should try and do and what he absolutely had to do in his own best interests. He was still awake, waiting and thinking, as the sunrise began to lighten the curtains on his windows.

At seven o'clock in the morning Lysander was third in the queue at the main door of the central post office on the Rue du Mont Blanc. It was a huge grand ornate building – more like a museum or a ministry of state than a post office – and when it opened he strode to a *guichet* in the vast vaulted vestibule and immediately sent a long telegram to Massinger in Thonon.

HAVE THE KEY COMPONENT STOP AS SUSPECTED THERE IS A SERIOUS MALFUNCTION IN THE MAIN MACHINERY STOP STRONGLY ADVISE NO EXCURSIONS IN THE IMMEDIATE FUTURE STOP ARRIVING EVIAN LES BAINS AT 440 PM STOP

The last Glockner letter had been intercepted little more than two weeks previously. It was reasonable to suppose that its detail of ordnance supply would be relevant for any attack due towards the end of the summer. The autumn offensive, whatever and wherever it would be, was well advertised now as far as the enemy was concerned.

He then posted the six transcribed letters to himself at Claverleigh and left the post office at 7.20. The first express steamer making the round trip to Nyon, Ouchy, Montreux and Evian left at 9.15. Madame Duchesne's note the night before seemed to imply that steamer points and railway stations might be watched – he had almost two hours or so to make sure he wouldn't be apprehended.

5. Tom O'Bedlam

HE LOCKED THE DOOR of the below-deck gentlemen's lavatory and placed his sack and seatless chair to one side. He sat on the WC and, with a sigh of relief, removed his shoes and shook the pebbles out. Then he washed the Vaseline off his upper lip and raked his fingers through his chopped hair trying to flatten it into some vestige of normality. Looking at himself in the mirror he could see he had gone a bit too far with the scissors.

After he'd left the post office he had made his other essential purchases as soon as the relevant shops on the Rue du Mont Blanc opened. First, was a coarse linen laundry bag into which he'd stuffed his raincoat and his golfing cap – he had left his cardboard suitcase and his remaining clothes in his room at the hotel – Abelard Schwimmer had no further use of them. Then he bought a glass jar of Vaseline and a pair of hair-scissors from a pharmacy before going on to a furniture shop where, after some searching, he found a cheap pine straight-backed kitchen chair with a woven straw seat. Any chair would have done – it was the straw seat that was important. By 8.30 he had re-crossed the river to the Jardin

Anglais and in a quiet corner, sitting on a bench, he had unpicked and unravelled the lengths of straw-raffia that made up the seat of the chair. He then looped and wound the straw into a loose figure-of-eight that he hooked on to the chair-back. He had his prop – now he just needed his costume.

His idea – his inspiration – came from a performance of his father's that he remembered when Halifax Rief had played Poor Tom, Tom O'Bedlam, Edgar in disguise, the madman whom King Lear meets during the storm. To feign Tom's madness his father had put axle grease in his hair to make stiff spikes, had smeared more grease on his lip below his nose and had filled his shoes with sharp gravel. The transformation had been extraordinary – unable to walk normally or comfortably, his gait had become at once rolling and jerky, and the smear of grease looked like snot from an uncontrollably running nose. The uncombed, outlandish greasy hair added an extra aura of filth and neglect. A tattered jerkin had finished off the transmutation.

Lysander couldn't go that far but he aimed in that direction. He picked up some round pebbles from the gravelled pathways and put them in his brown shoes that he loosely and partially laced. Then he unbuttoned the cuffs on his serge jacket and rolled them up towards his elbow, letting the link-free cuffs of his shirt dangle. He buttoned the jacket badly, fitting buttons to the wrong buttonholes so it gaped askew at the neck. He put his tie in his pocket. Then he scissored off clumps of his hair at random, adding swipes of Vaseline – not forgetting a thick snot-smear under his nose. Then he picked up his seatless chair and his looped skein of straw, slung it over one shoulder and his linen sack over the other and shuffle-limped off to the jetty where the steamer was berthed. He looked, he assumed, like some poor itinerant gypsy simpleton, earning a few centimes by repairing furniture.

He could see no police or evident plainclothesmen eyeing the small queue of passengers waiting to board. He let most of them embark before he clambered painfully up the gangway, showed his ticket and went immediately to the seats at the stern, where he sat down, head bowed, muttering to himself. As expected, no one wanted to sit too close to him. No passports were required as the steamer was making a round trip and would be back in Geneva at the end of the day. Massinger would have received his telegram and would have plenty of time to make his way to Evian in time for the steamer's arrival. Once they were together he could brief him on the essential contents of the Glockner letters. He imagined it would not take long to discover who was the source of the information in the War Office – only a few people could be privy to that mass of detail.

He heard the engines begin to thrum and vibrate through the decking beneath his feet and he allowed himself a small thrill of exultation. He had done it – it had not been easy, it had been the opposite of easy – but he had done the job he had been sent to do. What more could anyone ask of him?

The steamer began to ease away from the pier and head out into the open waters of the lake. The morning was cloudy with a few patches of blue sky here and there but, when the sun broke through, the dazzle from the lake-surface made his eyes sting so he sought the shade of the awnings. Soon they were out in the main water, at full steam, making for Nyon, and Lysander felt he could safely go below and remove his disguise.

In the lavatory, as cleaned-up as he could make himself, he stamped and levered the kitchen chair into pieces and stuffed the lengths of splintered pine and the bundle of straw into the dark empty cupboard that ran beneath the two sinks. He put on his Macintosh and his flat golfing hat and checked himself in the mirror, adjusting his cuffs and re-buttoning his coat correctly. Fine – just another tourist enjoying a tour of the lake. He tossed his empty linen sack into the cupboard as well – everything he needed was in his pockets. He flushed the lavatory for form's sake and unlocked the door.

After Nyon, the steamer ceased hugging the shore and made

directly across the lake for Ouchy, the port of Lausanne. From Ouchy the course was directly to Vevey before turning back a half-circle west, with Montreux and its wooded hills in full view, the wide mouth of the Rhône backdropped by the jagged peaks of the Dents du Midi in the distance.

He wandered down to the stern and leaned on the railings, looking out at the wake and the retreating vistas of Geneva and its ring of low hills and distant mountains. There were a few of the famous Genevan *barques* out on the water, low free-boarded, two-masters with big-bellied, sharply pointed triangular sails that seemed to operate independently. From certain angles they looked like giant butterflies that had settled for a moment on the lake, their wings poised and still, to drink. He watched their slow progress and waited until there was no other passenger near him and quickly tossed his small revolver into the water. He turned, no one had noticed. He walked away from the stern.

On any other day he would have enjoyed the spectacular views but he patrolled the decks restlessly, instead, his mind busy and agitated. There was a small glassed-in salon set behind the tall thin smoke stack where light meals and refreshments were served, but he didn't feel hungry; he felt suddenly weary, in fact, exhausted from the stress of the last twenty-four hours. He climbed some steps to a small sun-deck in front of the bridge where he hired a canvas deckchair from a steward for two francs. He sat down and pulled the peak of his cap over his eyes. If he couldn't sleep at least he might doze – some rest, a little rest, was what he needed, all he asked for.

He was dreaming of Hettie who was running through a wide unkempt garden holding the hand of a little dark-haired boy. Were they fleeing something – or were they just playing? He woke – upset – trying to remember the little boy's features. Had he somehow encountered Lothar in his dream – his son whom he had never set eyes on, not even in a photograph? But Lothar was only a year old, now – this little boy was older, four or five. Couldn't possibly be –

'You slept for nearly two hours.'

His head jerked round.

Florence Duchesne sat in a deckchair three feet away from him, in her usual black, a baggy velvet hat held on her head with a chiffon scarf.

'My god,' he said. 'Scared me to death. I was dreaming.'

He sat up, regaining his bearings. The sun was lower in the sky, the hills on the left were less mountainous. France?

'Where are we?'

'We'll be in Evian-les-Bains in an hour.' She looked at him – could that be the hint of a smile?

'I almost missed you,' she said. 'I thought you hadn't boarded. I had seen you – the chair and the sack, the curious limping way you had walked. Then, just as the steamer was about to leave, I realized. That's him, surely? I remembered Massinger had warned me – be alert, he won't look like the man you're expecting to see.'

'How would Massinger know that?'

She shrugged. 'I've no idea. He just warned me that you might be disguised. Anyway, bravo – no one would have guessed it was you.'

'You can't be too careful . . .' He thought for a second. 'But what're you doing here, anyway?'

'Massinger wanted to be sure you got away safely. Asked me to chaperone you, discreetly. I've had a nice day out – I'll just take the steamer back to Geneva.'

'What did you mean in your note when you said people were "concerned"?'

'Manfred Glockner is dead.'

'*What?*'

'He died of a heart attack. He was found unconscious in his apartment and rushed to hospital – but it was too late.'

Lysander swallowed. Jesus Christ.

'Do you know any reason why he should have died?' she asked him, casually.

'He was fine when I left him,' Lysander improvised, thinking of the meshed wire of the scourer, the strong domestic electric current . . . 'I gave him the money, he counted it, then he told me the key to the cipher and I left.'

She was looking at him very closely.

'The money was found in his attaché case,' she said.

'How do you know?' he countered.

'I have a contact at the German consulate.'

'What kind of contact?'

'A man whose post I opened. It contained photographs that he would prefer remained private. Some of them I kept in case I had to remind him. So when I need to know something he's very happy to tell me.'

Lysander stood up and went to the railing. He had to be very, very careful, he knew – yet he wasn't exactly sure himself why he had lied to her so instantly. He looked across the placid lake waters at the French shore – the hills were rising again and he saw a small perfect château situated right at the water's edge.

Madame Duchesne came to join him at the railing. He turned and had a good view of her profile as she stared at the slowly approaching shoreline. The perfect curve of her small nose, like a beak. Her nostrils flared as she inhaled deeply and her breasts rose. There was something about her that stirred him, she –

'Beautiful château – it's called the Château de Blonay,' she said. 'I'd like to live somewhere like that.'

'Might be a bit lonely.'

'I wasn't imagining living there alone.'

She turned to him.

'What's the key to the cipher? Did Glockner give you the text?'

'No. It's in my head. He told me how it worked – it's very simple.'

'What is it?'

'It's the Bible – in German,' Lysander said. He had never expected her to ask him this, directly. 'But the trick is that the first number doesn't correspond. It's a double-cipher. You have to subtract a figure or add to get to the right page.'

'What's the trick? It seems very complicated.' She didn't seem convinced, frowning. 'What makes it correspond?'

'It's probably best if I don't tell you.'

'Massinger will want to know.'

'I'll tell him when I see him.'

'But you won't tell me.'

'The information in the letters is extremely important.'

'You don't trust me,' she said, her face still impassive. 'It's obvious.'

'I do. But there are times when the less you know, the better for you. Just in case.'

'I've got something to show you,' she said. 'Perhaps when you see it, you'll trust me.'

She led him down the stairway and through a door and down further stairs. The churning grind of the steamer's engines grew louder as they descended through a bulkhead to another deck.

'Where are we going?' he asked, having to raise his voice.

'I've hired a little cabin, right down below.'

They found themselves in a narrow corridor. Lysander had practically to shout to make himself heard.

'There are no cabins down here!'

'Round this corner, you'll see!'

They turned the corner. A door said, '*Défense d'Entrer*' and there was a steep metal stairway rising to the upper decks again. They seemed right above the engine room.

'Wait one second!' she shouted, rummaging in her handbag.

She drew out her small, short-barrelled revolver and pointed it at him.

'Hey! No!' he yelled, completely shocked and knowing instantly that she was going to shoot him. He raised the palm of his left hand reflexively in a futile gesture of protection.

The first shot, misaimed, hit him in the left thigh, making him

Lysander walked behind him, and taking a short noose of rope from his grip, slipped it over Glockner's wrists and pulled it tight. Now he could put his revolver down and with more short lengths of rope bound Glockner's arms together and secured them to the back of the chair. He stepped back, put the revolver in his pocket and placed his grip on the desk, reaching in and removing the wad of 500 franc notes. He placed it on Glockner's knees.

'25,000 francs, first instalment.'

'Listen, you English fool, you moron –'

'No. You listen. I just need the answer to one simple question. Then I'll leave you alone to enjoy your money. No one will know that it was you who told me.'

Glockner swore at him in German.

'And if you behave yourself,' Lysander continued, unperturbed, 'then in another month you'll receive another 25,000.'

Glockner seemed to have lost something of his self-control and assurance. He spat at Lysander and missed. A lock of his fair, thinning hair fell across his forehead, almost coquettishly. As he continued to swear vilely at him the silver in his teeth glinted.

Lysander slapped his face – not hard – just enough to shut him up. Glockner looked shocked, affronted.

'It's very simple,' Lysander said, switching to German. 'We know everything – the letters from London, the code. We have copies of all the letters. I just need to know the key.'

Glockner took this in. Lysander would have said that this news had genuinely disturbed him somewhat, as if the full seriousness of his plight were suddenly made clear to him.

'I don't have it,' he said, sullenly.

'It's a one-on-one cipher – of course you have it. As does the person who is sending you the letters. We're not interested in you – we're interested in him. Give us the key and the rest of this Sunday is yours.'

As if to underline his words, the big bells from the cathedral a few streets away began to chime, sonorous and heavy.

stagger from its impact, though he felt nothing. He saw the second, immediately after, blast through the back of his raised left hand and felt the blow, like a punch, as the bullet hit his left shoulder, canting him round sideways for the third shot to slam into his chest, high on the right-hand side.

He went down heavily onto the studded metal floor and heard the noise of her feet clatter up the stairway. He raised himself off the ground on his elbows and caught the shockingly distressing sight of his own vibrant, red blood beginning to spill and pool beneath him before he slumped back again and felt his body begin to go numb, hearing the jocular, breathy phoot-phoot! phoot-phoot! of the steamer's whistle announcing its imminent arrival at the sunny bustling quayside of Evian-les-Bains.

PART FOUR

LONDON, 1915

1. Autobiographical Investigations

SO, THE ONE AGREEABLE bonus of all this is that I finally found a way of gaining admittance to Oxford University. Here I am in Somerville College on the Woodstock Road experiencing a simulacrum of the varsity life. While I have a room off a staircase in a quadrangle in a women's college there are no women (apart from nurses and domestic staff) – the undergraduettes having been decanted to Oriel College for the duration of the war. We are all men here, wounded officers from France and other battlefields with our various incapacities – some shocking (the multiple amputees, the burned) and some invisible: the catatonic victims of mental dementia caused by the concussion of huge guns and images of unconscionable brutality and awfulness. Somerville is now part of the 3rd Southern General Hospital, as the Radcliffe Infirmary, a few yards further up the Woodstock Road, has been renamed.

Florence Duchesne shot me three times and caused seven wounds. Let's begin with the last. Her third and final squeeze of the trigger sent a bullet through my chest, high on the right-hand side, entering two inches below my collar-bone and exiting above my shoulder blade. Her second shot blasted through my left hand – that I'd raised in futile protection – and sped on, undeterred, through it and through the muscle of my left shoulder. I remember seeing – in a split second – the flower of blood bloom on the back of my hand as the bullet passed through. The scar has healed well but I have enduring stigmata – one in the middle of my palm, and one on the back of my hand – puckered brown and rose badges the size of a sixpence. Her first shot was a miss, of sorts – a misaim, certainly: she hadn't raised the gun sufficiently when she fired and I was hit in the top of my left thigh where the bullet smashed into a small bundle of change in my pocket, driving some of the coins deep into the rectus femoris muscle. The surgeon later told me he'd extracted four francs and sixty-seven centimes – he gave them to me in a small envelope.

The shot in the chest caused my lung to collapse and I think produced the copious flow of blood that I saw before I passed out. My good fortune – if such a concept is valid in a case of multiple gunshot wounds – is that six of my seven wounds were entry and exit. Only the pocketful of coins denied egress and – now I'm feeling much better – only my thigh still causes me discomfort and makes me walk with a limp and, for the moment, compels the use of a cane.

I'm also lucky in that, after Florence Duchesne shot me and disappeared, some mechanic or stoker emerged from the engine room and found me lying there in the widening pool of my own blood. I was swiftly taken to a small nursing home in Evian and then Massinger, who eventually tracked me down, had me transferred immediately across country by private motor ambulance to the British base hospital at Rouen.

I convalesced there for four weeks as my injured lung kept filling with blood and had to be aspirated regularly. My left hand was in a cast as some small bones had been broken by the bullet on its way through but the persistent problem was my left thigh. The bullet and the small change were extracted in Rouen but the wound seemed continually to re-infect itself and had to be drained and cleaned and re-dressed. I was obliged to walk around on crutches for most of my stay there.

I was shipped back to England and Oxford towards the end of August. My mother came to visit me almost as soon as I was installed in Somerville. She rushed into my room wearing black and for a fraught, shocked moment I thought Florence Duchesne had returned to finish me off. Crickmay Faulkner had died a month before – while I was in Geneva, in fact – and my mother was still in mourning.

She told me that the worst night of her life had occurred when she received the telegram that I was 'missing in action'. Crickmay was close to death and she thought her son had been snatched away, also. The next morning, however, she had a visit from a 'naval officer' – bearded, with a most curious, eerie smile, she said – who had come all the way to Claverleigh to tell her that I was believed to have been captured, unharmed. She found it very hard to understand how it came about that I was now in hospital in England, 'riddled with bullets'. I told her that the naval officer (it could only have been Fyfe-Miller) had been well intentioned but not in possession of all the facts.

Despite her new status of widow she seemed in excellent spirits, I had to admit, and she'd made the most of her mourning subfusc with a lot of black lace and ostrich feathers on display. Crickmay's passing was a blessing, she said, much as she loved him, sweet old man, and Hugh was preparing a perfectly adorable cottage on the estate to serve as a kind of dower house for her. The charity fund was growing incrementally and she was to be presented at court to Queen Mary. After we had walked through the quadrangle and I had seen her into her taxi, one of my fellow wounded – who knew about my former life – wondered if she were an actress. When I told him no, he asked, 'Is she your girl?' War affects people in all manner of different ways, I suppose – in my mother's case she was flourishing, visibly rejuvenated.

I received a telegram from Munro today, commiserating and congratulating simultaneously, and saying that we needed to assess the intelligence from the Glockner letters. And when that moment came he had a proposition to put to me. I reasoned that with Glockner dead the pressure to find the War Office source might have reduced somewhat – whoever our traitor was would have to seek out someone new to communicate with and that would obviously take some time.

★　★　★

Hamo has just left. He was very affected to see me – I was in bed, having just had my lung aspirated again – a concern that took the form of very specific questions about my wounds: what exactly were the physical sensations I felt at the moment of impact? Was the pain instant or did it arrive later? Did I find that the shock anaesthetized me in any way? Did the numbness endure for the length of time I lay out on the battlefield – and so on. I answered him as honestly as I could but kept deliberately vague about the reality of who had shot me and where. 'I had the strangest feelings when I was wounded, that's why I ask,' Hamo said. 'I've seen men screaming in agony from a broken finger, yet there I was, blood everywhere, and all I felt was a kind of fizzing, like pins and needles.' When he left he took my hand and squeezed it hard. 'Glad to have you back, dear boy. Dear brave lad.'

I walked up St Giles this evening all the way to the Martyrs' Memorial and back – as far as I've walked anywhere since Geneva. I stopped in a pub on the return journey and had half a pint of cider. People looked at me oddly – my pallor and my stick signalling the 'price' I've paid, I suppose. I keep forgetting I'm an officer in uniform (Munro has arranged for me to be resupplied). Lt. Lysander Rief, East Sussex Light Infantry, recovering from wounds. It was a warm late summer evening and St Giles with its ancient, soot-black college to one side and the Ashmolean Museum on the other looked timeless and alluring – motor cars and tradesmen's lorries excepting, of course – and I rather envied people who had had the chance to study and live here. Too late for me now, alas.

I was sitting on a bench in the front quad this afternoon, around the corner from the porter's lodge, reading a newspaper in the sun, when one of the nurses appeared. 'Ah, there you are, Mr Rief. You've just had a visitor in your room. We didn't know where

236

you were.' And stepping diffidently into view came Massinger, in civilian clothes.

He sat beside me on the bench, very tense and awkward, and seemingly unwilling to look me in the eye.

'I never thanked you properly,' I said, wanting to ease the mood. 'Whisking me off to Rouen. Private ambulance and all that. The best of care, really.'

'I owe you an apology, Rief,' he said, looking down at his hands in his lap, fingers laced as if he were at prayer. 'I can't tell you how glad I was to see you alive in Evian. How glad I am today.'

'Thank you,' I said. Then, curious, asked, 'Why so? Particularly.'

'Because I think – I have this horrible feeling that I ordered you killed. Terrible error, I admit. I got it all wrong.'

He explained. There had been a rapid exchange of telegrams between him and Madame Duchesne on the Monday morning after Glockner's death had been discovered and reported. Madame Duchesne had been very suspicious, convinced that it had something to do with me and my meeting with him. They had even spoken by telephone about an hour before my steamer was due to depart. Massinger had received my telegram by then and knew from the steamer timetable when I would be leaving. At this point he had ordered Madame Duchesne to accompany me on the boat, interrogate me and, if she had any reason to believe I was a traitor, she was to take the necessary steps to bring me to justice.

I listened to this in some shock.

'Then when I saw her at Evian she told me she'd shot you,' Massinger said. 'You can imagine how I felt.'

'Saw her?'

'We met on the quayside. She said you had lied about the cipher-key – the source text. She said you were hiding something. She was convinced that you had murdered Glockner. She was incredibly suspicious of you. I think your disguise was enough proof for her.'

'Yes, how did you know that I'd disguise myself?'

Massinger looked a little taken aback at this, confused.

'Munro told me. Or was it Fyfe-Miller? About what happened in Vienna when I saw them there.'

'You were in Vienna?'

'Off and on. Mainly last year before the war began – while I was setting up the network in Switzerland. Everybody spoke about your escape.'

'I see . . .' I was puzzled to learn about my notoriety. I put it to the back of my mind. 'Anyway, I didn't think I was obliged to tell Madame Duchesne everything. Why should I? I was about to meet you and report in full, for Christ's sake – on French soil. And all the while you'd ordered me killed.'

Massinger looked a bit sick and grimaced.

'Actually, I didn't in so many words. Madame Duchesne was going on and on, raising her suspicions about you. So I said –' He paused. 'My French is a bit rusty, you see. I don't know if I made myself totally clear to her. I tried to reassure her and I said words to the effect that we cannot assume he – you – is not a traitor. It's unlikely, but, in the event it was confirmed, you would be treated without compunction.'

'Pretty difficult to say that in French even if you were fluent,' I said.

'I was a bit out of my depth, you're right. I got confused with "*traître*" and "*traiter*", I think.' He looked at me sorrowfully. 'I have this ghastly feeling I said you were a "*traître sans pitié*" . . .'

'That's fairly unequivocal. A "merciless traitor".'

'Whereas I was trying to say –'

'I can see where the confusion arose.'

'I've lain awake for nights going through what I might actually have said to her. We were all rather thrown by Glockner's death. Panic stations, you know.'

'That's all very well. The woman shot me three times. Point-blank range. All because of your schoolboy French.'

'How did Glockner die?' he asked, clearly very keen to change the subject.

'A heart attack – so Madame Duchesne told me.'

'And he was fine when you left him.'

'Yes. Counting his money.'

Why do I keep on lying? Something tells me that the less I tell everyone, the better. We chatted on a bit more and he informed me that Munro was coming to see me about the decryption of the letters. Finally he stood and shook my hand.

'My sincere apologies, Rief.'

'There's not much I can say, in the circumstances. What happened to Madame Duchesne?'

'She took a train back to Geneva. She's back there now, working away as Agent Bonfire. Worth her weight in gold.'

'Does she know I survived?'

'I'm pretty sure she thinks you're dead, actually. I thought it best not to raise the matter – I didn't want to upset her unnecessarily, you see. She thought she was acting on my orders, after all. She couldn't really be blamed.'

'That's very considerate of you.'

My mother had brought my mail from Claverleigh, including the letter I'd sent myself from Geneva containing the Glockner decrypts. I made fresh copies of all six and gave them to Munro when he came to see me yesterday.

We sat in what used to be the Junior Common Room. There was a foursome playing bridge but otherwise it was quiet. A rainy, fresh day, the first inklings of autumn in the air.

I spread the transcripts on the table in front of us. Munro looked serious.

'What's disturbing me is that this man seems to know everything,' he said. 'Look – construction of two gun spurs on the Hazebrouk–Ypres railway line . . .' He pointed to another letter. 'Here – the number of ambulance trains in France, where the ammunition-only railheads are . . .'

'Something to do with the railway organization?'

'You'd think so – but look at all this stuff about forage.'

'Yes,' I said. 'I don't get that.'

'There's one horse for every three men in France,' Munro said. 'Hundreds of thousands – and they all have to be fed.'

'Ah. So, follow the forage trail and you'll find the troop build-up.'

Munro mused on. 'Yes, where is he? Ministry of Munitions? Directorate of Railway Transport? Quartermaster-General's Secretariat? General Headquarters? War Office? But look at this.' He picked up letter number five and quoted, '"Two thou refrig vans ordered from Canada." Refrigerated vans. How can he know that?'

'Yes. What are they for?'

'You want your meat fresh in the front line, don't you, soldier?' Munro smoothed his neat moustache with the palp of his forefinger, thinking hard. Then he turned and looked at me with his clear enquiring gaze.

'What do you want to do, Rief?'

'What do you mean?'

'Do you want to return to your battalion? They're still in Swansea – but you can't keep your rank. Or you can have an honourable discharge. You've more than done your duty – we recognize that and we're very grateful.'

It didn't take much thought. 'I'll take the honourable discharge, thank you,' I said, knowing I couldn't go back to the 2/5th E.S.L.I. 'I should be out of here in a couple of weeks,' I added.

Then he stiffened, as though he'd just thought of something.

'Or you could do one more job for us, here in London. What do you say?'

'I really think I've more than –'

'I'm phrasing it as a question, Rief, to allow you to reply in the affirmative.' He smiled, but it was not a warm smile. 'You'll stay a lieutenant, same pay.'

'Well, when you put it like that – yes. As long as I don't get shot again.'

240

Just at that moment some catering staff came in and began to lay the long table for lunch, with much clattering of plates and ringing of silverware.

'Do you fancy a spot of lunch?' I asked Munro.

'I don't fancy hospital gruel,' he said. 'Can we go to a pub?'

We walked through the college and out of the rear entrance on to Walton Street.

'I've never been in this college,' Munro said. 'Though I must have walked past it a hundred times.'

'What college were you in?' I asked him, not surprised to be not surprised that he'd been an Oxford undergraduate.

'Magdalen,' he said. 'Other side of town.'

'Then you joined the diplomatic service,' I said.

'That's right, after my spell in the army.' He glanced at me. 'What was your college?'

'I didn't go to university,' I said. 'I started acting straight after my schooldays.'

'Ah, the University of Life.'

The pub was called The Temeraire and its sign was a lurid misrepresentation of Turner's masterpiece. It was small and wood-panelled with low tables and three-legged stools and prints of old ships-of-the-line on the walls. Munro fetched two pints and ordered himself a veal-and-ham pie with mashed potatoes and pickled onions. I said I wasn't hungry.

'There's a big attack due,' Munro said, sprinkling his pie and mash with salt and pepper. 'In a matter of days, in fact. Supporting a French offensive. In the Loos sector.'

I spread my hands and looked at him with some incredulity. 'For heaven's sake,' I said. 'I suggested strongly that we stopped all operations. I urged that we stopped. They'll be waiting for us – look at the last two Glockner letters. You can pinpoint the area yourself.'

'If only it were that easy. The French are being very insistent.' He smiled thinly, unhappily, obviously feeling the same way I was. 'Let's hope for the best.'

'Oh, we can always do that. Costs nothing, hope.'

Munro made a rueful face, said nothing and tackled his pie. I lit a cigarette.

'There's one thing our correspondent missed,' Munro said. 'Curious. We're going to use poison gas at Loos – though we refer to it as the "accessory".'

'Well, they did it to us at Ypres,' I said, carefully. 'All's fair in love and war.' I was wondering why he was telling me this. Was it some kind of test?

'I wonder why he missed it,' Munro went on. 'Maybe it'll help us locate him.' He took a sip of his beer. 'Have a week's leave when you get out of hospital. Then I want you to meet someone in London. We need to plan our course of action.'

'So I'm still to remain a lieutenant.'

'Absolutely.' Then he said, trying to make it sound throwaway. 'You never told me what the cipher-text was.'

'I told Massinger and Madame Duchesne.'

'Oh yes, a German Bible. But that obviously wasn't the truth.'

It's always dangerous to forget how clever Munro is, I now realize as I write this account up. He seems at times so boringly proper – the career soldier, the career diplomat, a neat and tidy man secure in his status and ever so slightly smug and superior, though he tries not to let it show. But not at all – that's what he wants you to think. I don't really know why – maybe because he had tried to test me with news about the 'accessory' – but I decided to test him, in turn.

'I decided not to tell them,' I said. 'In fact it was the libretto of an obscure German opera.'

'Oh yes? Called?'

I watched his face very carefully.

'*Andromeda und Perseus.*'

He frowned. 'Don't think I know it,' he said with a vague smile.

'No reason why you should, I suppose. By Gottfried Toller. Premiered in Dresden in 1912.'

'Ah, modern. That explains it. I was thinking of Lully's *Persée*.'

I felt a chill creep through me and I decided there and then not to trust Munro any more, however much I was naturally inclined to like him. Anyone living in Vienna in 1913 would have known about Toller's *Andromeda*. Anyone – certainly someone who was familiar with Lully's *Persée*. Why was he lying? Why were we both smilingly lying to each other? We were on the same side.

'Did Glockner give you his libretto?'

'Yes. In return for the money.'

'What happened to it?'

'I lost it. In all the fuss over the shooting. It was left behind somewhere in the nursing home in Evian, I assume. I haven't seen it since.'

Munro put down his knife and fork and pushed his plate aside.

'Shame. Could you lay your hands on another copy – through your contacts in the theatrical world, perhaps?'

'I could try.'

'Let's have another pint, shall we? Celebrate your speedy recovery.'

2. A Turner Two-Seater with a Collapsible Hood

LYSANDER WAS DISCHARGED FROM Somerville College a week later and decided to take his leave in Sussex as Hamo's guest in the cottage at Winchelsea. Hamo had acquired a motor car – a Turner two-seater with a collapsible hood – and together they went for drives over the Downs and into Kent to Dungeness and Bexhill, to Sandgate and Beachy Head and one epic journey to Canterbury where they stayed the night before motoring home. Lysander punctuated the motor tours with walks of increasing length as he began to feel stronger and his injured left leg showed signs of bearing up. The scar on his thigh was still unsightly, buckled and lurid – a lot of muscle had been cut away in search of the evasive coins – and after his walks, steadily progressing through half a mile, a mile, two miles, he felt the leg stiff and sore. Still, it was the best thing for it, he reckoned, as he felt his love of walking renewing and, as soon as his confidence had grown sufficiently, he threw his stick away with relief.

On his final Saturday before his return to London they motored into Rye for lunch and then went for a walk on Camber Sands. They made their way down a path through the barbed wire and the crude anti-invasion defences on to the beach. The tide was out and the huge expanse of sand seemed like the vestige of an ancient, perfect desert washed up here on the south coast of England, unbelievably flat and smooth. A mile away someone was flying a kite but otherwise they had the great beach to themselves. Lysander stopped – he thought he could hear the rumble of distant explosions.

'That's not from France, is it?' he said, knowing the offensive was due any day now.

'No,' Hamo said. 'There's a range up the coast – training gunners. How's the leg?'

'Getting better. No pain, but I'm still aware of it, if you know what I mean.'

They strode on in silence. There was a coolness lurking in the afternoon air.

'Do you know who I mean by Bonham Johnson?' Hamo asked.

'The novelist?'

'Yes. He lives not far away. Over by Romney. Turns out he's a great admirer of my African book. He's asked me to his sixtieth birthday party.'

'You can drive over.'

'He wants me to bring a guest. In fact he rather specified you – the actor-nephew – I think he's seen you on stage. You up for it? Week tomorrow.'

Lysander thought – it was the last thing he wanted to do but he rather felt Hamo's invitation was more entreating than its casual delivery inferred.

'Assuming I have weekends off – yes. Might be interesting.'

Hamo was clearly very pleased. 'Literary types – ghastly. Feel I need moral support.'

'You're the one who's written a book, Hamo.'

'Ah – but you're the famous actor. They won't notice me.'

Lysander went up to London on Sunday evening. The Chandos Place flat was still sublet so he booked himself into a small lodging house in Pimlico – with the grandiose name of The White Palace Hotel – not far from the river. He could walk to Parliament Square in thirty minutes or less. Munro had asked him to meet at a place called Whitehall Court on the Monday morning but had been vague as to who else would be there and what would be discussed.

As it turned out, on the Monday morning, Lysander realized that Whitehall Court was one of those London buildings he'd seen from a distance countless times but had never bothered to identify properly. It looked like a vast nineteenth-century château – thousands of rooms with turrets and mansard roofs, containing a gentleman's club, a hotel and many floors of serviced apartments and offices. It was set back from the river behind its own gardens between Waterloo Bridge and the railway bridge that serviced Charing Cross station.

A uniformed porter checked his name on a clipboard and told him to go up to the top floor, turn left at the top of the stairs, through the door, down a passageway and someone would be waiting. Lysander saw him pick up the telephone on his desk as he made for the foot of the stairway.

That someone turned out to be Munro – in civilian clothes – who showed him into a simple and severely furnished office with a view of the Thames through the windows. Massinger was there waiting, uniformed, and greeted Lysander stiffly, as if he were still guilty for his near-fatal error with his imperfect French. There was a large, leather-topped, walnut desk set back against a wall facing the windows with the chair behind it empty. Someone of greater eminence had yet to arrive.

The three men sat on the available chairs. Munro offered refreshments – tea – and was politely declined. Massinger asked Lysander how he was feeling and Lysander said he felt pretty much back to normal, thank you. A train clattered over the railway bridge from Charing Cross and, as its whistle sounded, as if on cue, the door opened and a grey-haired elderly man in a naval captain's uniform limped in. The clumping sound as he set his right leg down made Lysander think the limb was artificial. He had a mild, smiley manner – everything about him, apart from the wooden leg, seemed unexceptional. He was not introduced.

'This is Lieutenant Rief, sir,' Munro said. 'Who did the splendid job in Geneva.'

'Exceptional,' Massinger chipped in, proprietorially. Switzerland was his territory, Lysander remembered.

'Congratulations,' the captain said. 'So you're the man who found our rotten apple.'

'We haven't quite found him yet, sir,' Lysander said. 'But we think we may know what barrel he's in.'

The captain chuckled, enjoying the metaphor's resonances.

'So, what do we do next?' he said, looking at Massinger and Munro.

'Not really my area,' Massinger said, defensively, and once again Lysander wondered about the hierarchy in the room. The captain was the big chief, clearly, but who was the senior between Massinger and Munro? What autonomy did either of them have, if any?

'I think we have to get Rief into the War Office somehow,' Munro said. 'His best asset is that he's completely unknown – unlike us. Fresh face – a stranger.'

The captain was drumming his fingers on his desk top. 'How?' he said. 'He's just a lieutenant. Nothing but bigwigs in the War Office.'

'We set up a commission of enquiry,' Munro said. 'Something very boring. Send in Rief with authorization to ask questions and examine documents.'

'Sir Horace Ede chaired a commission last year on transportation,' the captain said. 'There could be some supplementary matters arising —'

'Exactly. That Lieutenant Rief had to cover and account for.'

'And there's a joint nations' conference coming up which would explain why we have to have everything ship-shape.'

'Couldn't be better.'

Massinger was looking increasingly uncomfortable at being sidelined in this way with nothing to contribute. He cleared his throat loudly and everybody stopped talking and looked at him. He held up both hands in apology. Then took out his handkerchief and blew his nose.

'How long would you need, sir?' Munro asked.

'Give me a couple of days,' the captain said. 'The higher the authorization the easier it'll be for Rief, here.' He turned to Lysander. 'Hold yourself in readiness, Rief. If we want you right at the heart of things then we need to give you some power.'

Massinger finally spoke. 'You don't think we're treading on M.O. 5's toes, do you, sir?'

'This wretched mess all originated out of Geneva,' the captain said with a trace of impatience in his voice. 'It was your show — so it's our show. I'll square things with Kell. He doesn't have any men to spare, anyway.'

Lysander didn't know what they were talking about. He picked at a loose shred of skin on his forefinger.

'Right, let me get on to it,' the captain said. 'We'd better give our rotten apple a codename so we can talk about him.'

'Any preferences?' Munro asked.

Lysander thought quickly. 'How about Andromeda?' he said, his eyes fixed on Munro. Munro's face didn't move.

'Andromeda it is – so let's find him, fast,' the captain said, and rose to his feet. The meeting was over. He crossed the room to Lysander and shook his hand. 'I saw your father play Macbeth,' he said. 'Scared me to bits. Good luck, Rief. Or should I say welcome aboard?'

3. The Annexe on the Embankment

MUNRO TOLD HIM TO go away and enjoy himself for a few days until he was called for. Once everything had been set up he would be briefed and given precise instructions. So he returned to the White Palace Hotel in Pimlico and tried to keep himself distracted and amused even though he was aware of a steadily increasing undercurrent of uneasiness flowing beneath the surface of his life. Who was this all-powerful captain-figure? What role and sway did he enjoy? To what extent, if at all, could he rely on Munro and Massinger? Could he trust either of them? And why had be been selected, once again, to do his duty as a soldier? Perhaps he'd gain some answers in the coming days, he reflected, but the complete absence of answers – even provisional ones – was troubling.

He went to his tailor, Jobling, and had a small buttonhole fitted for his wound-stripe – an inch-long vertical brass bar worn on the left forearm – sown into the sleeves of his uniform jackets. Jobling was obviously moved when he told him the nature of his injuries. Three of his cutters had joined up and two had already died. 'Don't go back there, Mr Rief,' he said. 'You've done your bloody bit, all right.' He also adjusted the fit of his jacket – Lysander had lost weight during his convalescence.

He went to see Blanche in *The Hour of Danger* at the Comedy. Backstage in her dressing room she didn't allow him to kiss her on the lips. He asked her to supper but she said she couldn't go as she was 'seeing someone'. Lysander asked his name but she wouldn't tell him and they parted coolly, not to say acrimoniously. He sent her flowers the next day to apologize.

He quickly organized a small dinner party in a private room at the Hyde Park Hotel for four of his actor friends with the precise intention of finding out the name of Blanche's new beau. Everybody knew and, to his alarm, it turned out to be someone he was slightly acquainted with as well – a rather successful playwright that he'd read for called James Ashburnham, a man in his late forties, a widower. A handsome older man with a reputation in the theatre as something of a philanderer, Lysander thought, feeling betrayed, though a moment's reflection made him realize he had no right to the emotion – he was the one who had broken off their engagement, not Blanche. As Blanche had reminded him, they had decided to remain friends, that was all, consequently her private life was her concern alone.

Of course, being rejected for someone else made him feel hurt and his old feelings for Blanche re-established themselves effortlessly. She was an extremely beautiful, sweet young woman and whatever they had shared together couldn't be simply tossed aside that easily. What was she doing having an affair with a middle-aged playwright old enough – well, almost – to be her father? He was surprised at how agitated he felt.

On the Friday morning there was a knock at his door and Plumtree, the young chambermaid, told him there was a gentleman to see him in the back parlour. Lysander went downstairs with some trepidation – it was underway, the play was about to start again – orchestra and beginners, please. Fyfe-Miller was waiting for him, smart in a commander's uniform, with a file of papers under his arm. He locked the door and spread them on the table. He and Munro had analysed the variety of information in the Glockner letter decrypts and were convinced they could only have come from one department in the War Office – the Directorate of Movements. This department was currently housed in an annexe to the War Office on the Embankment in a building near Waterloo Bridge. Lysander was to report there at once to the director, one Brevet Lieutenant-Colonel Osborne-Way, who would ensure that Lysander was provided with his own office and a telephone. He was expected this afternoon – there was no time to waste.

'Can't it wait until Monday?' Lysander asked, plaintively.

'There's a war on, Rief, in case you hadn't noticed,' Fyfe-Miller said, not smiling for once. 'What kind of attitude is that? The sooner we find out who this person is, the safer we shall all be.'

At two-thirty that afternoon, Lysander stood across the street from the seven-storey building that housed the Directorate of Movements. He was standing approximately half way between Waterloo Bridge and the Charing Cross Railway Bridge. Cleopatra's Needle was a few yards away to his left. The phrase 'searching for a needle in a haystack' came pessimistically into his head. The Thames was at his back and he could hear the wash of water swirling round the jetties and the moored boats as the tide ebbed. He was smart in his new uniform with his brass wound-bar and with highly polished, buckled leather gaiters encasing his legs from knee to boot. He took his cap off, smoothed his hair and resettled it on his head. He felt strangely nervous but he knew that, above all, he now had to act confident. He lit a cigarette – no hurry. He heard a flap of wings and turned to see a big black crow swoop down and settle on the pavement two yards from him. Big birds, up close, he thought – size of a small hen. Black beak, black eyes, black feathers, black legs. 'City of kites and crows,' Shakespeare had said about London, somewhere. He watched as the bird made its hippity-hoppity way towards half a discarded currant bun in the gutter. It pecked away for a while, looking around suspiciously, then a motor car passed too close and it flew off into a plane tree with an irritated squawk.

Lysander realized he could think of three or four symbolic, doom-laden interpretations of this encounter with a London crow but decided to investigate none of them further. He threw his cigarette into the Thames, picked up his attaché case and, watching out for the speeding traffic, made his way across the Embankment to the Annexe's front door.

Once he'd presented his credentials, Lysander was taken by an orderly up to the fourth floor. They pushed through swing doors into a lobby with two corridors on either side. On the wall were lists of various departments and meaningless acronyms and small arrows indicating which corridor to take – DGMR, Port & Transport Ctte, Railway and Road Engineering, DC (War Office), Ordnance (France), Food Controller (Dover), DART (Mesopotamia), ROD (II), and the like. Lysander and the orderly turned right and walked down a wide linoleum-floored passageway with many doors off it. The sound of typewriters and ringing telephone bells followed them all the way to a door marked 'Director of Movements'. The orderly knocked and Lysander was admitted.

The Director of Movements, Brevet Lt.-Colonel Osborne-Way (Worcester Regiment) was not at all pleased to see him, so Lysander recognized in about two seconds. His manner was unapologetically brusque and cold. Lysander was not offered a seat, Osborne-Way did not attempt to shake his hand, nor return his salute. Lysander handed him over his magic laissez-passer to the kingdom of the Directorate – a sheet of headed notepaper signed by the Chief of the Imperial General Staff himself, Lieutenant-General Sir James Murray, KCB, that said that 'the under-named officer, Lieutenant L. U. Rief, is to be afforded every possible assistance and access. He is acting under my personal instructions and is reporting directly to me.'

Osborne-Way read this missive several times as if he couldn't believe what was actually written down in black and white. He was a short man with a grey toothbrush moustache, and large puffy bags under his eyes. There were seven telephones in a row on his desk and a camp bed with a blanket was set up in the corner of his office.

'I don't understand,' he said, finally. 'What's it got to do with the C.I.G.S., himself? Why's he sending you? Doesn't he realize how busy we are here?'

As if to illustrate this claim two of the telephones on his desk began to ring simultaneously. He picked up the first and said 'Yes. Yes . . . repeat, yes. Affirmative.' Then he picked up the second, listened for a moment and said 'No,' and hung up.

'This is not my idea, sir,' Lysander said, reasonably. He was affecting a slightly drawling, nasal voice, faintly caddish and bored-sounding, he thought, conscious that this tone would make Osborne-Way like him even less. He didn't care – he wasn't entering a popularity contest. 'I'm just following orders. Some unfinished, supplementary business to Sir Horace Ede's commission of inquiry on transportation. Matter of some urgency given the up-coming all-nations' conference.'

'What do you need from us, then?' Osborne-Way said, handing the letter back as if it was burning his hand.

'I'd like a list of all personnel in the Directorate and their distribution of duties. And I'd be grateful if you'd alert everyone in the Directorate to the fact that I am here and have a job to do. At some stage I will want to interview them. The sooner I'm finished the sooner you'll see the back of me.' He smiled. 'Sir.'

'Very well.'

'I believe I have an office assigned to me.'

Osborne-Way picked up a telephone and shouted, 'Tremlett!' into the mouthpiece.

In about thirty seconds a lance-corporal appeared at the door. He had a black patch over one eye.

'Tremlett, this is Lieutenant Rief. Take him to Room 205.'
Then to Lysander he said, 'Tremlett will fetch you any files or
documents you need, any person you wish to interview and will
provide you with tea and biscuits. Good day.' He opened a drawer
on his desk and began removing papers. The meeting was clearly
over. Lysander followed Tremlett back along the wide passageway,
taking two right-angled turns as they made for Room 205.

'Good to have you aboard, sir,' Tremlett said, turning and giving
him a lopsided smile, the portion of his face below the patch not
moving. He was a young man in his early twenties, with a London
accent. 'I'm on extension 11. Give me a tinkle whenever you need
me. Here we are, sir.'

He opened the door to Room 205. It was a windowless box
with a dirty skylight. Here was a table, two wooden chairs and a
very old filing cabinet. On the table was a telephone. It was not a
room one would want to spend many hours in, Lysander thought.

'What's that curious smell?' he asked.

'Disinfectant, sir. Colonel Osborne-Way thought we should
give the place a good swab-out before you arrived.'

He told Tremlett to bring him Osborne-Way's list as soon as
possible, sat down and lit a cigarette. His eyes were already stinging
slightly from the astringency of the disinfectant. The battle lines
had been drawn – the Director of Movements had made a pre-
emptive strike.

There were twenty-seven members of the Directorate of
Movements on the fourth floor of the Annexe, and many clerical
and secretarial staff to serve them. Almost all of them were army
officers who had been wounded and were unfit for active service.
As he looked down the list of names Lysander found himself
wondering – which one of you is Andromeda? Which one of you
has been sending coded messages to Manfred Glockner in Geneva?
Who has access to the astounding detail those letters contained?
Where are you, Andromeda? Temporary Captain J.C.T. Baillie

(Royal Scots)? Or temporary Major S.A.M.M. Goodforth (Irish Guards)? . . . He leafed through the typed pages, wondering what had made him choose Andromeda as the name of the traitor in the Directorate. Andromeda – a helpless, naked, beautiful young woman chained to the rocks at the ocean's edge, waiting terrified for the approach of the sea monster Cetus – didn't exactly conform to the stereotypical image of a man actively and efficiently betraying his country. 'Cetus' might have been more apt – but he liked the ring and the idea of looking for an 'Andromeda'. The paradox was more intriguing.

But he quickly became aware as he contemplated Osborne-Way's list that it would not be an easy process. He picked a name at random: temporary Captain M.J. McCrimmon (Royal Sussex Regiment). Duties – 1. Despatch of units and drafts to India and Mesopotamia. 2. Inter-colonial moves. 3. Admiralty transport claims and individual passage claims to and from India. He picked another – temporary Major E.C. Lloyd-Russell (Retired. Special Reserve). Duties – 1. Despatch of units and drafts from India to France (Force 'A') and Egypt (Force 'E'). 2. Union of South Africa contingent. Labour corps from South Africa and India to France. 3. Supervision of Stores Service from the USA and Canada to the United Kingdom. Then there was Major L.L. Eardley (Royal Engineers). Duties – 1. Travelling concessions and irregularities. 2. Issue of railway warrants unconnected with embarkation. 3. General questions concerning railways and canals in the United Kingdom.

And so it went on, Lysander beginning to feel a mild nausea as he tried to take all this amount of work – these 'duties' – on board. He ordered a pot of tea and some biscuits from Tremlett. He thought of himself as a child on the roof of a vast factory peering down through a skylight at all the machinery and the people inside. Who were they? What were they doing? What was being made? All these strange jobs and responsibilities – 'Railway Engineering Services. Accounts for work services. Occupation and rent of

railway property. Shipping statistics. Labour Corps to France. Remounts to France. Long-voyage hospital ships. Despatches of
stores to theatres of war other than France. Construction of
sidings . . .' They went on and on. And this was only one
department in the War Office. And there were thousands of
people working in the War Office. And this was only one country
at war. The Directorate of Movements would have its equivalent
in France, in Germany, in Russia, in Austria-Hungary . . .

He began to feel dizzy as he sat there trying to conceptualize
the massive scale of this industrial bureaucracy in the civilized
world, all directed to the common end of providing for its
warring armies. What gigantic effort, what millions of man-
hours expended, day after day, week after week, month after
month. As he tried to come to terms with it, to visualize in some
way this prodigious daily struggle, he found himself perversely
glad that he had actually been in the front line. Maybe that was
why they employed wounded soldiers rather than civil servants
or other professional functionaries. These temporary Captains
and Majors in the Directorate of Movements at least knew the
physical, intimate consequences of the 'movement of stores' that
they ordered.

Lysander personalized it, grimly. When he had thrown that
Mills no.5 bomb into the sap beneath the ruined tomb it was the
final moment in the history of travel of that small piece of ordnance
– a history that stretched back through space and time like a
ghoulish, spreading wake. From ore mined in Canada, shipped to
Britain, smelted, moulded, turned, filled and packed in a box,
designated as 'stores to be transported from the United Kingdom
to France'. Perhaps new sidings had been built in a rural railway
station in northern France to accommodate the train carrying these
stores (and what was involved in constructing a siding, he
wondered). And from there it would be transferred to a dump or
depot by animal transport whose forage was supplied through
Rouen and Havre, also. Then soldiers would carry the boxes of

bombs up to the line through communication trenches dug by 'labour from the Union of South Africa'. And then that Mills no. 5 bomb eventually found itself in the kitbag of Lt. Lysander Rief, who threw it into a sap beneath a tomb in no man's land and a man with a moustache and a fair-haired boy struggled to find it in the dark amongst the tumbled masonry, hoping and praying that some defect in its manufacture, or some malfunction caused by its long journey, would cause it not to detonate . . . No such luck.

Lysander found that he was sweating. Stop. That way madness lies. He thought of tips of icebergs or inverted pyramids but then an image came to him from nowhere that seemed to cohere with what he had been imagining more fittingly. A winter bonfire.

He remembered how, on very cold days in winter, when you lit a bonfire the smoke sometimes refused to rise. The slightest breeze would move it flatly across the land, a low enlarging horizontal plume of smoke that hugged the ground and never dispersed into the air as it did with a normal fire on a warmer day. He saw all the monstrous, gargantuan effort of the war as a winter bonfire – yes, but in reverse. As if the drifting, ground-hugging pall of smoke were converging – arrowing in – on one point, to feed the small, angry conflagration of the fire. All those miles of broad, dense, drifting smoke narrowing, focussing on the little crackling flickering flames burning vivid orange amongst the fallen leaves and the dead branches.

Lysander left Room 205 and wandered the corridors of the Directorate, passing other officers and secretarial staff as he went. Nobody paid him any attention, the ringing of the phones and the dry clatter of the typewriter keys a constant aural backdrop. He peered into one room where the door was ajar and saw three officers sitting at their desks all speaking into their telephones. Two women typists faced each other typing, as if duelling, somehow. He walked down the stairs and saw the signs on the other floors –

MOVEMENTS, RAILWAYS AND ROADS
INLAND WATER TRANSPORT (FRANCE)
INSPECTOR-GENERAL (ALL THEATRES)
IRISH RAILWAYS

He stepped out, feeling exhausted and a little overwhelmed, on to the Embankment and took some deep breaths of dirty London air. He stretched, flexed his shoulder muscles, rolled his head around, easing his neck, feeling weak and almost tearful at the magnitude of the task he'd been set. Who the hell was Andromeda? And, when he found him, what would happen then?

4. English Courage

'YOU KNOW,' HAMO SAID over the noise of the engine, 'I never feel nervous about anything in life but I feel strangely nervous today.'

They were in the Turner two-seater motoring towards Romney on Sunday morning, heading for Bonham Johnson's lunch party.

'I know what you mean,' Lysander said, leaning towards him and cupping his hand around his mouth. 'I felt exactly the same the other day when I went into the War Office. First day at school.' He looked around and saw a signpost flash by – Fairfield, 2 miles. 'Let's stop at a pub or a hotel and have a drink first. Dutch courage. Why's it called Dutch courage? English courage is what we need.'

'Excellent idea,' Hamo said. He was wearing a flat leather cap, reversed, and driving goggles. They had the hood of the two-seater down as the day was fine, though breezy. They both wore greatcoats and Lysander had his Trilby tied securely on his head with his scarf.

They found a small pub in Fairfield and ordered whisky sodas at the bar.

Hamo said, 'I'm just terrified that one of these literary types is going to ask me about Shakespeare or Milton.'

'No they won't. You're the one they want to see and meet. You wrote *The Lost Lake*. That's what they'll want to talk about – not Keats and Wordsworth.'

'I wish I had your confidence, my boy.'

'Hamo, you've won the Victoria Cross, for god's sake. They're just a bunch of idle writers.'

'Still . . .'

'No. Do what I do. If I don't feel confident I *act* confident.'

'I'll try. That's exactly what your father would have said. D'you know, I think another whisky would help.'

'Go on, then. Me too.'

Lysander watched his uncle go up to the bar to order another round, feeling a kind of love for him. He looked slim and upright in his dark grey suit, the ceiling light shining off his bald pate like some incipient halo. Hamo's halo. Nice thought.

Bonham Johnson's house – Pondshill Place – was large and imposing – a Victorian farm of cut and moulded red brick and tall groups of chimney-stacks. At one end was a wide bow window looking over a terraced garden that fell gently to a reflecting pool surrounded by closely clipped obelisks of box trees. There was a barn and stable block to one side where the guests' motor cars were to be parked. A farm labourer waved them into the courtyard where there were already a dozen cars in two neat rows.

'Oh good,' Hamo said. 'Looks like a big crowd. I can hide myself.'

The main door to Pondshill Place was opened by a butler, who invited them to 'go through to the saloon'. This was the drawing room with the big curved bay window and was already occupied by upward of twenty people – all very casually dressed, Lysander noticed, glad that he had decided on a suit of light Harris tweed. He saw some men without ties and women in brightly coloured print dresses. He whispered, 'Relax!' to Hamo and they helped themselves to a glass of sherry from a tray held by an extremely pretty young maid, Lysander noticed.

Bonham Johnson was a very stout man with longish thinning hair and a grizzled pointed beard that made him look vaguely Jacobean, Lysander thought. He introduced himself and launched into a fluent and protracted hymn of praise to *The Lost Lake of Africa* – 'Extraordinary, unparalleled.' Even Hamo yielded in the face of this encomium and Lysander happily let Johnson lead him away across the room, hearing him ask, 'Do you know Joseph Conrad? No? You'll have a lot in common.'

Lysander headed back to the maid with the sherry and helped himself to another glass.

'What time is lunch being served?' he asked, fixing her with his eyes. She was strikingly pretty. What was she doing serving Bonham Johnson's guests?

'About one-thirty, sir. Still a few more guests to arrive.'

'This may seem a strange question. But have you ever thought of –'

'Lysander?'

He turned round and for a brief second didn't recognize her. The hair was darker, cut short with a severe straight fringe across the eyebrows. She was wearing a jersey dress with great lozenges of colour blocks – orange, buttercup-yellow, cinnamon. He felt himself shiver, visibly. The shock-effect was palpable, unignorable.

'Hettie . . .'

'I'm so glad you could come. I told Bonham that your uncle would be the best way to lure you here.' She leaned forward and kissed his cheek and he smelled her scent again, for the first time in a year and a half. Now he had tears in his eyes. He closed them.

'So it was all your doing . . .'

'Yes. I had to find a way of seeing you. You're not going to be beastly to me, are you?' she said.

'No. No, I'm not.'

'Are you all right? You've gone quite pale.'

'Is Lothar here?'

'Of course not. He's in Austria.'

This was impossible. He felt he was in some kind of emotion-race, feelings and sensations succeeding each other in a frantic, spinning helter-skelter.

'Can we get out of here?' he managed to say.

'No. Jago would be horribly suspicious. In fact he won't even like me talking to you for very long.'

'Who's Jago?'

'My husband – Jago Lasry.'

Lysander sensed he was meant to react to the name but he had never heard of the man.

Hettie looked at him sardonically.

'Come on, don't play those games with me. Jago Lasry, author of *Crépuscules*. Mmm? Ring a bell? The *Quick Blue Fox and Other Stories*. Yes?'

'I've been in the army since the war started – very out of touch.'

She moved closer and he was reminded of how small-made and tiny she was – the top of her head reaching his chest. She lowered her voice.

'I'm sitting beside you at lunch but we must pretend to be strangers – almost-strangers, anyway. And I'm not called Hettie any more. I'm Vanora.'

'Vanora?'

'A Celtic name. I always hated being called Hettie. It seemed fine in Vienna but it's all wrong here. Imagine being Hettie Lasry! See you at lunch.'

She walked away and Lysander, still in awful turmoil, mistily watched her ease her way through the crowd of guests to greet one of the tieless young men. A small wiry fellow, in his late twenties, Lysander supposed, with a dark patchy beard, wearing a maroon corduroy suit. Jago Lasry, author of *Crépuscules*. He saw the man's head turn to seek him out. So Hettie/Vanora had been behind this invitation . . . he wondered what she wanted of him. He drained his sherry glass and went back for a refill.

He heard the rest of Hettie's story at lunch – in fits and starts, out of sequence, with many a doubling-back and re-explanation, at his insistence. To his shock he discovered she had been living in England since the beginning of the year. She had left Vienna in November 1914 and had crossed into Switzerland, making her roundabout way back home via Italy and Spain.

'Why didn't you bring Lothar with you?'

'He's much happier in Austria. He's living in Salzburg with one of Udo's aunts. Happy as anything.'

'Have you got a photograph of him?'

'I have, but . . . not here. Jago doesn't know about Lothar, as it happens. Let's keep it between ourselves, if you don't mind.'

She had met Jago Lasry shortly after her return and they had married in May ('Love at first glimpse,' she said), so it transpired, and they were currently living in Cornwall in a cottage owned by Bonham Johnson. Lasry was a protégé of Johnson, who had been very generous with introductions to publishers and editors and the provider of small loans, when required, so Hettie told him. Lysander glanced across the table at Lasry – a skinny, intense man who appeared to eat his food with the same concentration and urgency as he spoke. He suspected Bonham Johnson was more than a little in love with his protégé.

'I told Jago that you and I had met briefly in Vienna,' Hettie said. 'That we were both seeing the same doctor there. Just in case he was suspicious.'

'Bensimon's back in London, you know. I heard from him.'

Hettie looked at him in that strange way she had. A bizarre mixture of sudden interest and what seemed like potential threat.

'Just like the old days, eh?' she said.

'What do you mean?'

She looked away and asked the person next to her to pass the salt. Lysander felt her hand on his thigh under the table and her fingers quickly searching for and finding the bulge of his penis. She gripped him hard through the cloth of his trousers, then ran her fingertips up and down. He reached for his wine glass, as if it would give him support – he thought he might swoon or cry out. She took her hand away.

'I have to see you,' he said, quietly, a little hoarsely, talking into his plate, trying not to look at her, slicing his lamb into small pieces to keep his mind occupied. 'I'm staying in London. A small hotel in Pimlico called The White Palace. They've a telephone.'

'I don't know if I can get up to London. Difficult – but I can try.'

'Send me a postcard – The White Palace Hotel, Pimlico, London, South West.'

Now she had turned to look at him again and he stared into those slightly-too-wide, pale hazel eyes. He realized that seeing her again here was a watershed. He felt he knew himself once more, understood the kind of person he was, what he needed, what he asked of life.

'I promise I'll do my best,' she said. 'Listen. You couldn't lend me some money, by any chance, could you?'

'Surprisingly nice fellow, that Bonham Johnson,' Hamo said. 'Put me completely at my ease. What a fuss I made for nothing – I could tell he was musical at once.'

'Musical?'

'One of us.'

'Ah. Right.'

'What did you need ten pounds for?' Hamo asked, stooping to crank the starting handle of the Turner. 'Lucky I had some cash on me.'

'I had to lend it to that woman I introduced you to. Vanora Lasry.'

'Very generous of you,' Hamo said, clambering on board the

now gently shuddering vehicle. 'To lend all that money to a perfect stranger.'

'That was her, Hamo,' Lysander confessed with relief. 'That was Hettie Bull – the mother of my son.'

'Good god!'

They pulled away out of the stable block and headed back across flat expanses of the marsh towards the main road to Rye. Lysander leaned close and shouted a brief explanation of what had taken place into Hamo's ear. As he listened, Hamo's head shook more regularly in bemusement and sympathy.

'I've got nothing to say to you, dear boy. Not a word of reproach. I know exactly what you're feeling. *La coeur a ses raisons*. Oh, yes!'

They motored along at a steady speed, the light fading, and when they caught glimpses of the Channel as the road took them closer to the coast they saw the setting sun burnishing the sea, like hammered silver. Lysander felt both exhilarated and confused. Meeting Hettie again made him achingly conscious once more of the irrefutable nature of his obsession with her. Obsession – or love? Or was it something more unhealthy – a kind of craving, an addiction?

He and Hamo sat up late, talking, drinking whisky – Lysander taking the opportunity to relate Hettie's story in more detail.

'Are you going to see her again?' Hamo asked.

'Yes. I have to.'

'Are you sure that's wise – now she's married and all that?'

'Very unwise, I'd have thought. But I can't see any alternative, Hamo. I'm sort of in thrall to her.'

'I understand. Oh, yes, I understand.'

Hettie had introduced Lysander to Jago Lasry after lunch was finished and Lysander felt himself being scrutinized, the suspicion and scepticism overt. Hettie linked arms with her husband, trying to emanate uxorious contentment.

'We both had the same doctor in Vienna,' Lysander said, searching for something bland and conventional to say to this coiled, angry, small man.

'Same quack, you mean.'

'I wouldn't go that far.'

'How far *would* you go, Mr Rief?'

'Let's say Dr Bensimon was a great help to me, therapeutically. Made a huge difference.'

'He just fed Vanora drugs.'

'Freud himself used Coca. Wrote a book about it.'

They then had a short, fervid discussion about the demerits of Sigmund Freud and Freudianism. Lysander began to feel increasingly out of his depth as Lasry spoke of Carl Jung and the 4th International Psychoanalytical Conference in Munich in 1913, subjects Lysander knew nothing about. He found himself trying to place Lasry's accent – Midlands, he thought, Nottingham coalfields – but before he could be any more precise Johnson drew Lasry away to meet 'the editor of the *English Review*'. Lysander stood there swaying, exhausted.

'I'd better join him,' Hettie said. 'I can see you've put him in one of his moods.'

'Why didn't you come to me the moment you were back in England?' Lysander said, suddenly aggrieved and hurt.

'I thought it was pointless – thought you'd never forgive me for Lothar. And the police. And all the rest.'

Lysander remembered his travails in Vienna at Hettie's hands, experiencing a sudden vivid recall of his anger and frustration. He wondered why he couldn't sustain these brief, intense rages that Hettie provoked. What was it about her? How did she undermine them so easily?

'I forgive you,' he said, weakly. 'Come and see me in London. Please. We'll sort everything out.'

And what did he mean by that? – he thought as he went up the stairs to his bedroom that night, his head numb and muddy with

264

all the whisky he'd drunk and the swarm of emotions that had persecuted him all day. As he undressed he remembered that the hunt for Andromeda was meant to begin in earnest the next morning. In his troubled half-drunkenness he thought that, actually, in a house in Romney in the heart of Romney Marsh he had met the real Andromeda herself once more, in all her importunate beauty.

Coincidence? What was the Viennese connection in the Andromeda affair, he wondered dozily. If Hettie hadn't accused him of rape, if he hadn't called on Munro at the embassy, if he hadn't artfully engineered his own escape, then his current life would be entirely different. But what was the point of that? The view backward showed you all the twists and turns your life had taken, all the contingencies and chances, the random elements of good luck and bad luck that made up one person's existence. Still, questions buzzed around his brain all night as he tossed and fidgeted, punched and turned his pillows, opened and closed the windows of his room, waiting for sunrise. He managed to sleep for an hour and was up and dressed at dawn, off to the Winchelsea Inn for a pony and trap to take him into Rye. Monday, 27th September, 1915. The hunt was on.

5. Autobiographical Investigations

I BOUGHT A NEWSPAPER this morning on my walk to the Annexe. 'Great offensive at Loos'; 'Enemy falls back before our secret weapon'; 'Significant advances across the whole front despite heavy casualties'. The vapid vocabulary of jingoistic military journalism. It had all started this weekend while I was at Winchelsea and at Bonham Johnson's lunch party as I was sipping sherry, feeling Hettie grip me under the table and arguing about

Freud with her obnoxious husband. There are long faces in the Annexe, however. Here in the Directorate we quickly know when the ambulance trains are full. Provision was made for 40,000 wounded men and already it appears inadequate. Not enough heavy artillery, ammunition dumps insufficiently supplied. Our cloud of poison gas seems to have had the most partial effectiveness – reports have come in complaining that it hung in the air over no man's land or else drifted back into our trenches to blind and confuse our own men waiting to attack. The one thing we can't supply from the Directorate of Movements is a stiff westerly breeze, alas.

Going through Osborne-Way's list it's at once obvious that a significant number of the officers in the Directorate could not possibly have access to all the information in the Glockner letters. However, I've decided as a matter of policy and subterfuge to interview everyone – I don't want to concentrate on any particular group and thereby raise suspicions. Andromeda, whoever he is, mustn't develop the slightest concern over this supplementary enquiry into Sir Horace Ede's Commission on Transportation. So, I've summoned Tremlett and given him the entire list of interviewees. I begin with one Major H.B. O'Terence, responsible for 'Travelling claims by land. Visits of relatives to wounded in hospital in France'. He's going to be a busy man in the coming days and weeks – best to finish with him first.

It has proved to be both a shock and unusually destabilizing to have seen Hettie. All my sex-feelings for her have returned in an instant. Incredible desire. Old images of her naked and what we did with each other. And all my contradictions and confusions about her crowd in as well. Vanora Lasry – I can hardly believe it. And what about Lothar? Your son, your little boy. Again, emotions wax and wane. One second he seems unreal, a product of my imagination, a fantasy – and then, the next, I find myself thinking of this little boy, this baby, living in a suburb of Salzburg with Udo Hoff's aunt. Does Hettie care? Why wouldn't she tell her new husband that he has a stepson? I bought Lasry's book of poems, *Crépuscules*. Modern nonsense in the main. Free verse is both seductive and dangerous, I can see – it can be a licence to be pretentious and obscure. Lasry often abuses it, in my opinion. I take more care.

SEVENTH CAPRICE IN PIMLICO

The dawn created itself
And turned to see what had been lit.

Rubbish, litter, broken glass and a bit
Of green England, unsmirched, a glance
At something beautiful. Behold the dance:
The girls advance,
The boys decline.
Emerging from the Piccadilly Line
I find the tropic odours of Leicester Square
Beguile and mesmerize.
I roam the streets at midnight. The glare
Of gaslights an artificial sunrise.

'*Les colombes de ma cousine
Pleurent comme un enfant.*'

I asked Tremlett to do me a favour and to look up the casualty lists of the Manchester Fusiliers – to check whether a Lt. Gorlice-Law or a Sergeant Foley appeared. He came back with the news that Lt. Gorlice-Law had died of wounds on June 27th and a Sgt. Foley was in a hospital in Stoke Newington. 'He must be blind, sir,' Tremlett said, pointing to his patch. 'That's where they took my peeper out.' So Gorlice-Law died the day after our raid into no man's land . . . I feel I have to try and see Foley and find out exactly what happened that night after I crawled away and left them. Feelings of guilt inexorably creep over me. Was it my fault? No, you fool. You were ordered to bomb that sap to create a diversion. After that the gods of war and luck took over and you were as much subject to their fatal whim as any of the thousands of soldiers facing each other on both sides of the line.

6. Unlikely Suspects

LYSANDER INTERVIEWED THE OFFICERS of the Directorate over the next three days in the cramped and antiseptic quarters of Room 205. All were conducted in the same tone of apologetic tedium and polite routine – he wanted to make no one remotely suspicious or alarmed. He asked for their understanding – he knew he was wasting precious time – and strove to be as amiable as possible, but the men he saw were uniformly wary and resentful – sometimes even contemptuous. Osborne-Way had obviously been at work preparing the ground.

He ended up with a list of six key names, including the Director, Osborne-Way, himself. All these men were capable, theoretically, of reproducing the specific type of information contained in the Glockner letters. Four of them were responsible for 'Movement and control of war material and stores to France'. One dealt with control of ports, one with railway material – 'tanks, road metal, timber, slag and coal'. One was a rare civilian in the Directorate who was solely concerned with the compilation of shipping statistics – so every fact ended at his desk. Apart from Osborne-Way (an unlikely suspect, though Lysander refused to rule him out – unlikely suspects were more suspect in his opinion) the two men who most interested him were a Major Mansfield Keogh (Royal

Irish Regiment) who was the Assistant Director of Movements –
Osborne-Way's number two – and a Captain Christian Vandenbrook (King's Royal Rifle Corps) who supervised the 'despatch to
France of ammunition, ordnance, supplies and Royal Engineers'
stores'.

In principle the Directorate of Movements retained no more
responsibility once stores were landed at Le Havre, Rouen or
Calais; at that moment the Quartermaster General's department at
headquarters in St Omer took over. However, in practice, there
were always problems – trains went missing, ammunition found
itself in the wrong depots, ships were sunk in the Channel.
Significantly, Lysander thought, both Keogh and Vandenbrook
had been to France independently on three occasions in 1915
(Osborne-Way had been twice) to liaise with the Director of
Railway Transport and his staff and to supervise the construction
of marshalling yards and sidings behind the lines. There was ideal
opportunity to discover everything the Glockner letters contained.

Keogh was a quiet, earnest, efficient man who seemed consumed
by some private sadness. He was civil and prompt with his answers
but Lysander felt he regarded him as a mere nothing – a buzzing
fly, a crumpled piece of paper, a leaf on the pavement. Keogh
looked at him with empty eyes. By contrast, Vandenbrook was the
most open and charming of his interviewees. He was a small, lithe,
handsome man with perfect, even features and a fair moustache
with the ends dashingly turned up. His teeth – he smiled regularly
– were almost unnaturally white, Lysander thought. Vandenbrook
was the only person he talked to who asked him about himself and
who seemed happy to acknowledge that he'd seen him on stage
before the war. Lysander knew his past life was common knowledge
in the Directorate – he had overheard Osborne-Way refer to him
as the 'bloody actor-chappie' more than once – but only
Vandenbrook made overt and unconcerned reference to his stage
career and Lysander liked him for it.

The War Diary of the Directorate had revealed the facts about

Keogh's and Vandenbrook's trips to France. Tremlett supplied him with the ledger that detailed all the departmental 'travelling claims by land'. Keogh had responsibility for the port of Dover; Vandenbrook for Folkestone. Both men visited the ports every few days, where the Directorate kept branch offices, and their expenses – train tickets, hotels, taxis, porters, meals and refreshments – were docketed, copied and filed. Lysander decided to investigate Keogh first, then Vandenbrook, then Osborne-Way. Save the biggest beast for last.

Lysander saw Keogh come out of the Annexe and walk through to Charing Cross. He followed at a safe distance though he thought it unlikely he'd be recognized. He was wearing a false moustache, a bowler hat and was carrying a briefcase. He had chosen an old dark suit and made it short in the arms to expose the frayed cardboard cuffs of his shirt, looking, he hoped, like one of the thousands of clerical workers who spilled out of the great ministries of state in Whitehall at the end of the working day and began their routine journey homewards by the various means of public transport – omnibus, tram, and Underground and Tube railway. He followed Keogh on to the Underground at Charing Cross and sat at the far end of the compartment from him as they rattled along the District Line and over the Thames to East Putney. He watched Keogh plod up Upper Richmond Road and then turn off into a street of semi-detached brick villas. Keogh went into number 26. From inside the house Lysander could hear the faint barking of a dog, quickly silenced. He saw that the blinds of every window were drawn down. It was still light – perhaps he was one of the few London households that observed a proper blackout against the Zeppelin raids, but there seemed little point in that if your neighbours were lax. A death in the family? . . .

He spotted a woman pushing a pram up the pavement on the other side of the road and so crossed and came up behind her.

Putting on a slight cockney accent he asked if she knew which house Mr and Mrs Keogh lived in.

'I been knockin' on the wrong door, missus, it seems.'

'You want number 26, dear,' she said. 'But don't go asking for Mrs Keogh, though.'

'Why's that, then?'

'Because she died two months ago. Diphtheria. Very sad, terrible shame. Lovely young woman. Beautiful.'

Lysander thanked her and walked away. So, a recent widower – that explained the vacant, indifferent stare. Did that rule him out? Or did the meaningless death of a beautiful young wife provoke feelings of nihilism and rage against the world? He would have to find out more about Major Keogh. In the meantime he would turn his attention to Captain Christian Vandenbrook.

Vandenbrook was rich enough to take a taxi home from work. Lysander sat in the back of a cab at the end of the afternoon outside the Annexe, watched Vandenbrook flag down a passing taxi and followed it to his club in St James's. Two hours later he emerged, hailed another cab and was driven home to Knightsbridge to a large white stucco house in an elegant sweep of terrace off the Brompton Road. Vandenbrook was doing very well for a captain in the King's Royal Rifle Corps.

Lysander dismissed his taxi and walked up and down the smart crescent of large houses. Through a window he caught a glimpse of Vandenbrook accepting a cut-crystal tumbler from a silver tray held by a butler. Staff, as well. Twenty minutes later another taxi pulled up and a couple – dressed for dinner – descended and rang the doorbell. Lysander returned to his small hotel in Pimlico, conscious that someone with Vandenbrook's manifest privileges had no real need to turn traitor. Osborne-Way was next.

At the hotel he found he had a postcard, sent from St Austell,

Cornwall. It read, 'Arriving Friday evening. Have booked room at White Palace, Pimlico. Vanora.'

Tremlett fetched him the ledger of 'Travelling claims by land' and stood there waiting for further instructions as Lysander flicked through the pages.

'Colonel Osborne-Way hasn't filed any expenses claims.'

'No, sir. He sends his direct to the War Office. He was on the General Staff – seconded here, like.'

'Seems odd. Can we get them?'

Tremlett sucked his teeth.

'We can try but it might take a while. We may need you to go yourself with your magic letter.'

'Thanks, Tremlett, that'll be all for the moment.'

He looked through Keogh's claims and noted the dates he'd been to Dover over the past months; then he turned to Vandenbrook and collated their respective journeys – some days they tallied, some days they didn't. However, he noticed that Vandenbrook very rarely stayed in Folkestone – his accommodation claims were for hotels in Deal, Hastings, Sandwich, Hythe and once in Rye. Probably keen to get some golf in, Lysander thought, leafing through the dockets, or else wanted to be away from the Directorate organization – sensible man.

There was a knock on his door. Lysander put the bottle of champagne back in the ice-bucket and crossed the room, trying to stay calm, and opened the door. Hettie stood there, smiling, as if this encounter were the most natural and normal in the world.

'What a funny little hotel you chose,' she said, stepping in. 'My room's minute.' Lysander closed the door behind her, feeling as if his chest were stuffed with hot, rough wool – an ill, constrained breathlessness stopping him speaking. He sensed a weakness flow through him, as though his knees might buckle and he'd fall to the floor.

'Aren't you going to give me a kiss?' Hettie said, unpinning her hat and throwing it on to a chair. 'Let's take our clothes off now – then we can drink our champagne.'

'Hettie, for heaven's sake –'

'Come on, Lysander. Race you.'

They kissed. He felt his lips on hers and then her tongue in his mouth. They undressed and Lysander opened the champagne and poured it. He noticed Hettie had kept her hosiery on and her high-heeled shoes and her jewellery. Jet beads at the neck, a cluster of ivory bracelets.

'Why are we doing this?' he asked, faintly. 'This way.'

'Because I *know* you, Lysander. Remember?' she said, almost scoldingly. 'Because I know what you like.' She strode around the room, unselfconsciously, checked that the curtains were properly drawn. 'It's exciting, isn't it? To be naked in a hotel room in Pimlico drinking champagne . . .' She glanced down at him. 'My – you seem to agree.'

She came over to him and he touched her breasts and drew her close. Again, oddly, he felt like weeping – as if some form of destiny were being fulfilled, here in this unassuming room; that he was here with Hettie in his arms, once more. This was the problem with her, he acknowledged – or, rather, this was *his* problem with Hettie – it was like being with no other woman. He had never felt this need, this strongly, with anyone else.

She kissed his chest and he put his arms around her. She hugged her small body against his.

She raised her face and whispered, 'I've missed you.' Then she took him in her hand and led him compliantly to the bed.

7. The Dene Hotel, Hythe

THE DIRECTORATE OF MOVEMENTS had opened and maintained branch offices in Dover and Folkestone since the end of 1914, the easier to supervise the loading and despatch of the millions of tons of stores that were sent out to France each week. They were staffed mainly with former port authority officials and clerical workers but, every few days, Keogh and Vandenbrook would make a routine journey to oversee the office work or, more likely, sort out problems.

Looking through the departmental memoranda on Monday Lysander saw that two cargo vessels had collided in the Channel, one of them sinking with the loss of '600 black labour drowned (approx.)'. Osborne-Way had added a note in the margin in his small crabbed schoolboy's hand, 'Attn. Capt. VdenB.' Lysander asked Tremlett where Vandenbrook was and he came back with the information that he had not come into the Annexe that morning but had gone straight to Folkestone to 'sort out the steaming mess'.

Lysander told Tremlett to have a railway pass made out for him and he caught a train to the coast from Victoria before noon. At Folkestone he negotiated with a taxi-driver who grudgingly agreed to stay with him until midnight for £5 cash. Lysander thought of the soldiers in the trenches earning their eighteen pennies a day for their unique version of the diurnal grind. Still, the mobility might be essential – he had a feeling Vandenbrook wouldn't be spending the night in Folkestone.

He had the taxi park a little way up the street from the Directorate offices in Marine Parade and settled down to wait. It turned out to be a long one, Vandenbrook not emerging until seven o'clock that evening. A motor car drew up and he climbed in. They headed out of town, going west along the main coast road towards Hythe. Vandenbrook was dropped off at the front door of the Dene Hotel – a neat brick and hung-tile, two-storey building with a garage at the rear and a modern extension, just off the high street on the lower slopes of the hill that led up to Hythe's principal church, St Leonards. The car drove away, returning to Folkestone. After five minutes, Lysander followed him in.

The reception lobby was a low, beamed area with doors off to a saloon bar and a dining room and a fine curved oak staircase that led to the bedrooms on the first floor. Far more comfortable than the Commercial Hotel, Folkestone, he was sure, and where Directorate staff usually stayed, so Tremlett had informed him. Lysander saw fresh flowers in a bowl on the reception desk and read the posted menu outside the dining room where he noted a simple but classic choice of English dishes – a roast, a saddle of lamb, devilled kidneys, Dover sole. He felt suddenly hungry – no wonder Vandenbrook preferred to find his own lodgings.

He went into the bar and chose a seat where he had a view of the lobby through the glass-paned door. He ordered a whisky and soda and thought he'd wait until Vandenbrook came down for dinner and surprise him. They would have a laugh about it and at least he'd eat a decent meal before he caught the last train back to London.

He sipped his whisky and lit a cigarette, his mind turning inevitably towards Hettie and the night they'd spent together. She could only stay until morning, she had said, as she had to meet Lasry in Brighton, where they were going to look for somewhere to live – Cornwall was beginning to pall, so far away, and Bonham Johnson was urging them to be closer to London. She promised Lysander that she would come back to London for several days as soon as she could think up an excuse that would appease her suspicious husband. Lysander thought he might rent a small service apartment in a mansion block somewhere central where they could safely spend time together – he was growing tired of hotel life, anyway, and god knew how long he'd be stuck in the Directorate of Movements, searching for Andromeda. He wasn't anticipating his investigation of Osborne-Way with any great pleasure. He'd have to be exceptionally cautious, take real pains not to be –

His mother walked into the hotel.

His first instinct was to rush out into the lobby and surprise her, but something made him shrink back in his seat. She was wearing a fur coat and one of the new, fashionably smaller hats. She spoke to the receptionist and a porter was called and sent away. Luggage? Was she staying the night? The mâitre d' emerged from the dining room and shook her hand, obsequiously. She must be known here . . . She was led away towards the dining room and out of his line of sight.

Lysander would have liked to put this encounter down as one of life's many coincidences. Coincidences – the most extraordinary coincidences – happened all the time, he knew, and in a manner that would make the laziest farceur blush. But life's strange congruences were not applicable here – every suddenly aching bone in his body was telling him that this was no accidental coming-together of the respective orbits of Vandenbrook, Rief and Anna, Lady Faulkner. Then he saw Vandenbrook come down the stairs, cigarette in hand, and turn into the dining room. He knew instantly that he was going to his mother's table, that this rendezvous had been planned, but decided to wait five minutes before he sought his 'ocular proof'. He strolled out of the bar and pretended to consult a map of Hythe conveniently hung to one side of the dining-room door. It was ajar and he could see at an angle into the salon. There was a fireplace and a dozen tables, half of them occupied. And there in the corner was his mother, accepting a glass of wine poured by the sommelier, and there across the table from her was Christian Vandenbrook. They toasted each other – they seemed familiar and relaxed – clearly this was not their first introduction. As they talked and consulted the menu, Lysander saw that they were displaying all the timeworn and conventional feints and poor disguises of lovers meeting in a public place and hoping the real nature of their relationship would be invisible.

8. The Colonel's Daimler

'I NEED A MOTOR car, Tremlett,' Lysander said. 'I have to do a tour of the south-east. Does the Directorate have transport?'

'There is Colonel Osborne-Way's motor, sir. A Daimler. Sits in the garage for weeks at a time.'

'That'll do nicely.'

'I think we'll have need of your magic letter, however, sir.'

It turned out to be a big, new, maroon-and-black, 1914-model, seven-seater Daimler that had been ordered and paid for straight from the Daimler works in Coventry by the director of a chemical firm in Leipzig. It had been seized by the authorities at the outbreak of war before it could be shipped to Germany, but how it had ended up as Osborne-Way's personal vehicle was something of a mystery. It was ideal for Lysander's purposes, however, and Tremlett quickly and enthusiastically volunteered to act as chauffeur. Armed with copies of the relevant claims, the two of them headed off the next day – Lysander reclining grandly in the rear on mustard-yellow kid-leather seats – on a circuit of all the hotels on the Kent and Sussex coast that Christian Vandenbrook chose to frequent.

One night in Ramsgate drew a blank, but Sandwich, Deal and Hythe confirmed the pattern. They were all small, relatively expensive hotels with ardent recommendations from the better guidebooks. The hotel registers revealed that whenever Captain Vandenbrook was booked in so too was Lady Faulkner. She didn't stay with him in Rye, nor in Hastings, however – perhaps a little too close to home, Lysander thought. All in all, over a period from September 1914 to this latest October encounter, they had spent the night in the same hotel nine times. He would not have been surprised to find similar evidence in London – they were bound to have met there also, she went up to town two or three times a month – but Vandenbrook could hardly present a claim for a night in a London hotel to the Directorate's accounts department.

An affair of over a year, then, Lysander considered, and one that had begun while Crickmay Faulkner was still very much alive. The thought of his mother with Vandenbrook, carnally, made him uneasy and disturbed – made him instantly think of her differently, as if she had suddenly become someone entirely separate from the woman he knew and loved. But of course she wasn't old, he told himself, she had other roles in life beyond that of his 'mother'. She was an extremely attractive mature woman, cultured, vivacious, confident. Vandenbrook himself – sophisticated, charming, handsome, amusing, rich – was exactly the sort of man she would be attracted to. He could see that, understand that, all too clearly. He tried not to condemn her for it.

In Hastings, at the Pelham Hotel, the last hotel on their itinerary, the staff had been particularly helpful and concerned. Vandenbrook had stayed there four times and must have been a heavy tipper, Lysander thought. The young receptionist was full of anxious enquiries.

'I do hope everything was to Captain Vandenbrook's satisfaction. We'd be most upset if he was in any way displeased.'

'Not at all. Routine enquiry.'

'Has something gone wrong, sir?'

'Well,' Lysander improvised, 'something's gone missing – we're just retracing the captain's movements over the last few weeks and months.'

'Are you a colleague?' the receptionist asked. She was young, eighteen or nineteen, and had arranged her hair in a curious low swipe over her forehead that was not particularly flattering, Lysander thought, it made her look a bit simple, though she evidently wasn't. He suspected she had been subjected to the full Vandenbrook charm on many occasions.

'Yes, I am. We work together in London.'

'Please do tell him that his envelopes were all collected as specified. Never more than two days later.'

'I will, thank you.'

He said goodbye, promised to pass on the affectionate good wishes of the staff of the Pelham Hotel, Hastings, to the captain and tried to walk casually back out to the street. Tremlett was smoking by the Daimler, cap pushed to the back of his head. With his eye patch he looked unusually slovenly. He threw away his cigarette as Lysander strode up to him and readjusted his cap.

'Back to London, sir?'

'Back to Hythe.'

'Thought we were done for the day, sir.'

'The devil's work is never done, Tremlett. Quick as you like, please.'

They drove back up the coast to Hythe and returned to the Dene Hotel. Lysander walked into reception, experiencing the curious sensation of his life repeating itself. This was his third visit to the Dene Hotel in forty-eight hours.

'Good evening, sir. Welcome back.'

'I was just wondering . . . Did Captain Vandenbrook leave anything – in his room, perhaps?'

'Oh, you mean the envelope. I should have said this morning. Usually a porter from the station collects it.'

The receptionist reached under his counter and drew out a large buff manila envelope. On the front was written, 'Capt. C. Vandenbrook – to be collected.'

Lysander thanked the clerk and went into the saloon bar. It was quiet – one old man smoking a pipe in a corner and reading a newspaper. Lysander felt a coldness fall from the nape of his neck over his shoulders and back, as if he were standing in an icy draught. Mysteriously, the wound in his thigh began to ache, suddenly, a kind of burning. He knew what the envelope would contain. He ripped it open with his thumb and began to read.

'145 thou six inch howitz shells to Béthune. 65 wagons-under-load at Le Mans. Repair of telegraph lines Hazebrouk, Lille, Orchies, Valenciennes. New standard gauge line Gezaincourt-

Albert. Gun spur engineer store depots Dernancourt. 12 permanent ambulance trains Third Army Second Army.'

He turned to the next page. It went on and on. He carefully placed the three sheets of paper back into the envelope, folded it longways and slipped it in his jacket pocket. He ordered a large brandy and tried to empty his mind. He concentrated on one fact alone, it was enough – for the moment further speculation was a waste of time. He had found his Andromeda.

9. Autobiographical Investigations

I DECIDED, FOR THE moment, to tell no one and do nothing. Something was violently and differently wrong here – not least the presence of my mother. I had opened the envelope expecting to see the usual columns of figures as in the previous six Glockner letters, but instead saw pages of close-written factual prose – all the raw intelligence that Vandenbrook's role in the Directorate could provide. Not for the first time in this whole affair I felt myself wantonly adrift – seeing a few details but making no connection – and also consumed with the feeling that invisible strings were being pulled by a person or persons unknown and that I was attached to their ends. I needed time to take this new information in, time to deliberate, and I realized I had to be very careful over what my own future movements and decisions were. Perhaps it was the moment for me to go on the offensive, myself. Certain facts needed to be established before I could return to Munro and Massinger with my astounding discoveries. The first course of action was to confront Vandenbrook and see what explanation he would fabricate about the contents of his envelope. Then there was the urgent need to have a conversation with my mother.

★ ★ ★

John Bensimon's beard has turned quite grey since I last saw him in Vienna. He's put on some weight also, yet there's something strangely diminished about him, I feel, though on reflection it was perhaps the fact that it was England where we eventually met again that was responsible. To be a psychoanalyst practising in Vienna, with your smart consulting rooms just a few blocks away from Dr Freud's, was a more dramatic and self-enhancing state of affairs than showing your patient into a converted bedroom at the back of a terraced house in Highgate.

Bensimon seemed genuinely pleased to see me, I sensed — perhaps I came trailing clouds of his former glory — and he shook my hand warmly, even though I had knocked on his front door unannounced at the end of the afternoon. He introduced me to his wife, Rachel — a demure, timid woman — and his twin daughters, Agatha and Elizabeth, before he showed me up to his study with a view through the windows of the sooty backs of terraced houses and the long thin gardens that trailed scruffily from them, containing the usual assortment of various-sized, dilapidated sheds that haunt the cluttered ends of these city plots, with their blistered tar-paper roofs, broken windows and creosoted weatherboarding, washing lines and brimming rainwater barrels.

He still had his desk, his turned-away couch and armchair and, I was glad to see, the silver African bas-relief from Wasagasse.

'Not quite the same,' he said, as if reading my thoughts. 'But we must try to do the best with what we have.'

'How's business?' I asked.

'Slow, let's say,' he conceded with a rueful smile. 'People in England haven't yet realized how much they need us. It's not at all like Vienna.' He offered me the couch or the armchair. 'Is this a social visit, or can I help you professionally?'

I told him that I wanted to reinstate our old relationship — perhaps a weekly consultation, I said, going to the armchair. I sat down and focussed on the familiar fantastic beasts and monsters, for a moment enjoying the illusion that I was still in 1913 and nothing had happened to me since. In a very real sense, the disturbing thought came to me, I had changed enormously, irrevocably – I was a different person.

'Is it the old problem?' he asked. 'I still have all your files.'

'No, that seems well and truly solved, happily,' I said. 'My new problem is that I can't sleep at night. Or, rather, that I don't want to sleep at night because I always seem to dream the same dream.'

I told him my dream – the recurring jumbled experience of my night in no man's land that always culminated with my bombing of the sap and the image of the two torchlit faces looking up at me – the man with the moustache and the fair-haired boy.

'What happens next?' he asked.

'I wake up. Usually my face is wet with tears, though I don't recall weeping in the dream. I'm taking chloral hydrate – it's the only thing that makes me sleep the night through.'

'How long have you been taking that?'

'Some months – since Switzerland,' I said without thinking.

'Oh, you've been to Switzerland. How interesting. Were you there long?'

'A matter of days.'

'Right.' Discreet silence. 'Well, we'd better take you off the chloral – its long-term consequences can be rather drastic.'

'What do you mean?'

'You can become over-dependent on it. Its effects can be disturbing. You can – how shall I put it? – you begin to lose your grip on reality.'

'Whatever reality is . . . Sometimes I want nothing more than to lose my grip on reality. I just want to get to sleep at night.'

'That's what everyone says. And then . . .'

'Well – perhaps we could try hypnosis once more.'

'Actually, I think this is a perfect opportunity for Parallelism. But let's take you off the chloral first.'

He wrote me out a prescription for another 'somnifacient' and told me that his fee in England was two guineas an hour. We made an appointment for the following week. Cheap at the price, I thought, suddenly hugely relieved that I'd come to see him. I believed that Dr Bensimon could cure me of anything. Well, almost anything.

Talking of which, I told him as I left that I had seen Hettie Bull again and his face darkened.

'It's none of my business, but I'd have nothing to do with that young woman, Mr Rief,' he said. 'She's very dangerous, very unstable.'

This evening I was leaving the Annexe when I heard a shout, 'Rief! I say! Over here!' I looked round to see a man standing on the other side of the Embankment, leaning on the river wall. I crossed the roadway and saw that it was Jack Fyfe-Miller – but dressed as a stevedore in a flat cap with a scarf at his throat, moleskin trousers and heavy boots. We shook hands and I looked him over, professionally.

'Almost convincing,' I said. 'But you need some dirt under your nails – rubbed into your cuticles. You've got the hands of a curate.'

'The expert speaks.'

'Black boot polish,' I advised. 'Lasts all day.'

'Where're you headed?' he asked, staring at me with his usual strange intensity.

'Walking back to my hotel.'

'Ah, hotel life. Lucky for some.'

'There's nothing special about it. A small hotel in Pimlico – very average.'

'Have you got a girl, Rief?'

'What? No, not really. I used to be engaged to be married, once upon a time . . .'

'When I find my girl I'll get married – but she has to be spot-on right for me. Hard, that.'

I was inclined to agree, but said nothing as we walked along in silence for a while, Fyfe-Miller doubtless preoccupied with thoughts of his spot-on girl. From time to time he kicked at the fallen leaves on the pavement with his hobnails like a sulky adolescent, scuffing the stone and sending sparks flying. We walked under the railway bridge that led to Charing Cross and up ahead I saw the grand château-esque rooftops of Whitehall Court. I wondered if that was where he had come from, and perhaps the sight of the building and memories of our last meeting there stirred him as he suddenly became animated again and stopped me.

'Any sign of Andromeda? Any news?' he asked abruptly.

'Ah, no. But I think I'm getting close.'

'Getting close, eh?' He smiled. 'Hard on Andromeda's trail.'

Not for the first time I wondered if Fyfe-Miller were entirely sane.

'It's a question of narrowing the investigation down,' I said, playing for time. 'Analysing exactly who had access to that particular information.'

'Don't take too long, Rief, or your precious Andromeda may fly the coop.' At which point he took his hat off, gave me a mocking theatrical bow and then turned back the way we had come, shouting at me, over his shoulder, 'Boot polish under the fingernails, I'll remember that!'

I wandered back to The White Palace thinking about what he had said. It was a fair point, actually – I couldn't take my own sweet time – Vandenbrook could easily grow suspicious. Was this some kind of a warning I'd been given? Had Munro and Massinger ordered Fyfe-Miller to turn up the pressure on me? . . . I bought the *Evening News* and read that Blanche Blondel had opened at the Lyceum the previous night in *The Conscience of the King* to triumphant acclaim. Blanche – perhaps I'd pop in a note at the stage door . . . Fyfe-Miller had inadvertently reminded me of her and I thought it might be a good moment to see her again.

10. The History of Unintended Consequences

LYSANDER DID SOME QUICK research on Christian Vandenbrook's life and background. Vandenbrook had been caught up in the mass retreat from Mons in the first hectic weeks of the war and had been knocked unconscious by an artillery explosion that left him in a coma for three days. He suffered thereafter from periodic bleeding from the ears and his sense of balance left him for some months. He was declared unfit for active service and joined the General Staff in London. Lysander wondered how this agreeable move had come about, then he discovered that Vandenbrook's father-in-law was Brigadier-General Walter McIvor, the Earl of Ballatar, hero of the Battle of Waitara River in the Maori Wars in New Zealand. Vandenbrook was married to the earl's younger child, his daughter, Lady Emmeline, and they had two daughters themselves, Amabel and Cecilia. A very well-connected man, then, married into wealth and prestige. That explained how he achieved the grand house in Knightsbridge and the other quietly munificent trappings of his life on a captain's pay. But did it explain why he should choose to betray his country? Or why he was having an affair with Anna, now the dowager Lady Faulkner? Obviously the sooner he confronted Vandenbrook the sooner answers to these questions might ensue.

But he felt a kind of inertia seize him as he wondered what the outcome of these next actions and investigations would be – and felt the near-irresistible urge to procrastinate. He knew that the moment he laid out his evidence in front of Vandenbrook everything would change – not just for Vandenbrook but for himself, also. And, perhaps, for his mother. But all history is the history of unintended consequences, he said to himself – there's nothing you can do about it.

At the end of the day Lysander strolled along the Directorate's corridors towards Vandenbrook's office, feeling more than somewhat nervous and on edge. Vandenbrook was dictating a letter to his secretary and waved him to a chair. There was a green plant in a worked brass pot in one corner, a Persian rug on the floor, and on the wall, hung a nineteenth-century portrait of a whiskered dragoon with his hand on the pommel of his mighty sabre.

'– Whereupon,' Vandenbrook was saying, 'we would be most grateful for your prompt and detailed responses. I have the honour to remain, obedient servant, etcetera, etcetera. Thank you, Miss Whitgift.' His secretary left.

'Applying leather boot to lazy arse,' he said to Lysander with a wink. 'What can I do for you, Rief?'

'I wonder if we might have a discreet word, in private.'

'"Discreet"? "Private"? Don't like the sound of that, oh, no,' he said with a chuckle, taking his overcoat off the back of the door. 'I'm heading home – why don't you come with me? That way we can have a proper drink and still be "private".'

They took a taxi back to Knightsbridge, Vandenbrook explaining that his wife and daughters had gone to the country – 'to Inverswaven,' he said, as an aside, as if Lysander should know where and of what he was talking. Lysander nodded and safely said, 'Lovely time of year.' He was feeling surprisingly tense but was acting very calm, and he thanked his profession once again for the trained ability to feign this sort of ease and confidence even when he was suffering from its opposite. He offered Vandenbrook a cigarette, lit his and his own with a flourish, flicked the match out of the window and kept up – in a loud, sure voice – a banal flow of conversation about London, the weather, the traffic, the last Zeppelin raid, how the blackout was a risible farce – 'What's the point of painting the tops of street lights black? It's the pool of light they cast that you see from up in the air. Farcical. Risible.' Vandenbrook picked up the mood and the two of them bantered their way west across London. Vandenbrook asked him what he recommended at the theatre. Lysander said he simply had to see Blanche Blondel in *The Conscience of the King*. Vandenbrook said he would pay good money to hear Blanche Blondel read an infantry training manual – and so the two of them chatted on until they found themselves in Knightsbridge in no time at all.

Vandenbrook's butler served them both brandy and sodas and they settled down in the large drawing room on the first floor. It was a little over-furnished, Lysander thought, a grand piano taking up rather too much of one corner of the room and thereby making the rest of the furniture seem jammed together. There were many vases filled with flowers, he saw, as if someone were seriously ill upstairs, and heavy gilt-framed paintings on the walls of Highland scenes in various seasons – perhaps painted around Inverswaven, he surmised.

'I think you'd better have your discreet word with me,' Vandenbrook said, not smiling for once. 'The suspense is affecting my liver.'

'Of course,' Lysander said, standing and taking the envelope out of his inside pocket, unfolding it and handing it to Vandenbrook. 'This was yours – "Capt. C. Vandenbrook – To be collected."'

He could see his shock, suddenly visibly present. His lips pursed, the tendons on his neck flexed, his Adam's apple bobbing above the knot of his tie.

'There are some sheets of paper inside,' Lysander added.

Vandebrook drew the pages half out, glanced at them and shoved them back in again. His eyes turned, to fix themselves on the painting above the fireplace – a stag on some moorland hill, mists swirling.

'Where did you get this?' he asked, his voice suddenly a little shrill.

'Where you left it – the Dene Hotel, Hythe.'

Vandenbrook hung his head and began to sob – a low keening sound, like an animal's pain. Then he began to shake and rock back and forward. Lysander saw his tears fall on to the manila envelope on his lap, staining it. Then Vandenbrook toppled off his chair, slowly, and fell face forward, pressing his brow into the pile of the carpet, making a grinding, moaning noise as if some deep agonizing internal ache were forcing the sound from between his clenched teeth.

Lysander was shocked, himself. He hadn't seen a man collapse so abjectly and so suddenly ever before. It was as if Vandenbrook had become instantly dehumanized, changing into a form of atavistic suffering unit that precluded any reasoning, any sentience.

Lysander helped him to his feet – now absurdly conscious of their situation, two uniformed English officers in a Knightsbridge drawing room, one a spy-hunter and the other the sobbing spy he had hunted and caught – and yet every instinct in him was concerned and humane. Vandenbrook was a man *in extremis*, gasping and snuffling, hardly able to stand.

Lysander sat him down and found some crystal decanters in an unlocked tantalus on a table beside the grand piano and poured him an inch-deep draught of some amber fluid. Vandenbrook took a gulp, coughed loudly and seemed to compose himself, his breathing more measured, his sobbing ceased. He wiped his eyes on his sleeve and stood up, taking some paces towards the fireplace and back. It struck Lysander that, should Vandenbrook attack him, he had no defensive weapon to hand – but Vandenbrook seemed docile, cowed: no threat at all.

He sat down again, smoothed his jacket, smoothed his hair and cleared his throat.

'What're you going to do?' he asked, his voice still quavery and frightened.

'I have to give you up. I'm very sorry.'

'That's why you appeared at the Directorate, didn't you? To find me.'

'To find whoever was passing information to the enemy.'

Vandenbrook started to sob quietly again.

'I knew this would happen,' he said. 'I knew someone like you would come one day.' He looked Lysander full in the face. 'I'm not a traitor.'

'We'll let the courts decide –'

'I'm being blackmailed.'

He asked Lysander to follow him and they went up half a flight of stairs to a small mezzanine room off a landing. This was his 'study', Vandenbrook explained – some bookshelves, a small oak partners' desk with many narrow drawers and a green-shaded reading lamp. In a corner was a large jeweller's safe, the size of a tea-chest. Vandenbrook crouched by it and turned its combination. He opened the door, reached in and removed an envelope, handing it to Lysander. The address said simply, 'Captain Vandenbrook, Knightsbridge'.

'It's always put through the letterbox,' Vandenbrook explained, 'in the middle of the night.'

Lysander lifted the flap and drew out a photograph and two pages of grubby, typewritten paper. The photograph was of a young girl – ten or eleven, he thought, staring blankly at the camera. Her hair was thick and greasy and the cotton blouse she wore seemed too big for her. Around her neck, incongruously, was a single rope of fine pearls.

'I have a problem,' Vandenbrook said, weakly. 'A personal failing, a vice. I visit prostitutes.'

'You're saying this girl is a prostitute?'

'Yes. So is her mother.'

'How old is the girl?'

'I'm not sure. Nine. Eleven . . .'

Lysander looked at Vandenbrook as he stood by his big safe, hunched, swaying, looking at the floor.

'Good god,' Lysander said flatly. 'This girl is younger than your daughters.'

'It's not something I take any pride in,' Vandenbrook said, his voice regaining some of its old arrogance. 'It's a terrible weakness in me. I confess – fully.' He opened a cigarette box on his desk, took out and lit a cigarette.

'Have you ever been to the East End of our great city?' Vandenbrook asked. 'Down by Bow and Shoreditch, those sort of places. Well, if you've got a little bit of spare cash you can get anything you want. Little boys and little girls, dwarfs and giants, freaks of nature, animals. Anything you can imagine.'

'Tell me about the blackmail.'

'I used to visit this girl – with her mother's compliance – once a month or so,' he said. 'I became fond of her. She was unusually unconcerned by what I asked her to . . .' He stopped himself. 'Anyway, out of affection for her I gave her a pearl necklace. That was my mistake. It was in a box, there was the jeweller's name, it was traced back to me. Her mother, a conniving, evil person – she wrote the deposition – now knew my name and who I was.' He sat down on the edge of the desk, suddenly looking exhausted. 'About a year ago, the end of last year, 1914, this envelope arrived with precise instructions. I was to pass on all the information I was party to at the Directorate. Everything I knew – movement of stores, munitions, construction of railway branch lines, and so on. If I didn't comply then this photograph and the girl's testimony would be sent to the Secretary of State for War, my commanding officer, my wife and my father-in-law.' He gave a weak smile. 'I assume you know who my father-in-law is.'

'Yes, I do.'

'Then you'll understand. A little. So I wrote down what I could find out and, as directed by the instructions, left the envelope to be collected by a person unknown in a particular hotel.'

'The same hotel?'

'Various hotels on the south coast. No doubt you've visited them all.'

Lysander looked at the girl's blank face and read a few lines of the deposition. 'The captin use to come and akse me to sit on his nee . . . He took my close off and then he told me to opin my legs as wide as I could . . . Then he woud wash me with a flannel and warm water and tell me to . . .'

Vanderbrook looked at him as he scanned the page, his eyes

dead, the dashing uptilted blond moustache like a bad prop, the affectation of a different man altogether.

'Did you try to find this woman and her daughter?'

'Yes, of course. I hired a private detective agency. But they were long gone from their usual haunts. They obviously sold me on. To someone. Who may have sold me on again. Many men are trapped in this way. You wouldn't believe it. There's a whole trade in this blackmail, passed along, from one person to another –'

'Many?'

'We're all capable of anything,' he said. 'Given the means and the opportunity.'

'The pervert's quick and easy excuse,' Lysander replied, coldly. 'Since time immemorial.'

'I don't excuse myself, Rief, as it happens. I hate myself, I loathe my . . . my sexual inclinations . . .' he said with real feeling. 'Just spare me your sanctimonious moral judgement.'

'Continue with your story.'

'Whenever a copy of this photograph and the witness statement arrived it was a sign that I should supply more information. I was also told which hotel I should leave it at. Another one came two weeks ago. The Dene Hotel, Hythe – the one you have.'

'How do you encode it?'

'What're you talking about?'

'Your previous letters were all in code. This one wasn't.'

'What code? I just write down the facts and figures and leave them at the hotel.'

Lysander looked at him, feeling a new panic. Somehow he knew at once Vandenbrook wasn't lying. But then he checked himself. The man did nothing but lie, it was his *raison d'être*. However, he thought on, furiously investigating the ramifications of this news – if Vandenbrook didn't transform the data into code then who did? If Vandenbrook was lying, then why did he not encode the last letter? There must be another Andromeda – or else

Vandenbrook was playing another game with him. He began to feel his brain cloud.

'What should I do, Rief?'

'Do nothing – go to work, act as normal,' Lysander said, thinking – this would buy him some time. He needed more time now, definitely, the complications were multiplying rapidly.

'What's going to happen to me?' Vandenbrook asked.

'You should hang as a traitor, if there's any justice – but perhaps you can save yourself.'

'Anything,' he said fiercely. 'I'm a victim, Rief. I didn't want to do this but if my . . . my peccadillo was to become known . . . I just couldn't face that, you see. The shame, the dishonour. You've got to help me. You've got to find out who's doing this to me.'

Lysander folded up the deposition and the photograph and slipped them inside his jacket pocket.

'You can't take that,' Vandenbrook said, outraged.

'Don't be stupid. I can do anything I like as far as you're concerned.'

'Sorry. Sorry. Yes, of course.'

'Go to work as usual. Try to act normally, unaffectedly. I'll contact you when I need you.'

11. The Sensation That Nothing Had Changed

IT WAS STRANGE BEING in the Green Drawing Room again, Lysander thought, walking around, letting his fingertips graze the polished surfaces of the side tables, picking up a piece of sheet music and laying it on a window seat. Again, he felt this sensation that nothing had changed and indulged it, letting it linger in him. He was still an adolescent, the century was new, they had just moved to Claverleigh and in a minute or two he would see his mother come into the room, younger, pretty, frozen in time, years back. But he knew how fast the world was spinning, faster than ever. Time was on the move in this modern world, fast as a thoroughbred racehorse, galloping onwards, regardless of this war – this war was just a consequence of that acceleration – and everything was changing as a result, not just in the world around him but in human consciousness, also. Something old was going, and going fast, disappearing, and something different, something new, was inevitably taking its place. That was the concept he should keep in mind, however much it disturbed him and however he found he wanted to resist it. Perhaps he should bring it up with Bensimon – this new obsession he had with change and his resistance to it – and see if he could make any sense of his confusion.

His mother swept through the door and kissed him three times on both cheeks in the continental manner. She was wearing a pistachio-green teagown and her hair was different, swept up on both sides and held in a loose bun at the back of her head, soft and informal.

'I like your hair like that,' he said.

'I like that you notice these things, my darling son.'

She went to the wall and turned the bell handle.

'I need tea,' she said. 'Strong tea. English fuel.'

He had one of those revelations and understood at once why a man would be irresistibly drawn to her – the casual, ultra-confident beauty coupled with her vivacity. He could understand why a Christian Vandenbrook would be ensnared.

Tea was served by a maid and they sat down. She stared at him over the top of her held teacup, her big eyes looking at him, watchfully.

'Do you know, I haven't seen you for ages,' she said. 'How are you? Fully recovered? I must say I do like you in your uniform.' She pointed. 'What're these?'

'Gaiters. Mother – I have to ask you a few rather pointed questions.'

'Me? "*Pointed*"? My goodness. On you go.'

He paused, feeling on the brink again, as if he were about to initiate a causal chain that could lead anywhere.

'Do you know an officer called Captain Christian Vandenbrook?'

'Yes. Very well. I deal with him all the time about Fund business.'

The Fund, Lysander thought, of course. The Claverleigh Hall War Fund. He relaxed ever so slightly – perhaps there was nothing in it after all.

'Did you see him at the Dene Hotel in Hythe three nights ago?'

'Yes. We had an appointment for dinner. Lysander, what's all this –'

'Forgive me for being so blunt and horribly obtuse and impolite but . . .' He paused, feeling sick. 'But – are you having an affair with Captain Vandenbrook?'

She laughed at that, genuinely, but her laughter died quickly.

'Of course not. How dare you suggest such a thing.'

He saw the real anger in her eyes and so closed his as he pressed on.

'You stayed in the same hotel as Captain Vandenbrook nine times in the past year.'

He heard her stand and he opened his eyes. She was looking out on the park through the high, many-paned window. It was drizzling, the light was fading – silvery, tarnished.

'Are you spying on me?'

'I'm spying on *him*. I was following him and I saw him meet you.'

'Why on earth are you spying on Captain Vandenbrook?'

'Because he's a traitor. Because he's been sending military secrets to Germany.'

This shocked her, he saw. She swivelled and stared at him alarmed.

'Captain Vandenbrook – I don't believe it . . . Are you sure?'

'I have the evidence to hang him.'

'I can't . . . How . . .' Her voice trailed off and then she said, incredulously, 'All we talk about is blankets, ambulances, pots of honey, village fêtes and nurses – how to spend the money I raise. I can't believe it.'

'Do you know that every time he meets you he leaves an envelope at the hotel to be collected?'

'No, of course not.'

'He's never asked you to deliver one of these envelopes?'

'Never. Honestly. Look, I met him because the War Office appointed him as the officer to liaise with the Fund when I started everything up. He was incredibly helpful.'

'He's a charming man.'

'He's even been here. Two – no, three times. We've had meetings here. Crickmay met him. He dined with us.'

'Here? He never mentioned it to me.'

'Why would he? I never mentioned you to him. I assume he hasn't the faintest idea that you're my son. That the man with the evidence to hang him is my son,' she added, a little bitterly. 'Or even that I have a son. For heaven's sake – all we talked about was the Fund.'

Lysander supposed that if you are an attractive woman in your very early fifties you don't advertise the fact that you have a son who is almost thirty. And it was true – nothing in Vandenbrook's demeanour, no sly implication or hint, had ever given away that he knew his mother was Lady Faulkner.

'Do you think I might have a drink?' he asked.

'Excellent idea,' she said and rang the bell for the footman who duly brought them a tray with two glasses, a bottle of brandy and a soda siphon. Lysander made their drinks and gave his mother hers. He took big gulps of his. Despite all the denials and the plausible explanations he had a very bad feeling about this connection with Vandenbrook. It was not a coincidence, he knew – there would be consequences. Fucking consequences, again.

'May I smoke?'

'I'll join you,' she said. Lysander took out his cigarette case, lighting his mother's cigarette and then his own.

'Why are you spying on Vandenbrook?' she asked. 'I mean, why you in particular.' She stubbed her cigarette out – she was never much of a smoker. 'You're a soldier, aren't you?'

'I'm attached to this department in the War Office. We're trying to find this traitor. He's causing terrible damage.'

'Well, you've found him, haven't you?'

'Vandenbrook is only handing over information because he's being blackmailed, it seems. So he claims.'

'Blackmailed for what?'

'It's very . . . unpleasant. Very shaming.' Lysander wondered how much to tell her. 'He'd be ruined, totally, if it ever came out what he'd done – marriage, career, family. He'd go to prison.'

'Goodness.' He saw that the vagueness of his reply was more disturbing than anything explicit. She looked at him again. 'So who's blackmailing him?'

'That's the problem – it looks very much as if you are.'

12. Autobiographical Investigations

PERHAPS I SPOKE TOO unthinkingly, too bluntly. She seemed very shaken all of a sudden – not incredulous, any more – as if the shocking but irrefutable logic of the set-up had struck her just as it had struck me. I made her another brandy and soda and told her to go over everything again for me, once more. It started with the first meeting with Vandenbrook at the War Office in September 1914 and subsequent regular contact followed as the Claverleigh Hall War Fund began to generate significant amounts of money. He first came to Claverleigh in early 1915 shortly after his transfer to the Directorate of Movements.

'Why didn't he pass on the War Fund to someone else? The work in the Directorate is frantic.'

'He asked if he could stay on board if he could,' she said. 'He was very impressed by what we were doing, he said, and very concerned that any hand-over to someone else would be detrimental. So I agreed without hesitation. I was very happy – we got on very well – he was extremely efficient. In fact I think I even suggested we meet when he came to Folkestone on business – just to make it easier for him. The first hotel I stayed in was at Sandwich. I offered to motor over.'

'Did you meet him in London?'

'Yes. Half a dozen times – when I went up to town.' She paused. 'I won't deny I enjoyed our meetings . . . Crickmay wasn't well and for me these nights away were, you know, a little escape. Of course, he's an attractive, amusing man, Captain Vandenbrook. And I think we both enjoyed the . . . The mild flirtation. The mildest. But nothing happened. Never. Not even after Crickmay died.'

'I completely understand,' I said. 'I believe you. I'm just trying to see things from his point of view.'

'It's because I'm Austrian, of course,' she said, flatly, almost sullenly. 'I've just realized – that's the key. That's why they'll suspect me. Instantly.' He felt the depression seize her, almost physically, as her shoulders seemed to bow. 'When they connect me with him . . . The Austrian woman.'

'I'm half Austrian too, remember,' I said, worriedly. 'Everything's too neat, too pat . . .'

'What're you going to do?'

'Nothing yet – I have to dig a little more.'

'What about me?'

'Carry on as if nothing has happened.'

She stood up, new anxiety written on her face. She seemed as troubled as I'd ever seen her.

'Have you told anyone about Vandenbrook and what you discovered?'

'No. Not yet. I don't want the rest of them blundering in. I have to be very careful what I say.'

She went over to the window again – it was now quite dark and I could hear the nail-tap of steady rain on the glass.

'You're making things worse for yourself by not telling anyone,' she said, quietly and steadily. 'Aren't you?'

'It's complicated. Very. I don't want you involved in this mess,' I said. 'That's why I need a bit more time.'

She turned and held out her arms as if she wanted to be embraced so I went to her and she hugged herself to me.

'I won't let you be dragged down by this,' she said softly. 'I won't.'

'Mother – please – don't be so dramatic. Nobody's going to be "dragged down". You've done nothing – so don't even think about it. Whoever's blackmailing Vandenbrook has been very clever. Very. But I'll find a way, don't worry. He can be outsmarted.'

'I hope so.' She squeezed my shoulders. I enjoyed having her in my arms. We hadn't held each other like this since my father had died. I kissed her forehead.

'Don't worry. I'll get him.'

I hoped I sounded confident because I wasn't, particularly. I knew that as soon as I told the Vandenbrook story to Munro and Massinger then everything would emerge rapidly and damagingly – the Fund, the meetings, the hotels, the dinners. To my alarm, as I began to think through this sequence of events, I thought I could see a way in which even I could be implicated. Which reminded me.

'I'd better go,' I said, releasing her. 'I just need one thing. You remember I gave you that libretto, the one with the illustration on the cover of the girl. *Andromeda und Perseus.*'

'Oh, yes,' she said, with something of her old wry cynicism returning. 'How could I forget? The mother of my grandchild with no clothes on.' She moved to the door. 'It's in my office.' She paused. 'What's the news of the little boy?'

'Lothar? He's well, so I'm told – living with a family in Salzburg.'

'Lothar in Salzburg . . . What about his mother?'

'I believe she's back in England,' I said evasively.

She gave me a knowing look and went to fetch the libretto. I glanced at my wristwatch – I was still in good time to catch the last train to London from Lewes. But when my mother came back in I could see at once she was unusually flustered.

'What is it?' I said. 'What's wrong?'

'It's the strangest thing. Your libretto – it's missing.'

Sitting in the Lewes–London train. Brain-race, thought-surge. Her office is a study on the top floor where she does her charity administration. Two desks for secretaries, a couple of white wooden bookshelves with a few books and a mass of files slid into them. She said she was convinced this was where she'd put the libretto. We searched – nothing. Books go missing, I said, it wasn't important. It was a book I gave to her almost eighteen months ago, after all. Anything could have happened to it.

As I write this, a man sitting opposite me is reading a novel and, from time to time, picking his nose, examining what he has mined from his nasal cavities and popping the sweetmeat into his mouth. Amazing the secrets we reveal about ourselves when we think we're not being observed. Amazing the secrets we can reveal when we know we are.

Back in my room at The White Palace I find a small bundle of post is awaiting me. One envelope contains a list from a letting agency of four furnished mansion flats, available for short lease, in the Strand and Charing Cross area. I'm excited by the prospect of having my own place, again – and of Hettie being able to stay with me there, incognito and unembarrassed. Another telegram, to my surprise, is from Massinger. He suggests a rendezvous in a Mayfair tearoom at four o'clock tomorrow. The Skeffington Tearooms in Mount Street.

Later. I've spent the last hour drinking whisky from my hip-flask and writing down lists of names in various configurations and placements, joining them with dotted lines and double-headed arrows, placing some in parentheses and underlining others three times. At the end of this fruitless exercise I still find myself wondering why Massinger could possibly want to talk to me.

13. 3/12 Trevelyan House, Surrey Street

LYSANDER CHOSE THE SECOND of the four furnished flats he was shown by the breathless, corpulent man from the letting agency. It was on the third floor of a mansion block in Surrey Street, off the Strand, called Trevelyan House: one bedroom, a small sitting room, a modern bathroom and a kitchen – though the kitchen was no more than a cupboard with a sink and an electric two-ring heater and a bleak view of the white ceramic bricks of the central air-well. In truth, any of the flats would have served his rudimentary purpose perfectly well but there was something newer about the curtains, the carpets and the furniture in number 3/12 that was immediately appealing – no greasy edge to the drapery, no flattened worn patch before the fire or cigarette burns on the mantelpiece. All he needed now, he felt, was something bright and primary coloured – a painting, a couple of new lampshades, cushions for the sofa – to make it more personal, to make it his rather than everybody's.

He signed the lease, paid a month's deposit and was given two sets of keys. He had his linen and his household goods from Chandos Place in store and would hire a porter to bring them around to Trevelyan House right away. He could walk to the Annexe from here in under ten minutes, he reckoned – another unlooked-for bonus in his and Hettie's 'love nest'. He felt the old excitement mount in him at the prospect of seeing her again – at the prospect of being naked in a bed with her again – and noted how the promise of unlimited sensual pleasure blotted out all rational, cautious advice that he might equally have given himself. Hettie – Vanora – was a married woman, now; moreover, her new husband was a jealous and angry man. Hoff and Lasry: two men with fiery, irrational tempers, quick to take the slightest offence – what drew Hettie to these types? Also, the current complications of Lysander's own life should have dictated against the introduction of new circumstances that would add to them. 'Gather ye rosebuds while ye may,' he said to himself, as if that old adage took care of all sensible matters. He had a new home and, perhaps more importantly, only he knew its address.

The Skeffington Tearooms in Mount Street were unabashed about their striving for gentility, Lysander saw as he approached. Elaborately worked lace curtains screened the tea-drinkers from the curious gaze of passers-by; the name of the establishment was written in black glass in a very flourished white copperplate, tightly coiled curlicues ending in gilt flowerlets or four-leafed clovers. A serving maid in a tiny bonnet and a long white pinny was sweeping the pavement outside. It didn't seem a Massinger type of place at all.

Inside was a single large long room lit by crystal chandeliers and lined on three walls by semi-circular maroon velour Chesterfield booths. Two rows of highly polished tables with neat doilies and a centrally placed flower arrangement filled the rest of the area. The hushed tinkle of silverware on crockery and a low murmur of discreet conversation greeted him. It was like entering a library, Lysander felt, with a library's implicit prohibitions against unnecessary noise – quiet footsteps, please, coughs and sneezes to be muffled, no laughter at all.

An unsmiling woman with a pince-nez checked that Massinger's name had been entered in the ledger and a summoned waitress led him across the room to a booth in the far corner. Massinger sat there, smoking, wearing a morning suit, of all things, and reading a newspaper. He looked up to see Lysander and did not smile, merely holding up the newspaper and pointing to a headline. 'English County Cricket to be abandoned in 1916.'

'Terrible business, what?' Massinger said. 'Where does that leave us? Shocking.'

Lysander agreed, sat down and ordered a pot of coffee – he didn't feel like tea; tea was not a drink to share with someone like Massinger.

'What do you want to see me about?' he asked as Massinger crushed his cigarette dead – with conspicuous force – in the ashtray, smoke snorting from his nostrils.

'I don't want to see you, Rief,' he said, looking up. He gestured. 'She does.'

Florence Duchesne stepped up to the table, as if she had suddenly materialized.

Lysander felt a lurch of instinctive alarm judder through him and had the immediate conviction that she was about to pull a revolver from her handbag and shoot him again. He stared at her – it was Florence Duchesne but a different woman from the one he'd last seen on the steamer on Lac Léman. The black weeds and the veil were gone. She had powder and lip rouge on her face and was wearing a magenta 'town suit' with a cut-away jacket and a hobble skirt and a little fichu at the neck of her silk blouse. She had a velvet Tam o' Shanter set on a slant on her head in a darker purple than the suit. It was as if Madame Duchesne's fashionable twin sister had walked in, not the melancholy widow who lived with the postmaster of Geneva.

She slipped into the booth beside him and, despite himself, Lysander flinched.

'I had to see you, Monsieur Rief,' she said in French, 'to explain and, of course, to apologize.'

Lysander looked at her, then Massinger, then back at her again, quite disorientated, unable to think what he could possibly say. Massinger stood up at this juncture and distracted them.

'I'll leave you two to talk. I'll see you later, Madame. Goodbye, Rief.'

Lysander watched him stride across the room to collect his top hat – he looked like a superior shop assistant, he thought. He turned back to Florence Duchesne.

'This is very, very strange for me,' he said, slowly. 'To be sitting here with someone who's shot me three times. Very strange . . . You were trying to kill me, I suppose.'

'Oh, yes. But you must understand that I was convinced you were working with Glockner. I was convinced you had killed Glockner also. And when you lied to me about the cipher-text – it seemed the final clue. And Massinger had ordered me not to take any risks – said you were possibly a traitor, even. Was I meant to let you step ashore at Evian and vanish? No. Especially with all the suspicions I had – it was my duty.'

'No, no. You were absolutely in the right.' The irony in his voice made it unusually harsh, like Massinger's throaty rasp. He recalled Massinger's schoolboy French blunder. She bowed her head.

'And yet . . .' She left the rest unspoken.

'I wonder if they serve alcohol in a place like this?' he asked, rhetorically. 'Probably not, far too plebeian. I need a powerful drink, Madame. I'm sure you understand.'

'We can go to a hotel, if you like. I do want to talk to you about something important.'

They paid and left. At the door to the tearoom she collected a dyed black musquash coat with a single button at the hip. Lysander held it open for her as she slipped her arms into the sleeves and smelled the strong pungent scent she wore. He thought back to their supper on the terrace of the Brasserie des Bastions in Geneva and how he'd noticed it then – thinking it an anomaly – but now he realized it was a trace of the real woman. A little clue. He glanced at her as they walked along the road in silence, heading for the Connaught Hotel.

They found a seat in the public lounge and Lysander ordered a large whisky and soda for himself and a Dubonnet for her. The drink calmed him and he felt his jumpiness subside. It was always amazing how one so quickly accustomed oneself to the strangest circumstances, he thought – here I am having a drink with a woman who tried to assassinate me. He looked across the table at her and registered his absence of anger, of outrage. All he saw was a very attractive woman in fashionable clothes.

'What're you doing in London?' he asked.

'Massinger has brought me out of Geneva. It was becoming too dangerous for me.'

She explained. Her contact in the German consulate – 'the man with the embarrassing letters' – had been arrested and deported to Germany. It would only be a matter of time before he gave her name up. 'So Massinger pulled me out, very fast.'

'I assume you're not a widow.'

'No. But it's a most effective disguise, I assure you. I've not been married, in fact.'

'What about your brother?'

'Yes, he's really my brother – and he's the postmaster in Geneva.' She smiled at him. 'Not everything is a lie.'

The smile disarmed him and he found himself unreflectingly taking in her looks – her strong curved nose, her clear blue eyes, the shadowed hollow at her throat between her collar-bones. He could forgive her, he supposed. In fact it was very easy – how absurd.

'How are you?' she asked. 'I mean, after the shooting.'

'I have seven scars to remember you by,' he said, showing her the stigma in his left palm. 'And my leg stiffens up sometimes.' He tapped his left thigh. 'But otherwise I'm pretty well. Amazingly.'

'Lucky I'm a bad shot,' she said, smiling ruefully. 'I can only say sorry, again. Imagine that I'm saying sorry to you all the time. Sorry, sorry, sorry.'

Lysander shrugged. 'It's over. I'm alive. You're here in London.' He raised his glass. 'I'm not being facetious – despite everything, I'm very pleased to see you.'

She seemed to relax finally – expiation had occurred.

'And you remembered I liked Dubonnet,' she said.

They looked at each other candidly.

'You like Dubonnet and you don't drink champagne.'

'And you used to be a famous actor.'

'An actor, certainly . . . You said you wanted to tell me something.'

She looked more serious now.

'My contact at the consulate told me an interesting detail – I obliged him to tell me an interesting detail – before he was arrested and taken away. They were paying funds to the person who sent the letters to Glockner. A lot of money, transferred through Switzerland.'

'I imagined money was the reason. Was there a name?'

'No.'

'You're sure?'

'This is all he said. But the money they sent was a lot. Already over two thousand pounds. It seems a lot for one man. I thought – maybe there is a cell. Maybe there are two, or three . . .'

Lysander wasn't surprised to have this confirmed but he feigned some perplexity – frowning, tapping his fingers.

'Have you told this to anyone else?'

'Not yet. I wanted to tell you first.'

'Not Massinger?'

'I think with Glockner dead he feels the matter is closed.'

'Could you keep this to yourself for a while? It would help me.'

'Of course.' She smiled at him again. 'Very happy to oblige, as they say.'

He sat back and crossed his legs.

'Are you going to stay in London now?'

'No,' she said. 'Massinger wants to put me into Luxembourg – to count troop trains. He wants me to become the special friend of a lonely old station master.'

'*La veuve Duchesne*, once more.'

'It's very effective – instant respect. People keep their distance. No one wants to trouble you in your terrible grief.'

'Why do you do it?'

'Why do *you*?' She didn't bother to let him reply. 'Massinger pays me very well,' she said, simply. 'I appreciate money because at one stage in my life I was without it. Completely. And life was not easy . . .' She put her glass down and turned it this way and that on its coaster. They were silent for a moment.

'How do you find Massinger?' she asked, still looking down.

'Difficult. He's a difficult personality.'

Now she looked him in the eye.

'I find it difficult to trust him entirely. He changes his mind – a lot.'

Was this a subtle warning, Lysander wondered. He decided to remain neutral.

'Massinger's worried about his job, his role. They want to shut down Geneva and Switzerland – concentrate on Holland.'

'I'm going to Luxembourg via Holland. I have to meet a man called Munro.'

'Munro runs Holland – I think. There's some rivalry, inevitably.'

'I could have gone to Luxembourg from Switzerland very easily. Do you think that's significant?'

'I don't know,' he said, honestly. He reflected that they shouldn't actually be talking to each other like this but he felt her constant doubts and suspicions were exactly like his. You thought you had possession of key facts, of certainties, but they disappeared and were facts and certainties no more.

'I'm just like you,' he said. 'Following instructions. Trying to think ahead. Be aware of potential problems. Trying not to slip up.' He smiled. 'Anyway, I wish you luck. I'd better go.' He rose to his feet and she did the same. She took a card out of her bag and handed it to him.

'I expect to be in London a few more days,' she said. 'It would be nice to see you again. I remember our dinner in Geneva – *un moment agréable.*'

He looked at her card – a card supplied by the hotel she was staying at, Bailey's Hotel, Gloucester Road. There was a telephone number.

'I'll telephone you,' he said, not really knowing why – or even if – he should try to see Florence Duchesne one more time. But somehow he didn't want this to seem like a final parting so he held out this prospect, at least, that they would meet again.

At the front door, outside on the pavement, they made their farewells. She was going to explore, she said, this was her first visit to London. They shook hands and Lysander felt the extra pressure as her squeeze on his fingers tightened and she looked him directly in the eye again. Was that a warning – was he to be careful? Or was it a covert reminder that she expected to be telephoned and would like to see him again? Lysander watched her walk away, the cut of her musquash coat making it sway to and fro, and he speculated about different short-term futures, courses of action, of how he had once imagined Florence Duchesne tipsy on champagne, naked, laughing . . . it didn't seem such a fantasy any more. He hailed a passing cab and asked to be taken to the Annexe.

He knew he would have to work late that night. Tremlett, with the aid of the magic letter from C.I.G.S., had managed to secure all of Osborne-Way's claims for travel and expenses that he had submitted to the War Office. The proviso for their release was that they could only be out of the building for one night.

Tremlett dumped the heavy ledger on his desk.

'Is Captain Vandenbrook in his office?' Lysander asked.

'Captain Vandenbrook is in Folkestone, sir. Back tomorrow morning.'

That was good, he thought – Vandenbrook carrying on as normal. 'Right,' he said to Tremlett. 'Bring me the War Diary and the travelling-claims-by-land dockets.'

He spent the next two hours going through Osborne-Way's claims and collating them with Vandenbrook's movements but there was no visible overlap. In fact Osborne-Way had been in France on at least two occasions when Lysander was sure that Glockner's letters had been left at hotels in Sandwich and Deal. One thing was clear, however – Osborne-Way had enjoyed himself in France. Nights in expensive restaurants in Amiens; a weekend in Paris at the Hôtel Meurice – on what business? – everything charged to the War Office and the British taxpayer. Frustrated, Lysander wondered if he could score some petty revenge and have Osborne-Way's extravagance brought to the attention of someone senior to him, a quiet word that might have the effect of –

He became aware of loud voices and hurrying feet in the corridor outside Room 205.

Tremlett knocked on the door and peered in. His eye patch was slightly askew.

'We're going up top, sir. Zeppelin coming over!'

Lysander unhooked his greatcoat from the back of the door and followed him out and up the stairs to the roof of the Annexe. Half a dozen people were gathered on the flat area by the lift housing staring westwards where the long lucent fingers of searchlights stiffly searched through the night sky, looking for the dirigible. There was the distant popping of anti-aircraft fire and every now and then a shrapnel star-shell burst high above them.

Lysander looked out over the night city, some seven storeys up from street level. To his eyes it could have been peacetime – motor cars and omnibuses, headlights gleaming, shop fronts lit beneath their awnings, ribbons of streetlamps casting their pearly glow.

Here and there were areas of approximate darkness but it was almost inviting, he imagined, to the captain of this airship somewhere overhead. Where shall I drop my bombs? Here? Or there? And, as if his thoughts had been read, the first searchlight found the Zeppelin and then another two joined it. Lysander's first thought was, my god, so huge – gigantic – and serenely beautiful. It was very high and moving forward steadily – how fast, he couldn't tell. The increasing noise from the artillery fire blocked out the sound of its engines as it seemed to float unaided above them, driven on by night winds rather than its motors.

Another gun, nearer, began to fire – *Pop! Pop! Pop!*

'That's the gun in Green Park,' Tremlett said in his ear, then shouted out into the darkness, 'Give 'em hell, lads!'

More cheers came up from the others on the roof as Lysander looked up at the Zeppelin, awestruck, he had to admit, at the vast lethal beauty of the giant silvery flying machine caught in the crossbeams of three searchlights, now almost overhead, it seemed.

'It's eight thousand feet up,' Tremlett said. 'At least.'

'Where are our planes? Why can't we shoot it down?'

'Do you know how long it takes one of our planes to climb to eight thousand feet, sir?'

'No. Not the faintest.'

'About forty minutes. He'll be long gone. Or else he'll drop ballast and jump up another thousand feet. Easy as pie.'

'How do you know all this, Tremlett?'

'My little brother's in the Royal Flying Corps. Stationed at Hainault. He's always – WOAH! FUCK ME! –'

The first bomb had exploded. Not far from the Embankment – a sudden violent wash of flame, then the shock wave and the flat crack of the explosion.

'That's the Strand,' Tremlett yelled. 'Fuckin' hell!'

Then there was a short series of explosions – *Blat! Blat! Blat!* – as bombs fell swiftly one after the other, Tremlett bellowing his commentary.

'They're going for the theatres! Fuckin' Ada! That's Drury Lane! That's Aldwych!'

Lysander felt a bolus of vomit rise in his throat. Blanche was in a play at the Lyceum. Jesus Christ. Wellington Street, corner of Aldwych. He held his watch up – it would be just about the interval now. He looked up to see the Zeppelin turn slowly, heading northwards, up towards Lincoln's Inn. There were more thumps as bombs fell, out of sight.

'Big fire there!' Tremlett yelled. 'Look, they got the Lyceum!'

Lysander turned and raced through the roof access door and pelted down the stairway. He burst out on to the Embankment – the noise of police bells and fire engines, whistles, shouts, all coming down from the Strand and, in the distance, the sound of even more bombs dropping. He ran up Carting Lane past the Hotel Cecil to the Strand. Here he could see the flames, tall as the buildings, a bright unnatural orange lighting the façades on Aldwych and Wellington Street. Gas, he thought, a gas main's gone up. People were rushing along the Strand towards the source of the fire. He pushed his way through them and sprinted up the slope of Exeter Street. There was a thick dust cloud here and all the street lights had been blown out. He turned the corner to see glass and bricks scattered on the road and the first fuming crater. The earth itself seemed to be burning at its centre and fringes. Three bodies lay huddled at the side of the road, like tramps sleeping. The fire was blazing garishly at the end of the street and he ran towards it. He could see it was at the side of the Lyceum itself, the gas main billowing flames forty feet high. Bells, shouts, screams. A woman in a sequinned gown stumbled out of the darkness past him, whimpering, the frayed stump of her right arm twitching at her shoulder. A man in an evening suit lay on his back, both arms thrown wide, not a mark visible on him.

Half a gable-end had come down here and the way forward was blocked by a wall of tumbled bricks six feet high. He could hear women screaming and the shouts of police in Wellington Street bellowing, 'Keep back! Keep back!' He scrabbled up the brickwork and slipped, bashing his elbow. He tried again on the north side of Exeter Street where he could at least gain some purchase from the opposite façades. Glass shone here, glittering shards of orange-diamond jewels – every window in the street blasted out. He was thinking of the Lyceum, where the dressing rooms were – his father had played there all the time in the eighties. Maybe it hadn't been the interval – Blanche would have been safer on stage – but he hadn't seen the wretched play yet so he had no idea where she would have been.

He hauled his way up the sliding brick wall. At the top the gas flare made his shadow monstrously huge on the building front, flickering and undulating. The crater was immense, ten feet deep. More bodies and bits of bodies were scattered about it – the pub at the corner, The Bell, was ablaze. People went to the pub from the Lyceum at the interval – the bomb had caught it at its fullest. Beyond the blaze he could see the police forming a cordon to keep the appalled but curious onlookers away from the soaring flames of the venting gas main.

He heard bricks falling to the road, a sharp egg-cracking sound, and looked up just in time to see a window embrasure topple outwards and drag down the half wall beneath it. He flung himself out of the way and fell awkwardly down the slope to the pavement, winded. Lights were flashing in front of his eyes as he struggled to regain his breath. He hauled himself to his knees and saw a figure a few yards away across the street, standing still in the shadows, apparently looking straight at him.

'Give us a hand, will you?' Lysander shouted, wheezily.

The figure didn't move. A man with a hat and the collar of his coat folded up – impossible to see anything more with the street lights gone. The man was standing at the right angle of Exeter Street where it turned down to the Strand, where he'd seen the first dead bodies.

Lysander rose to his feet shakily, perturbed, and the figure stayed where it was, apparently staring directly at him. What was going on? Why was he just staring, doing nothing? The gas main flared again and for a moment more light was cast – the figure raised his hand to shield his face.

'I see you!' Lysander yelled – not seeing him but wanting to provoke him, somehow. 'I know who you are! I see you!'

The figure immediately turned and ran around the corner – disappeared.

There was no point in chasing, Lysander thought, and anyway, he had to find Blanche. He climbed up and slithered down the other side of the brick pile and ran up to the stage door of the Lyceum. A policeman was sheltering inside.

'The actors! I've a friend –'

'Can't come in here, sir. Everyone's gathered down on the Strand.'

Lysander realized there was no way through by Wellington Street so he had to go back the way he'd come. He picked his way cautiously up the brick wall and saw now that there were policemen and ambulances collecting the bodies. Safe. He ran past them and down to the Strand heading for Aldwych. There was a big surging crowd here. The Strand Theatre opposite had emptied and the streets were full of well-dressed theatre-goers milling about, smoking and chatting excitedly – bow ties, feathers, silk, jewels. He looked around him. Where were the actors?

'Lysander! I don't believe it!'

It was Blanche, a mug of coffee in one hand, a cigarette in the other. Someone's overcoat was thrown around her shoulders like a cape.

He felt weak finding her like this, unmanned suddenly. He went towards her and kissed her cheek, tasting greasepaint. In the rippling light from the gas main she looked almost grotesque in her white Regency wig – a painted loon with dark, arched eyebrows, a beauty spot and red lips.

'Were you caught in the blast?'

He looked down at himself. He was covered in brick dust, the left knee of his trousers was ripped and flapping, he had no hat, a knuckle was dripping blood.

'No. I was working and saw the bombs and so came looking for you. I was worried . . .'

'Ah, my Lysander . . .'

They hugged each other, held each other close. Her whole body was shaking violently, trembling.

'You can't go home in that state,' he said, softly, taking her hands. 'Come to my flat and tidy up. Have a proper drink. It's two minutes away.'

14. Autobiographical Investigations

BLANCHE HAS GONE. IT'S nine in the morning. She sent to the Lyceum for her clothes. The newspapers say seventeen people died in the raid – the 'Great Raid on Theatreland'. Bizarrely, I owe everything to the pilot of that Zeppelin – my first night in 3/12 Trevelyan House was spent with Blanche. Blanche. Blanche naked with her wide low-slung breasts, her jutting hips, long slim thighs like a boy, her white powdered face, the beauty spot, lipstick kissed away. How she slipped her fingers in my hair, gripping, and held my face above hers, eye to unblinking eye, as I climaxed. Deliverance. Relief. Watching her cross the room naked to find my cigarettes, standing there, pale odalisque, lighting one, then lighting one for me.

Question: who was that man in the shadows watching me?

Only now do I sense the after-shock, feel my nerves set on edge. The Zeppelin, the bombs, the dead bodies, the screams. Seeing Blanche again, being with her, made me push everything else to the back of my mind, including that strange meeting in

Exeter Street – part of the madness and horror of the night. Was somebody trying to frighten me? A warning? Vandenbrook was in Folkestone, in theory – but I can't believe that he'd ever try anything so self-destructive, so against his best interests. I'm his only hope.

I sit here and re-run the seconds' glimpse I had of him sprinting away. Why do I think of Jack Fyfe-Miller? What makes me think that? No – surely mistaken identity. But, this much is clear, someone was waiting outside the Annexe, saw me dash out and followed me as I ran towards the bombs . . .

Last night as we lay in each other's arms we spoke.

ME: I still have the ring – our ring . . .

BLANCHE: What are you trying to say, my darling?

ME: That, you know, maybe we should never have broken off our engagement. I suppose.

BLANCHE: Am I meant to read that as a re-proposal of sorts?

ME: Yes. Please say yes. I'm a complete fool. I've missed you, my love – I've been living in a daze, a coma.

Then we kissed. Then I went and took the ring from the card pocket inside my jacket.

ME: I've been carrying it with me. Good luck charm.

BLANCHE: Have you needed a lot of luck, since we split up?

ME: You've no idea. I'll tell you all about it one day. Oh. Perhaps I should ask. What about Ashburnham?

BLANCHE: Ashburnham is a nonentity. I've banished him from my presence.

ME: I'm delighted to hear it. I just had to ask.

BLANCHE [putting ring on]: Look, it still fits. Good omen.

ME: You won't mind being Mrs Lysander Rief? No more Miss Blanche Blondel?

BLANCHE: It's better than my real name. I was born [Yorkshire accent] Agnes Bleathby.

ME [Yorkshire accent]: Thee learn summat new every day, Agnes, flower. Happen.

BLANCHE: We're all acting, aren't we? Almost all the time – each and every one of us.

ME: But not now. I'm not.

BLANCHE: Me neither. [Kissing renewed fiancé] Still, it's just as well that some of us can make a living from it. Come here, you.

I've drafted out a telegram – I'll call in at a telegraph office on the way to the Annexe. Everything's changed now.

DEAR VANORA SAD NEWS STOP YOUR AUNT INDISPOSED SUGGEST POSTPONE LONDON TRIP STOP ANDROMEDA.

At a halfpenny a word that's probably the wisest seven pennies I've ever spent.

15. A Dozen Oysters and a Pint of Hock

LYSANDER TIMED HIS WALK to the Annexe from Trevelyan House and discovered that, at a brisk pace, it took him slightly more than five minutes. He felt briefly pleased at the economies of time and money such proximity to his place of work would supply, but then abruptly reminded himself that his days in the Annexe must, surely, be nearly over. Matters were coming to a head, and fast – still, he had one more trick left to play.

As he sauntered up the Embankment, past Cleopatra's Needle, about to cross the roadway to the Annexe, he saw Munro coming towards him. Too many impromptu meetings, he thought – first Fyfe-Miller, now Munro. Anxiety must be building in Whitehall Court.

'Well, what a coincidence.'

'Cynicism doesn't suit your open, friendly nature, Rief. Shall we have a coffee before your daily grind begins?'

There was a coffee stall under Charing Cross Railway Bridge. Munro ordered two mugs and Lysander lit a cigarette.

'Quite a raid last night,' Munro said.

'Why can't we shoot down something that big? That's what I don't understand. It's vast. Sitting up there in the sky, lit up.'

'There's only one anti-aircraft gun in London with a range of ten thousand feet. And it's French.'

'Couldn't we borrow a few more from them? The Zeppelins will be back, don't you think?'

'Let others worry about that, Rief. We've got enough on our plate. Actually, I will try one of your "gaspers", thank you.'

Lysander gave him one and he lit it, then spent a minute picking shreds of tobacco off his tongue. He wasn't really a practised smoker, Munro, it was more of an affectation than a pleasure.

'How are you getting on?' he asked eventually.

'Slow but steady –'

'– Wins the race, eh? Don't go too slow. Any suspects?'

'A few. Better not single anyone out, just yet – in case I'm wrong.'

He saw Munro's jaw muscles tighten.

'Don't expect us to tolerate your due caution for ever, Lysander. You're there to do a job, not sit on your arse sharpening pencils. So do it.'

He was suddenly very angry for some reason, Lysander saw, noting the patronizing use of his Christian name.

'I'm not asking for your tolerance,' he said, trying to seem calm. 'I've got to make this enquiry look as boring and routine as possible. You wouldn't thank me if I scared someone off or presented you with the wrong person all for the sake of gaining a day or two.'

Munro seemed visibly to regain his usual mood of thinly disguised condescension as he thought about this.

'Yes . . . Well . . . I understand you sent for Osborne-Way's claims from the War Office.'

'Yes, I did.' Lysander concealed his surprise. How did Munro know this? An answer came to him at once – Tremlett, of course. Munro's eyes and ears in the Directorate of Movements. *Eye* and ears, rather. He would keep Tremlett's divided loyalties very much in mind from now on. 'Osborne-Way potentially knows everything that was in the Glockner letters, he's –'

'You had no right.'

'I had every right.'

'Andromeda's not Osborne-Way.'

'We can't be complacent; we can't risk easy assumptions.'

He could see Munro's anger returning – why was he so on edge and quick-tempered? He decided to change the subject.

'I saw Florence Duchesne the other day.'

'I know.'

'Is she still in London?'

'She's left I'm afraid.'

'Oh. Right. I was rather hoping to see her again.' Lysander felt a brief but acute sadness at this news – maybe something had been lost there. For some reason he thought of her as his only true ally – they seemed to understand each other; they were both functionaries following orders from a source neither of them knew or could identify. Their strings were being pulled – that's what linked them . . . He looked at Munro, puffing at his cigarette like a girl. He decided that attack was the best means of defence, now.

'Are you telling me everything, Munro? Sometimes I find myself wondering – what's really going on here?'

'Just find Andromeda – and fast.' He threw some coins on the counter, gave him a hard smile and walked away.

Lysander went back to the Annexe with a plan forming in his head, slowly taking shape. If Munro wanted action, then he would give him action.

Tremlett was waiting for him outside Room 205 and seemed unusually chirpy – 'Nice cuppa tea, sir? Warm the old cockles?' – but Lysander looked at him suspiciously now, wondering what Tremlett might have gleaned from their trip to the south-coast hotels. On reflection it seemed unlikely that he'd make the connection with Vandenbrook; Lysander had never told him what he was doing, making Tremlett wait outside each time. But he was no fool. Would he have passed on the details of their journey to Munro, in any event? Probably – even if he couldn't explain it. Was that what was making Munro and Fyfe-Miller so jumpy? Did they have a sense that he was ahead of them, was unearthing facts that they had no inkling of? . . . The unanswered questions piled up and yet again Lysander felt himself sinking in a quagmire of uncertainties. He opened a drawer in his desk and took out a booklet of pre-paid telegraph forms. He'd give them something that would make them think again.

He picked up the telephone and dialled Tremlett's extension.

'Yes, sir.'

'Is Captain Vandenbrook back from Folkestone?'

'I believe so, sir.'

'Would you ask him to step into my office.'

Lysander treated himself to a lunch at Max's oyster bar in Dean Street in Soho. He ordered a dozen oysters and a pint of hock and allowed his thoughts to return pleasingly to Blanche and the night they had spent together. She was tall, almost ungainly under the sheets – sheets that they had spread and tucked in themselves in a kind of frenzy, snatching them from his trunks, delivered by porter that morning – she was all knees and elbows, lean and bony. Her flat wide breasts with tawny nipples. It was obvious she'd had many lovers before him. That way she held his head, his hair gathered in her fists holding him still . . . Where or from whom did that trick come? He had no regrets about spontaneously asking her to take back his ring – though he wondered now, as he emptied oysters down his throat, if he had been too precipitate, over-happy, over-relieved that his old 'problem' hadn't recurred with her. No – it had been as good as with Hettie. Hettie, so different. There was no sense of danger with Blanche, however, it was more a kind of rigour. Refreshing, no-nonsense Agnes Bleathby. It was the end of Hettie, of course. But that was only right as Hettie had let him down shockingly, had betrayed him instantly and without a qualm to save herself despite the fact that she was the mother of their son. Lothar meant little or nothing to Hettie Bull, he realized. Furthermore, he – Lothar's natural father – clearly played no part in her life unless he could be useful to her in some selfish way – the marriage to Jago Lasry was the perfect example. No, Blanche had always been the girl for him. She had asked him back to her mews house in Knightsbridge for supper – her show was cancelled until the damage to the theatre was repaired. He smiled at the idea of Blanche cooking supper for him on his return from the office – a little forerunner of their domestic bliss? For the first time in many months he felt the warmth of security wash through him. Contentment – how rare that feeling was and it was only right that it should be cherished. He ordered another round of oysters and another pint of hock.

He returned to the Annexe in good spirits. He had a course of action to follow and Munro would have his answer soon, however unwelcome it might be. Vandenbrook was poised and ready. Yet again Tremlett was waiting by his door, agitated this time.

'Ah, there you are, sir. I was beginning to think you'd gone for the day.'

'No, Tremlett. What is it?'

'There's a man downstairs insisting on seeing you. Claims to be your uncle, sir – a Major Rief.'

'That's because he *is* my uncle. Send him up at once. And bring us a pot of coffee.'

Lysander sat down with a thump, realizing his head was a little blurry from all the hock, but pleased at the prospect of seeing Hamo. He didn't come up to town often – 'London terrifies me,' he always said – so this was an unfamiliar treat.

Tremlett showed Hamo in and Lysander knew at once something was very wrong.

'What is it, Hamo? Nothing to do with Femi, is it?' The fighting in West Africa was over, as far as he knew – everything had moved to the East.

Hamo's face was set.

'Prepare yourself for the worst possible news, my boy . . .'

'What's happened?'

'Your mother is dead.'

16. Autobiographical Investigations

THERE IS THIS MYTH that death by drowning is the best of all deaths amongst the dozens or hundreds available to us human beings –

that with drowning your end arrives simultaneously with a moment of pure exhilaration. I will hold on to that idea but the rational side of my brain asks who provided this testimonial? Where's the evidence?

When I saw my mother's body in the undertaker's at Eastbourne she did, however, look serene and untroubled. Paler than usual, a slight bluish tinge to her lips, her eyes closed as if she were dozing. I kissed her cold forehead and felt a pain in my gut as I remembered the last time I'd made that gesture, holding her warm in my arms. 'I won't let you be dragged down by this.'

Hamo tells me there is an unopened letter at Claverleigh waiting for me but I don't need to read it to know that it will be her confession. Hamo, in his kindness, bless him, ventured the theory that it might have been some awful accident – a slip, a fall, unconsciousness. But I told him I was convinced it was suicide and the letter would merely confirm that. Her body had been found at dawn on the shingly beach at Eastbourne, left by the retreating tide – the proverbial man out walking his dog at first light – she was fully clothed, all her jewellery removed and one shoe missing.

I find myself, all of a sudden, remembering something Wolfram Rozman said to me – it seems eons ago, back in that impossible, unimaginable world before the war began, before everybody's lives changed for ever – when, having been asked what he would have done if the tribunal had found against him, Wolfram had said – blithely, inconsequentially – that he would have taken his own life, of course. I can bring him into my mind's eye effortlessly – Wolfram standing there in his caramel suit, swaying slightly, tipsy from the celebratory champagne, saying in all seriousness, 'In this ramshackle empire of ours suicide is a perfectly reasonable course of action.' Wolfram – was it just bravado, the swagger of a born hussar? No, I recall, it was said smilingly but with absolute rigid logic: once you understand that – you will understand us. It lies very deep in our being. '*Selbstmord*' – death of the self: it's an honourable farewell to this world. My mother had made her honourable farewell. Enough.

Hugh and the Faulkner family are deeply shocked. I feel my grief burn in me alongside a colder, calmer anger. My mother is as much an innocent victim of this whole Andromeda affair as are those two men I killed in a sap one June night in no man's land in northern France. The causal chain reached out to claim them just as it did Anna Faulkner.

My darling Lysander,

I will not allow myself, or my stupidity, to harm you or endanger you in any way. You should understand that what I am about to do seems an entirely reasonable course of action to me. I have a few regrets at leaving this world but they are wholly outweighed by the benefits my imminent non-being will achieve. Think of it that way, my dear – I am no longer here, that's all. This fact, this state, was going to arrive one day therefore it has always seemed to me that any day is as good as the next. I already feel a sense of relief at having taken the decision. You are now free to move forward with full strength and confidence and with no concerns about your foolish mother. I cannot tell you how upset I was after our last conversation, how you were intent on imperilling yourself, on taking a course of action that was plainly wrong, only to spare me. You were prepared to sacrifice yourself for me and I could not allow that, could not live with that responsibility. What I am about to do is no sacrifice – you must understand that for someone like me it is the most normal of acts in a sane and rational world.

Goodbye, my darling. Keep me alive in your thoughts every day.

Your loving mother.

Images. My mother. My father. How she wept at his funeral, the endless tears. The grim flat in Paddington. Claverleigh. Her beauty. Her singing – her rich mellow voice. That terrible sunlit afternoon in Claverleigh Wood. At meals when she talked the way she would unconsciously tap the tines of her fork on her plate to emphasize the point she was making. That night I saw my father kissing her in the drawing room when they thought I was asleep. The way they laughed when I walked in, outraged. The cameo she wore with the letter 'H' carved in the black onyx. How she smoked a cigarette, showing her pale neck as she lifted her chin to blow the smoke away. The confidence with which she walked into a room as if she were going on stage. What else could I have been with those two as my parents? How can I best avenge her?

Dr Bensimon saw me two hours ago. I telephoned him as soon as I had returned from Eastbourne.

'I wish I could say it was an effort fitting you in at such short notice,' he said. 'But you're my only patient today.'

I lay on the couch and told him bluntly and with no preamble that my mother had killed herself.

'My god. I'm very sorry to hear that,' he said. Then, after a pause, 'What do you feel? Do you feel any guilt?'

'No,' I said immediately. 'Somehow I want to feel guilt but I respect her too much for that. Does that make any sense? It was something she thought about and decided to do. In cold logic. And I suppose she had every right.'

'It's very Viennese,' Bensimon said, then apologized. 'I don't mean to be flippant. Choosing that option, I mean. You've no idea how many of my patients did the same – not spontaneously – but after a great deal of thought. Calm, rational thought. Have you any idea what made her do it?'

'Yes. I think so. It's connected with what I'm doing myself . . .' I thought again. 'It's to do with this war and the work I'm doing. She was actually trying to protect me, believe it or not.'

'Do you want to talk about her?'

'No, actually, I want to ask you about something – about someone else. Do you remember that first day we met, in Vienna, at your consulting rooms?'

'The day Miss Bull was so insistent. Yes – not easily forgotten.'

'There was another Englishman present, from the Embassy – a military attaché – Alwyn Munro.'

'Yes, Munro. I knew him quite well. We were at university together.'

'Really? Did he ever ask you anything about me?'

'I can't answer that,' he said, apologetically. 'Very sorry.'

I turned my head and looked at Bensimon who was sitting behind his desk, his fingers steepled in front of his face.

'Because you can't remember?'

'No. Because he was my patient.'

'Patient?' I was astonished at this news. I sat up and swivelled myself around. 'What was wrong with him?'

'Obviously I can't answer that, either. Let's just say that Captain Munro had serious problems of a personal nature. I can't go any further than that.'

I sit in 3/12 Trevelyan House with a bottle of whisky and a cheese-and-pickle sandwich I bought from the pub on the corner of Surrey Street. I telephoned Blanche and told her what had happened and she was all sympathy and warm concern, inviting me to come round and stay with her. I said that day would come soon enough but I had to be on my own at the moment. There will be an inquest, of course – so we must wait before we can bury her – my mother, Annaliese. I want tears to flow but all I feel is this heaviness inside me – a leaden weight of resentment, this grinding level of anger that she should have felt she had no more choice than to do what she did. To take her jewels off and walk into the sea until the waters closed over her.

17. A Cup of Tea and a Medicinal Brandy

THE NEXT DAY PASSED slowly, very slowly, Lysander felt, as if time were responding to his own desultory moods. He kept to himself as much as possible, staying in Room 205 with the door closed and locked. At midday he sent Tremlett out to buy him some pastries from a luncheon-room in the Strand. He ran through the plans he had made for the evening again and again. He was trying to convince himself that this exercise would be significant, possibly revelatory. At the very least he would be wiser – one step closer, perhaps.

In the middle of the afternoon, Tremlett called him on the telephone.

'The White Palace Hotel on the line, sir.'

'I don't stay there any more.'

'They say your wife has been taken ill.'

'I'm not married, Tremlett – it's obviously a mistake.'

'They're very insistent. She had a fainting fit, it seems.'

'All right, put them on.'

He waited, hearing the clicks and buzzes as the connection was made. Then the manager came on the line.

'Mrs Rief is in a very, ah, agitated state.'

'There is no "Mrs Rief", as it happens,' Lysander said. Then he realized. 'I'll speak to her.'

He heard the receiver being held away and footsteps approaching.

'Hello, Hettie,' he said.

'You've moved,' she said accusingly, angrily. 'I couldn't think how else to find you.'

'I'll be there in ten minutes.'

He took a taxi to Pimlico and found her in the resident's lounge of The White Palace with a cup of tea and a medicinal brandy. He locked the door so they wouldn't be interrupted but Hettie took this as an invitation to intimacy and tried to kiss him. He pushed her away gently and she sulkily sat down again on the sofa.

'I've got three whole days,' she said. 'Jago thinks I'm on a sketching holiday on the Isle of Wight. I thought being on an island would convince him more.'

'I can't see you, Hettie,' he said. 'There's a flap on – I'm working day and night. That's why I sent you the telegram.'

She frowned and tucked her knees up underneath her. She pouted and tapped her forefinger on her jawbone – one, two, three – as if counting down, mentally. Then she pointed the finger at him.

'There's someone else,' she said, finally. 'I'm right, aren't I?'

'No . . . Yes.'

'You're a swine, Lysander. A bloody fucking swine.'

'Hettie. You went and got married. We have a child but you didn't even bother to tell me.'

'That's different.'

'Please explain how.'

'What have you done to me, Lysander?'

'Hang on a second. Can I remind you of events in Vienna in 1913? You had me in prison with your damned lies. How dare you?'

'I was helping you. Well, maybe not at first, but I was later.'

'What're you talking about?'

'Those men persuaded me to drop the rape charge so you could be set bail. Udo was furious, practically threw me out –'

'What men?'

'Those two at the embassy. The attachés – I forget their names.'

'Munro and Fyfe-Miller.'

'If you say so.'

Lysander began to think fast.

'You saw Munro and Fyfe-Miller?' he asked. 'While I was under arrest?'

'We had a few meetings. They told me what to do – to change the charge. And they gave me money when I asked for some. After you escaped they were very helpful – offered to take me to

Switzerland. But I decided to stay – because of Lothar.' She looked at him aggressively, as if he were somehow to blame for all the mess. 'They asked me lots of questions about you. Very curious. And I was very helpful, I can tell you that. Told them all sorts of interesting titbits about Mr Lysander Rief.'

Was she lying again, Lysander wondered. Was this pure bravura? He felt confusion beginning to overwhelm him once more. He reached over and finished off her brandy. First Munro turned out to have been Bensimon's patient and now there seemed to be some form of collusion between Munro, Fyfe-Miller and Hettie. He tried to see what the connections and consequences might have been but it was all too perplexing. What had really happened in Vienna in 1914? It made him very uneasy.

Hettie leapt up from the sofa and came over to him, sliding on to his lap, putting her arms round his neck and kissing him – little dabbing kisses on his face, pressing her breasts into his arm.

'I know what you like, Lysander. Think what fun we can have – three whole days. Let's buy lots to eat and drink and just stay in. We can take all our clothes off . . .' She reached for his groin.

'No, Hettie. Please.' He stood up, slipping easily out from under her – she was so small, so light. 'I'm engaged to be married. It's over. You should never have come. I explicitly told you not to come. You've only yourself to blame.'

'You're a bastard,' she said, tears in her eyes. 'A fucking mean bastard man.' She carried on swearing at him, the volume increasing, as he put on his greatcoat and picked up his cap. He left the room without looking round. He didn't mind the abuse but the last thing she screamed at him was, '– And you'll never see Lothar in your life!'

The New London Theatre of Varieties, just off Cambridge Circus, was indeed new to Lysander. He would never have acted there as it was mainly a variety and vaudeville hall, although one that specialized in 'ballets, French Plays and Society Pieces'. In the theatre guide he'd consulted – he wasn't interested in the programme but the facilities – he had read that 'the tourist will find that the audience forms part of the entertainment'. This was a code, he knew, for 'prostitutes frequent the lobby bars'. The New London was an obsolescent type of Victorian theatre where the public could drink at the theatre bars without having to pay for the show. It was originally a way of supplementing the night's takings but the system inevitably brought other trade with it. Lysander remembered some old actors of his acquaintance reminiscing fondly about the prices and the quality of the streetwalkers available – the higher up you went in the theatre – from the stalls to the bars at the dress circle, upper circle, amphitheatre – the cheaper the girls. A better class of gentlemen also came to these public theatre bars because it provided perfect camouflage – there was plenty of time to scrutinize and select while ostensibly doing something entirely innocent: going to the theatre – how very cultural and educative.

The show had begun by the time Lysander slipped into his seat. A 'ballet' of French maids and a hairdresser as far as he could tell.

'Sorry I'm late,' he said to Vandenbrook and turned slightly to gain a better angle on him. He was in a suit, his hair was oiled flat with a middle parting and he had combed down the uptilted ends of his moustache. He already looked entirely different from the usual person he presented to the world – weaker-looking and much less attractive.

'Got the spectacles?'

Vandenbrook fished in his pocket and put them on.

'Ideal. Keep wearing them.'

They were clear-lensed, plain glass with wire rims, borrowed from a theatrical props agency in Drury Lane. As the ballet continued Lysander ran through the plan once more, making sure Vandenbrook understood exactly what to do. There was no need to whisper or even lower his voice as the auditorium was loud with a sustained growl of conversation and the to-ing and fro-ing of people leaving their seats and going to the bars and drinks counters that ringed the stalls. Many of them, Lysander noticed, were uniformed soldiers and sailors. Almost everyone seemed to be smoking so he offered Vandenbrook a cigarette and they both lit up as the ballet ended and the comedy sketch began.

When the curtain came down the Master of Ceremonies reminded them that the top of the bill in the second half of the evening's entertainment was the 'celebrated West End actor' Mr Trelawny Melhuish, who would be reciting the soliloquies of Hamlet, Prince of Denmark. Lysander and Vandenbrook filed out into the aisles and headed for the stalls' lobby bar. To be or not to be, Lysander thought.

'We'll split up here,' he said, as they reached the curtained doorway that led to the lobby.

The stalls' lobby was a wide, curving, low-ceilinged corridor, dimly lit with flickering gas sconces and very crowded with people who had come in off the street and those who were now pouring out of the auditorium. Lysander edged his way towards the central bar opposite the stairs leading up from the entrance. Standing some way back, a silent trio, in civilian clothes as he'd specified in the telegrams he'd sent to them, were Munro, Fyfe-Miller and Massinger. He glanced back to make sure that Vandenbrook was nowhere near him but couldn't spot him in the throng. Good.

He approached the three men, circling round behind them. They all looked ill at ease, uncomfortable in this bibulous, flushed, shouting crowd. Even better, Lysander thought.

'Gentlemen,' he said, suddenly appearing in front of them. 'Thanks for coming.'

'What're we doing here, Rief? What kind of tomfoolery is this?' Massinger snarled at him.

'I had to make sure I wasn't followed,' he said. 'I don't trust anyone at the Directorate.'

'What's going on?' Munro said, his eyes flicking around the

faces of the crowd. 'What's your game, Rief? What was so damn urgent to bring us all here?'

'I've found Andromeda,' Lysander said, immediately gaining their full attention.

'Oh, yes?' Fyfe-Miller said with undue scepticism, Lysander thought. Over Fyfe-Miller's left shoulder Lysander could see Vandenbrook circling closer. The disguise was excellent, Lysander thought – Vandenbrook looked like a timid accounts clerk out on the town looking for sin.

'Yes,' Lysander said. He had to draw this out a little, give Vandenbrook as much time as possible. 'It's someone quite high up.'

'It's not Osborne-Way – don't waste our time.'

'It's his number two,' Lysander said. 'Mansfield Keogh.'

The three looked at each other. They clearly knew who Keogh was.

'Mansfield Keogh,' Massinger said. 'Good god almighty.'

'Yes, Keogh,' Lysander said, half aware of Vandenbrook moving around their group. 'Everything fits. The trips to France tally. Only he had all the information in the Glockner letters.'

'But why would he do it?' Munro said, sounding unconvinced.

'Why does anyone?' Lysander said, looking at all three of them pointedly. 'There are three reasons why someone betrays their country – revenge, money.' He paused. 'And blackmail.'

'Nonsense,' Massinger said. Munro and Fyfe-Miller kept quiet.

'Think about it,' Lysander said.

'How do any of those categories fit Keogh?' Fyfe-Miller said, frowning.

'His wife died recently, very young – maybe it's driven him a bit insane,' Lysander said. 'But I don't know, in the end. I was just gathering evidence, not looking for motives.'

'Well, we can ask him when we arrest him,' Munro said with a thin smile. 'Tomorrow – or maybe tonight.'

Everyone fell silent contemplating the reality of the situation.

'So – Keogh is Andromeda,' Massinger said, almost to himself.

'Well done, Rief,' Munro said. 'You took your time but you got there in the end. I'll be in touch. Keep going to work in the Annexe as usual.'

'Yes, good hunting, Rief,' Fyfe-Miller added, allowing himself a wide smile. 'We thought you'd be the man to winkle him out. Bravo.'

A bell began to clang, announcing the second portion of the evening's entertainment. The crowd began to drift back into the auditorium and for the first time Lysander became aware of the painted women standing around.

'I'll leave you chaps here,' he said with a smile. 'I'm going to watch the rest of the show. Best to go out one by one.' He turned and walked away, glad to see no sign of Vandenbrook.

'Evening, my lord,' one of the doxies said to him, smiling. 'Doin' anything after?'

He glanced back to see Massinger leaving. Fyfe-Miller and Munro were talking urgently, their heads close together. I'll give it twenty-four hours, Lysander thought, pleased with the way everything had run – something would happen.

Vandenbrook was in his seat already, smoking, waiting for the curtain to go up.

Lysander joined him and handed him a pint of lager beer. He had one for himself.

'Well done,' he said. 'Do you like this stuff? I developed quite a taste for it in Vienna.'

'Thanks.' He seemed a bit subdued and sipped at the froth at the top of the glass.

'Well?'

'I didn't recognize any of them. Except that fellow with the step-collar. He looked familiar somehow.'

'Massinger?'

'I think I may have seen him before. In my War Office days. Is he an army man?'

'Yes. So – conceivably he might know who you were.'

331

'Possibly – he seemed familiar.'

Lysander thought – it was hardly evidence. The orchestra in the pit began to play a military march and the curtain rose to reveal a chorus of girls in khaki corsets and bloomers carrying wooden rifles. Cheers, whoops and whistles went up from the audience. This was what they wanted to see – not Mr Trelawny Melhuish reciting soliloquies.

'So Massinger could be Andromeda,' Lysander said.

'Andromeda? What's that?'

'That's the codename we gave you. When the search began.'

'Oh, right.' Vandenbrook looked a little uncomfortable at the thought he had been identified by a code word, Lysander supposed. 'Why Andromeda?'

'It was my choice, actually. Taken from a German opera. *Andromeda und Perseus* by Gottlieb Toller.'

'Oh, yes. It's a bit saucy that one, isn't it?'

'Never saw it,' Lysander said, his eye suddenly caught by a tall, leggy dancer who reminded him of Blanche. He put a sixpence in the slot that freed the catch on the opera glasses fixed to the back of the seat in front of him and raised them to his eyes for a closer look. Might as well enjoy the show, he thought.

18. No Eureka Moment

LYSANDER COULDN'T SLEEP SO sometime between three and four in the morning he went through to his kitchen and made himself a draught of chloral hydrate. Bensimon's somnifacient didn't work at all and he was beginning to suspect it was a placebo. He put half a teaspoon of the crystalline powder in a glass of water, stirred it vigorously and drank it down. Not much left in the packet he saw – he was rather racing through it. Bad sign.

As he waited for the familiar effects of the drug to start, he ran over the events of his elaborately planned encounter at the New London Theatre of Varieties. In a way he was disappointed – there had been no Eureka moment, no detonation of understanding and clarity – but something had been said this night, something inadvertently given away that he hadn't quite grasped. Yet. Perhaps it would come to him. More and more he was convinced that Vienna held the key – those last months before the war began . . . He felt the chloral begin to work – the room swayed, he sensed his balance going. Time for bed and sleep at last. He walked carefully back through to his bedroom, a hand on the wall to steady himself. God, this stuff was strong – he flung himself on the bed feeling consciousness blissfully slipping away. Vienna. That was it. So it must be . . .

'You all right, sir?' Tremlett said. 'Look a bit under the weather.'

'I'm perfectly fine, thank you, Tremlett. Got a lot on my mind.'

'Going to have a bit more on your mind, I'm afraid, sir. Colonel wants to see you.'

Lysander smoked a quick cigarette, checked his uniform thoroughly so that Osborne-Way wouldn't have the satisfaction of claiming he was 'improperly dressed', and walked briskly down the passageway to the Director of Movements' office.

Osborne-Way's secretary could not meet his eyes as she showed him in. Lysander saluted and removed his cap, stood at ease. Osborne-Way sat behind his desk looking at him and did not offer a chair.

'Captain Keogh was arrested at his house this morning at six o'clock. He's being held at New Scotland Yard.'

Lysander said nothing.

'No answer, Rief?'

'You didn't ask me a question, sir. You made a statement. I assumed a question would be following.'

'People like you make me wonder why we're fighting this war, Rief. You make me sick to my stomach.'

'I'm sorry to hear that, sir.'

'How some actor-popinjay like you wound up as an officer is a disgrace to the British Army.'

'I'm just trying to do my bit, sir. Like you.' He pointed to his wounded-in-action bar on his sleeve. 'I've done my time in the front line and have the scars to prove it.' He enjoyed the fleeting look of discomfort that crossed Osborne-Way's face – the lifelong staff officer in his cushy billet with his all-expenses-paid weekends in Paris.

'Mansfield Keogh is one of the finest men I know. You're not fit to tie his bootlaces.'

'If you say so, sir.'

'What evidence have you got against him? What's your grubby little enquiry dug up?'

'I'm not at liberty to tell you, sir.'

'Well, I'm damned well ordering you to tell me! You filth! You scum of the earth!'

Lysander waited a second or two before replying – accentuating the drawl in his voice, ever so slightly.

'I'm afraid you'll have to talk to the Chief of the Imperial General Staff about that, Colonel.'

'Get out of here!'

Lysander put his cap back on, saluted and left.

Back in Room 205 he found a telegram waiting.

ANDROMEDA. SPANIARDS INN. 7 AM TOMORROW.

Not even twenty-four hours, Lysander thought, impressed. So, something had happened last night after all. He had just enough time to make sure everything was prepared.

19. Waiting for Sunrise

LYSANDER HAD THE TAXI drop him at the top of Heath Street, in Hampstead, by the pond and the flagstaff, deciding he'd rather approach the Spaniards Inn on foot. It was 5.30 in the morning and still dark night, as the French would say. He was wearing a black overcoat and scarf with a black Trilby. It was cold and his breath was condensing thickly in front of him as he began the half-mile walk from the flagstaff to the inn along Spaniards Road, along the top of the heath. He could see very little – the streetlamps were very widely spaced on Spaniards Road – but he knew that all London lay to his south and he could hear the noise of the wind in the great oaks of Caen Wood on his right hand side – the creak and rub of huge branches like the masts and cross trees of a sailing ship at sea – timber under strain. The wind was growing, fierce and gusty, and he jammed his hat more firmly on his head, telling himself as he marched along that the key element at the moment was calmness – stay calm at all costs, whatever happened. Everything was planned, everything was in place.

Soon he stood by the little toll-house where the road narrowed opposite the Spaniards Inn and he smoked a cigarette, waiting for sunrise. Sunrise and clarity, he thought – at last, at last. In the final minutes of darkness he felt more secure, oddly, his back against the wall looking across the road at an inn – there was a light now on in a dormer window – where Charles Dickens himself had enjoyed a drink or two. In his pocket he had a torch and a small hip flask with some rum and water in it. A little tribute to his soldiering life – the tot of rum before the morning stand-to in the trenches – a life that he was about to abandon for ever, he hoped.

He shone his torch at his watch – 5.55 – an hour to go. He sensed the faintest lightening – tree trunks in the thick wood behind him beginning to emerge and solidify in the thinning darkness and, looking upwards through the branches with their remaining autumn leaves, he thought he could make out the sky above, the faintest lemony-grey, the packed clouds bustling by on the stiff westerly breeze.

He took a nip of rum, enjoying its sweetness, its warm burn in his throat and chest. A horse and dray clip-clopped by, a coal merchant. Then a telegraph boy buzzing past on a motorbike. The day beginning. He hadn't even tried to sleep last night – no chloral – but instead had written up a long account of his investigation into the Andromeda affair, its history, his suppositions and his conclusion. It had kept him occupied and made sure his mind was alert even though he was fully aware that the document he was producing was a contingency – a contingency in case he didn't survive the next few hours.

He decided not to follow that line of thought – everything was geared to triumphant, vindicatory success – he had no intention of risking his life if he could help it. It was definitely lightening now. He stepped away from the toll-house and moved a few yards into the wood. The sun's rays would be spearing over Alexandra Palace through the hurrying clouds, slowly illuminating the villages of Hornsey and Highgate, Finchley and Barnet to the east. Now he could actually see the heave and sway of the branches above his head, feel the gusts of wind tugging capriciously at the ends of his scarf. The inn was revealed to him, opposite, its white stucco façade glowing eerily; lights were on in many of the windows and he could hear a clanging sound from the yard behind. He moved a little way further back into the trees. Whoever was coming should think that he or she had arrived early and first – he didn't want to be spotted.

He smoked another cigarette and sipped at his rum. He could read his watch now without the aid of his torch – twenty minutes to go. For a moment he had another attack of doubt – what if he was wrong? – and he ran through his deductions again, obsessively. It seemed entirely conclusive to him – his only regret being that he had not had the time or the opportunity to try his theory out on anyone. The rationale and the judgement had to stand on its own terms, its inherent credibility self-sufficient.

A motor taxi puttered up the hill from Highgate and continued on its way. There was a little more traffic on Spaniards Road – a man wheeling a barrow, a dog-cart with two boys driving – but it was ideally quiet. He had a sudden urge to urinate, quickly unbuttoned his fly and did so. Trench-life again, he thought – a tot of rum and a piss before you went over the top. Think of the big attacks – tens of thousands of soldiers suddenly emptying their bladders. He smiled at the image this conjured up and –

A taxi pulled into the yard beside the inn.

Inside he saw a man in a Homburg lean forward and pay the driver.

Christian Vandenbrook stepped out and the taxi drove away.

Lysander shouted furiously from the shelter of the trees.

'Vandenbrook! What the hell are you doing here? Get away!'

Vandenbrook hurried across the road. He was wearing a long tweed coat that almost reached his ankles.

'I sent you the telegram!' he shouted, peering into the wood, still not seeing where Lysander was. 'Rief? I know who Andromeda is! Where are you?' He saw Lysander and ran up to him, panting. 'It came to me after the theatre – I just had to confirm a few things before I told you.' He stepped behind a tree and looked down Spaniards Road where it sloped towards Highgate. 'Someone's following me, I'm sure. Let's get away from here.'

'All right, all right, calm down,' Lysander said and they headed down a beaten earth path that led deeper into Caen Wood. Vandenbrook seemed unusually tense and watchful. At one point he pulled Lysander off the pathway and they waited behind a tree. Nothing. No one.

'What's happening?' Lysander asked.

'I'm sure I was followed. There was a man outside my house this morning. I'm sure he got into a motor and followed my taxi.'

'Why would anyone follow you? – You're imagining things. So – tell me what you know.'

They were deep in the wood by now. In the grey, pearly dawn light Lysander saw that the trees around them – beech, ash and oak – were ancient and tall. Stands of holly grew at their feet and the undergrowth on either side of the pathway was dense. They could have been in virgin forest – it was hard to believe they were in a borough of north London. The wind was growing stronger and the trees above their heads whistled and groaned as the branches bent and yielded. Lysander gathered in the flying ends of his scarf and tucked them in his coat.

'D'you want a nip of this?' he held out his hip flask. 'It's rum.'

Vandenbrook took a couple of large gulps and handed it back.

'Tell me,' Lysander said. 'So, who's Andromeda?'

'It's not a he – it's a she. That's what was confusing you.'

'And? –'

'The person who's blackmailing me is a woman – a woman called Anna Faulkner. Don't be confused by the name. She's Austrian. The enemy.'

'She's dead. She killed herself.'

'I know but –' Vandenbrook stopped, looking suddenly shocked. 'How do you know this?'

'Because she is – she was – my mother.'

Vandenbrook stared at him and Lysander saw his expression change from excited near-panic to something colder, icier. All pretence gone. Two men in a wild wood at dawn with a gale blowing about their heads.

Vandenbrook reached into the pocket of his coat and drew out a revolver. He pointed it at Lysander's face.

'You're under arrest,' Vandenbrook said.

'Under arrest? Are you mad?'

'You and your mother – you were in it together – two Austrian spies. You were both blackmailing me.'

Lysander didn't mean to laugh but one burst out of him all the same.

'I have to hand it to you, Vandenbrook – you're exceptional.

338

You're the best actor I've ever seen. Better than any of us. Best ever. You missed your vocation.'

Vandenbrook allowed himself a small smile.

'Well, we're all actors, aren't we?' he said. 'Most of our waking lives, anyway. You, me, your mother, Munro and the others. Some are good, some are average. But nobody really knows what's real, what's true. Impossible to tell for sure.'

'Why did you do it, Vandenbrook? Money? Are you stony broke? Did you want to get back at your father-in-law? Do you hate him that much? Or was it just to feel important, significant?'

'You know why,' Vandenbrook said, evenly, unprovoked. 'Because I was being blackmailed – blackmailed by that bitch Andromeda –'

A fiercer gust of wind whipped Lysander's hat off and, an instant later, Vandenbrook's head seemed to explode in a pink mist of blood, his body thrown violently down to the ground by an invisible force.

Lysander closed his eyes, counted to three and opened them. Vandenbrook still lay there, the left half of his skull gone, matted hair, brains bulging, spilling, blood flowing thickly, like oil. Lysander picked up his hat, put it on and backed off so he couldn't see. He turned to find Hamo striding through the trees, shouldering his Martini-Henri.

'You all right?' Hamo asked.

'Sort of.'

'I would have plugged him earlier – soon as he drew his gun – but I was waiting for your signal. What took you so long?'

Lysander wasn't really concentrating. He was looking at Vandenbrook. From this angle all he could see was a small red hole under his right ear.

'Sorry, Hamo, what were you saying?'

'Why did you wait so long to take your hat off?'

'I was trying to squeeze some more information from him, I suppose. Get a few more answers.'

'Risky thing to do when a man is pointing a gun at your nose.

339

Strike first, Lysander, and hard. That's my motto. That's why I used a dum-dum. One-shot kill required, no messing about.'

Hamo went to check on the body and examine the effects of his expanding bullet. Lysander took a notebook from his pocket and tore a sheet from it.

'So this is the man responsible for your mother's death,' Hamo said, looking down on Vandenbrook.

'Yes. And he managed to kill her without so much as laying a finger on her. He was going to use her – and me – as his ticket to freedom.'

'Then may he rot in hell for several eternities,' Hamo said. 'A good morning's work, I say.'

Lysander scribbled a word on the sheet of paper and unclipped a safety pin from behind his lapel. He stooped and pinned the note to Vandenbrook's chest. It read, 'ANDROMEDA'.

'I assume you know what you're doing,' Hamo said.

'Oh, yes.'

Lysander prised the revolver from Vandenbrook's fingers and walked a few yards away before firing one shot into the ground. Then he fitted the gun back into Vandenbrook's hand, pushing the forefinger through the trigger guard.

'That little pop-gun couldn't do that damage,' Hamo said, almost sounding offended.

'They won't care. Andromeda killed himself – that's all they need and want. We won't hear another word about it. Where's your motor?'

'Round the corner on Hampstead Lane. I think he thought he was being followed – had the taxi take all sorts of turnings and doublings-back. Didn't want to risk him spotting me.'

Lysander put his arm around his uncle's shoulders and squeezed. He had tears in his eyes.

'That was absolutely the right thing to do, Hamo. I can't thank you enough.'

'I told you to call on me, my boy. Any time.'

'I know, now we have our secret.'

'Silent as the grave.'

They walked away from Vandenbrook's body, through the wood towards Hampstead Lane, as a weak sun managed to spear through a gap in the rushing clouds and, for a few seconds, the light was burnished, a pale gold.

20. Autobiographical Investigations

MY MOTHER'S GRAVE IS in the north corner of St Botolph's graveyard, Claverleigh's parish church. It is a bare and rather cold patch but away from the vast spreading yews that line the path to the porch and that make the place look dark and grim. I wanted some light to shine on her. Hugh Faulkner has planted two flowering cherries on either side of the headstone. I'll come again in the spring when they're in blossom and think about her in more tranquil times. Her headstone reads,

ANNA LADY FAULKNER

1864–1915

Widow of Crickmay 5th Baron Faulkner

1838–1915

Formerly wife of

Halifax Rief

1840–1899

Mother of

Lysander Rief

'For ever remembered, for ever loved'

So our complicated personal history is edited down to these stark facts and these few words and numbers.

I never went back to the Annexe – I kept nothing in Room 205 – and was glad to be rid of the place with its persistent, lingering odour of antisepsis. I did return to The White Palace Hotel in Pimlico to collect my unforwarded mail and provide the management with my new address. I had grown strangely fond of flat 3/12 Trevelyan House and I gave up the lease on Chandos Place when the news reached me of poor Greville Varley's death in Kut-al-Amara, Mesopotamia, from dysentery. Amongst my mail – mainly circulars and commercial solicitations (the bane of any serving officer's postal life) – was a letter from Hettie:

Lysander, darling,

Can you forgive me? I was so horrible to you because I was so upset. However, I should never have said the things I did (particularly about Lothar – photograph enclosed). I feel ashamed and I rely on your tolerant and understanding nature. I have decided to divorce Jago and go to the United States. I want to live in a peaceful, neutral country – I'm sick of this ghastly, endless war. A friend of mine runs an 'artists' colony' in New Mexico, wherever that may be, so I am going to join him and become a teacher.

I have to tell you that Jago is not taking this at all well and, perversely, thinks you are to blame. Apparently he has been going up to London and following you. When you saw him the night of the Zeppelin raid he panicked and confessed all to me.

I know we will always be friends and I wish you every bit of good luck for your forthcoming marriage (lucky girl!).

All my best love, Hettie (never more Vanora)

PS. If you could possibly find your way to send £50 to me care of the GPO in Liverpool I'd be undyingly grateful. I set sail for 'Americay' in two weeks.

LINES WRITTEN
UNDER THE INFLUENCE OF CHLORAL HYDRATE

The heat, that summer in Vienna, was immense.
It slammed down out of a white sky, heavy as glass.

I do not hope
I do not hope to see
I do not hope nor see

Why were those bands playing in the Prater?
No one told me what was going on.

She was *schön*.
She was *sympatisch*.
We couldn't be left alone
At the Hôtel du Sport et Riche.

I do not see hope
Hope does not see me

Blackblackblackblackwhiteblackblackblack

We turned on our backs in the flax
We strove in the shadows of the apple grove
We found bliss beneath the trellis of clematis
Roll me over, lay me down and do it again.

It's black, alack – I can't see a thing.

Tara-loo, Madame, tara-lee, tara-loo-di-do

I dream of a woman.

★ ★ ★

Blanche and I have set a date for our wedding in the spring – May 1916. Hamo is to be my best man. Blanche and I spend many nights together but I find I still need chloral hydrate to sleep. I visit Dr Bensimon in Highgate once a week and we talk through the story of the last two years. Parallelism is working, slowly – I'm beginning to live with a version of events in which the man with the moustache and the fair-haired boy scramble out of the sap before my bombs explode. They're both lightly wounded but both regain the German lines. The more I concentrate on this story and manufacture its precise details the more its plausibility beguiles me. Perhaps one night I'll sleep peacefully, unaided by my chemicals.

I wrote to Sergeant Foley at the Stoke Newington Hospital for the Blind but have received no reply to date. Perhaps it might be better if I don't learn any more facts about that night – it's been hard enough dislodging the ones that are haunting me – but I feel I need to see Foley and explain something of what was really going on.

I have an audition tomorrow – my old life returning. A revival of *Man and Superman* by George Bernard Shaw.

I sit here looking at Hettie's photograph of Lothar that she sent me. A studio portrait of a little glum boy – close to tears, it seems – dressed to all intents and purposes as a girl in some embroidered pseudo-peasant smock. Long, dark curly hair. Does he look anything like me? One minute I think – yes, he does. And the next I think – no, not at all. Is he really, truly mine, in fact? Hettie betrayed Udo Hoff with me – might she not have been betraying me with somebody else? Can I ever be certain?

And on this note I think back, as I often do, to that October dawn on Hampstead Heath as I was waiting for sunrise, waiting for Vandenbrook to arrive. I knew it would be him and I hoped that sunrise that day would bring understanding and clarity with it – or at least clearer vision. And I thought I had it as I pinned 'Andromeda' to Vandenbrook's coat. Everything solved, explained. But as the day wore on other questions nagged at me, troubled me and set me thinking again, until by dusk all was confusion once more. Maybe this is what life is like – we try to see clearly but what we see is never clear and is never going to be. The more we strive the murkier it becomes. All we are left with are approximations, nuances, multitudes of plausible explanations. Take your pick.

I feel, after what I have gone through, that I understand a little of our modern world now, as it exists today. And perhaps I've been offered a glimpse into its future. I was provided with the chance to see the mighty industrial technologies of the twentieth-century war machine both at its massive, bureaucratic source and at its narrow, vulnerable human target. And yet, for all the privileged insight and precious knowledge that I gleaned, I felt that the more I seemed to know, then the more clarity and certainty dimmed and faded away. As we advance into the future the paradox will become clearer – clear and black, blackly clear. The more we know the less we know. Funnily enough, I can live with that idea quite happily. If this is our modern world I feel a very modern man.

I met Munro at noon by the north-east lion at the foot of Nelson's Column in Trafalgar Square. It was a grey, cold day of intermittent rain and drizzle and we were both wearing rubberized trenchcoats, like a couple of tourists. A heavy shower had passed through ten minutes before and the paving stones were glossy and lacquered, the wet smoky façades of the surrounding buildings – the Royal College of Physicians, the National Gallery, St Martin's – almost a velvety black. The brief sun was trying vainly to break through the thick grey clouds, managing only to illumine some breeze-blown interstices, and this, coupled with the gloomy effect of the heavy purpley mass of more rain coming up the Thames estuary, cast a curious gold-leaden light on the scene, making the vistas down

Pall Mall, Whitehall and Northumberland Avenue seem lit by arc-lights, artificial and strange, as if the city blocks could be struck like stage scenery and re-assembled elsewhere. I felt uncomfortable and edgy, troubled by the weather and the curious light, almost as if I were in a theatre, acting.

MUNRO: Why are we meeting like this, Rief? All very melodramatic.

LYSANDER: Indulge me. I like public spaces at the moment.

MUNRO: We found 'Andromeda', of course, up on the heath, with your note on him. The police called us . . . Everything tidied up nicely. We're grateful, I must say.

LYSANDER: He was very clever, Vandenbrook. Very.

MUNRO: Not clever enough. You caught him and dealt with him. I read your deposition – very thorough.

LYSANDER: Good. He was never being blackmailed, you see. That was the first of his clever ideas. He had everything prepared in case he was ever found out. There was no ten-year-old girl, no genuine statement, no pearls. It gave him an excuse – and it might have saved him the hangman if he hadn't shot himself.

MUNRO: Yes . . . How did you know it was him – in the end?

LYSANDER: I admit – I'd been completely convinced by his blackmail story. Then he gave himself away – just a little slip-up. Even I didn't notice it when he said it – it was something I remembered a few hours later as I was trying to get to sleep.

MUNRO: You're going to tell me what it was, I'm sure.

LYSANDER: That night we all met at the theatre, Vandenbrook made a reference to the cover of *Andromeda und Perseus*.

MUNRO: Glockner's source-text –

LYSANDER: Exactly. I mentioned it – the opera – and he said he had heard it was a 'saucy' opera. How could he know? He'd never seen it. But he had seen the libretto with its provocative cover because he'd stolen it from my mother's office and used it as the master-text for the Glockner code.

MUNRO [thinking]: Yes . . . What was that meeting in the variety theatre all about?

LYSANDER: I wanted Vandenbrook to look you over – you, Fyfe-Miller and Massinger. See if he could identify you. I still believed he was being blackmailed at that stage.

MUNRO: Are you saying you suspected one of us?

LYSANDER: I'm afraid so. It seemed the obvious conclusion at the time. I was convinced it was one of you three – that one of you was the real Andromeda. Until he made his slip-up.

MUNRO: I don't understand –

LYSANDER: When I was in Vienna I knew this Austrian army officer who had been accused of stealing from the officers' mess. I'm sure now that he was guilty but there were eleven other suspects. So he hid behind a screen of other suspects and manipulated them very adroitly – just like Vandenbrook. And he got away with it. When there are many suspects the inclination is to suspect anyone and everybody – which means you probably never find the real suspect. It's a very clever ruse. But I had this strong feeling that the whole business was connected to Vienna in some way. You had been in Vienna, Fyfe-Miller as well – and so had Massinger, apparently.

MUNRO: Yes, Massinger came to Vienna. And you were in Vienna, also.

LYSANDER: So I was. And Hettie Bull. And Dr John Bensimon. The only person who hadn't been there was Vandenbrook. And that's what gave him away. He hadn't been there, yet he knew about *Andromeda und Perseus*. And, most importantly, what was on the cover of the Viennese libretto. Glockner's Dresden libretto had no 'saucy' cover. Just plain black lettering on white. A tiny, fatal, error. But I was the only person who knew that. The only one.

Munro looked thoughtful, stroking his neat moustache with his middle finger in his habitual gesture. I sensed that he was desperate to find something wrong with my reasoning, some flaw in the logic – almost as a matter of intellectual pride and self-esteem, as if he was annoyed by the case I had built and wanted to bring it down, somehow.

MUNRO: All of the Glockner letters were posted in London.

LYSANDER: Yes.

MUNRO: So you're saying Vandenbrook took them to a south-coast hotel. Left them there. Then had them picked up the next day by a railway porter and brought back to him in London. He then encoded them and sent them on to Geneva.

LYSANDER: It was part of his cover. He was unbelievably thorough. Everything was thought through. Everything had to fit his essential blackmail story – that there was another person controlling him. Another Andromeda, if you like. A more important one.

MUNRO: He certainly took pains.

LYSANDER: And they nearly paid off for him. By the way, how did you know the Glockner letters had London postmarks?

MUNRO: You told me.

LYSANDER: Did I? I don't remember.

MUNRO: Then it must have been Madame Duchesne.

LYSANDER: Must have been . . .

MUNRO: How can you be sure that Vandenbrook was Andromeda?

LYSANDER: How can you be sure about anything? It's my best guess. My most considered deduction. My most cogitated interpretation. Vandenbrook was very shrewd – and an exceptional actor, incidentally, far superior to me. I wish I had half his talent. And he had established an invisible layer of power above him that made him look like a victim, a dupe, a pawn. Don't look at me, I'm small fry, he was saying – the real control lies elsewhere. I believed it for a while but it was a total fabrication.

MUNRO: Then why did he try to deliver the last letter?

LYSANDER: That was the beginning of the ruse. He saw I had come into the Directorate and he knew exactly what I was looking for – and that I might very well narrow the suspects down to him – so he put his escape plan into operation. Of course he encoded the Glockner letters himself. He had the master-text. But he had to cover himself in case I found him out. And of course I might never have come upon the last letter, but he couldn't risk it.

MUNRO: Isn't that a bit too subtle? Over-subtle? Even for Vandenbrook?

LYSANDER: This is your world, Munro, not mine. I think 'too subtle' or 'over-subtle' are its defining features, don't you? The triple-bluff? The quadruple-bluff? The third-guess? The tenth-guess? Normal currency in my limited experience. Why don't you ask an expert like Madame Duchesne? Ask yourself, come to that.

Munro frowned. He looked like a man who was still not convinced by the argument.

LYSANDER: You don't look convinced.

MUNRO: Well, next summer's offensives will give us a final answer, I suppose, as to whether the leak is staunched or not.

LYSANDER: I suggest you go and spend a few days in the Directorate of Movements and its associated departments. It's all there. Mountains upon mountains of hard fact – so easy to read. It's too big, Munro. The war machine is too gigantic and gigantically obvious – you can't hide anything when it's on that massive scale and when you're as close as I was. Anyone could have been Andromeda – it just happened to be Vandenbrook.

Munro looked at me, quizzically, as if I were some fractious and rascally schoolboy who was forever disrupting his classroom.

LYSANDER: Think of our armies as cities. There's a British city, and a French city and a German city and a Russian city. And then there's the Austrian city, the Italian and the Turkish. They need everything a city needs – fuel, transportation, power supply, food, water, sanitation, administration, hospitals, a police force, law courts, undertakers and graveyards. And so on. Think how much these cities need on a daily basis, how much they consume, on an hourly basis. There's a population of millions in these cities and they have to be kept running at all costs.

MUNRO: I see what you mean. Yes . . .

LYSANDER: And then there's the final, unique ingredient.

MUNRO: What's that?

LYSANDER: Weaponry. Of every imaginable type. These cities are trying to destroy each other.

MUNRO: Yes . . . It does make you think . . .

He was silent for a while and kicked out a foot at a pigeon that was pecking too close to his brilliant shoes. The bird flapped away a few feet.

MUNRO: Why did you kill Vandenbrook?

LYSANDER: I didn't. He killed himself. When I confronted him with the evidence about the libretto. He drew a gun and shot himself. Search his house – you'll find the vital clue. The *Andromeda und Perseus* libretto is the key to all this.

MUNRO: We can't search his house. It wouldn't do. Grieving widow, little weeping girls who've lost their father. Distinguished officer who took his own life, injured in battle, suffering from the awful pressures and stress of modern warfare . . . No, no. And his father-in-law would have something to say about us sending men in and tearing the place apart.

LYSANDER: Then you'll have to take my word for it, won't you?

Silence. We looked at each other, giving nothing away.

MUNRO: I was sorry to hear about your mother.

LYSANDER: Yes. It's a real tragedy. She just couldn't cope, I suppose. But it was something she wanted to do. I respect that.

MUNRO: Of course . . . Of course . . . What about you, Rief? What do you want to do now?

LYSANDER: I want my honourable discharge. No more army for me. My war's finished.

MUNRO: I think we can arrange that. It's the least you deserve.

We shook hands, said a simple goodbye and walked away from each other, Munro heading back down Northumberland Avenue to Whitehall Court and me strolling up the Strand to Surrey Street and 3/12 Trevelyan House. I didn't look back and I assume Munro didn't, either. It was over.

21. Shadows

IT IS A DARK, foggy, drizzly night in London, near the end of 1915. The fog, pearly and smoky, seems to curl and hang – as if from a million snuffed candles – around the city blocks like something almost growing and sinuously weedy, blanketing and vast, seeking out doorways and stairways, alleyways and side streets, the levels of the roofs quite invisible. The streetlamps drop a struggling moist yellow cone of luminescence that seems to wane as soon as the light hits the shining pavement in its small hazed circle, as if the effort of piercing the engulfing murky darkness and falling there were all it could manage.

You are standing shivering in the angle of two walls in Archer Street, peering out, trying to discern the late-night world go by, your attention half-caught by the small crowd of enthusiastic theatre-goers waiting with their programmes for an autograph as the cast of *Man and Superman* leaves the stage door after the show. Exhalations of rapture, an impromptu smatter of applause. Eventually the people drift away as the actors come through, sign, chat briefly and leave.

The light is switched off but you see that the door opens one last time and a man appears with a raincoat and a hat in his hand. He looks up at the opaque night sky, checking on the dismal weather, and you will probably recognize him as Mr Lysander Rief, who is playing the part of John Tanner, the leading role in *Man and Superman*, by Mr George Bernard Shaw. Lysander Rief looks tired – he looks like a man who is not sleeping well. So why is he quitting the theatre so discreetly, the very last to leave? He puts his hat on and sets off and – vaguely curious – you decide to follow him, left into Wardour Street and then quickly right into Old Compton Street. You keep your distance as you watch him make his way home through the thickening condensations of the night. He pauses frequently to look around him and, as he goes, he takes an odd swerving course along the street, crossing and re-crossing the roadway, as if keen to avoid the bleary yellow circles cast by the streetlamps. You give up after a minute – you've better things to do – and you leave Mr Lysander Rief to make his erratic way home, wherever that may be, as best he can. Good luck to him – he's evidently a man who prefers the fringes and the edges of the city streets, its blurry peripheries – where it's hard to make things out clearly, hard to tell exactly what is what, and who is whom – Mr Lysander Rief looks like someone who is far more at ease occupying the cold security of the dark; a man happier with the dubious comfort of the shadows.

ABOUT THE AUTHOR

WILLIAM BOYD is also the author of *A Good Man in Africa*, winner of the Whitbread Award and the Somerset Maugham Award; *An Ice-Cream War*, winner of the John Llewellyn Rhys Prize and shortlisted for the Booker Prize; *Brazzaville Beach*, winner of the James Tait Black Memorial Prize; *Restless*, winner of the Costa Novel Award; and *Ordinary Thunderstorms*, among other books. He lives in London.